THE
CANNABIS
PREACHER

SERMON TWO

*A financial thriller about resurrecting a failed company,
navigating love, betrayal, old secrets, and murder.*

SABINE FRISCH

Publishing Services provided by Paper Raven Books LLC

Printed in the United States of America

First Printing, 2023

Hardcover ISBN: 978-0-9878580-6-1

Paperback ISBN: 978-0-9878580-5-4

PROLOGUE

Vaomar Island at one o'clock in the afternoon made for an amazing, picturesque postcard view. Though, owing to its proximity to the equator, temperatures could hit about 35 degrees Celsius before you knew it, sucking the energy and enthusiasm out of anyone foolish enough to venture outside.

Fucking South Pacific, Reverend Bartholomew thought, struggling up the hill to his little wooden church, wiping his face with a kerchief that had once been white. He quickly made the sign of the cross and raised his eyes to heaven. No one was around, but better safe than sorry—you just never knew.

Fucking South Pacific. Paradise all right, but you ended up chasing a cool breeze like a man who owed you money, and stared at the same insane temps every single day. Unless it was the rainy season, of course, when you stared at the same insane temps every day and tried to keep all your worldly goods from being washed away in the torrential downpours. South Pacific paradise—what sort of insane fool would move here and then want to live here anyway? Unless said fool needed a place far away from the prying eyes of the law, a place that was safe from extradition.

A fool like Connor Beauregard potentially.

Reverend Bartholomew threw open the door to his church and stood, breathing hard for a moment, letting his eyes get accustomed to the dim interior, letting the cool breeze caress him gently. When the locals noticed that his ramshackle little church always seemed to be the coolest spot on the entire island, they talked about the reverend's direct line to the good Lord. The Lord who kept his church at a comfortable 20 degrees.

Reverend Bartholomew only encouraged them. 'And the Lord holds his sheltering hands around our little church,' he often lectured from the little rough-hewn pulpit. 'The Lord wants you to relax and feel nothing but the comfort of his word, delivered by his faithful servant.'

Enjoying the cool, they hung on his words. His wonderful, amazing flock of parishioners followed him and praised his miracles.

"Carrier is the true miracle," he said sarcastically, flipping off the portable generator that powered the portable air conditioner, all concealed by a massive carved statue behind his pulpit. His private little miracles had been smuggled in one night shortly after his arrival on the island and installed with much cursing and bloodied knuckles. No need for any of his parishioners to officially know that miracles were made in China and on sale at Shenzhen Electronics, though he suspected they did.

"You ever worry they'll find you out and drive you out of paradise?"

"About as much as you worry they'll unmask you for the drunk and fraudster you are and throw your ass off the island. What are you doing in here, Cristos? Doesn't look like you came for prayer and reflection."

His friend Cristos, known by many here just as the 'Portuguese Man,' shrugged and rose from the pew where he'd been napping.

"Hey, it's still the coolest place on this damned island."

"Given some basic tools and a day of being sober, you could install your own air conditioning in that ramshackle hut you call home."

"I could." Cristos shrugged and yawned. "Then again, I keep promising myself I'm going to leave in a couple of months anyway, and it's no longer going to be worth it."

"Leave this island," Barry snorted. "As if. The moment you leave here, you'll have no less than five different government agencies looking for your ass, or you would have gone home already. So, what the hell?"

"A man's gotta have a dream."

"Dream on. Now help me clean up this church."

"You ever get tired of bossing people around—Reverend?"

"You ever get tired of being a sarcastic old drunk?"

"Probably not."

They worked in silence, tidying up the church and, most important of all, polishing and arranging the wooden collection vessels so they shone in quiet prominence. His father would be so proud, the reverend thought—or not. Last he had heard of his father, he was condemning his one and only son as a cheating, philandering drug dealer.

Some days he got up in the morning and instantly felt like the God-fearing Reverend Bartholomew himself, the man whose persona he had taken on when he arrived on the island. It made him want to go out and beat someone senseless. Or get rip-roaring drunk or find the nearest drug dealer on this godforsaken island and buy out his supply. Maybe both.

Was this life he had taken on really so much better than jail? Get real! It was more comfortable—marginally, better than being locked up at night and having to shower in groups, anyway.

"This island," he groused, pushing newly delivered candles into their holders. "This fucking island is starting to drive me stark raving mad."

"Oh, my dear Barry, and you've only been here for a short while. Look at me—I've been hiding on this rock in the middle of the goddamn ocean for over ten years, and then some. You think you ought to go mad? Please." Cristos raised his hands and rolled his eyes to the ceiling.

"Yeah, well, you stole money from the wrong people and then tried to get away with it by offing one or two. Which makes this island the only place where you wouldn't be in jail or a graveyard. Same difference."

"I need to drink less," Cristos said, scratching his enormous beer belly. "You know too much about me by a long mile. What is it you are here for again?"

"Shortcuts—nothing but a couple of shortcuts."

Cristos laughed so hard his belly shook.

"That's what they're calling it now, shortcuts is it? If I had to make a guess, I would say your government did not entirely approve of your shortcuts now, or you would not be here either."

"How about you stop talking and take a look at that goddamned air conditioner. Every now and then, it rattles and groans like a herd of elephants with diarrhea. It's a little disruptive while I'm trying to deliver a fucking sermon."

Cristos chuckled and went behind the altar for his tool box.

"My, my, do you want your good parishioners to hear you cursing like that—Reverend? What are we preaching about today, dare I even ask?"

"You don't need to know that. Just get to work and fix it."

"Oh, but I do need to know. I have to listen to your joyous parishioners when they tell me how wonderful your sermons are, and how I need to clean up my sinful lifestyle and start coming to church on a regular basis. So at least give a guy some sort of warning. What is it going to be this time?"

"Cris, just move your ass and get the AC fixed, will you? Grease it or trim it or beat it for all I care—I only want it to cool the fucking building when I tell it to do so, without making that godawful racket. Is that too much to ask?"

Cristos scratched his belly again, belched, and proceeded to take off the wood paneling that hid the clever device.

"I used to think that thing was the only reason they came to you every Sunday morning and twice during the week on afternoons."

"Gotta give 'em a good reason, is what my daddy would say. And if it's not the Lord's word they are rushing in here for, they might as well be coming 'round because it's the only comfortable place on this damned island. Collection plate don't care."

***

Cristos shook his head and went to work. He really did want to blame it on the AC—the only one on the island, by the way. Most of the rough-timbered bars down along the waterfront did not even have walls, never mind air conditioning. No way to cool off but in here. If he could have blamed that blasted AC, he would happily have watched his friend mesmerize the great unwashed population of this island and pull whatever coins they had out of their pockets. But there was something else.

In his gut he knew that Barry had something akin to magic. He had a talent Cristos couldn't explain, but when the good reverend Bartholomew opened his mouth, time refused to move on until his sermon was over.

People did not just want to listen. They had no choice but to take in every word. Barry could spin a tale out of thin air and dust, and create paradise in the air in front of them—complete with unicorns, fairies and dragons. And he did not have to use a single thing but his damned words and that soothing, mesmerizing voice of his.

The air conditioner—the air conditioner was just stage effect and window dressing, and Cristos would have given the remainder of his small fortune to figure out how Barry did it.

Damn that man anyway. He smiled, said amen, passed around those silly homemade collection plates of his, and voila. Eager hands slipped into frayed pockets, and money these people did not even know they had, never mind had to give away, would end up on the plate.

Damn that man anyway.

When he was totally and brutally honest with himself, which to a man like Cristos did not happen excessively often, when he was really honest, he'd have to admit that Barry had caught him out once or twice too.

Officially, he hung around the church to shoot the breeze with the reverend, the only other white, educated, smart and halfway normal guy on the island. When no one was looking, he had found himself staring at the man, mouth agape, listening to his words as if... Well, as if they were the gospel itself, as a matter of fact.

So how did he do it? It had become his ongoing obsession to answer that question. Cristos could run a con—any con. Just name it, he had done it. As a matter of fact, that's why he was spending his old age in this godforsaken place. Barry was annoying, but not entirely wrong about his alternatives. Cristos knew every easy con there was, how it worked, and how much money there was in it. Period.

Then there was Barry.

He remembered the day when he had come to the island as a wandering preacher—please! Of course, he'd recognized him for what he was, one con man to another. And then he had seen the talent.

Barry wasn't a man who had to bother with small-time stuff, one mark at a time. Cristos listened to him speak, and he knew Barry could run the big ones. The kind of con that's measured in 'real money,' capital M. The kind you did once and never worried about a single thing again, even if you lived to be 100.

All Barry would have to do was open his mouth and spin the story. He'd never met anyone with that kind of magic before—real magic. And let's face it, if you spoke well enough to fascinate Cristos Castaneda, you had a marketable talent.

So, there it was, Cristos's other reason to hang around the good reverend Bartholomew and his silly pretend church—he wanted to learn. If he could pick up just a percentage of what Barry knew about the way to work a room... shit, he would not be on this island much longer.

Leaving just one more question...

Cristos arranged all the little collection plates Barry had ordered from China (*carved with my own two hands, praising the Lord with every scrape of the knife*, as he would say) and looked over to where Barry stood, deep in thought. He had closed his eyes and put his hands together, looking real pious. Shit, if you knew him like Cristos knew him, you would realize that prayer was the furthest thing from his mind just before his so-called sermons.

The good reverend Bartholomew had a little voodoo kind of ritual that put him into what he called 'the mindset.' That 'thing' that allowed him to mess with his parishioner's minds. At least that's what Cristos called it, 'messing with their minds.' A) Because that's what was happening and B) because he hadn't discovered any other explanation that made sense.

Leaving the other questions Cristos had pondered ever since he'd met Barry, when his name was still Connor something or other. Why was he here? And what on earth was he waiting for?

Because sure and enough, he was waiting for something.

At regular intervals, Iskandar, the man who drove the mail boat, would bring large boxes of mail-ordered supplies for Barry, candles, prayer books, incense and nonsense… And mixed in among them were always these envelopes—big brown manila envelopes, sealed with enough tape that no one but Barry could actually open them without it being obvious.

When he got one, Barry would usually drop everything he was doing, sometimes even postponing a sermon for some sort of pretend emergency—and then he would disappear with his envelope.

Presumably reading the papers and documents it contained.

Cristos was dying to get his hands on one of these, but as much as they shared everything else over a bottle of rum, nothing was ever said about the reason that had brought Barry to Vaomar Island. Except for the vague term 'business trouble.'

Business trouble could mean anything from cheating on your taxes to conning your closest business partners.

"I know it's tempting to believe in miracles, seeing as you're in a church, Cristos, but I'm pretty sure those collection plates and hymnals are not going to arrange themselves, you know."

"Bugger off, Barry."

Another irritating thing about the good old reverend that never failed to piss off Cristos. The man could stand there with his eyes closed and still know everything that was going on.

"As for hymnals, Reverend…"

"I know—beautiful, are they not? My contact bought the lot at a used bookstore in Melbourne. I think they're great. Add a bit of class to this here outfit."

"Not sure you should be calling a church an outfit, but whatever. What else does your contact say then?"

"This and that. You just about ready?"

"You know I am."

Same old Barry—never give anything away. Not when he was sober, not when he was drunk, not when he was getting ready to preach. Cristos comforted himself with the fact that he had lived on this island far longer than Barry, and he possessed the one thing Barry did not have: patience. He would find out, one day.

In the meantime, he hung around the church, enjoyed Barry's company, halfway decent conversation, and the liquor he brought in through obscure channels on a regular basis. Barry at least knew how to hide in style, Cristos thought, painfully remembering his own ramshackle hut down by the beach.

"Did your contact at least put something enjoyable into your magical chest of supplies this time?"

"London gin good enough for the gentleman?"

"Praise the Lord."

Cristos raised his beautiful alto voice and began singing, filling the little wooden church.

He was soon to find out what Barry's sermon was all about this afternoon. One of Barry's favorite themes: thieves. For some reason, he could raise his hands and thunder judgment against the two thieves who were crucified alongside Jesus. "*The thief comes only to steal and kill and destroy,"* he would preach. *"But I came that they might have life and have it more abundantly."*

Barry had a thing about thieves. Cristos himself kept an eye on things, making sure nobody would come around and help himself from the liquor supply or the locked ancient vault where Barry kept the contents of the collection plates—but Barry. Barry could talk himself into a lather about thieves.

As a result, the incidents of thievery had almost become nil on Vaomar Island. Apparently, nobody had a desire to get on Reverend Bartholomew's bad side. He made it sound like hellfire and then some, if one got caught.

Thievery it was then. Hallelujah.

Cristos got ready to assist the great master in his sermon and to collect and share what spoils there might be at the end of the day.

ONE

They moved silently and cautiously, testing the room with barely concealed discomfort. Coats stayed buttoned, ties firmly tied. Rafael shivered a little, but knew it had nothing to do with the temperature in the blandly neutral, rented conference room. More like nobody trusted anybody. If you put a really nice pen down in front of you, you'd sure as hell check if it was still there 10 minutes later. Something like that.

Personally, Rafael only carried his trademark, cheap Bic pens with a logo from a local bar, The Lighthouse. Dozens of them he had demolished in his busy, twitchy fingers when a meeting got particularly uptight and his friend…

Correction—his former friend…

Rafael did not allow himself to think about Connor Beauregard very often. He hadn't thought of him in ages, as a matter of fact. Not since the day Rafael's wife received the shattering diagnosis of cancer and passed away so quickly, he still couldn't quite wrap his mind around it.

He hadn't had the time to think about his closest friend during the turbulence of those days or the emptiness of the days that followed— but today, today memories weighed heavily on him.

They wormed their way into his brain, no matter how hard he tried to push them out. Being in a conference room like this one brought it all back, and he would have given money to put on his heavy boots and be out on a construction site somewhere.

1

"How's it going?" Simon Graff asked him, sitting down next to him. "Construction business running OK?"

"Most of the time." Rafael nodded cautiously and forced his mind back to this meeting at hand. "You?"

"Same old same old." Simon shrugged. "Security business—you know. Everybody thinks their neighbor is going to rob them blind when they aren't looking."

"Good news for you," Rafael said and nodded slowly. He picked up his pen and put it back down again. Too early in the meeting to mangle another one. Way too early.

"You heard anything?" Simon asked, almost covertly, and Rafael looked down at his notebook, not admitting that he had thought along those lines just a minute ago.

"'Bout what?"

"You know—Beauregard?"

They always asked. At least Simon did—and Kayla Montecito every now and then, when he saw her, and every single time he had to tell them the same thing.

"Nothing. Not one thing."

"Where do you think he…?"

"You know what, Simon? Let's not go there. Not now, not today—not ever."

The venom in his voice startled even him, but the hell with subtlety right now. Jesus—they all ought to know Connor had scammed him as much as everyone else in the room.

Simon wanted to apologize, but just then the door opened, and a young woman sauntered in. Instantly, Rafael wanted to grin, and ended up coughing to cover it. Same old Tessa—dressed head to toe in black and silver, heels that could drill a hole through a man's skull if she so chose, and purple hair this time.

The hair always changed; the rest stayed the same. No matter how many people dismissed her because of her looks and attitude, Rafael knew she hid a sharp brain under that purple hair and godawful black makeup. If it had a monitor and a keyboard, Tessa could make it dance. Connor had known it too.

Jesus. He had not seen her since just before the shit hit the fan big time. Hadn't even thought of her, but if time had been a bitch to him, it had been kind to her. She looked good, better perhaps than she had a right to, if Connor had been right about her.

"Hey, Tess," he called out, and she nodded at him.

"Rafael."

It burned on his tongue, the same stupid question Simon had just asked him—'did you hear anything'—but one look at Tessa, and he thought better of it.

Tessa would be among the last person Connor would contact. Way back when, she had been his favorite excuse and escape hatch. Connor always got away with saying, 'Oh, Tessa did this, or she forgot that,' and she never complained about it. Thought it part of being the big man's PA, so she took it in stride and in private told Connor to get his shit together, and soon.

The three of them had been one tight group right up to the very end. Connor was convinced she had gone over to the enemy camp just before he himself took off. Had she?

Rafael never heard of her being questioned the way he and Kayla, Simon, and Josh had. She'd never been dragged onto a TV news show to make an official statement. Had the police come knocking at her door?

He did not know. Looking at her, he would guess not. They had protected her then, looked out for her. Guess they did at least that right, Rafael thought, and watched her unpack.

Tessa opened a roll-aboard case and set up a small laptop, connecting it to the monitor on the wall, running cables and pushing buttons without saying a word to anyone. She moved with the confidence of one who knew what was going on while everyone else in the room just waited.

So, they were going to have a little presentation today, were they? Was that why they had all been called to a rented conference room in the hotel district of town, the kind of room that saw dozens of meetings and hundreds of people every single week of the year?

"Wonder what that's all about," Simon asked in a low voice, nodding at the AV equipment, and Rafael shrugged again.

He couldn't even guess what Al might be planning, or if in fact it was even going to be Al chairing this very meeting. The email, calling an extraordinary meeting of the board of directors of Perfect Cannabis Corporation, had been infuriatingly vague. The usual 'your attendance is required.' No opportunity to express regrets, no chance to say you couldn't make it for whatever reason, just 'be there.' Period.

Rafael looked around with mild curiosity. They all lived in town or within a reasonable distance, they all had offices around here, and still someone went through the trouble of renting a conference room in a mid-range hotel, really? And this was the best they could do? Connor would have…

Well for starters, Connor would likely have picked a place where he could land his goddamn helicopter on the roof; this much was certain. There would have been a small buffet if it were breakfast time, and champagne starting around lunch. Connor would rather drop dead than chair a meeting in a boring room like this one…

No style, no pizzazz, no go.

Finally, Rafael allowed the memory and smiled. Dammit, Connor had had style, and panache and guts and everything else a businessman like him needed to fake it till you make it. He had been a damned magician, and nobody had ever come close to beating him—nobody.

Those had been the good times, and they felt about a million years ago.

Tessa straightened and pushed a few more buttons on her laptop, testing a microphone quietly. Still no clue as to what was about to happen. Not your everyday presentation, for sure. Shit.

If he had to hazard a guess, it would be something he wouldn't like, especially considering the fact that Tessa could not even look his way.

Had she not always had a joke for him, and given him a hard time about his slovenly appearance and nonexistent manners, pointed out every loose button and dangling thread? Once, he'd been in a meeting with Connor, and she'd walked in with a pair of shoelaces for him because she could no longer look at the cable ties holding his right shoe to his foot. Today, she could not get herself to say hello to him? Go figure.

The door to the conference room opened again, and two more men stepped in. Rafael lifted a hand in greeting. Josh, real estate broker extraordinaire, and more than ever peeved at having to step through the door of the conference room with a man he most certainly considered beneath him.

"Dante, long time no see," Rafael called out and nodded at Josh. "And you, Josh—where you been?"

"I have been taking care of business," Josh said stiffly. "My business, as if you did not know. Since this—venture—you talked me into does not appear to be skyrocketing, Rafael. There are moments when I wish..."

Rafael tuned him out. Most people tuned out Josh Novak in his experience. The man had an excessive fondness for the sound of his own voice and would have made a fabulous college professor. In his dreams, he probably stood in front of an audience and babbled all day long, going on and on and. Rafael grinned at the thought, and Dante did likewise, sitting beside Rafael.

"He does go on, doesn't he," Dante said softly, and Rafael nodded looking down at the pad in front of him.

"Any progress at all on the production facilities?"

"Some." Dante shrugged. "You know yourself everything turned into a nightmare when—I mean, when things started to come apart."

"You can say it. When Connor Beauregard made a mess of it and took off. Go on. Nothing I have not said myself."

Dante only nodded. "Like that. Sorry. I know you two were best friends, that's all."

"Friends, of a sort. There was a lot of stuff even I did not know."

Rafael looked around, but Josh, meanwhile, had found another victim to listen to his monologue in Simon, and Tessa paid no attention to the men in the room, still adjusting and fine-tuning the controls of her laptop and the wide screen on the wall.

"Like when he tried to make a backroom deal with your brother…"

Dante struck his chest with the palm of his hand. "Jesus, why don't you go straight for the heart, Rafael. But you're right. Roberto had a big hand in this thing going down."

"Sure did. And yet, in the end, he must have made up with your father in order to set up Connor, make him look guilty as sin."

Dante said nothing. There probably was not anything he could say, and suddenly, Rafael became as impatient as his friend Josh. He had construction sites to go to, to take care of his own business and immerse himself in some sort of hands-on task, like operating a bulldozer, until the noise of his own thoughts disappeared.

"Hey, Tess, is anything going to happen here? Seeing as how once again we were all hauled away from our regular, money-earning jobs and businesses to attend… here."

"Patience, Rafael—things are about to go on."

"Go on?"

Tessa merely nodded and buried her face in her laptop screen without saying anything else, although now she had a little microphone and earpiece attached. Great, Rafael thought, the queen of gadgets and her toys. In her dreams she probably ran loose at the local Best Buy all night long.

For a minute, he wondered how much money Al's family had paid her. Certainly more than outstanding wages because she had been loyal to him and Connor for years and years.

Then from one day to the next…

Money did odd things to people. Connor himself would have been the prime example if you needed one. Rafael smiled again when he remembered sitting at The Lighthouse bar with his best friend, coming up with the idea for Perfect Cannabis Corporation. 'Hey, let's go be drug dealers.'

Nobody could screw up being a drug dealer—right? That was not possible, and with the country just about to legalize marijuana for medical purposes, they decided this one was 'no-fail.' And it would have been. Rafael still believed it would have been an absolute no-fail business.

All they needed was a bit of capital, and they would have been fine.

That's when he had brought in Josh and Simon. Those two lacked any kind of imagination and creativity, but they had lucked out in their respective field, and they had what Connor and Rafael needed the most—cash. Cash that needed a place to be invested, cash that was burning holes into their pockets. Match made in heaven.

At least for a while.

Once he looked at Connor's basic business plan, which the man had thrown together in less than a day, mind you—no matter what you said about Connor, when he was fired up, there was no stopping him... Once Rafael took a long look at Connor's business plan, he realized two things. One, this was going to be the biggest thing they had ever started, and two, they were going to need a lot more cash that even Simon and Josh together could provide.

Enter Al.

The famous, charismatic, mysterious Al... No one in the group even knew his last name. Rafael rested his chin in his hand so he wouldn't shake his head. Al had been—something of a legend in the circles he and Connor ran in. Al had more money than God, they said. Al never mentioned more than his first name. Al never stayed longer than the first, important half hour of any meeting and never wrote anything down.

If you knew Al, you had a story about him—who he was, what he was doing, and why he was that way.

Rafael thought he had heard all of the stories. He knew Al's father, the cunning brain behind a complicated mostly legal network of corporations and even odder than Al. Could you improve on odd?

Was odder even a word? The man who had fathered Al and Dante and, as they found out later, Roberto, certainly defined odder.

He ran his more or less illegal empire out of the back room of a rundown little family diner—a diner that rarely saw any actual customers. Called himself the 'Original Chef' and wielded enough power in the shady world of strip clubs and prostitution that even the heads of the local motorcycle gangs obeyed every word he said.

Why not, Rafael had thought, why not Al and his family? He had seen enough of Al to know the man did not voluntarily screw anybody he did business with. He had all the cash they needed, readily available. Where did you get all that in one package anyway?

Besides that, they were going into the "marijuana for medical purposes" business. They would need some sort of protection, no? Were they going to rely on the local police to keep the local hoodlums at bay? Or the drug addicts who might try to break in late at night looking for the goods? Please! Of course not.

So yes, it had been a good idea at the time. To this day it was a good idea—except Connor and Al and his father had disliked each other at first sight.

Water and oil be damned. Connor and that family were like chemical elements causing an explosion on contact. You need not worry if they were going to blow up at one another; you just wanted to be elsewhere when they did.

"Give it time," he had counseled his friend again and again. "Do your thing and don't worry about what Al's family members are doing. Things will work out eventually."

Reluctantly, they had taken Dante into the company in charge of production, and Al in charge of—well—operations, most likely, if they had ever progressed that far.

The money just rolled in as investors everywhere realized what a sexy little business they were starting. They had everything, until Connor became obsessed with being the big man in charge and with getting rid of Al and his family, while at the same time Al's father became obsessed with seeing Connor as a clueless loser and with getting rid of him.

Wasn't it damned handy—wasn't it bloody damned handy, then, that his third son, the one he never spoke about, the one he himself had put into prison, got out just then? Wasn't it handy that third son, Roberto, would put an illegal grow op into Connor's building and then find ways and means to blame Connor for the very thing? Videotaped confessions and everything.

He would have wondered how they had done it, but watching Tessa at the end of the table with her electronic gadgets, he knew he need not. Tessa always needed money, and Connor had not paid her in quite some time, so they'd had access to everything they needed to make Connor take a hard fall.

Sure, Connor had made a ton of mistakes, and Rafael could list them without effort.

Trying to bribe the minister of health—please!

Acquiring a luxurious helicopter while suppliers and workers like Tessa went unpaid? Unwise to say the least. His girlfriend leased the helicopter, he said, true, but it did nothing for the company image.

Taking shortcuts, 'copying' investor's signatures, making a general mess of anything remotely considered proper procedure—that was Connor.

People did not understand Connor. They expected him to live in the real world, while he inhabited his castles in the air, his stories, his magical places. Those were completely real to him, and that was what made him such a goddamn good salesman.

Trying to understand Connor from an everyday level, you might as well send a rhinoceros to preschool. He defied description as much as Al's father, the Original Chef, did. Maybe that was why they hated each other so much.

All of his little shortcomings could and would have been excused. Because he was a trailblazer, because he made things happen when nobody else could. But the one thing even Rafael could not excuse was trying to betray them all.

You went too far, buddy, Rafael thought, not for the first time, and traced abstract linear doodles on the pad in front of him. *You went too far trying to make a deal with Roberto to have an illegal grow op in the building, right under everybody's nose, making the illegal money while we were pursuing a license to grow.*

Trying to dance at several weddings simultaneously. That, too, was Connor Beauregard.

And Rafa could have forgiven him that—on a good day—but why did he have to betray Rafael, his best friend?

"Morning, Rafa, everything OK?"

Rafael's head snapped up, and he looked straight into Al's coal-dark, unreadable eyes, and realized he had drawn hard, straight lines through his pointless doodles with enough pressure to tear the paper. Like shooting arrows, or bullets maybe.

"Just fine, thanks. Yourself?" he choked out. He put his pen back into his pocket and forced a smile. "Now that you're here, perhaps this show is going to get on the road. I know we are all impatient to know what's going on with Perfect Cannabis and how we are going to get out of…"

Al raised his hands, palms out, and shook his head.

"I would if I had the answers, Rafael, sorry. I'm afraid I know little more than you do."

"Come again?"

Rafael looked around and blinked, as if he had awakened from a nap just now. What? Al—not in charge? But—who else could it be?

Dante sat at his left, relaxed, scrolling through messages on his phone as if he were bored. Josh and Simon had started a discussion about the viability of the medical marijuana business and paid no attention whatsoever, and he himself most certainly was not in charge. So, who…?

"Kayla?" he asked, knowing the moment he said it that it was not an option. Kayla ran a rather successful gossip magazine—true—but there ended her competence in business, as far as he knew. Unless you wanted to decorate your offices real pretty and know all the executives' innermost secrets.

"Kayla has been invited," Al confirmed with a slight nod of his head. "And I believe if she wishes it, she may even be offered a seat on the board of directors going forward. After all, she was involved in this company from the very beginning, and her contacts in and experience with the media are invaluable."

"That's why Connor thought she was useful," Rafael said slowly, still more dumbfounded than ever.

If the company was to survive the recent scandals, and keep going as a viable concern, interest investors again and become the money-making enterprise it could be, someone needed to be in charge. Someone with the experience, the knowledge, the contacts, and the image to inspire trust and confidence.

Simon or Josh?

Rafael looked across the table to where the two of them were still arguing and involuntarily made a face. Right. Even he would not want to invest in a new, innovative and risky project with either one of those two in charge.

Still, Al's father, Ivers Senior, as he had started to think of him, must have something in mind. The man never did anything without having a proper plan in place, and a backup just in case. Connor had had to learn that the hard way, hadn't he?

"I can't tell you what his plan is," Al said and settled in on his other side. "Even if I wanted to, he hasn't shared it with me."

Something there he couldn't put his finger on. It made no sense that Al would not be part of the grand plan. None, unless his father felt Al had a hand in screwing this up somehow.

"I'm not blaming you," Rafael said, but even to him, the words sounded wooden, made up.

"Thank you. But if I were you, I sure would. My brother ruined everything we had worked for, and I failed to keep an eye on him. The moment he got out of jail, I should have…"

Rafael raised a hand, stopping him. "Hey, Al, it does not much matter now, does it? We're stuck with a company that is in tatters, we own most of the shares in it, we have some smaller shareholders banging on our doors, wanting to know what happened… I suggest we don't go around looking for fault. It's a waste of time."

Al nodded slowly. "That is generous of you, Rafael, indeed. I do hope we can work together if this company is to have any kind of future at all."

"I don't know about that…"

Rafael wanted to say more, but the words stuck in his throat. The door opened once again, and floating on a cloud of Chanel, Kayla entered.

Kayla never walked into a room and closed the door behind her. Kayla only did grand stage entries, and she paused in the doorway to make sure all heads were turned her way.

Today, she wore white from head to toe, including the fluffy white fur stole wrapped around her shoulders. Kayla would not worry a moment about the anti-fur lobby that kept most women wearing faux hides. She would always do exactly as she pleased.

She also did not care one whit that she ran 20 minutes late, and quite obviously everyone had been waiting for her. The world did indeed wait for Kayla Montecito.

"Hello there, darlings," she said, tossing her blonde mane. "I dare say, traffic downtown gets more dreadful every single day. Rafael, my dear, I have not seen you in ages. How are you…?"

With that, she enveloped him in a great big hug and kissed him on both cheeks.

"If you have heard anything from Connor and did not tell me, I will personally strangle you," she whispered into his ear, and indicated with a nod that Al should vacate the seat to Rafael's right to make room for her.

Obediently, Al rose and moved up one seat, while Kayla arranged her furs, her hat, her sunglasses, portfolio, and fine leather gloves. Rafael watched with an amused smile. Whatever else she did, Kayla had always provided a certain amount of entertainment. Things did not get dull while she was around.

Then again, she was the source of the helicopter.

"I miss that helicopter," he said, bending low so only she could hear, and took her wrist. "It was the highlight of the day at the grand opening."

"Oh, Rafa, why did you not say so? Of course I kept it. The lease ran an extra few months. It would have been such a waste. Come around any time. We'll take a little jaunt somewhere."

Vintage Kayla Montecito.

Rafael smiled despite himself. He knew it had hit her just as hard when Connor up and left town. After all, they had been living together for the longest time, and her magazine had run a suspicious number of wedding stories just around the end, but Kayla had kept it together, held her head high and made the best of things.

As they all had, holding their broken promises.

"Well now that I am here, boys, would anybody like to tell me what is so important that I had to give up a morning interview with the delicious Anderson Cooper?"

"Actually, we would all like to know that," Josh said and looked at Al as if all of the answers were written in his face. "It's not like we all want to be in here for coffee and cake all morning, you know, Al? Just let me know what."

"Folks, I have no idea," Al said again and shrugged. "Much like you, I was summoned here for a meeting, away from my regular…

business activities. Like you, I am waiting to hear what the fate of this company might be."

All eyes turned to Tessa now. She lounged in her chair, one leg slung over the other, her laptop pulled across her lap, her fingers pecking away at the keyboard.

"Tessa," Rafael finally asked. "You're the one who came prepared. What do you know that we don't?"

"They are kind of getting restless," Tessa whispered into the mouthpiece at her neck and listened for a moment. "OK, couple of minutes at the most. Stand by now."

"Tess?"

Tessa tapped against the chassis of her laptop and stared at the screen as if no one had spoken, indeed, as if no one else were in the room. Rafael ground his teeth.

When they worked together, at Connor's office, he would frequently call her 'Brat,' and for good reasons.

Connor should have kept an eye on her, should have known she would be vulnerable to large amounts of money being thrown at her. They all should have known. Startup companies did not make you rich, at least not in the beginning and not at her level. But shit, they had worked together for years and through a number of projects.

You just did not expect it out of your own ranks. You did not go looking behind you after all this time. 'We only steal from other people—not from each other,' Connor would say, making everybody laugh.

Until he went insane with funds, did not pay anyone, and kept making and breaking promises. How much did Ivers pay her, Rafael wondered, not for the first time, and how much information did he get for it? Everything? Almost everything?

"OK, go ahead."

The room suddenly became very quiet at Tessa's words, and Rafael saw eyes darting around, waiting for the door to open.

Above them, the flatscreen TV flickered, and an image appeared, flickered, pixelated briefly, and reassembled again.

An older gentleman, dressed impeccably in a black suit, starched shirt, and tie, sitting in a comfortable leather chair, smiled down at them, almost benevolently. For a moment, no one spoke, trying to make sense of what they were seeing.

"Father," spoken so softly, Rafael thought he might be the only one who had heard it, but the glance that passed between Al and Dan proved otherwise.

"Did you know anything about this?" Dan mouthed, and Al shook his head.

"Welcome, ladies and gentlemen," Ivers Senior said jovially and folded his hands on the table before him. "Welcome to your new Board of Directors for Perfect Cannabis Corporation. I thought we should all meet and get a few things settled before everyone runs off to attend to their own business again."

Can he see us? Rafael wondered. Then a hard look met Al and Dan from the screen, and something passed in that look, telling Rafael that indeed he could. Those two men had just been given orders without the need for words. *Shut the hell up and listen.*

Both men looked down at their hands and obeyed.

Josh, on the other hand…

"Well, I'll say, sir—I have no idea who you are or why you feel we ought to listen to you just now. I would not ordinarily care, except for the fact that I have been dragged out of an important meeting to attend here. To do what, I am not sure."

"Patience, Josh, it is a virtue, my mother would say. Of course, my mother did not have a virtuous bone in her body, so I don't know how she would be the expert on it. Let's leave that for the moment…"

"Yes, let's dispense with homilies," Simon said sarcastically. "I have sort of an idea who you are, and Al's reaction does fill in some blanks, but unless you have a way to pull this company out of the pile of

15

excrement the previous management steered us into, I think we are all wasting each other's time."

"As you wish. Right down to business then." The man on the screen folded his hands and sat a little straighter, cold grey eyes passing from one to the next. "I personally prefer to get to know the people I am going to be working with, but it is not actually required now, is it? Thank you for your comments, Mr. Graff. You and Mr. Novak can make your apologies and leave at any time; I don't have any further use for you at this point."

"What the hell..."

Josh stood now, and took a step closer to the monitor, bringing him face-to-face with the oversized face on the screen.

"With all due respect, what the hell are you talking about? We here are the founding members of this company. What authority do you take to dismiss us and presume to take charge?"

The man on the screen smiled. An odd little twitch, Rafael thought. One that only moved his mouth, as if he had practiced the expression in the mirror. Ivers's eyes stayed locked on the little group, hard and unreadable as they had been before. Something about those eyes made Rafael shiver just a little. He wouldn't want to be the target of that man's angry stare, not without good reason.

"Well then, allow me to introduce myself, Mr. Novak. My name is Tadeo Ivers, and as of two weeks ago, I own the majority of voting stock of Perfect Cannabis Corporation. So, you see, it does not much matter who you are or what you do. If I say goodbye, you are gone. Is that understood?"

"Well, I'll..."

Josh sat back down, his eyes never leaving the face on the screen.

"I was not aware..."

"Of course not. Nobody knew, and I made sure information did not get out unless I wanted it to get out, you see?"

Rafael shivered again, even though he was sure the temperature in the conference room was as balmy and pleasant as it had always been.

Ivers used the word 'I' the way he imagined God himself might. 'I made sure the information did not go out,' and it would not. Period.

"Are you uncomfortable, Mr. Covin?"

Rafael head snapped up, and he found Ivers's dark, cold eyes boring into him. Damn this technology anyway. He'd have to talk to Tessa, well... no.

"Not at all, sir. I am fine," he said simply and forced his shoulders to square.

Damn the man if he was going to make him shiver. There was money involved here, nothing else, just money. And Ivers had tons of it, but Rafael was not exactly looking for handouts either.

"Good, because we want our executives and future executives to be as comfortable as possible. Now then, let us continue..."

"You own the company," Josh said, a little confused, and shifted in his chair. "That changes things, a bit, I believe."

"Of course I do not own the company, Mr. Novak. It is a public company after all, as you are well aware. I just own stock, lots and lots of stock. So, in a way, yes, what I say around here will happen, but no need to panic."

No need to panic, just because the insane were running the asylum. If he hadn't known Ivers was watching him, he would have chuckled, but Rafael did not care to draw attention a second time. *No need to panic, people. The Titanic is now being captained by a criminal of questionable ethics and experience, but don't worry about it.*

"I have no desire to become involved in the day-to-day running of this business, although I will keep a very close eye on it this time around."

Ivers paused and dramatically looked at each man and woman in turn. "Anyone who is not comfortable with this would be best advised to vacate their chair immediately, just so I can make plans."

Nobody moved. Heck, it was just getting good now, and they could always leave a little later, if necessary. Rafael was tempted to leave, and leave that portion of his life behind, but for sheer curiosity.

He still wanted to see Ivers's plans for the company. PerCan was not a company he could run.

Oh, he could try for a while, but he would not get very far, no matter how much money he spent, or how many of his sons he installed in executive positions. For starters, if he thought anyone in the Ministry of Health was inclined to issue a license to grow marijuana for medical purposes to him, he had to be dreaming. A man with a criminal record, shady business deals, and even shadier underground connections would never be in charge of such a company.

Not even if he bribed his way through the ranks of public servants. Connor had tried to go that route and failed spectacularly. Not just failure, grandiose, amazing, spectacular public failure. So, what was Ivers's plan?

"Wonderful. I like it when people try to get along. Let's get the easy things out of the way right off. Then we can concentrate on the—more involved issues, shall we?"

Josh and Simon nodded, dumbfounded. Rafael could feel the steely gaze on him again and inclined his head ever so briefly.

"You see how easy this is. Now then, Kayla..."

Kayla's head snapped up, and her voice actually trembled a little. "Yes?"

One-word answers had never been her style, but then again, she had just recently watched the man she loved be torn to shreds by that fellow on the screen. Whatever she and Connor had had, they had been good together. Even if they were two strange peas in a pod.

For a moment, Rafael felt sorry for Kayla. She'd been a working girl most of her life—polite term—married Hanson Montecito, the publisher of magazines and trashy novels, and ended up a very wealthy widow a few years later. She did well as long as she stuck to publishing gossip, but she would lose against this man.

"Kayla, I think ours is a very useful relationship. And if not a friendship, at least one filled with goodwill to one another, don't you think?"

"I don't wish anyone ill," Kayla managed to say, probably just then imagining what the man up there could do to her little publishing house if he so chose... Better not to think about it.

"Good, then I would like you to remain in charge of publicity and public information if that is acceptable to you. You will retain your seat on the board of directors, and my office will work out a suitable compensation package for you. I leave the details to them; I am absolutely sure you can come to a mutual satisfying arrangement."

Kayla blinked once and exhaled visibly. Apparently, she had expected anything but this.

"I am sure we can," she finally said, and Ivers smiled again. Rafael wished he would quit smiling. That grimace scared the daylights out of him, and Ivers knew it.

"Very well then, splendid."

Ivers rubbed his hands and smiled broadly, and Rafael could almost feel Kayla relax into her chair. Kayla was a fighter, a tough cookie, who had been through worse. She would get along with Ivers just fine, especially if he let her do her job—which she happened to be good at.

"I am pleased you will be working with us. You are very good at what you do, Kayla."

His gaze wandered around the table again and eventually fastened on Dan.

"Most of you would agree the same holds true of my son Dante. Now, I could simply assign a post to him if I wished to do so, but for the sake of agreement in the group..." Ivers spread his hands. "I would propose to have Dante Ivers become head of the growing operation, if there is no opposition from anyone here."

As if. Rafael barely stopped himself from shaking his head.

"I think none of us know anything about growing," he finally said and briefly glanced at Simon and Josh, who nodded their agreement. "When things were still going well down at the building, Dante did an excellent job, so I would support him."

A cold glance from the monitor met him. *You know,* that glance said, *you know all about Roberto and Dante, don't you?* This time Rafael held steadfast and returned the stare. *Fucking yes, I do.* He refused to take his eyes off Ivers until the other man smiled again. For long seconds, the room lay in silence.

"We are all in agreement," Josh finally said, breaking the moment.

"Splendid. We are moving just right along here. I have great expectations all of our board meetings will turn out to be so agreeable and efficient."

"This is an official board meeting then?"

"Why yes, Rafael, why do you ask?"

"There are certain—requirements and conventions. But never mind, sir. Just making sure."

Rafael looked back down at his notepad. He wanted to laugh at Ivers's presumption. This had never been called as a board meeting, no regular invitation, no agenda, no notes—just the guy with a ton of shares saying 'be there.' Period. If he truly wanted to run this business, and run it well, Ivers had a lot of homework to do.

But he only smiled that reptilian smile again. "Do not worry about it, Rafael. We are not formal around here. Everybody can say what is on his or her mind. I find prepared meetings terribly stiff and boring."

Stiff and boring. Christ. Rafael barely managed to keep a straight face while the pen in his fingers suffered. Connor would have…

Screw it, he thought, he had nothing to lose here. His friend and cofounder of the company had left the country in disgrace, the share price stumbled all over the place, Connor's friends and fiancé/girlfriend regularly used him for a shoulder to cry on, and if someone ever used the words 'have you heard anything' again, he would explode. So, in fact, Rafael decided, he had nothing to lose.

"If I might ask a question that's on my mind then."

"But of course. That is what this meeting is all about. And why don't you call me Tadeo? Just to make us all a little more comfortable."

"Well, Tadeo, if you don't mind, a few minutes ago, you mentioned you were not interested in an active role in managing Perfect Cannabis Corporation."

"Correct. I have too much to do to worry about the day-to-day running of a corporation like this one. I have my own interests."

Criminal interest, most likely, but let's let that remain unspoken for a minute, Rafael thought and nodded.

"Surely, being the businessman you are, you understand that there needs to be a defined corporate structure in place, to make the engine run, so to speak. It's all good and well to say we will keep carrying on, but this company has lost its founder."

Rafael paused for a minute, but Ivers did not speak or move.

"One of the key people. Gone. Connor Beauregard was Perfect Cannabis in every way, no matter what we think about him. He sold it to our investors because he lived and breathed the company. He was…"

"Its heart?" Ivers suggested softly, and Rafael shrugged.

"If you want to put it that way, sure. Nobody is irreplaceable. I know that. I just can't see a way the four of us…" His hand circled once around the table. "Are going to be able to do all of the lifting he used to. So, unless you hire a magician…"

"There will be no need for heavy lifting or miracle workers, Rafael. I understand your concern. I was not going to do this until later on, but, oh well, change of plans." He nodded at Tessa, who in turn went to open the conference room door and beckoned to someone outside.

A tall, lanky man appeared, nodding at the people in the room and at the monitor.

"Good morning, gentlemen. Mr. Ivers."

Rafael sat thunderstruck for a moment.

"Roger Carmichael," he said as if he were seeing a ghost, and he shook his head to clear it. "You—in here?"

"You gentlemen know each other then? Splendid." The reptilian grimace shone from the screen again, but Rafael was too busy shaking hands with the newcomer to mind.

"We met a few years ago, and you don't work in the construction industry long without having come across Roger's name," Rafael said, smiling a little because he felt in his own element again, finally. "Roger Carmichael here made magic happen for a tiny little construction company by the name of Omni, ended up being the biggest damned outfit in the country. I heard you retired?"

"Spent some time in Asia and Hawaii," Roger said, taking a seat, shifting comfortably. "Got bored. Heard there was a need for some decent management here."

Roger was tall and tanned, clad in khakis and work boots, with the broad hands that could grab a tool and get to work anywhere.

"So, you're the one who will manage PerCan?"

They could have chosen worse. From what he'd heard, Roger had indeed worked miracles for Omni, taking it from the brink of insolvency to being the first stop in high-rise, low-rise, and any-in-between-size construction, if you wanted it done well. This was a man he could respect in the board-room, or out of it. But cannabis? Was that not a bit of a leap for the man?

From concrete and steel girders to leafy green plants and growing rooms? Management was management, though, and if Roger thought he was up for it... But Roger stretched his long legs away from him, folded his hands behind his head, and shook it.

"I don't think I have a green thumb or any kind of body part in me, Rafa. Not my thing at all."

"Rafael, Mr. Carmichael is not going to be running Perfect Can-nabis Corporation," Ivers said in that soft, patient tone again that immediately raised all sorts of alarms in Rafael's brain.

"Mr. Carmichael is going to be managing Covin Construction Corporation."

Rafael dropped into his chair, waiting for the rush in his brain to abate. But what the fuck?

"What the... that's my company! Damn it."

He fired his broken pen onto the table, forcibly straightened his shoulders as he had seen Connor do, and looked Ivers straight in the eyes.

"I'm quite sure you are at this point the majority shareholder in Perfect Cannabis Corporation, Tadeo, and what you say in here goes, but, with all due respect, you will please leave your hands off my private company, are we clear on that?"

"Perfectly clear."

"Then, again, with all due respect, what the hell? What is Roger doing here? No offense, Roger, I admire and respect you. But this..."

Ivers raised his hands again, and Rafael could feel his own forming fists he did not even bother trying to conceal. This was bullshit, beyond bullshit. If Ivers had been in the room...

"Calm down, Mr. Covin."

"Oh, I am perfectly calm, Tadeo. And if I am telling you to stay away from my company, then you had best do that, because..."

"Because what, Rafael?"

What was he doing? Nobody threatened Tadeo Ivers—nobody. At least no more than once. How often had he heard that? Had that been Connor's line? *Fuck. And fuck you, Connor, for disappearing on me and leaving me with this pile of...*

He could not, he would not let him anywhere near the construction company he had spent his life building and planning on leaving to his sons one day. Not while he still had one thing to say about it. Rafael took a breath and started over.

"Nobody is threatening you. But we're talking about PerCan here, a publicly traded corporation that's in trouble right now, not a small, privately owned construction company. I fail to see..."

"Correct, and that is why you will sit down and listen."

Rafael sat, and Kayla took his hand under the table and gave it a reassuring squeeze. Rafael pulled away roughly and shook his head. Ivers had not just threatened to take her magazine away from her, had he?

"Are you ready to listen?"

"I am not five years old, Tadeo. Enough with the games. Speak your mind."

"Nobody is trying to take your company away from you. Roger Carmichael, from what I have heard, is a rainmaker when it comes to construction companies."

Roger winked at him, and Rafael still had a hard time keeping his hands still and clenched away out of sight.

"Yes, and?"

"And I thought you might appreciate having his advice and—hands-on support—while you tried to grow your company into something worth leaving to both of your sons. Mike and Tyler, is it? Admirable young men, I am told. Smart, talented and…"

"Leave them out of it. I still don't see…"

"Free-of-charge advice and support, Covin, that sound pretty good to you?"

"Naturally, but what does that have to do with the price of oranges in Spain? I've been doing fine on my own—not spectacular, not like Carmichael here, but still OK. So somewhere in there, there has to be a hook. And I would like to know what that is."

Ivers sighed and looked off into the distance.

"You're suspicious, Rafael," he finally said. "That is not necessarily a bad thing, but I tire of it. Now if you had just let me roll out the whole plan the way I wanted to, and show it to everyone in a logical manner." He threw up his hands and shook his head. "I simply thought that it would be easier for you to know your company and your legacy was in good hands back home while you stepped in as CEO of Perfect Cannabis Corporation—just until the company is in smooth waters again. Until such a time as we can talk about a future for Perfect Cannabis Corporation. I also figured you were more likely to say no, knowing that you cannot handle both Covin Construction and Perfect Cannabis at the same time. So, I came up with a brilliant solution, if I might say so myself."

Ivers? The man before whom the heads of motorcycle gangs, small-time drug dealers, and other assorted criminals trembled in fear, pouting?

Rafael had to look again to be sure. Besides, he still wasn't entirely sure the whole monologue had sunk in yet. But Ivers was definitely pouting. Shit, what had he just said? One of the best construction managers in the country was going to be running Covin Construction for free while he patched together PerCan?

"Well…"

"Well what, Rafael?"

"I did not expect this."

"Of course you did not." Ivers made a face again. "I actually put some thought into this. I did not simply purchase the company and hope for the best."

"Wait a minute," Josh piped up. "And you just assumed this would be OK with the rest of us? I mean, you never bothered to ask either Simon or me how we felt about it? Perhaps we might have had a suggestion as well."

"And do you, Josh? Do you have an alternate suggestion? Speak up now. I assure you I did look at your company and background as well, but for some reason, you did not strike me as the perfect CEO for a publicly traded company."

"I have plenty of experience, just for your information."

"Naturally. 20 years in the commercial real estate business. You've made a small fortune, and you can quite rightly be proud of your achievement. The thing is Rafael was one of the founding members of Perfect Cannabis. People remember him. They remember his connection to Connor Beauregard."

"Exactly my point, Mr. Ivers, Tadeo. As far as I remember, Rafael and Connor were best of buddies. Nothing against you, Rafael, but if people see your name, and they remember Connor, well, I fail to see how that would inspire confidence."

"You might have a point, Josh." Tadeo cocked his head and shrugged. "And believe me, I thought of that too. Then… my contacts confronted me with Rafael Covin's, er, reputation."

Rafael's head snapped up, and he glowered at the screen.

"Excuse me?"

"Don't get excited again, Rafael, please. To answer your question, Josh, every time I talk to someone about Rafael Covin, they can't tell me enough about how honest the man is, how much of a straight shooter. How he tries to make a guy whole even after the deal goes sideways. When I hear something like that, I want the man with that kind of a reputation on my team. How can I lose with him in charge? Do you see my point?"

"He never screwed me in a deal, even the ones that went south. You're right about that," Josh said and sat back down. "But you might have prepared us instead of springing this thing at a meeting like this one."

"Oh, now where would the fun be in that?"

Ivers grinned again as Rafael tried to assemble scattered brain cells into rational thoughts and thoughts into something that at least approached a sensible answer.

"I—well…"

So much for sensible answers. Rafael looked down at his hands and started again. "Mr. Ivers, Tadeo, I am honored by the trust you put in me. However, let me assure you I am not Connor Beauregard."

"Oh, I would hope you are not, Rafael. After all, Connor is the man responsible for all of the problems this company faces at the moment."

"Perhaps 'all of them' is a bit sweeping. Be that as it may, Connor had a talent. Some might call it magic. Investors, people with the kind of money we need, they listened to him. I own a construction company. I have no illusions about my talents in that area."

"Don't sell yourself short," Josh all of a sudden said and rested his chin on his closed fist. "While I am not in favor of this so-called meeting, I have to say, the thought of you becoming CEO does have a certain appeal."

"Josh, I appreciate your support, but…"

"And you were there, at the very beginning," Kayla said, putting her hand on his wrist once again. "You were there when he thought of the idea, even before I joined. It was you and him working together. This is perfect. Who else could lead this company in the spirit in which it was started?"

"Has everyone gone mad all of a sudden?" Rafael looked around the table into the faces of Josh, Simon, Kayla, and Al and Dan. They all looked at him with eager smiles, expecting great solutions from him. As if he could jump up suddenly and say, *Sure, I will solve all of your problems. Just give me a minute.*

But he knew he couldn't. Moreover, he didn't want to. He just wanted to go back to the life he'd had before anyone mentioned cannabis. This company was in a hole so deep there was likely no digging out, and he was not going to try. No. Rafael shook his head again.

"This company is out of money, it is nowhere near getting a license to grow, and until it does, nobody will want to invest, and that is on top of the public relations nightmare about the illegal grow op. What do you think I can do? Wave a magic wand and make everything right? I hate to tell you people—I am not so sure this company will survive as a viable entity. Even if it does, it would take extensive financing to set things right. Moreover, I just don't believe it can be done."

"You let the financing be my problem for the moment," Tadeo said from the screen. "I will make sure you won't have to rattle a tin can for a while."

"For a while, Tadeo? I'm sure you have seen the financial statements, such as they are. You know how much cash an operation like this bleeds every single day. Do you want to commit your personal funds indefinitely?

None of us does, at least not me. So, hear me when I am telling you. I am not Connor; I cannot talk us out of this problem. I want out."

"And again, Rafael, we are fortunate you are not Connor, and talking is what caused many of our problems in the first place. We could sit here and argue about this until the end of days, but let me cut this short right here. If you are turning me down, fine. Even though you are forcing me to go look elsewhere for a suitable CEO. I thought you might want to preserve the memory of what you started."

Some memory! Rafael said nothing for a moment. He burned to step outside for a minute, gather himself and think rationally, something he had not done in God knew how long, while he'd been busy putting out one fire after another.

"I know you are tired, Rafa, but I also know you can do this."

"Jesus, Kayla, this is a mess…"

"A mess you would not have to unravel all by yourself. There's still Kayla, Simon, and myself." Josh looked across the table at Al and Dan and shrugged. "And those two."

"Indeed," Ivers chuckled, another sound that gave Rafael the chills. "It looks like your troops are raring for you to lead. So, what do you think, Mr. Covin? Would you at least give it a try?"

Rafael looked into the eyes of the men and woman in the room and back up to the man on the screen.

Go and fuck yourself, he wanted to say. *You and your constant battles against Connor caused a large portion of the shit-pile this company has crashed into, so why don't you just go and fuck yourself? I can't, and I don't want to fight against the windmills you put up there.*

"I understand if you are going to tell me to go and fuck myself, Rafael, but for the sake of the people in this room and the shareholders…"

"I would appreciate it if you did not try to read my mind, Tadeo. You have no idea how I think."

"Keep your own company in mind, Rafael. If you were to say no to me today—well, if you were to say no to me, number one, Roger would leave, and you miss out on a wonderful opportunity, and number two..." Ivers paused for a moment and locked eyes with Rafael onscreen. That dark cold glance that made every man shiver, no matter who he was. "Number two, I can go look for another CEO, but who knows what else might happen? It's a dangerous world out there."

Ivers spread his hands, shrugged, and the room became so still Rafael thought the very air had stopped moving.

He fought to swallow past a lump in his throat. He still wanted out.

On the screen, Tadeo still smiled and held his eyes with that reptilian, laser-focused stare.

In less than a second, he made up his mind. What else was he going to do, really? Damn Ivers and his brood. *I hear you, Connor!*

"I—truly appreciate the vote of confidence from all of you. I really do... I told you. I am not Connor, and I will not be able to perform the way he did..."

"But?"

"But if only for the sake of the shareholders who have entrusted us with money they have had to work hard for, I think I ought to at least try."

Kayla took his hand, Simon and Josh exhaled visibly, and Ivers up on the screen grinned. Rafael didn't see a grin; he saw pure evil. He wanted to wipe that grin off the man's face, and he finally understood why Connor and Ivers had gone to loggerheads so many times.

Al and Dan sat completely still, their eyes on their folded hands. If it bothered them, they did not let it show.

Josh and Simon rose and shook Rafael's hand, as if no threat had been uttered. Kayla hugged him, enveloping him in a cloud of blonde hair and Chanel Number Five, and throughout all of this, Rafael's and Tadeo's eyes stayed locked on the big screen at the far wall of the conference room.

An entire conversation took place in that look, without a word being spoken.

TWO

In short order, Tadeo offered Simon and Josh seats on the board of directors once again, which they graciously accepted. No need to make huge and sweeping changes in a company that was barely alive. The collective sigh of relief became a physical thing in the room. Someone had taken over. Someone who had at least been there all along.

"I'd say this calls for a drink at The Lighthouse," Kayla said with a brittle edge of false cheerfulness when everyone had left and they were the last two people there. "What say? Shall we? Come along."

"Kayla, with all due respect, but I am not in the mood for celebrating."

"Why ever not? I bet since your wife passed away, you have not been out once. And we've just scored a huge victory. So, let's go…"

"A victory—is that what we are calling it? From where I am sitting, I've just been handed an enormous shit sandwich, Kayla. If this company isn't dead, it barely has a pulse, and that man pretty much threatened what's left of my family if I don't get it done. I have several hundred thousand dollars of unpaid bills sitting there somewhere, I have no idea what happened to the company documentation, investor confidence is nil, and the one thing everyone wants to ask me is if I have heard from Connor."

"Well—yes—but…"

"The man is at the moment languishing in the Cayman Islands for all I know."

"Caymans are not what they used to be, Rafa, not if you're thinking of hiding from the law or stashing away illegal cash. They are getting really careful down there."

"Well, aren't I glad to have an expert on malfeasance on my team. Grand. Fact remains, people are just waiting for me to screw this up. There's a cheering section out there for 'bring down Covin' and 'let's see how dreadful bad can get.' The only reason I just agreed to go near this damned company is because Ivers left me no other choice. It was that or personal ruin."

"You know, you never used to swear like this."

"I do now. Get the hell used to it."

"You know what I think? I think you are doing it for Connor—for his memory."

"Connor," Rafael spat. "And where is he, huh? The brilliant man who screwed all of us—including you if I might remind you. The woman he supposedly loved."

"I am well aware of that," Kayla said tightly, put her gold leather portfolio under her arm, and shrugged into her cloud of white fur. Just as she slipped on oversized designer sunglasses to hide her eyes, he thought he could see it: the same kind of sadness and betrayal he'd been carrying around. She had lived with him after all.

"Sorry. I'm just a bitter old man. Don't mind me. I shouldn't have snapped at you, but the hopelessness of this affair is getting to me." He pressed his hands into the side of his head for a moment and looked at his watch. "I suppose it is lunchtime anyway. I think I am going to need your advice on an office and immediate staffing needs."

Kayla managed a smile, held out her elbow, and waited for him to take it.

"You can have an office at the publishing house for the time being, Rafa. You need not even ask, and you're going to need a capable PA, not like..." She nodded in the direction where Tessa had sat.

31

She had left in the meantime, packing up her electronics and leaving the room as if the entire scene had nothing to do with her. "Not like Ivers's puppet over there. Leave it with me. I'll make sure to find you someone who knows what she is doing."

"She?"

"Rafa, I might be a little old school, but most capable PAs are women, has something to do with organizing and multitasking, you know."

"You are too much, Kayla."

***

Much as Josh and Simon had been happy to let him step in to take care of the company, he now let Kayla step in. In less than a week, he had moved into a small but elegant corner office at Montecito Publishing and said good morning to an attractive woman in her thirties, who knew exactly what needed to be done, when and how. She scared the lights out of him the moment he met her.

Connie dressed in conservative business suits, carried her long blonde hair in a precise braid, and presented him with an itemized to-do list every single morning.

He called his sons every day, until they tired of him asking if they were OK, and he looked over his shoulder regularly. The dread that had formed in his stomach the moment Ivers had made him CEO would not go away, no matter how hard he tried.

He really had no idea how he could save Perfect Cannabis, and what would happen to him if he failed. Jesus, he could barely talk to his new PA.

***

"Old school," he said to Roger Carmichael one evening.

He'd made a regular habit of dropping in at Covin Construction every day, visiting his old office and unloading on Roger.

"Old school indeed. Originally, I was not fired up about having an actual PA. I barely know what I need to do, never mind telling somebody else, you know? But Connie runs the place without me. Knows exactly where I need to be every single minute and what I need."

"And you are complaining about this exactly why?"

Roger leaned back in what used to be Rafael's chair and crossed his feet on Rafael's desk. Former desk. "I know you ran this place basically single-handed, but you were wasting time doing shit. Do you know there now exists a perfect filing system in your office?"

"No kidding—an official filing system?"

"Exactly. Offers, tenders, records. Everything you had piled into the back room in that rickety old bookcase."

"Hoping to find it when I needed it," Rafael said ruefully. "I remember."

"All organized now. You can ask about any one project from the last five years, and my girl will find everything on the inside of an hour. She even has students scanning and digitizing it all, so paper will be history before long."

"Fabulous, I think."

"Point being, Rafael, I don't need you to drop in every single day. If I were to be completely honest, you are making people a little nervous."

"People?"

"Your staff. The construction workers, accounting department. They're not quite sure if you trust me, and I really don't like it."

"Well, it's still…"

"It's your company. I know that, Rafael. But I was hired to run it. Let it go. I have it in hand. You ought to have your hands full with getting Perfect Cannabis back on the map. How is that going anyway?"

"It's a lot of work, you know."

"Exactly. So why are you here, Rafa? Bluntly speaking, we don't need you in this office. It's working better than it ever did before. Your company is in good hands, even when you're not looking over my shoulder every step of the way. So once again, why are you here?"

Rafael looked around. The office, his former office, the one that used to overflow with paperwork, receipts, bits and pieces of construction equipment, material samples and tools in a state of disassembly, his office suddenly had become neat, clean and organized. Things had their place, and a man who needed information had only to reach for it. It never had been like this during his time.

He'd created the chaos he thrived on. And nobody, except for Rafael Covin himself, could make sense out of it.

Until now.

He took off the annoying reading glasses he had to wear nowadays, dangling them from his fingers.

"Right…"

"I know you inherited a pile of crap with PerCan, to put it mildly. I wouldn't want it. I got the easy end of the stick. Covin Construction is a breeze to work for and build into something great. But it will not end well if you come around every day checking on things, confusing people."

"Are you throwing me out of my own company?"

"No. I'm telling you to tend to the job you said you would. PerCan. Nobody expects you to be Connor Beauregard. Heck, people hope you won't turn into him. Fervently hope you won't turn into him, but win or lose, you have to try."

"So?"

"So go do what you need to do, Rafael. You've got nothing to lose, at least not your own company."

Nothing to lose. Nothing to lose, unless he did not manage to save PerCan.

***

Connie presented him with a neat little signature folder upon his return. Checks to be signed, agreements to be read, accepted or rejected… Rafael found himself longing for the simplicity of a seven-story shopping complex with a three-level underground parking garage, several elevators, and moving sidewalks. Shifting uncomfortably, he settled into his new executive leather chair.

"Fine then, Connor. Not the first time I have to clean up your mess."

He shuffled his rear end around the new chair again and called Connie back into his office.

"Could you do me a favor, Connie?"

"Of course, all you need to do is ask."

"Call Roger Carmichael, over at Covin Construction, ask him to ship my old chair here."

"Your… chair?"

"Yes, my chair. This damned thing was made for a candy-assed MBA, and if I have to spend any kind of time in this office, I need my old chair back."

"Very well, Mr. Covin," she said, her tight features radiating disapproval, and out of the corner of his eyes, he thought he could see her shaking her head as she disappeared into her own space.

Next, he sifted through Connor's odd collection of notes and loose papers to find David's phone number. Last he'd heard, the accountant had been involved in a hot battle with the SEC and a stubborn crew of auditors to get the company's quarterly filings up to date. Surely no easy task, given the state of Connor's desk and indeed his affairs, but as Roger had so timely reminded him, he had to try.

"Connor, for God's sake, you ever heard of organizing anything?" he cussed, digging through the bottom of a large pile of paper.

"Mr. Covin? Something else you needed?"

"Connie. Sorry for cussing. I am indeed looking for something. I need David Custer's phone number. David used to be…"

"The accountant in charge of Perfect Cannabis Corporation. Of course, Mr. Covin. If you look on your phone system, you will find his number stored on your speed dial list. Number nine to be precise."

"Oh... I never thought to look."

"No need to apologize. I should have told you, sir."

"Connie, could you do me another favor?"

"Of course, sir. That is why I'm here after all."

"Will you please stop calling me sir? Rafael will perfectly suffice. Rafa if you are in a good mood. Mr. Covin makes me feel like you are talking to the guy behind me."

Connie did not move. Only her lips pursed a little while she considered his words.

"I mean it. Everybody in my company always called me Rafa. Connor did. Tessa did. Even that, err, Tadeo Ivers. So, I would really appreciate it."

"If it makes you feel better."

"It does. And Connie, one more thing?"

"Yes?"

"PerCan never has been and never will be an ordinary company doing things the way they are usually being done. I think all of us will have to get used to this. Perhaps embroider it on a kerchief or something."

Connie said nothing, just nodded and disappeared into the outer area of their office. Kayla really had outdone herself, Rafael thought, looking around. His office was small, but decorated with taste and comfort in mind. He could get used to this, the desks and bookcases from finest, polished mahogany, the soft plush carpeting underfoot and the matching abstract prints on the walls. The construction offices he frequented were usually freezing, furnished with something that had come out of the Goodwill store and featuring blueprints and construction schedules taped haphazardly to the walls.

This was kind of nice for a change, so much comfort and luxury, even as he reminded himself not to get used to it. Soon enough, he would have to get out of here and decamp for their own building on the outskirts of town, if he survived that long. If.

"Check on building," he put on the next page of his hand-scrawled to-do list.

While they had purchased an enormous building to serve as PerCan's head offices and production facilities, he had not seen the place since— well actually since the grand opening months ago, except for a middle-of-the-night visit when Connor had shown him the illegal grow op.

Buying what Connor called the biggest and ugliest building to grow an empire had literally bankrupted them, but his construction crews had managed to make it look decent for the grand opening. They had made a mess look like a palace, at least in the areas accessible to the public and press. The pictures had been fantastic.

Behind the scenes, though. Behind the scenes, the loan shark had waited, the man Connor had promised everything and then some to hide the fact that he was running through funds like nobody's business.

"Check on Mirko," he added to his list. No need to expound on who 'Mirko' was; he would remember without any trouble. After all, they'd had a showdown in the utility room the night of the grand opening. Connor trying to bluff his way out of trouble and Mirko doing everything but threatening to shut down the building.

Rafael chuckled. In a fit of chutzpah Connor had actually promised to write the man a check!

Good old days, standing shoulder to shoulder with Connor.

His phone rang, startling him out of the reverie and making him drop the pen he'd been mangling in his fingers. The insistent ringtone definitely would take some getting used to.

"Rafael Covin," he said with more bravado than he felt.

"It's David. David Custer. Your private secretary called me, said you needed to speak to me?"

Good old Connie. She too would take some getting used to.

"Indeed, David. Thanks for calling. Long time no speak. I'm sure you've endured enough interviews and hearings, and I don't have to tell you what happened over the last few months."

David laughed without mirth.

"Aside from the fact that I almost lost my license because of your mess and never got paid to boot? Are you trying to be funny? Right now, I'm wishing I had never heard the name Beauregard in my entire life. And yours is not far behind."

"There are a lot of people who feel about Connor that way right now, David. A lot of them. I would in fact say there's a line. Rather than get into that line, what say we do something useful and help me put this company back together? From what I hear…"

It took Rafael a moment to understand that the harsh, cackling sound he heard was David's impression of hearty laughter. To him it sounded like someone shaking a tin can filled with nails, but to each his own.

"Forgive me, Rafa, but are you fucking kidding me?"

"Wish I were. Alas, what I have in my hands is a ruin…"

"A ruin? A ruin, Rafael? Go for broke and say a bit of a mess. Connor left a shit-pile behind, plain and simple. No matter where you reach, your hand will be covered in excrement. Nothing was done the way it should have been—nothing."

"Well then, we have a lot of work to do to clean it up, don't we?"

"Were you listening a minute ago? I told you I never got paid. So, give me one good reason why I'm even on the phone with you, instead of telling you to go fuck yourself."

I can manage David, Rafael heard Connor say in his head. *You know why? Because he has a couple of small issues with gambling, and he always needs money—always. As long as I give him a little bit, he just keeps coming. He is too greedy and too desperate to tell me to go fuck myself, as he rightly should.*

"One good reason, David? One, how about I do have money for you? Not everything at once, but I have enough to make a decent good-faith payment, so we can get started to put things right. If you'd rather walk away from everything, though, and forget about the money we may or may not owe you…"

"You do owe me."

"Maybe, maybe not. You said it yourself. Connor left a mess behind. A big mess. I can't find anything around here—heck, I can't even find any positive evidence that you ever worked here."

"The auditors—the auditors were dealing with me all along."

"Oh good, then they ought to be familiar enough with you to pick up where you left off back when. Put it this way, I have enough cash here to put you right for now. Cash. No checks, no games, you come in, you pick it up, you start working again. Sound good to you?"

"I don't want to work for you or your goddamn company again."

"That's fine then, David. Like I said, there's a lineup outside my door of people who have a bone to pick with Connor, and it's a long one. A really long one. No hard feelings then. You can get in back of it. I just thought I'd give you a ring. I am sure there are other…"

"Wait, wait just one goddamn minute."

"What do you mean, David? You just told me to go fuck myself."

"I might have…"

"What? Overreacted? Made a mistake? 30 seconds, only one answer is possible. Do you want to continue with this, take the money and do the best job you can, yes or no?"

"You really have cash there?"

"I have cash here."

Thanks to Tadeo Ivers. Not like cash deals were not the everyday normal in the construction business. He had just never thought…

"I'll be down there in half an hour."

"Montecito Publishing, ground floor, David. Ask for me. And if I were you, I would not dawdle too much. Offer expires the moment I leave my office, you got that?"

He hung up without another word of greeting and sat there for a moment, shaking his head as if he'd been underwater, surfacing just now. If that was how it was going to be with each and every goddamn person he had to deal with… How the hell had Connor done it anyway, promising and making people believe all day long, keeping people happy, knowing damn well that at the end of the day there was no way to follow through? Except he usually had, damn him!

One down, how many more to go?

He asked Connie to get cash ready for David, just enough to keep him interested and hungry, not enough to make him walk, cursing all the way.

You see, Rafa, there's an art to paying people. Always know how much a guy owes. You need to give them what they need, not what they want or what they're hoping for. That way you're keeping the hope alive, the dream alive. So, they will come back and work for you, as long as there's hope. You are mortgaging their dreams, you see.

"Get out of my head, Connor."

"Pardon me?"

He looked straight up at Connie, holding a sealed envelope out to him.

"Just as you asked, sir—Rafael."

"Thanks."

He took the envelope and lined it up on the desk in front of him, perfectly parallel to the dark green leather desk mat Kayla had purchased him. When had he become a "green leather desk mat" guy anyway? Probably at the same time he had become a CEO with an office and an uncomfortable leather chair, instead of a guy happily running around in dirty boots on construction sites, drinking coffee with his workers. Rubbing his eyes, he allowed himself to daydream for just a moment, until Connie knocked on his door again.

"Mr. Custer for you?"

He nodded and managed a smile. "Sure, might as well let him in."

"Did you want me to bring you some water, coffee, anything?"

"Don't bother. David will not be staying long."

David eyed the envelope on Rafael's desk with hungry eyes and did not bother to sit in the visitor's chair.

"Is that it?"

"This is it." Rafael snatched it just out of reach of the man's greedy hands as he reached for it.

"Just a minute, if you will. I'm going to need a few assurances here."

"Fuck assurances, Rafa, I have…"

"You have—let me tell you what you have. You have three clients, two of whom are almost ready for bankruptcy. You owe money to your bookie, the bank, and anyone else foolish enough to lend you some. So let me tell you what I have. I have a company that is ready to get back on its feet and pay you better than you've ever been paid in your entire booze-filled life. This…" He waved the envelope in the air. "This is just enough to pay off the people who are seriously on your tail, but it's only the beginning. You take this. You make my filings happen. You square me with the SEC, and the rest is going to be right here right the same way the moment we are done. You need any resources, you ask Connie out there. If your request is reasonable, she will grant it. No excuses, no delays, no fucking around, do I make myself clear? I don't want to hear what Connor did or did not do. He's gone. This is my game now."

"You can't tell me how to do…"

"I can and I will. My rules. You say yes, you do your damn best, and we're going to make this thing happen together. Shit, this is going to be the biggest goddamn medical marijuana manufacturer the world has ever seen. You say no, you walk away, no hard feelings. In that case this…" He took the envelope and put it into the inside pocket of his jacket. "Stays right there waiting for the next guy who knows finance and is willing to work with people, even when the shit hits the fan. My rules all the way or nothing at all. What is it going to be, Custer, going forward, or your last stand?"

The lanky accountant licked his narrow lips nervously, his eyes focused on the bulge in Rafael's jacket where the envelope had disappeared.

"I'm not going to do anything illegal for you, like Connor used to all the time. I could lose my license."

41

"Wait," Rafael said and cocked his head, listening. "Did you hear me ask you to do anything illegal? I sure did not. And just for an extra bonus, if you don't quit drinking and gambling, you're going to lose your license anyway, no matter what, so what the fuck are you talking about?"

"I don't…"

"You don't, you don't what? I'm tired, David. Yes or no. Do you want this job or not? I don't have all day here, so just tell me and get back to work. I have a company to run if you did not notice on your way in here."

He balled his hand to a fist, just for emphasis, and then opened his hands. "So, what's it going to be, David?"

"I suppose I could…"

"You suppose you could. Whole sentences, David, whole sentences, at least try, OK? You could what?"

"I suppose I could try to get the filings up to date. It's not going to be easy…"

"Nothing's easy, David, not in this company."

"It's not going to be easy because of all of the… irregularities. But we do have a bit of a basis to build on."

"Good for you. Build on it. Can you get started right away?"

"I have another client, but I guess I could."

"Do that and be in touch with Connie. Every other day, let her know what is happening, where you're at, and if there's anything you need. Is that clear?"

"Yes."

"Then we understand each other. I like it when people understand each other."

His hand slipped back into his jacket, and he brought the envelope back, offering it to David. Shit, had he really just used the very same words as Tadeo Ivers? *I like it when people get along? Shit. And if you don't do as I ask…*

"Your down payment."

"I swear to you, if there are not regular payments after this—"

"There will be. There's a new sheriff in town."

A greedy hand snapped up the envelope, and it disappeared into David's jacket just as fast as it had shown up.

"I don't think you know what you are getting into, Rafael. Shit, there are so many landmines buried in the old statements."

"Why do you think you're here? Identify them, tell me about them, and let me know what I need to do so they don't blow up in my face. We need to get back into the good with the SEC."

"I can…"

"David? Just get out of here and do it. Standing here talking about getting your job done is not getting your job done. You dig?"

David ducked down a bit and finally nodded.

"I will be in touch."

Rafael waved his hand, shooing him out the door, while already looking at Connie's notes for the rest of the day. Damn, if each and every one of the vendors made a fuss like David, he'd have a heart attack. But he needed David. Many of the others he did not need. Damage control, it all came down to damage control.

THREE

But first, Rafael thought, first, he was going to check on the building they had purchased for Perfect Cannabis Corporation just a few short months ago. If he were perfectly honest with himself, all the construction he had done for the grand opening had been nothing more than window dressing, making a big and ugly box look decent for a party. He had not done anything useful or anything even approaching making the building fit to grow marijuana in.

If they were ever granted a license.

For starters, he needed to stand inside the old building, feel the floor and the walls, do what Connor would have done, which was imagine their operation in full swing in there. Maybe that would help him. Perhaps then he would be able to talk to prospective investors the way he needed to, to loosen their wallets and get the big checks. *This is our dream—be part of it.*

"Going out to check on the building," he said to Connie on his way out. "Anybody wants me, I'm on my cell."

Going out to the building site served as a valid excuse for a multitude of sins in the construction sector, and he'd used it freely before. Suddenly, though, he noticed a raised eyebrow from Connie. She would not indulge BS; he'd better remember that.

He drove out to the building at the edge of town—too fast, he realized, which was not usually his style. More like Connor's. The hell with that too.

The far end of the parking lot resembled a small anthill, with trucks and cars from the existing tenants coming or going moving this way and that. Thank God he'd had the foresight not to let Connor throw all of the tenants out of the north end of the building. He'd reasoned they might as well use it as warehousing space while Perfect Cannabis built up the business until they needed the room. Thank God the incoming rents had at least kept the building safe from bankruptcy. Rafael shook his head remembering the rousing fight Connor had put up. He wanted the entire building to himself, for all sorts of purposes, no doubt.

As if they were taking an ugly sister to the prom, Rafael's crews had begun to dress up the left-hand side of the building for PerCan the moment they took possession. It had been spectacular on the night of the grand opening, but now that side lay in complete darkness. Dark, silent, and deserted, except for a sleek, black limousine, parked reasonably close to the PerCan entrance, making him think that was where its occupant had gone.

The limo driver lounged in the front, reading a magazine and looking up every now and then with a bored expression on his face.

Rafael pulled up beside him, intent on giving the man one hell of a hard time for being parked out here, where he most certainly had no business being, when it occurred to him without the usual tirade of swear words. Of course, Al.

The only person he currently knew who travelled around in a black, chauffeur-driven limo was Al Ivers. The man that Rafael had introduced to Perfect Cannabis right at the beginning. Al, the man who had brought about their eventual downfall in the person of Tadeo Ivers. It could be no one else.

Rafael parked his pickup truck haphazardly in the vicinity of the front entrance and slammed the door.

He stomped inside and found Al standing in the main warehousing space, much as he had found Connor only a few months ago, standing there, his head cocked to the side just a fraction, listening into the dark.

"So, you still can't drive, or you just don't want to be alone in a car all day?" he asked by way of greeting, and Al almost smiled.

"Rafael, I see you needed to plant your feet inside our building as well."

Our building, indeed, why don't you pee into the corners, and claim it for yourself, as Connor wanted to do, Rafael thought, but he kept his mouth shut and stood, feet squared, hands in his pockets.

"Could be. What about you, measuring for your new office space or checking on the damage your own brother caused?"

"Let's not go there."

"Oh, let's. You want me to show you? It's at the far wall, right over there behind that pillar. That's where the concealed door led to the space Roberto had carved out for his own use. And what perfect use he had for that space, an illegal grow-op. It was really quite a showpiece."

"And if you remember, I knew nothing of the entire operation."

"No, of course not. Except I don't really believe that."

"Well, believe it, Rafael. What good would it do now to lie to you? My father put you in charge, not me. You've won."

Won? You think I've won, Rafael thought.

"Tell me," he asked instead, "what happened to Roberto anyway? I didn't see him at the so-called director's meeting. From what I hear, Roberto is indeed the country's first and foremost authority on growing marijuana. Perhaps the cannabis professor has some insights for us?"

Al shrugged and spread his hands in a somewhat helpless gesture Rafael had seen him use more than once recently.

"There are moments when I would like to know that myself, Rafael. After everything happened…"

"After you blamed Connor for Roberto's grow op and managed to run him out of the country, you mean. Might as well call a spade a spade."

"After—that—I did not see Roberto again. I would suspect father gave him some money to go away and bury the incident."

"Go away. Impressive. Your father is quite good at making things and people go away, isn't he?"

"Yes, making people go away and handing out money, Rafael, don't you think? After all, did he not just purchase you?"

Rafael did not even notice his own hands flying out of his pockets, hands balled to fists, ready to strike Al. Only when the other man flinched and took a step back did he stop and relax his hands by his side.

"Tadeo did not purchase me. He hired a man to take care of my business affairs while I took care of his, which happens to be your business as well, and mine. And I would still have said no if he hadn't implicitly threatened my family."

"I was in the same meeting. I remember my father saying if you turned him down, he could not give any guarantees Covin Construction Corp would survive. I understand."

Rafael lowered his eyes and said nothing.

"Look, Rafael, let's not stand here arguing about my father. He screwed both of us."

"I don't know—did he?" Rafael did his best to stand relaxed again and stuff down the seething anger that always seemed to bubble just below the surface these days.

It hadn't gone away. Not since—well, not since his wife Alice had died, and he hadn't even had the time to mourn her properly because he'd been in the middle of an investigation about activities at Perfect Cannabis and what he did and did not know about an illegal grow op in a hidden partition of the building. Not since Tadeo Ivers had handed him this wreck of a company. Revive it or else.

"You're used to it, Al. You grew up with it. You know how he operates. Me, I thought I was bringing an investor into the company, somebody who would put up some money and let us grow the company the way we thought it should be done."

"Don't blame my father for the things Connor did, Rafael. It doesn't suit you, and it does not excuse you. Do you know how many mistakes all of us made? Way too many to pick them apart and point fingers now. You said you would do your best to save this company, so I say go do it, and best of luck."

"Then why don't you tell me what you are really doing here, Al?"

Al looked down at his shoes for a long time, and for a moment, Rafael thought he might just up and leave.

When Al spoke again, his voice had a wistful softness Rafa had never heard before.

"The hell if I know. I thought there might be something left back here. Something we—worked on, together."

"Well, there's a lot, and there's a lot of work to be done, still."

He really did not know why he said it. Maybe it was the lost look on Al's face when he had walked in here and seen him standing alone in the great hall. Maybe it was the fact that Ivers would install Dante, Kayla, and Rafael in positions in the company and leave out Al, who had brought the investment to him, and Roberto…who had of course screwed it up.

Nice bookends.

"Why didn't he?"

"Didn't what?"

"Your father. He made Dan head of the grow op. Why didn't he make you COO or something equally suitable? You introduced this to him. You worked for it."

Al shrugged. "Who knows why he does anything these days? I can't even guess. Moreover, he does not share his reasoning with me, but that's nothing for you to be concerned about."

With that, he did turn to leave, and Rafael acted in one split second.

"Wait, wait, Al. This really sucks."

"Sucks, Rafael?"

"You know what I mean. You were part of this thing—almost from the very beginning, and you're a straight shooter."

"A straight shooter, am I? A minute ago, you wanted to hit me."

"Don't repeat everything I'm saying. It annoys the shit out of me."

Al raised a single eyebrow and said nothing.

"I know your old man is queer as folk, and I have no idea half the time what to make of what he says and does."

"He has that effect on people." Al nodded. "On purpose, at least most of the time."

"So, I'm thinking I'm going to need help around here. Look at this shit-pile." He kicked at a bit of debris on the ground and winced when it turned out more solid than anticipated. "Just look at it. We need to get our financials back on solid ground, we need to clear the shit out of here, we need to start with construction in a logical manner, and we finally need to get serious again about obtaining a license to grow."

"Then I suggest you get started. Sounds like you don't have the time to stand here and chat."

"Right. And I only have two hands. So, what do you say, help me out a little? You already know the operation; you've worked with us before. And you can translate your father for me."

"All of a sudden you would trust me? I find that a little hard to believe."

"Well, trust—trust is an odd thing. But I do know you were not actually involved in the illegal grow op."

"Well, hallelujah."

"And Connor, bless his heart, hated your guts. So, there's my guarantee you were not involved in any of his shady deals."

Al shook his head, and a tiny smile crossed his face. "You do know that's pretty stupid-ass reasoning there, Rafael, right?"

"And you know that stupid-ass is a pretty lame cuss word, right? Say *fucking idiotic* and we all know where we're at."

"Your language has seen better days too, Rafael."

"What can I say? Too many construction sites, too much time on a badly financed project involving growing drugs. You get that way. So?"

"So what?"

"So, help me get this operation back on its feet. For now, you can just share in my task load, and I'll pay you consulting fees. Any company you choose. Name it. When we have this thing dragged out of the mud, I'll make a strong pitch for an official position for you, whatever you want."

Al stood undecided and steepled his hands before his face.

"I don't know, Rafael, my father…"

"Your father tasked me with getting this company back on its feet. To do this, I need help, so I'm hiring someone to help me make sure it happens."

"He wouldn't…"

"Like it, no. I get that. But you have the experience and the know-how to help me out here. Question is, do you have the time, do you want to, and do you have the guts?"

Again, Al hesitated, and Rafael gave it one last push. "Come on, your old man is going to be livid when he finds out I've hired you."

"Which won't take too long."

"No, it won't. But he did say I would have all the means at my disposal to make this happen. You're it."

"I'm it?"

"You're it. So?"

"So, I think I might be certifiably crazy, but I am actually thinking about this."

"Then be crazy and keep thinking. Just tell me I won't have to deal with all of this shit all by myself."

"You may need to clean up your language. It is… distracting."

"And Dante—what kind of a name is Dante anyway? Somebody is going to have to keep an eye on him, and the hell if I know anything about growing."

"I hate to tell you. I don't know much about growing marijuana either."

Rafael gave him a sideways glance, and Al spread his hands. "What? It was not exactly encouraged at our house when I was younger. Roberto, he was the rebel, if you wish. He accumulated the knowledge and made himself the expert."

"That's another thing I don't get, Al. Why wouldn't Tadeo want him on board if he is that good? Why leave him to another marijuana company, the competition?"

"Trust? Would you trust my oldest brother?"

"Hell no. But you can keep an eye on him, can't you?"

"Nobody keeps an eye on Roberto. That is a given."

"What about Dante then?"

"Dante? Dan is weak. He won't betray you, but not because he is honest. It would simply be too much effort and bother to come up with a scheme to betray you."

"So basically, I've ended up with a lazy-ass copycat and the girlfriend of the man who fucked up the company in the first place. And you ask me why I need you."

Al walked away to the far end of the warehousing space and looked across at Rafael.

"It would take both of us committing every spare moment of the day to get this done, you realize that?"

"I realize that. What else have I got to do now? Roger Carmichael is running the construction business. My two sons are happily studying business administration, though I don't know what good that shit will do them when it comes to running a construction company. Point is there's nothing waiting for me back home, so let's do this."

"And there are no guarantees, even if we both give it all we've got. And my father…"

"Al, I swear to god, one more excuse and I'm personally going to kick you in the ass until you are out of my building."

"Your building? Last time I checked it was still ours."

"Goddamn right it is—it is our building. PerCan, Perfect Cannabis Corporation. You and I are going to fix this goddamn thing, even if I have to punch out somebody every single day. And if your father feels like threatening me again, I guess I'll have to learn to fucking live with it."

"Language, Rafael, language."

"Fuck that. Yes or no?"

Al sighed and stuck out his hand. "I don't know why I feel like I just signed a deal with the devil."

Rafael took his hand, shook it, and threw back his head with laughter.

"You want to know something really hilarious, Al? Those are the exact words Connor used the day he signed the letter of intent with you and your father."

FOUR

He felt better. For the first time since… Rafael tried to calculate. Well, indeed for the first time since about six months ago, when Connor had called him in the middle of the night. For the first time since then, he actually felt better. About PerCan, about the chances of success it may or may not have, about himself, his abilities and the people he was working with.

Person, actually.

So far all he had officially on Team Rafael was Al.

He was not going to count Dante into the thing until he had a man-to-man talk with him, looked him in the eye, and decided if he could trust him. And since about an hour ago, he knew that could take a while.

Kayla couldn't be much help, other than writing glowing articles in her paper, so Al was it.

And Connie. But she was really Kayla's employee, and he still had to warm up to the entire idea of a PA. Never had one in his entire life. Never needed one either. If he wanted something done, he either did it or assigned a task to one of the many people swirling around in his construction company. Jesus.

Connor, though, Connor had always been keen on having someone follow him around all day, if possible, carry his briefcase and read his mind for every one of his wishes before it came out of his mouth to become a request.

Rafael operated more on a, *hey, Joe, can you make sure this gets down to the purchasing department* kind of manner. Different approaches was all.

And then there was still Tessa.

Brilliant young girl, lived attached to her computers and electronic devices, never said she couldn't do something or didn't feel like trying. Connor asked her so many goddamn things, but she got it done. Every time, she got it done.

"Got it done in the end too, didn't she," he muttered as he flung his beat-up leather portfolio back on his desk and slipped into his old, comfortable chair. The chair elicited a grin.

Aaah!

Now he wanted to lean back and put his feet up onto the fancy desk Kayla had insisted on buying for him. The beat-up old chair looked as if someone had dragged it in from the recycling yard, while the black leather, ergonomic, electrified, heated, something-or-other he'd sat on earlier had been relegated to a corner.

Oh well. Dan could use it when he came to visit.

Another grin. Things starting to look up.

He dragged his notepad closer and sighed. He still had barely made a dent into the long list of people to speak to and tasks to get done.

Like a stubborn child he took out a pen and wrote, *Bring Al into the team*, at the very top of his list, squashing it into the margin of the paper, and then crossed out the task with glee. There, who said he didn't get anything done?

He looked up and straight into Connie's bemused face.

With a little chuckle, he put his paper and pen away and shrugged.

"Just checking my long list. Er, what did you have in mind? Do you need any signatures or anything?"

"No. I am about to leave. I wanted to ask you the same thing. And no again on the signatures. Mr. Ivers had me courier the check requests and completed checks, and he will sign those approved and have them brought back."

"Oh, will he now," Rafael said and sat up a little straighter. "I know he's one of the major shareholders, and also the major source of funding and financing at the moment, but I'm the one who is responsible for the running of this company. So, no offense, Connie, but the next time something like this happens, if you will please go through me first? I will involve Mr. Ivers as required. Got it?"

"Yes, sir." Connie couldn't meet his eyes.

"No criticism implied. I know Ivers can be hard to contradict when he wants something, but I run things around here, capisce?"

For the first time since they had met, Connie actually cracked a smile.

"My former husband used to say that, capisce. Said the Italian construction workers who were his clients regularly used the word."

"Where do you think I got it from? What did he do, your husband, I mean?"

"Former. He was a labor lawyer."

"Interesting."

Rafael nodded. Baby steps, he thought. At least he had managed to have a half decent conversation with her. Baby steps.

"Look, Mr. Covin—Rafael—I did not think it was right either, Ivers just stepping in here issuing orders. He just made it sound…"

"Oh, he always makes it sound… Connie. He always does. Number one rule: Rafael is the boss. Matter of fact…"

He got up and rummaged through the closet in the corner, where he had stashed all the personal stuff he had brought with him from Covin Construction Corp. He came up with a large framed picture of four men crowded around a shovel and a small hole dug in front of them.

"Groundbreaking of the first high-rise Covin Construction ever built. I think I'm gonna put it over here. Find me a nail tomorrow."

He leaned the picture against the wall on a sideboard and grinned again, remembering. In the picture, a very much younger Rafael Covin wore a bright yellow hard hat onto which he had written in large black letters "Da Boss."

The picture looked horribly out of place in Kayla's chic office, and yet Connie grinned almost as broadly as he did.

"It will be on the wall when you come in tomorrow, Boss…"

"Rafa, Rafa will do, thank you very much. Now, I won't keep you any longer. I'm sure you have an actual life to get back to."

He went back to his list after Connie had left and looked up at his picture every few minutes. Maybe that was just the inspiration he needed. He'd done well in the construction business, independent of Tadeo Ivers's opinion. He'd started as a guy with a truck doing odd jobs, moved on to building substandard residential subdivision houses, and finally turned it into a respected large corporation. No mean feat considering how many construction companies went under every year.

So, it ought to be no stretch of the imagination that he could do the same thing again here at PerCan. If he put his mind to it. And if he remembered—always remembered—what might happen if he failed.

His face darkened again, and he picked up his phone and made an appointment to see Dante first thing the next morning. Might as well get it all out there.

Dante could have been the wild card in this entire deal, but maybe he just needed to start over with him too. Put Connor behind them and start building a relationship. Because hell if that wasn't what he needed the most: relationships with people who knew what they were doing.

Rafael leaned back in his chair and laced his fingers behind his head.

The dynamics on a large and involved construction site were always difficult too: who bribed whom, who gave orders to whom, and, most importantly, who had to be paid off. Some days it was a never-ending puzzle, a game of 'don't step on anyone's toes,' and anytime the unions got involved, forget it.

Now suddenly that part of his life seemed like child's play!

Why had Ivers frozen out Al, what on earth had happened to Roberto, and how did Dante fit into this scenario?

Two camps were starting to build here, Rafael's side, and Ivers's side, and he did not like it at all…

***

"You look like a man who is either asleep or meditating on the weight on his shoulders."

His eyes flew open, and he smiled at Kayla.

"Well, hey there, doll, you always blaze into people's offices interrupting a well-deserved afternoon nap?"

"Only with special people. I saw Connie leave, thought you might want to grab some dinner."

"Dinner…" Rafael shook his wrist and checked the watch crawling out from under his shirt sleeve. "Indeed, it's late enough. But don't you have, I don't know, places to go, people to spend dinner time with, rather than a washed-up construction manager turned drug dealer?"

"Legal drug dealer. Don't forget that."

"Legal drug dealer then. I have a few things on my mind. I am warning you I may not be the best of company tonight."

"It was never going to be easy, Rafa. We all knew that."

Kayla stepped fully into the office and stood there before his desk. Today, she wore a dress of bright scarlet, and Rafa could not fend off the impression that a bright flame had been kindled right there in his little office.

Kayla moved slowly and sat in the visitor's chair David had vacated such a short time ago.

"Give yourself a break. You are fighting some huge old demons here, and from what I hear, you're winning."

"From what you hear? Connie's got your ear, does she?"

"I'm not spying on you, Rafa. We are on the same team, trying to patch this company back together."

57

"Funny you should mention that, on the same team. You reading my mind? I have very little on Team Rafael so far."

"In what way?"

"Ivers decided to keep on Dante, who copied everything he says he knows about cannabis from Roberto. He dismissed Al, who has been a major force in the building of PerCan, and nobody knows about Roberto. Roberto may be the hidden ace in someone's sleeve here. I'm trying to figure that one out. What does Ivers want with PerCan, I wonder? Build it back up or have it fail? And why bully me into it in the first place?"

Kayla frowned and crossed her long legs at the knee. Not without the intention of giving him something to look at, Rafael thought and smiled inwardly.

Kayla rested her chin on her hand. "Maybe he just wants to surround himself with people he thinks he can control. Myself, Josh, Simon, Dante."

"Thanks a lot. Not sure what that says about me. And you shouldn't count yourself out either. In any case, I've brought in Al today."

"You did?"

"I need help. Nobody said I couldn't hire people. Al is good, period. If Ivers does not like it…"

"He will most likely not."

"Tough shit, Kayla. Connie informs me he installed himself as the final authority on the checkbook and who gets paid when and how much."

"He is the major shareholder."

"Major shareholder, yes. CEO, no. He forced that role on me, so I think it's time to wear the hat properly. He wants to float us some capital, fine, I appreciate it. He wants to remain outside of the active circle of the company, fine too. I understand it. Now step back and let me do the job I have to do."

Rafael rose and stretched, holding his hand out to Kayla. When she got to her feet, he pecked her lightly on the cheek and pointed toward the door.

"I am sorry. I'll take a rain check on that dinner, my dear, although it pains me."

"You have a plan?"

"I, dearest Kayla, will take dinner at a rundown old diner in the seedy part of town."

"Do I have to understand that?"

"Better you don't. I'm going to see our old friend Ivers in person and lay down a few ground rules."

"Should I be concerned?"

"I don't think so." Rafael grinned and shrugged into his jacket. "He needs me, and he knows it. So, he will stand there and posture and threaten without half saying it to make me toe the line. But at the end of the day, he knows, without me, the job is going to be ten times harder. That's why he hired me. What I don't need is people starting to pick 'sides.' Ivers's side, or my side. That happens, we are done, and I'm going to make sure it does not happen."

FIVE

Most people walked into other people's offices for a meeting, Rafael thought. They might stop at the front desk and chat up the receptionist, a worthwhile effort as far as he was concerned. Or they might simply walk into the office of the person they were meeting. Either one worked. Apparently, Dante did not think so. Dante Ivers swaggered in as if the entire building were his and everyone in it merely his employees. Which might have been funny if the building, the company, and indeed this office did not belong to Kayla.

Rafael looked up from his stack of papers, put down his chewed-up pen, and smiled at the youngest Ivers as best as he could.

"Morning, Dante, thanks for coming at this early hour."

"Not an issue, Rafa. I'm an early riser myself." He sat and looked at Rafael without bothering to hide the attitude. "Well, what you got? I'm planning to head out to the building this aft, just getting everything back on track."

Rafael folded his hands on the desk in front of him, if only to have something to hold on to and to contain his irritation. He remembered Connor did not much care for Dante, and suddenly, he could see why. Overconfident, snobby, entitled, lazy.

Without the backing of Tadeo Ivers, Rafael wouldn't have hired him at a construction site. At the same time, he needed Dante. *Be nice*, he told himself, managing a noncommittal smile.

"Good. Please do and let me know what you find. It seems to me you are one of the few people who was there when we started this project. It's up to us to get the job done."

Dante leaned back in the chair, stretching his legs away from him, and shrugged.

"Hey, I wouldn't grieve the end of the Connor Beauregard reign if I were you. I know the two of you were friends and all, but he really knew shit about the business."

Growing marijuana, no, but about business, Connor knew more than you will ever know, Rafael thought, and dug his fingers in a little more. Still, he smiled.

"You see, Dante, if there's one person who knows Connor was no angel, that would be me. No need to repeat it. Fact remains. He is gone, this company is in a mess, and you and I have a job to do here. The purpose of this little meeting is none other than to make sure you are all-in, as they say."

Dante shrugged. "Why wouldn't I be, Rafael? My father owns most of the company. Don't you think it would be in my best interest to see it succeed?"

"No doubt," Rafael said, nodding slightly, still forcing the smile on his face. "But I'm talking about more than doing a good job. I'm talking about going out there every day and doing the goddamn best you can to make this the best medical marijuana grower there has ever been. There's a difference. Do you understand?"

Dante shrugged. "Sure."

Rafael shook his head. "You see, Dante, I don't think *sure* is going to cut it with the mountain we have ahead of us. If I want sure, I can go out there..." He pointed vaguely toward the front door and the road beyond it. "Out there, find some kid good at growing pot, and give him a ton of literature to read and a couple of consultants who will teach him what he needs to know. It's going to work. But I don't want it to just work. I want this to be the best."

"My father would have something to say about that, you going out and hiring a couple of consultants, you understand that, right?"

Now Rafael leaned back and opened his arms. "If I don't miss my guess, I would say your father made enough money to ensure you will never have to go look for a job again, for the rest of your life. I'm pretty close, no?"

Dante shrugged. "So, what business of yours is that? You work for my father. That's all."

"Your father wants the same thing we all want, to see this company where it belongs, at the top. And despite his questionable hiring practices, he has assigned me the task of getting it done. He needs me to do that, or lose it all… and he knows it. And another thing? He knows that I am going to do this my way, by my rules, or not at all. That includes staffing matters."

Dante came half out of his chair, making himself bigger than he was.

"My father made me the head of the growing operation. Were you in the same meeting, or were you sleeping when that happened?"

No missing the threat in his voice this time, but Rafael forced himself to stay cool.

"Not sleeping, Dante, listening. Your father is still a businessman. He wants the growing operation to be the best there ever was. If you can do that, great, we're all happy and carry on. If not…" Rafael shrugged. "He's given me a budget, and I can go out and hire a grower who can. Your father is a smart man, Dan. He believes in putting the best people into the right place."

"I can do the job. No matter what my… what somebody else might tell you."

What my brother might tell you. Yes, Roberto, the self-declared pope of pot. The man who really did know everything there was to know about growing marijuana, or so he had heard. Rafael took a step back and put his palms together.

"Dan, all due respect to your father and the fact that he's already made you head of the growing operation, but I can't use a guy who comes to 'a job' every single day. I need a guy who jumps out of bed before the sun is up because he's excited about the project he left behind. I need a guy who can't wait to get back at it because he loves what he's doing, because he can't even imagine doing anything else. If I find him, I don't care what his background, his education, or his family connections are. My question is this: are you that guy, Dante?"

Dante said nothing and shrugged.

"Because if you are not, no hard feelings. I know your father wants you here, and you can be anything you want to in this company. For crying out loud, be in marketing, or sales or IT, anything that stokes you. This is a big company, and it's going to be one of a kind. But my grower... My grower needs to be a guy who lives and breathes it, who would do anything to see those little plants grow. The kind of guy who can create magic. You understand that?"

"There's a lot of information," Dante said weakly, and the man who had walked in full of piss and vinegar suddenly did not know where to look. Rafael hid a smile and spread his hands.

"Doesn't mean you have to know everything right this minute and have all the answers ready. Shit, does it look like I do?" He swept his hand around his office. "I'm still trying to figure out how to function in an office that is this... pretty, you know what I mean?"

This time, Dante grinned and nodded.

"Nobody has ever done anything on the scale we are planning in this country, and we're all learning. Where I am trying to start is making sure we're all committed to this process and to the company. Not infighting and politics. And your father, well, your father is just going to have to give us the time and opportunity to figure this thing out. If that means he has to cool his jets until we do, tough shit. So, what's it going to be?"

He rose, walked around his desk, and offered his hand to Dante.

"What's it going to be, Dante? Are we going to work together and beat away at this thing until we've got it done, or killed it… whichever comes first?"

Dante hesitated for a moment. Then he rose himself and finally took Rafael's hand.

"Not exactly what I was thinking when I came in here," he admitted, "but you got it. You've got yourself a deal."

They shook hands awkwardly, and Rafael sat again.

"I had a long talk with your father last night."

"Interesting way of putting it. Not a lot of people say those words sitting comfortably behind a desk like you do."

Rafael spread his hands. "We just had to get a few things out on the table. One, I run this company the way I think it ought to be run, or I might as well not even start, no matter what he wants to do to me. Two, I build a team around me consisting of the people I want there, without his input being necessary."

"And he went for it? Without giving you grief or throwing one of his little fits?"

"Did not say that. But despite his 'little fit' as you call it, he did not really have much of a choice. Like it or not, we are stuck with one another for now. At least until I get PerCan back to where it needs to be. That will be the point in time when every one of us can decide what to do. Fair enough?"

"Fair enough."

"One last thing. And you might not like it. I made Al my right-hand man."

"My brother Al?"

"The one and only. If that's a problem for you, let me know right now. I don't know your family dynamics, and I can, uh, limit the time and extent to which you have to work together, but I cannot avoid it entirely."

"Why should that be a problem? It's just unexpected."

"That's what your father said. Why, I'm not sure, because personally I think Al is a smart and talented business man. We make a great team, and we can get this thing done. But I'm not going to hold anyone's hand, OK?"

"Fair enough."

Dante nodded again and rose. "That it? Because I really need to get back out to the building and check…"

"Yeah, end of speech." Rafael waved his hand toward the door. "Please, do what you need to do. And let me know what you find."

He leaned back with a sigh when Dante had left. Taciturn cooperation was probably the best he could get right at the moment, and that only because the entire Ivers clan needed Rafael Covin to get this thing done. For the moment.

And what would happen when that moment was gone, or when, God forbid, he tried and failed to get PerCan going again? What then? If Ivers lost all of his money and came to him?

"Don't go there," he reminded himself. "Not now."

"Did you need something, Mister—Rafael?"

"Connie. If we're going to keep working together, I might have to insist you start wearing high heels, or a little bell around your neck so I can hear you coming into my office. This sneaking up on me is not entirely healthy at my age."

"Nothing wrong with your age, Rafael, and I can knock if you rather."

Rafael waved his hand. "Just joking, never mind. Oh…" He looked at the extra-large cup of coffee Connie had brought him and sighed with pleasure.

"This looks like the beginning of a beautiful work relationship, Connie. I'm not sure how you did it, but you seem to have figured out my likes and dislikes relatively quickly."

"No magic required. Ms. Montecito filled me in."

"Kayla? When did she have time to figure me out, I wonder?"

He took a sip of his coffee and sighed.

"Perfect. Better than the stuff they serve on construction sites, I tell you."

"Not now... what?"

"Come again?"

"When I came in, you said 'not now.' Is there anything I can help you with?"

Rafael opened his mouth to say 'never mind' and closed it again. Connie, he was beginning to realize, had the smarts and the experience to be a great asset here in this team he was building, so perhaps...

"I'm trying to put an A-team together. Growing, management, expansion, build-out, financing. We have about this much to do..." He held his hands a good five feet apart. "And this much time to do it in, before we are dead in the water." Now his hands indicated about five inches. "So, you can see my problem. Making it worse, I have no idea who from the old gang I can still trust, who had a bone to pick with Connor, and who is plain pissed off enough to want me to fail, and make sure that happens."

Connie pulled up his visitor's chair and sat, folding her hands in her lap.

"I don't know all the politics and personal details about what went on before... before you came in here."

"You're probably lucky you don't. It was a mess. I'll be the first to admit that, even if my friend Connor caused most of it. While I'm in charge, I want it to be done logically and straightforward."

"If you can."

"If I can. I know how to build a shopping center from the ground up. Building a medical marijuana grower is a little like trying to learn knitting here for me, you know."

"Not really." Connie shrugged. "For what it's worth, it sounds like you've got the right idea. One step at a time. Just like building a shopping mall. Put together a great team and start taking baby steps."

Rafael closed his eyes and squeezed the bridge of his nose.

"It sounds good when you say it fast. But I'm quickly finding out how many moving parts there are to this whole business model, and, frankly, it scares the crap out of me. No offense."

"None taken. But don't look at it as one massive task. Just take all of the little steps, one at a time, and once you get your team behind you and everybody starts pulling their weight, you're in business."

"Your mouth to God's ears, lady." Rafael opened his eyes again and took another sip of his coffee. "And this—this is helping a lot, just so you know."

SIX

"That Connie is pretty sharp," he said to Kayla a little while later over dinner. "Thanks for bringing her into my team, even if..."

"Even if you were not that keen on having a PA there in the first place," Kayla suggested when he hesitated. "I knew that."

"Yes, well, it's just not the way I work—at all. In the construction business..."

"In the construction business, things are different, yes, you mentioned that, Rafael, numerous times. But you're here now, in this business, whether you want it or not."

"A drug dealer? Not."

"A builder of businesses. Doesn't matter what you're selling, marijuana or magazines or ladies' shoes, for all that matters. You just need to build this company, like you built your own."

"Oh, why didn't you say so right away?" Rafael put down his fork and stared intently at his wine glass. "It just sounds like so not a big deal."

"It shouldn't be, not for you."

"Thanks for the vote of confidence, but as I'm sure you have noticed, I'm no Connor Beauregard."

"Will you quit saying that? I'm sure you've noticed the rest of us are getting pretty tired of hearing it. Tadeo Ivers trusted you enough to make you CEO. The rest of the board trusted you enough to agree. What else do you want?"

"A way to raise $30 million in a hurry would be good." Rafael said darkly, draining the wine in his glass almost in one. "I don't think the rest of you understand..."

"No, we do understand, Rafa. And we are here for you. Whatever you need, whenever you need it, and we have all said as much to you. We're all counting our lucky stars not to be in your position, but if you give up now... Well, don't. I don't want that on my conscience. None of us do. We're here to help. I had Connie put a few contacts together for you."

"I saw that."

"So? What are you waiting for? It's fundraising, plain and simple. Just do it, Rafa. You've gone there before. You've done this before. I don't understand what the problem is."

"The problem—the problem is..."

"The problem is you're telling yourself you are not Connor. Nobody is. Raising funds was like breathing to him. You're different. So quit trying to be him and do this thing like Rafael Covin would. Whatever gets you through the day. If you have to open every single meeting by saying, 'I am not Connor Beauregard,' do that. People will laugh. If you need to hire a coach, do it, but do something. The longer you wait, the harder you are going to make it on yourself. And before you go telling me that's easy for me to say, what do you think it was like after Hanson died? A woman like me, trying to run a publishing business? Get real. Same damn thing."

"End of speech?"

"End of speech, as long as you go out do something."

Rafael glared deeply into his wine glass.

"Yeah, you're right. Sorry. I'm sitting here getting myself into a funk because I don't know where to start fundraising. I'm well aware I have to start somewhere."

"Good. Then you are going to go out and see the people Connie has lined up for you—tomorrow."

Rafael watched the waiter refill his glass and startled. All of a sudden, Kayla's hand covered his on the table and gave him a reassuring squeeze.

"I know you are the right man for this. You can do it."

"From your mouth to God's ear."

Her hand remained on his, and Rafael felt a little stir of panic. What, wait? Kayla here was his best friend's girlfriend. Well, his former best friend... and former girlfriend. Shit, talk about complicated.

"Tadeo said it better than any of us could have. The fact that you are not Connor is your best calling card. People know that. They want to hear that—they need to hear it."

"Thanks, Kayla, I'm going to have to stop looking at our capex tables. $30 million is just the beginning. This company needs a lot of money to just get started, never mind to succeed. I've run some big construction jobs, but sh—man, this is going to be a huge one. It's downright scary."

"I'm sure it is." Kayla squeezed his hand again. "And I've heard the two of you say it a dozen times sitting at the bar at The Lighthouse while the drinks were going down. This is going to be the biggest thing we've ever done. You knew it back then. And you got into it, and you brought your people into it. So, you can't turn around now and tell me it can't be done without Connor."

Rafael nodded, drank more wine, and finally managed to pull his hand away. Enough. People were going to start staring. If they weren't already.

"Guy sitting behind and to the left of me," he asked Kayla. "You ever seen him before?"

"No, should I have?"

"Maybe—it's just... I don't know, like he's watching us or something."

"You getting paranoid on me, or are you trying to change the subject?"

"I hope not. But the other day I was walking through the lobby at Montecito Publishing..."

"Yes?"

"There was a guy hanging around the lobby."

"There's always 'a guy' hanging around the lobby at the publishing house, Rafa. Weirdoes trying to sell their stories and their photos. They are desperate, and they're looking for a buyer. If you see one doing something he should not, call Hank down in security."

"I know. Don't get me wrong. It's just, the last few days… I can't shake the feeling that somebody is watching."

"Watching? You?"

"Yes—no. Watching me. Maybe watching the company. To see what's going on with PerCan, to see what we're going to do."

"If somebody is watching the company, at least they are going to learn something," Kayla said, and laughed. A sound that filled Rafael with anything but mirth. "We're going to build the company back up. Watch and learn."

She sat back and twirled her own wineglass idly in her hands, but out of the corner of her eyes, looking without looking, Rafael could see her checking out the man who sat behind him. LaCosa really was not the kind of restaurant that attracted a single gentleman dining on his own, was it now?

"You're being paranoid, Rafa. He's just eating. Enjoying his prime rib, as well as he should. This is a first-class restaurant, and you'll offend me as well as the chef if you don't at least try your food."

***

Paranoid, he reminded himself the next morning, on his way to his office. He was just being paranoid. In the lobby at Montecito Publishing, seven or eight people were hanging around idly. Waiting for an appointment perhaps, waiting to speak to one of the journalists, who knew?

Kayla was right. There were always people hanging around this office and this lobby. Just another day at a publishing house. The sooner he moved into his own office in the building, the better. What he wouldn't give for a plain old construction site.

He crossed the lobby to his corner office and forced himself not to turn his head to check behind him. It was only paranoia, that feeling he suddenly had of eyes boring into his back. Paranoia, nothing else.

That, and perhaps an excuse to get out of fundraising, his least favorite task on any project. He had always left that to Connor, who thrived at going out, selling his story to any willing audience. When it was just him and the shaving mirror, Rafael had to admit that he missed Connor's crazy bubbly energy, the force that never settled down for more than five minutes, and never admitted the existence of a problem, even if it stared you right in the eye.

SEVEN

Predictably, Connie had made a nice little tracking sheet for him, with all of the contacts Kayla had managed to come up with. All he had to do was call these people, make an appointment, go see them and convince them to give him their hard-earned money so he could go and rebuild a drug company somebody else had all but trashed.

Easy.

No big deal.

How did you do this every day, all day, Connor, without sounding desperate—how?

Rafael checked to make sure Connie was not in the outer office, then closed his office door anyway. He really did not care to have anyone barge in on him right now. What he was about to do was embarrassing, at best. He had watched Connor operate a dozen times. Heck, they had tag-teamed, so why did he feel like a teenager, watching his first X-rated flick?

Irritated with the pit in his stomach, his task, and the rest of the world, he popped a DVD with the taping of Connor's corporate presentation into his laptop.

It's all in the hands, Connor's voice said in his head, even as Rafael watched Connor's long fingers underscore every word. *It's all in the hands. People think it's in the face or the suit or the haircut, but they follow my hands, and my voice. Watch.*

"Light-deprivation technology," Rafael muttered, trying to emulate Connor's gesturing, "300 pounds of cannabis from every 20,000 square feet growing space dedicated, dedicated to—to this technology… Dammit."

Connor could go on quoting facts and figures all day long, as if he lived and breathed this stuff. He hardly had to take notes or take his eyes off the investor to check his presentation. How did he do it?

"Like you're telling people how you are going to build their damned shopping plaza," he muttered, nervous fingers flying through the papers before him to find one particular table with quick facts on it. "Know what you are talking about, make it your own. Back to basics, Covin. Annual gross revenues of over—of over 70 million US… Damn, that's a shitload of money."

He sat back in his chair and finally turned off Connor prattling on, on the little laptop screen, and rubbed his tired eyes with the heels of his hands.

This wasn't going to work. This was Connor's way, not Rafael Covin's. He was not Connor, period. He wasn't going to do things the same way, now was he? He shouldn't. He posed in front of the window to his office so he could see his own reflection, pushed his hands into his pockets, and relaxed his stance.

"This company," he said, trying to sound confident, "this company, ladies and gentlemen, is going to make one hell of a lot of money." He smiled, relaxed a little more, and shrugged at his reflection. "Hey, we are drug dealers. We grow marijuana. How can anybody screw up being a drug dealer?"

He chuckled, pointed a finger at the Rafael in the window, and started over. "When we are done building this thing, we are all going to make so much money, we'll be looking behind us, waiting for someone to yell thieves!"

Better. He'd used that particular sentence presenting a construction project. It might be universal at that.

"This has every potential of being the biggest and best… No. This project will be the biggest and best any of us has ever seen, and believe me, ladies and gentlemen—believe me, I have seen a lot of them. I've been involved in building some of the finest companies there ever were. And I am personally 100 percent committed to make this a success."

That sounded good—that definitely sounded good. Personally committed. *Because if I don't, if I don't… best not to go there.*

"As I am sure you're aware, Perfect Cannabis Corporation has experienced some trouble recently." No point in hiding anything; they would know. Anyone even tempted to invest in this company would know and wait to see what he came up with in his defense.

"But again, ladies and gentlemen, I am not Connor Beauregard. I will lead this company in the manner and with the ethics many of you have come to expect from me. I will lead this company to our collective prosperity."

Collective prosperity, hot damn, Rafael thought. Hot damn, he was on a roll here. This stuff wasn't half difficult if you just gave yourself a chance.

Before he could change his mind, he pressed the buzzer on his intercom phone to summon Connie.

"Connie, darlin', I need you to do something for me."

"Certainly, Mr. Covin."

Uh-oh, it was Mr. Covin again this morning.

"Sorry for the darlin', just my construction site manners. No offense."

"None taken, what can I do for you?"

"Well, for starters, you could take that list of contacts Kayla gave you and make appointments with these people. Tomorrow if we can. Stagger them, so I get an hour with everybody solid, and another one between appointments."

He would need at least that to recover and get his nerve back up, but maybe in time, it would be second nature like it had been for Connor.

'Goin' out to see some guy about some money.'

Connor had always been 'going out to see a guy,' always about money… most of the time successfully.

"Shit, brother, I wish the shoes you left weren't a size 20. A good set of construction boots would be just fine right about now."

Not much of a choice. He knew that as well as anybody else.

And what was the point in working in a publishing house if he couldn't make use of some of the in-house talent?

An hour later, Rafael went into a less familiar part of the building and recruited some of Kayla's graphic design staff to make up a corporate presentation for him, glossy, professional, and impressive.

Connor would have ordered one just like that, if he wanted to show off his latest idea.

***

"What do you think?" he asked a little while later at The Lighthouse, showing the presentation to Al on the little tablet he had taken to carrying.

"Not bad."

"Not bad? Al, Kayla's staff spent hours on this. I happen to think this is pretty damn good, you know?"

He flipped through the slides, from projected sales, to anticipated users, fast facts on medical marijuana, growing space, proprietary technology—he'd have to work on that one.

"I kinda threw that proprietary technology in, to fluff up that particular area. Honestly, I know nothing about growing."

"Probably don't need to."

"But it always looks better if you say you have something nobody else has, even if it is just the accumulated knowledge of—well…"

"My brother Roberto," Al sighed. "I agree, proprietary technology has a much catchier ring to it. But why go through all of this trouble?"

"What, a presentation? In case you had not noticed, I need to start hitting the pavement to raise some serious funds here. All credit to your father, but he's not going to fund us forever. Neither do we want him to."

"We most certainly do not, Rafael, but a glossy brochure is not the answer to all of life's questions. I remember when you put on your first presentation."

"Yes, I remember." Rafael snapped his tablet shut again and shoved it into its sleeve with an angry push. "I know. Connor only brought a handful of brochures, and he never even looked at them while telling you how great and wonderful it was all going to be. Well, I'm not Connor. If I want to make a presentation holding something in my hands or referring to the material I have, then that's how I am going to do it, OK?"

"That wasn't where I was leading, Rafael, no need to get cross with me. All I was trying to say was that you don't need a glossy brochure or presentation to hang on to. You can sell this one by your own convictions, and you know it."

"Thanks for the vote of confidence, but for the moment, I'd rather have it in my back pocket. This thing is—bigger than anything I have ever done. And as you well know, screwing this up is not an option."

"Then don't think about it."

"Easy for you to say," Rafael said, staring down at his drink. "I don't think any of you know…"

"We do know. And none of us wants to be in your shoes right now, but if needed, we're here for you."

"What, you're tag-teaming with Kayla now? That's exactly what she said to me last night."

"Last night, is it?" Al asked with a chuckle. "I hope you were having a good time then, despite the business talk."

"It's not like that." Rafael shook his head. "Not at all. Moron."

Al did not answer, but he also did not stop grinning so Rafael dug through his papers and brought out the now-familiar checklist.

"Moving right along here, my friend, just try to keep your mind on business, will you? You hear anything from Dante? Last I heard he was heading out to the building to get comfortable there again."

"Dante sent in his wish list all right," Al said with a sigh. "Looks like the renovations and build out have gone from 'major' to 'tremendous.' And I can't fault him anywhere. His calculations are solid."

He pushed a few printed spreadsheets across to Rafael and made a face.

"I realize this is not what you were expecting…"

"Never mind. Might as well look at it. Shit…" Rafael scanned over the figures and coughed discreetly into his hand. "Your brother does not believe in restraint, does he?"

"The thing is, if you want to…"

"Save it. If you want to do it right, you have to spend the money. Connor coined that phrase, so it's nothing new to me. The license?"

"Stalled for the moment, I am afraid." For the first time since he had known him, Rafael thought he detected a bit of embarrassment in Al. Al, the man who never lost his cool and never let anything get to him. Interesting to say the least.

"In the wake of Connor Beauregard's disappearance and the subsequent involvement of my family…"

"Shit."

"That is one way of putting it quite succinctly. At the moment, the officials at the Ministry of Health do not have any confidence in this company. Nor do they see such confidence out in the market. So, the inside scoop I am getting is they've taken a wait-and-see attitude."

"Great. Just awesome, Al. Why don't we add another shovel to the pile of crap I'm already faced with? Now it's your family's reputation…"

"In all fairness, Rafa…"

"In all fairness, Al, just can it. I already know what everybody is going to say when they look at me. Get out there, build this company and its reputation back up to where they were when all of this started, and let's talk again. I got it, and I am working on it, OK?"

EIGHT

"Damn."

He spilled coffee on his brand-new suit the next morning and started in on the cussing before he had even a small chance to say good morning to Connie, preparing his paperwork for the day.

"Are you all right?"

"Just coffee, Connie. I'll live." He dabbed away at the stain on his pant leg with a tissue, making no real headway. "Goddammit."

"Cussing isn't going to take care of a stain. Here, let me."

She reached for a real paper towel and bent over his desk before he managed to push her away.

"I said leave it. God. I don't need you to clean my clothes, OK? I'll be back."

Irritated with himself and the world, he ran straight out of his office. If he wanted to have a half a chance to get home, get changed, and still be in time for his first meeting, he had better hurry. Dammit, this was all he needed right at the moment, showing up for his first presentation looking like a duck. Right. And what was with Connie anyway, trying to dry up coffee on his leg, right on the heels of Kayla putting her hands on him, and Al joking about it?

"Don't think about it, Covin." He adjusted the rearview mirror and pushed a little harder on the accelerator of his truck.

Talking to himself, another good sign he wasn't really himself.

'Then who the heck are you,' his late wife would have joked. Rafael smiled wistfully.

"Time to get myself together, right, so lend me a hand here."

WWCD. What would Connor do? Connor would have spent a couple of minutes alone, working on his winner's mindset if it were a big presentation, or just walked in and opened his mouth, if it were an informal meeting. Nothing to it.

NINE

"Mr. Covin." His intended target rose from his chair and shook his hand. "Kayla speaks highly of you. Nice to finally meet you. How are you?"

Rafael smiled and shook the man's hand. "Mr. Seaway." His mind clocked off the facts he'd been given: Randy Seaway, owned a successful chain of sports supply stores, and a few exclusive and expensive fitness studios. Probably Kayla's personal fitness guru and specialist. He looked the part too, tanned, fit, and at least a couple of inches taller than the squat Rafael.

"We have our work cut out for us, as you might imagine," he said and smiled. "Perfect Cannabis Corporation has a history and a legacy to overcome, but I am here to tell you that I'm the man who is doing just that."

He opened his briefcase and took out the tablet with his presentation. "Let me show you how I'm going to do this."

***

His day became much like his glossy presentation and slideshow, a progression of moments and images, one much like the next. Rafael tried to do what Connor would have done: *just open your mouth, say what's on your mind, and don't worry about anything else.*

TEN

"Did it work?"

Kayla had ordered red wine, the good stuff, and the wait staff at LaCosa fawned over her, as always.

"Did what work?"

"Your presentations. Did everything work out?"

"I don't know. I don't think I remember anything past the first hour, and right now, I'm too beat to know what worked and what didn't. Guess I'll find out when they put up some money, or not."

"It was just the first…"

"No need to repeat something I already know. Just the first round, just the first time out there trying to do what Connor did every single goddamn day." He picked up his glass and downed most of it. Probably 50 bucks right there in that one gulp, he thought and watched the waiter refill. "Whatever, back at it tomorrow, you know."

"You see any more strangers in the lobby at Montecito Publishing?"

"I think today a guy in a Superman costume could have snuck up on me and hit me over the head. I would never have noticed."

"We're going to do this, Rafael." She had taken his hand again, and Rafael thought he did not even mind any longer.

"Damn straight we will," he said, taking more of the wine. "Damn straight we will."

***

He was sitting in his office the next morning, staring pretty smugly at the phone messages Connie had brought in. *He scores!* For once Rafael didn't care that he had a stupid-ass grin on his face. Randy Seaway wanted to see an official prospectus and information about putting money into the company, and quickly. The fitness guru of all people.

"That's what I get for freaking myself out in the first place," he said to David, who'd been camped out in Connie's office for a couple of hours, waiting for the mildly hungover Rafael to show up. "Nothing to it."

"That's what Con—let's just say I've heard it before. I'm glad you're in a good mood then."

"Thus far I am, so please don't go and ruin it."

"I afraid I may."

"Why does that not surprise me, David? Just let me have it straight up. How are you going to ruin my good mood, this time, might I add?"

"Your review and signatures are required on a number of filings, a good number of filings actually."

"Filings, catch me up here," Rafael asked, snapping his fingers, groping for fragments of memory. In the old days, they had referred to this kind of thing as 'technical stuff,' and Tessa had handled most of it. Tessa, who had taken all of her knowledge with her and sold it to the Ivers clan. She and David had kept them from needing to pay attention to most of it.

"SEC filings, I presume," he finally added, lest David believe he was a complete idiot. "Financial statements, quarterly filings, that kind of thing?"

"Well, a little more than that, I'm afraid." David pulled several two-inch black binders from his bag.

"Shoot, David! Is that what you do? I'm trying to keep us from drowning, and you are handing me more ballast?"

"You don't need to deal with all of it at once, Rafa. But you need to start on it, that's all. Now, being a public company, there is a requirement..."

"I know why I have to file public statements, yes. It's not my first time at the rodeo. I also know that we are delinquent, horribly delinquent, most likely. But with everything that's been going on—I—er, I guess I just assumed there was some sort of grace period, you know? A time they give us to get everything sorted again."

"I hate to disappoint you, but there really isn't."

"Twist the knife, why don't you?"

"Fortunately, it's not as horrible as all that."

"Glad to hear it."

"The company did file notices with the SEC of our—er—inability to file in a timely manner. Basically, we told them things are a mess for a bit, and we are cleaning up. So yes, we are delinquent, but as long as we pull together now, nothing is unfixable."

"You're serious? You and Tessa kept it up while the shit was going down? Jesus, that is—well, that is excellent news. Happy to hear it."

"You see, what happened was…"

"I can't believe you and Tessa did those filings."

"Well, yes, mostly me. But you need to know that…"

"Nothing, David, I really don't need to know more than that. The company is delinquent, but not in the bad books with the SEC, to the point of being delisted. Nothing unfixable, you said."

"Yes, but…"

"Good, I'll have Connie issue a check to you. Leave your binders. I'll review whatever you need me to review. Heck, I'll sit at it all night if need be. This is excellent news. Nothing to ruin my day. Thank you. When you're trying to raise funds, being on the stock exchange is rather important."

He looked up from the ominous black binder, only to find that David still looked as if he were in pain. "What?"

"Nothing—you know what, nothing." David forced a smile, a foreign sight from the lanky accountant, and slipped the rest of his binders across the desk.

"Let's just get it done. You know you need to file material changes?"

"Vaguely, yes."

"Any big change in the company structure. So now you have the new board of directors as per the meeting last week, and one of Ivers's companies is going to put in a lot of money, so that needs to be disclosed too."

David flipped through the pages as he spoke, and Rafael hid a grin. For all that he could be a pain in the ass, David had prepared everything for him. All he needed to do was review and sign and make sure he was comfortable with it.

A bit of the weight that had been on his shoulders for the past few months started lifting away. The looming nightmare of an SEC investigation gone. The company and the shareholders were safe, as long as he got his rear into gear and signed all of this paperwork. Jesus Christ, what a gift!

"I'm going to right now liberate some serious money from the coffers for you, David. Just for the loyalty you've shown me by keeping up those filings, so we wouldn't be dead in the water by the time this day finally came."

"You don't really need to, Rafael."

"Oh, yes I do. I've been struggling since I took this job to figure out who I could trust in this here game. And you've just shown me a big sign. So, if you want to come back in a couple of hours, Connie will have a check for you. And these reviews will be ready for you by tomorrow morning. Deal?"

"Deal," David said, smiling rather thinly.

Something still bothered the accountant, but Rafael felt too good for the moment to worry about it.

More things were coming off his list. The financing was shaping up, and David kept the SEC at bay. For one day, he really couldn't ask for more.

"Maybe you always had it, Covin," he said to himself, grinning, and eyed the pile of binders at the edge of his desk.

He almost felt confident enough to call up Ivers and give him a status update on the company. One of Connor's chief complaints had been that he could never get hold of the man who called himself the 'Original Chef' when he met him for the first time and had decided to become involved in the company.

Rafael had won something of a minor victory when he pried a phone number out of the man so he could speak to him whenever he felt necessary. Why Tadeo Ivers continued to be so evasive about his availability, he could only guess at, and every time he guessed, he had to shiver, so he generally avoided the thought.

He had started to punch in Ivers's number and changed his mind. What the hell? This was his game now. Ivers had decided to make him CEO of this company and to make him revive it. No need to announce every five minutes that he was still on the job. Ivers could ask if he needed information. He could wait on Rafa for a change, wondering what was happening, wondering if there was any news.

A tap at his door frame brought him back to reality and to Kayla.

"You look knee-deep in paper."

"I am. Nothing I can't handle, though."

"You're smiling. Good news?"

"Basically, yes. Just a bit of a pain. Our friend and big brother the SEC believes in total transparency for public companies that are trading."

"I would assume that's a good thing?"

"It is. But it also means that every time somebody farts—pardon the language—you have to disclose said fart, explain it, and file it to be out there on their website for everybody and their grandma to look up."

"But there was some good news, right?"

Kayla pointed at the stack of black binders on his desk, one eyebrow raised almost all the way to her forehead. Finally, she shook her head. "That right there looks like torture instead. What is all of this?"

"That indeed is the good news, Kayla. Every quarter we should have filed financial statements and another statement every time something happened—a director leaving, a new one coming in, how much money they were offered, that kind of nonsense. To tell you the truth, Kayla, when Connor disappeared, I thought all of that went down the drain with him."

"And?"

"And, as it turns out, David quietly kept it up in the background. Basically, he filed a notice that there were good reasons why we couldn't file and to be patient with us. No big deal, but the mere fact that he did so, and did so when we weren't even paying him, that's huge. It saves us from a whole lot of trouble."

"David is not usually the giving type."

"That's what I thought. But I'm looking at it right here." He tapped his tower of binders with a pen. "Looks like all I have to do is review this stuff one at a time, make sure I can comfortably put my name to it, and go ahead and file it."

Kayla chewed on her thumb, and Rafael felt a little stab of irritation.

"What, you think I'm missing something? Now you're the one getting paranoid? I've done all of this stuff before, when Connor was still around, you know."

"That's not it, Rafael. It's just that I know the Davids of this world. The concept of him doing anything for free seems foreign. So, pardon the suspicion, but where's the catch?"

"Thanks for the cold shower, Kayla. No catch. David did all of this... This..." He tapped the stack of binders again, a little harder this time. "This is his work, while we were off worrying about the investigations into Connor. I know I didn't give him any money for it, and Connor? Forget it. So, if you don't mind, I'm not going to look a gift horse in the mouth and take it, with gratitude, as one of our problems solved. Solved, and without the usual wrangling and sweating."

He sat back and forced down his irritation.

"Anyway... We are making headway. That's all that counts."

"Yes—I am sorry for raining on your parade. I hear Randy Seaway signed on."

"He did."

Rafael shrugged and didn't bother to hide the shit-eating grin.

"Came up with the cash. Nothing earth-shaking, but a start. And all I had to say was I am not Connor. No offence."

"None taken, Rafa, I'm happy for you."

She came around his desk and enveloped him in a great big hug.

"Whoa, Kayla."

"You can do this, Rafael. I knew it. I knew you were the one."

"The one—er, Kayla…"

"The one to save this company."

As long as that is all you're expecting here. The comment sat on the tip of his tongue, and at the last possible moment, he shoved it back down. What was wrong with him anyway?

"Thanks." Awkwardly, he patted her back. "Thanks. We try, you know."

"Excellent. Then we can…"

"Before you say we need to celebrate, stop. Give my poor head a little break here."

"Aww."

"We've done enough partying to last for a while."

Rafael returned to his desk and awkwardly shuffled a few pieces of paper around.

"You mean when Connor was still alive."

"Still alive, good God, Kayla."

"Around. You know what I mean."

"Yes, I know what you mean, and at times, it might be like he died. But please don't say it like that again, please."

"Why? You think he's coming back one day? Good luck with that one, Rafael. They do say hope dies last."

"I don't know. Is he coming back? This company was his baby, his one big shot at making it huge and showing everyone how it's done. I would think he would have a hard time staying away, but who knows?"

"Coming back and going straight to jail, you mean," she said, plucking invisible pieces of fluff off her blazer. "There are a couple of minor legal matters waiting for him here, not the least of which was operating an illegal grow op."

"Well, I guess more good news might be in order then, depending on how you look at it."

"I don't follow."

"You haven't heard then. The prosecution did the best they could, but the case they were able to put together against Connor was weak at the best of times. Just of late, the wheels have come off totally."

"Really?"

"Really." Rafael lined the corner of a binder up exactly to the edge of his desk mat before he spoke. "I'd obviously not like for this to leave this room, but there's a young clerk down at the court office who gets some—consideration—from me now and then, just to keep me in the loop."

"You are bribing…"

"I am making sure information gets to me, that's all. And I'm only sharing it with you because I thought you might want to know."

"I do, yes, but…"

"But nothing. The case against Connor is going to be history before you know it. Evidence that's been mishandled or disappeared entirely, witnesses who don't remember what when or where. He couldn't have set it up any better if he were controlling it."

"Wow."

"Yes, wow. Spelling it out, if he wanted to come back, he could."

"But, Rafael, he is not…?"

"Not yet," Rafael said. "Now, can I get back to restoring the reputation of this company he started, preferably without going down the same roads he did?"

"Sure. Yes, do that. And Rafael?"

"Yes?"

"Thanks—thanks for letting me know."

"No prob." He nodded and pulled his paperwork closer. No need to look up to see the disappointed look on her face, or the sadness in her eyes.

ELEVEN

Time to kick it up a notch. He asked Connie to make more appointments with potential investors for him and stopped working on his finely honed investor presentation. What on earth had made him think he needed it in the first place?

'Believe it, live it, breathe it, ask for the money and make it real. That's all there is to it.'

He would never admit to it, but Connor's voice in his head had become a stand-in for his friend. He liked that voice, and he was grateful for the advice it offered. *Couldn't have done it without you, buddy.*

***

Rafael took a deep cleansing breath, allowing himself a rare moment just standing at the window of his office staring out at Cross Avenue. It was working. Even if he had had no idea what to do when Tadeo Ivers had asked him to step in as CEO, to guide the company back to prosperity, it was working. Bit by tiny bit, they were coming back.

"Damn it if I am not fixing this thing," he muttered to himself, leaning his shoulder against the window frame. "Just by being here."

As long as nobody asked him exactly how he did it or what he was doing because he didn't have an answer, and "I don't know" sounded pretty stupid.

Perhaps without realizing it, he had picked up a few tricks in the years of running deals with Connor. Osmosis, perhaps. He must have absorbed it, Rafael concluded, just by hanging out with Connor Beauregard, the man who could run a deal like nobody else.

Rafael knocked on the window ledge three times, just for good luck. Perfect Cannabis was coming back, and coming back strong.

He was turning away from the window to gather his materials for the next meeting when something caught his eye.

Down there, on the intersection of Cross Avenue and Water Street, a man stood leaning casually against the lamp pole at the corner. Rafael wouldn't have thought anything of it if the man had been staring down at his cell phone, if he had even been reading a magazine, or standing close enough to the bus stop on Water Street to make one think that's what he was waiting for.

But he wasn't.

He just stood at the intersection, leaning against the lamp post, staring up at Montecito Publishing. At Rafael Covin's office.

"What in blazes..."

Rafael suddenly tensed and stood closer, gripping the edge of the window ledge, his breath fogging the glass.

"Who are you...?"

He simply stood there, clad in jeans and a grey hooded sweatshirt, the hood pulled so far over his head that his features were a mere dark shadow even in the bright light of day.

Rafael couldn't see anything about the man, but something—some sixth sense—convinced him the kid was looking up at the building, his floor, and at this very window.

This was real. He wasn't hallucinating. He wasn't dreaming. This guy stood down there on the street, staring at him.

Two steps took him to his desk, and angry fingers stabbed out the number of the front desk downstairs. What did Kayla say the name of the main security dude was—Hank? Hank would know what to do.

Bouncing on the balls of his feet, he picked up the remote handset and went back to the window.

"Hank—er, I think it is Hank, right?"

"What can I do for you, Mr. Covin?"

"I need you to look into something. There's a suspicious character hanging around the building, and I think..."

"Right away, where did you see him last, Mr. Covin?"

"He's—he's gone."

Rafael stared down at the spot where he had been only moments ago, the very corner of Water Street and Cross. Nothing. He had disappeared as fast as Rafael had seen him standing there.

A soft curse escaped Rafael.

"Never mind, Hank, he's gone now."

"Are you sure, Mr. Covin? It's not a problem. I can go and check if you like."

"Forget it. Thanks. I was wrong, I guess."

His hand holding the phone sank slowly to hang by his side, and Rafael peered through the glass as if he could find his answer out there on the other side of the window. He had been there—he was sure of it. A moment ago, when he stood there, congratulating himself on his success, there'd been a young man standing there by the street light.

At least he thought it had been a man, and he thought he'd been young. Somehow, he had disappeared into thin air.

"Good God, Covin," he muttered. "Hallucinating, are you?"

He threw the phone onto his desk carelessly and paced the perimeter of his office, unwilling to let it go. That guy had been there.

He swiped his phone off the desk again, almost dropped it dialing, and bounced on his feet until it was answered.

"Al, you got a minute?"

"For you I do, Rafael. Although I have to note..."

"I'm not in the mood for jokes just now."

"Did something happen?"

"Honest answer, OK?"

"Always."

"Honest answer, Al."

"All right already, Rafael, ask away. I will answer as honestly as I can. That's all I'm giving you. What happened?"

"Does your father have someone watching me?"

"What? Not that I know of. Why?"

"Just indulge me."

"Like I said, not that I'm aware of. He could always hire somebody without telling me, but I don't see a good reason for him to do so. What would be the point?"

"To know what I'm up to, who I'm seeing, how much money I'm raising."

"Nothing he couldn't get from your update memos."

"Unless he did not trust me and thought perhaps I was cheating him. Then, then he might hire somebody, you think...?"

Al took a moment to answer, and Rafael could almost see him leaning back in his chair, or wherever he hung out just now, closing his eyes the way he did when he had to work out something in his mind, stroking his chin.

"I don't think so," he finally said. "Mind you, I still might be wrong, but if Father wanted some information on you or on the company, he would not do something as obvious as hiring someone to follow you."

"Instead?"

"Instead, he would pay off someone close to you to keep tabs on you. Rafael, do you mind telling me where all of this is coming from?"

Rafael walked back to the window and stared out into the lengthening shadows. For a long moment, he said nothing.

"Guy was hanging around the building," he finally said. "And I kind of get the feeling I've seen him before. And if not him, then somebody else who's been lurking around."

"Your office is in a publishing company. I would imagine..."

"There are always people lurking around the halls and in the entry. I know. Kayla said the same thing."

"And?"

"And—I don't know, Al. I got the distinct impression this guy was looking straight at the window where I was standing."

"I wouldn't dream of questioning your instinct, Rafael, but for all the reasons I just mentioned, I don't think my father is involved. He trusts you to run PerCan. He told me as much."

"Forgive me for saying this, but your father says a lot, given the chance to do so. And he was not impressed when I told him I brought you on. Never mind. Let's drop it for now. I'm just going to have the security fellows here keep an eye out."

"If you feel this is necessary, but I can assure you..."

"You don't think your father would do anything like this. I get it. Thanks anyway, Al."

He hung up knowing less than he had before. It made little sense for Ivers to send someone to spy on him—he had to admit that, but it irritated him. And then there was the casual tone Al used when he said, 'Oh, he might bribe somebody close to you.'

Shit. Rafael made a fist. Who would Ivers choose? Connie maybe? He'd tried to bully her before when it came to payments, and Rafael had shut that down. Ivers wasn't above using tactics like that one. But Connie had a smart head, and she was loyal.

Loyal to Kayla, perhaps, and only to a certain extent, he thought. Remember Tessa. Tessa, who had known everything in the old Perfect Cannabis Corp and had been bought by Ivers. Keep your eyes open and your ear to the ground; that was the only advice he could give himself for the moment, and it all but ruined his earlier good mood.

With a jerk, he grabbed his jacket off the back of the chair and decided to head down to The Lighthouse for some early R and R. No wonder Connor had started drinking. God, what he wouldn't give for a nice 15-story shopping mall to construct, something easy for a change.

TWELVE

Rafael slowed down a bit after the incident with the watcher. He looked over his shoulder on a regular basis. If anybody indeed was trying to follow him, he or she had become more careful.

And now, after the first rush of signing up a few investors and getting things off the ground, he had hit a patch of rough ground.

The last week and a half of pounding the pavement hadn't netted him more than an extremely polite, 'thank you, we will revisit the issue of investing when you are further into the rebuilding process of the company.'

Not that he could blame them.

You'd be hard-pressed to find anyone in the country who had not seen the lurid headlines when Connor ran the company: bribing government officials, gallivanting around the country in his fancy helicopter and, finally, the crowning bit, an illegal grow op in the building. Not since Bre-X had CEO bashing been this much fun.

How did you even start to overcome all of that and make the public believe everything was going to be different now that Rafael Covin was in charge?

He took a fat folder from Connie in the morning and sighed.

"More bills to be paid, I assume."

"Afraid so. It's like they're crawling out of the woodwork now that you're resurrecting the company."

He flipped through the top few invoices and sighed again. Of course, he recognized some of the names.

"It's not really your fault, you know. All this…"

"Of course it's not my fault, Connie. Neither would there be any purpose in pinpointing whose fault exactly it might be. It wouldn't move us one iota forward. These people did work for the company, presumably. And they deserve to get paid. That's all. David is going to faint when he sees what this means to his financial statements."

"Adjustments?"

"And then some. All of this should have been posted and reported last year."

"Didn't that girl you had…"

"Tessa? If she knew about it, maybe." Rafael sighed and waved a hand. "Onward and upward. Anything else?"

"Well…" Connie folded her hands and failed to look directly at him. "When you're through checking all of those invoices and statements…"

"Yes?"

"I kind of did a quick tally. With those, and what's due at month's end, and, well, my own salary… We're overdrawn."

"Shit."

He'd quit apologizing for swearing around Connie. She either had become used to it, or she didn't hear it any longer. But right now, she looked as if she'd rather have a root canal without the benefit of anesthetic.

He sighed and put his hands on the folder.

"You go and pay yourself first, Connie. Let me worry about this bunch here. I will work something out."

"Are you sure? I wouldn't want to…"

"This is not the time to be generous. Make up your paycheck and come see me for a signature. Everything will work out, I promise."

Borrowed time. The phrase kept buzzing around his head. Borrowed time. Tadeo Ivers had given them enough to keep hope alive, and when Rafael ran out of money, he would have to come to him, hat in hand, and ask for more.

Like an old Dickens play. *Please, sir, can I have some more?*

And the real work had just begun. Just out of the gate, and here he had stumbled over hundreds of thousands in unpaid bills—not just a few, but hundreds of thousands.

***

"Even I don't understand how Connor could have run through that amount of money in that short a time," he said to Al, as they stood at the bar in The Lighthouse in the afternoon. It could have been early or late afternoon. He didn't know, nor did he care.

The mere fact that he had taken on this enormous task and now depended on the goodwill of Tadeo Ivers if he were to have any chance of success needed to be washed down with copious amounts of liquor.

No wonder Connor had drunk heavily.

"Wonder if he still does."

"Does what?" Al asked, raising one eyebrow, his customary indication that he had no idea what Rafael was talking about.

"Drink." Rafael lifted his glass. "Connor was never shy to toast to the success of our current venture, regardless of what the venture actually was or how it was doing, but I wonder if he still... you know, lifts a glass now and then."

"Remembering?"

"Remembering, and perhaps repeating," Rafael said, staring into his glass. "Don't assume he would change his style anytime soon."

"I've heard you talk about Connor an awful lot in the past few days. It couldn't be good for you."

"It happens if you're the one who has to clean up the mess."

"No. You're the one who has to straighten up the company. Doesn't matter who made the mess."

"I'm also the one who has to talk to your father, asking for more money."

"Then I suggest you do that, and quickly too, before the mess becomes any bigger and he himself comes around asking questions."

"He himself?"

"One of my guys called him that, when he thought no one was listening, of course."

"Of course. If you don't mind my asking something?"

"Even if I do, you will ask anyway," Al said, looking out into the busy bar.

"Well, yes, but…"

"Go ahead, Rafael." Al sighed. "I suspect you want to know about my father."

"What's his deal?"

"His—deal?"

"Yeah, his deal, you know. He hardly leaves that dingy diner. He conducts an empire from the back room, which kind of gets me to thinking that most of that empire conducting is not entirely, how shall I put this—kosher, no?"

"Rafael, you knew all of this when you took on the job, right?"

"I knew he was involved in some deals, and he had money, but that's the extent of it."

"Tadeo is always involved in 'some deal.' And most of his days, I hate to tell you, he spends scheming how to hide his money from the government without the burden of paying excessive amounts of taxes on it."

"That's it, huh?"

"As far as I know. But then again, as you found out, he does not always let me in on everything he is doing either."

"But…"

"He built this godfather persona for himself, and he likes it. He owns every strip joint and a majority interest in every seedy bar between here and the next county. There's a lot of business being conducted there in old-fashioned, untraceable cash, and yes, I assume there are plenty of drugs being consumed in those places. The persona of the 'Original Chef' served his purposes, nothing else."

"Jesus, and you…?"

THE CANNABIS PREACHER : SERMON TWO

"I've never been party to any such transaction."

"But you took care of things for him. Ran errands, did all of the outside work…"

Al spread his hands. "So? That was my job. Tadeo liked to have somebody else running around 'outside' so his own hands could be kept clean. Plausible deniability."

"I never knew that. Moreover…"

"Rafael, just go ask the man for money if you need to do so. What does it matter to you anyway?"

"What does it matter? I'm just a little bit worried about the source of his funds, aren't you? I don't want to run into any… issues."

"You won't. The books are completely clean. I told you that before. You want to know what I think?"

"What does it matter if I want to or not?" Rafael fired back.

"Touché. What I think is you don't want to go ask Tadeo for money. Period. I understand that, and I empathize. But you need to do it, and that is why you are sitting here drinking instead of carrying on business."

"Your advice?"

"Make a choice."

Rafael sighed and downed his beer in one huge gulp, signaling for another.

"Have I told you recently that I hate your guts, Al?" he grumbled, but his voice carried no malice. Whether he would admit it or not, Al was right.

***

Before he could change his mind the next morning, he made one of his rare phone calls and drove out to Decantur Street and the seedy part of town, to meet the man Connor had known as the 'Original Chef.'

THIRTEEN

Rafael played the game as always, sitting in the diner, ordering something—anything—waiting for Dinah, the waitress who was actually one of Tadeo's former 'entertainment girls,' to go check with the big man himself if it were OK to see him.

Moments later, he walked down the hallway past the kitchen and storage rooms, feeling quite like a man going for his last meal.

"Rafael, you are looking splendid. Come on in and close the door behind you."

As always, two men sat with Tadeo, doing nothing but sitting there and looking dangerous, and Rafael remembered Al's words. *It's this godfather persona he created.*

He nodded a brief greeting to the men and waited for Tadeo to offer him a seat.

"What brings you here, good news, I hope?"

"We are making progress, slowly but surely. I was just talking to David yesterday, and the next set of SEC filings is basically..."

"Paperwork, I know." Tadeo waved his hands in front of his face as if he meant to dispel a bad smell. "There's always paperwork. It is one of the perils of running a public company. Nothing new."

"Oh, dear, someone told you. I had hoped my staff would wait for me to give you all of the news."

"Rafael, what is this?" Tadeo sounded like a kindly old grandfather, Rafa thought. Probably time to be careful. "Are you accusing me of something?"

"No, not at all. If you want to know something about the company, you are smart enough to come directly to me."

Tadeo smiled again and shrugged.

"So, no matter if David told you. I gave him a little money to keep up those filings up when things went bad. I thought he could be useful. And I would get the most up-to-date information. No big deal."

Now things started to make sense. David's discomfort, the surprising good news about the filings. Al's comment. *My father would bribe one of your staff.* So, they'd got to David, too. Dammit, was he surrounded? Did Ivers really have his hands in everything at PerCan? And what did that make him?

Don't screw it up, Covin, he thought and bit the inside of his cheek. *Ivers is just waiting for you to screw up. Don't give him the satisfaction.*

Tadeo inclined his head just a fraction. "Well then, what brings you here? Other than good news, that is."

"We are—progressing," Rafael said slowly, still clenching his fists and trying to hang on to the temper that wanted to erupt all over this man. "However…"

"Ah, there it is, the however."

"The however. Yes, you see… Now that the company is in business again, a lot of people are showing up on our doorstep."

"Yes?"

"Presenting invoices."

"Really? Well, that is surprising."

"Does it really surprise you, Tadeo? And perhaps it would be better if we quit this cat-and-mouse game. A lot of decent and honest businesspeople did work for Connor and got screwed when the company went south. I would like to set them right. That's what I've done thus far. After all, you knew my reputation and banked on it."

"I did at that; it was one of the reasons I chose you."

Chose you, as if there had been several contenders. Or any kind of choice for that matter. Rafael did not recall having much of a choice in that meeting room with Roger Carmichael sitting there taking over his company. The thought of Covin Construction did not occur to him often these days, but when it did, he knew his company and his sons to be safe. As long as he played Tadeo Ivers's game.

"Then you also should know that I would pay all of these people, without dickering about a thousand dollars here or there. They've waited long enough."

"Quite a long time in some cases, I understand."

"Then understand this, Tadeo: we are out of funds."

There it was, out on the table. Was this how Connor had felt when he finally went to Mirko, the loan shark? That had been a decidedly bad choice, but Ivers here was not really much better.

Tadeo made him squirm for long moments.

He folded his hands in front of his face and shook his head a few times, making an annoying *tsk tsk* sound. Then he looked left and right at the two bookends sitting there, making a 'can you believe this guy' face. Both of the bookends shook their heads sadly and looked down at the table in front of them, heads lowered in shame.

What's it gonna be, for crying out loud? I'm too old for this shit. The words sat right at the tip of his tongue, but he held them back. Sometimes it was just better to keep your mouth shut if opening it wouldn't do any good.

"Besides," he said when he had himself under control again. "Besides all of the old bills, I'm also going to have to beef up security a bit."

"Oh?"

"I saw a guy hanging around my office, more than once actually. Would you know anything about that?"

"And why would I know anything about some guy hanging around your office?"

"Just mentioning it, Tadeo. On the heels of my finding out you bribed my accountant for information. I'm sure Tessa has outlived her usefulness, now that she doesn't work for me any longer. For the last time, if you want me to run this company, you're going to have to let me do it my way or not at all."

"That's still on the table," Tadeo said and put his hands on the table in front of him. "You walking in here telling me you're out of money. What happened to all of the investors you've been seeing? Am I to believe you raised nothing... nothing at all?"

"I raised some," Rafael said, irritated with the defensiveness in his voice. "But people are careful, Tadeo. They want to see where we are going with this thing before they sink money down a hole." He shrugged and shook his head. "And I can't blame them."

"You're not supposed to empathize with them. You are supposed to get money out of them."

"That's not how I roll, and you know it," Rafael said and struck the table before him. "I don't pull money out of unsuspecting marks and damn the consequences. You know that. So again, and with all due respect, please don't tell me how to do my job."

"Big words, Rafael, very big words. Are you sure you can back them up?"

It's just a persona he puts up. Rafael sat up a little straighter and put his hands on the table just like Tadeo had.

"I am confident I can, so let's quit wasting time fucking around and get down to business. We need another infusion of cash. Are you going to give it to us, or do you want me to quit right here? Dealer's choice."

The two bookends sat up a little straighter and fixed Rafael with their most menacing looks, which he refused to acknowledge. He sat perfectly still, eyes locked on Tadeo—and won.

A nod calmed down the bookends, and Tadeo sighed.

"How much is it you need?"

"500,000, at least, to start with."

Never go cheap and never show a figure you can't live with, even if it's negotiated.

"Are you out of your mind? I just gave you..."

"I know exactly what you gave me—us, actually. It's gone. And I didn't spend it wildly. I spent it on cleaning up old bills and generating much-needed goodwill for this company. Of which you own a large portion. Now we need to continue on the construction and make sure people keep doing their jobs. Is that what you want to do, Tadeo, or not?"

"I want you to fix this company without bankrupting me."

His voice had risen a couple of decibels, and the bookends looked down at the floor between their legs. *Crunch time, boys. We either live or die right now. Literally, at least.* Rafael refused to finish that thought.

"Maybe that can't be done, Tadeo," he said very softly. "I told you that at the outset. I don't know how much it's going to take until I get further along in the process."

"You had better not be telling me I am screwed, Rafael, for all of our good."

"Not screwed, no. But you are the majority shareholder of a company that is in deep, deep trouble."

"Unacceptable."

Now Tadeo's flat hand hit the table with a dry cracking sound much like a gunshot, and Rafael forced every muscle in his body to still. *Just sit there, Rafael, just sit there. He'll get it.*

"Shut the goddamn thing down, now."

"Then you lose everything." Rafael nodded and rolled his shoulders getting ready to rise. "OK."

"Wait."

His body settled back into the chair, his hands perfectly still in his lap. And still, he did not say one word.

"Wait. That is the only other option?"

"A miracle could happen, Tadeo, correct. But if I want to keep this company afloat, just afloat, while I go out there pounding the pavement trying to talk nervous investors into this sinking ship, then I need the cash and the opportunities to do so. So yes, essentially, it is the only option."

Tadeo folded his hands and rubbed them as if he were trying to crush something between the rough palms. Rafael most likely. Better not to think about it.

He settled his body into the chair and forced himself to think of something more pleasant. Pouring concrete foundations in minus 20-degree weather, browbeating suppliers who tried to sell you sub-standard materials while collecting huge fees, unions muscling in on a job and becoming…

"You drive a hard bargain, Covin."

Rafael only shrugged.

"You would really walk?"

"I refuse to fight a war while my hands are cuffed behind my back."

"And your company?"

"If you chose to bankrupt me out of malice or spite, nothing in this world or perhaps in the next one could save my ass or my company. We both know that. I've had to accept that the moment I said yes to your proposal. Connor learned it a lot sooner and found a country where you could not get to him."

"And your sons?"

Every fiber in Rafael's body told him to jump to his feet, put both his hands around Ivers's scrawny neck, and squeeze until no more sound came from the hated throat. The goons expected it and sat ready, wound tight as watch springs.

"My sons are men now, Ivers. Men with the instincts and powers of men. They would not thank me for thinking them weak enough to be in need of my protection."

"Words, little man."

Rafael barely suppressed the grin. He had seen Ivers standing up, back at the grand opening when he had snuck into the building and made a surprise inspection. He knew as a fact that he was the taller man. Not that it mattered, not to him. The first crack in Ivers's tight façade?

He shrugged lightly and put his hands on the table before him again.

"You know what happens when you have nothing to lose, right?"

"What does happen when you have nothing to lose? Tell me."

"Then you can try everything… anything." Rafael leaned forward a bit, right into the other man's face and lowered his voice to a whisper. "And life becomes real easy to manage!"

"Enough with the cute quotes."

"Then don't threaten me, ever again."

Rafael leaned back and picked up the notepad he had brought with him. "You hired me to do a job, and I told you months ago—either I do it my way, or not at all. You agreed. Whether you like it or not, you agreed, Tadeo. You want to change your mind now, fine by me. I will shut down the operation and find some other way to occupy my time."

He rose and nodded to the bookends. "I think we're done here."

"I didn't say we were done."

"Didn't you? I must have missed that. Let me rephrase it then. I think we're done. If you don't want to fund the company any longer, it's dead in the water, and I'm going to shut it down before it bleeds to death. If you change your mind, you know where to find me."

He did it. He grabbed his stuff, walked out of the room, and shut the door behind him with just enough force to make everyone know that he meant it. Rafael Covin had no need to go slamming doors. He had made his point.

He left through the main section of the diner without looking left or right and drove down the highway for a block or two until he finally pulled over by the side of the road and became violently ill.

***

He made it back to Montecito Publishing somehow, driving back-roads, drinking copious amounts of water to wash the taste of this meeting out of his mouth, and finally sneaking into the building through the back door, dropping into his old chair as if he had just finished a marathon.

Nobody spoke to him, which suited him just fine because right this minute, there was nobody he wanted to see or speak to.

Except perhaps Connor. *Damn you, Connor.*

Jesus H. That was the worst meeting he had ever had to live through in his entire life, bar none. He uncapped another bottle of water, drank half of it in one gulp, and leaned back, thinking of the ups and downs he had endured in construction during his long career.

Bar none.

"Stupid man," he muttered. "Trying to get into this business and thinking he can do it on a dime."

Even someone with Ivers's access to funds would run out of money, and quickly. This couldn't be done on one person's private fortune—it couldn't.

So where did that leave him? He leaned back in his chair and pressed the balls of his hands into his eyeballs. Dammit all, he should have known when he took this job that it was a near impossible thing to do, and yet…

Somewhere along the line of fighting Ivers and pounding away at the company, his stubborn streak had come up, and he wanted this to work—wanted it badly. Maybe because Connor and he had started it, maybe because everybody else would take one look and tell him it couldn't be done. Maybe just because he wanted to, Goddammit. And that had to be enough.

He picked up the phone and dialed Al's number, not thinking twice about the fact that the most elusive business man in town, a man whom everyone else in his life described as exceedingly odd at best, suddenly had become his best friend.

"Is this a good time?" he asked when Al answered, and Al, knowing the backstory, and most likely what had happened at the diner earlier, didn't even hesitate.

"You need some advice from me, Rafael?"

"I do—I don't—I don't know, dammit."

"Well, that covers the range, Rafa. You went to see Father, I presume."

"He didn't tell you about it?"

A long pause. Rafael fidgeted, and Al finally sighed. "I told you. Father does not share his plans with me these days as he used to."

"Well, he's an idiot if he doesn't, but that's just one man's opinion."

Al chuckled softly. "Generous. I gather it did not go well?"

"*Not well* is an understatement. He threw one of his little fits, and when I did not bite, he threatened my business me and my sons again."

Al cursed softly. "I am sorry, Rafael; you know that I would never condone…"

"Violence, I know. And thanks for the tip. He was just posturing anyway."

"Most of the time, Rafael. He does have a tendency to become mean when he is challenged and angry."

"So can I, Al, if you push me into a corner long enough. But leaving that aside, he is not totally wrong."

"Oh?"

"We are trying to get into the marijuana business, in grand style, on a budget supplied by one man, fighting a legacy and debts created by another man. Investors have lost confidence, and right now, I simply cannot raise the kind of funds we need. We rely on your father to pull this cart out of the muck, and right at the moment…"

"Right now, he is unwilling to do a lot of pulling?"

"I don't even know if we are still in business, Al. If he doesn't come through, we can close the doors, such as they are, again in a couple of weeks and—sayonara. Nice knowing you. This time there won't be any coming back."

"I didn't know it was that serious."

"Nobody did. There was a lot of stuff Connor let fall through the cracks. He ran this business with an ignorance of generally accepted practices that was unparalleled. Never mind. We need cash, or we are dead, period. What happens to me and my family after that, anybody's guess."

Al said nothing for a moment, and Rafael heard him breathe in the background, evenly, without rushing. That was the Al he knew and appreciated, ready, aim, fire.

"And there's another huge piece of the puzzle. We don't even have a license to grow yet. That's probably the largest sticking point with our investors."

"I know this will sound a little off the wall," Al finally said. "But hear me out before you say no. Have you ever thought about a merger with another company?"

"A merger?"

"Yes, one of the smaller producers who have a license already and a small operation somewhere, struggling to get by. Connor's business plan was ambitious but sound, or I would never have bought into it. If you were to take over a small producer, pull the new concept over the old company so to speak, and went back to doing what you were doing…"

"We'd have a license and part of our credibility restored," Rafael said softly. "I never thought about it. That is a damn fine idea, Al, really."

"Been around the block a few times. Does that sound like something you want to think about?"

"Think about, hell yeah. Let's you and I kick a few ideas around. By the time we find out what your father intends to do with the company, and us, maybe we have a concept that makes sense. Something he can buy into. Dare I say something to make everybody happy?"

"I will make myself available tomorrow," Al said. "Let's talk."

"Somewhere private," Rafael threw in quickly. "Not Montecito and not the building. The boat. Why don't we meet on the boat?"

"You have a boat?"

"Dinky little thing. My wife always wanted something to spend weekends on the lake. *Denpasar Mood*, down in the main harbor. Fingers crossed the old thing still starts. We'll drive around a bit and toss some ideas around."

"You are a careful man, Rafael."
"I'm getting there, Al, slowly but surely."

***

For the first time in a while, he called both of his sons, away at college studying business or some such nonsense, and as usual, they didn't have much to say to one another. At least he got a bit of a rise out of them when he told them he managed a medical marijuana company now, he noticed with a bit of satisfaction. They would be OK. No matter what happened, he believed they would be OK.

FOURTEEN

Reverend Bartholomew had unpacked the crate of hymnals ever so carefully. At the bottom of the crate, he had found what he was looking for, one of the hymn books that looked just a minute bit different from the others in the load. The cover was a deeper shade of maroon, the size off by just a tiny bit.

Now, looking left and right to make sure no one saw his unholy deed, he took a penknife and loosened the inner from the outer covers, carefully tore off the flypaper, and smiled. There it was, wrapped into a bit of plastic wrap to protect it from moisture, carefully glued into the extra hymnal.

He knew both Cristos and Iskandar had started to go through his crates and boxes before handing them over, wanting to know what in blazes was so damned important about them, so he had become more careful. Neither one of these men would ever figure out what was going on; they were too lazy and too stupid. He would never have to worry, but if there was one lesson Reverend Bartholomew had learned it was this one: always err on the side of caution.

Slowly, he unwrapped and unfolded one sheet of paper and flattened it out in the sand before him. The sun blazing almost directly overhead all but cooked him, dressed as he was in black robes, but it ensured no one would be foolish enough to hang around at the beach during the hottest hour of the day.

He read the few lines on the paper once, twice, and threw his head back, roaring with laughter.

"Nice move, Rafael," he said hoarsely. "Nice move, almost worthy of me."

Then he found a box of matches in his pocket, dug a small hole in the sand, and burned the letter until nothing but a pile of ashes was left. When the ashes had cooled, he mixed them with sand over and over and finally dumped the lot into the ocean. What he needed was already committed to his perfect memory.

He rose and brushed the sand from his pant leg, taking a cleansing breath and letting it out slowly. His time had come. The heat that had been bothering him to the brink of madness for the past months suddenly did not register any longer. He stood at the shore and looked out over the glittering ocean. Diamonds—they were all diamonds out there on the waves, and each and every one of them waited for him to take them.

Time for Reverend Barry to take a small trip. He would have to plan this carefully. For starters, he needed more information, lots and lots of information, his stock in trade, more than his current contacts could give him.

Once he had identified his target, he would need to move himself into place ever so carefully without anyone noticing. That was key to the whole operation, no one noticing. People were stupid. They didn't pay attention; they saw what they wanted to see.

"Well, dear Reverend, are you planning a hostile takeover, or your next sermon while you are standing in the blazing sun?"

In one smooth move, Bartholomew flexed his knees and swung around, his fist clenched and extended, his body ready to strike, until he recognized Cristos and caught his motion short.

"Cristos, I almost slugged you. How often do I have to tell you not to sneak up on me like that?"

The Portuguese man had reflexively ducked and now stumbled trying to regain his footing.

"Fuck, Barry. What is your problem? I was just asking a harmless…"

The reverend, quite unlike his normally jovial and peaceful self, grabbed a handful of the man's shirt and pulled him up close until they were face-to-face.

"What are you talking about, a hostile takeover? Who…? What makes you say that? Tell me quick."

"Have you gone mad?"

Cristos finally found his feet again and pushed away from the reverend, with a little more force than quite rightly necessary, but the fire in the holy man's eyes and the hard set of his mouth bore nothing but bad news.

"I was joking, you fool, but now I am thinking something's going on."

"Joking?"

"Joking, yes. Ha ha, remember. You've lost your mind, Barry. Get out of the sun and quickly."

The reverend ran his hands through his sweat-damp hair and forced a smile.

"Forgive me. I was deep in thought, and you merely—disturbed me."

"Disturbed, my foot," Cristos muttered, collected his aged liquor bottle, which had rolled into the sand somewhere, and put a few giant steps between himself and the reverend. "You've gone insane," he hollered before Barry could grab him once again.

"Wait, just tell me what made you say that?"

"I was joking, you damn fool," Cristos hollered now, from a decent and safe distance. "Go sober up or chill out or whatever you need to do. I was fucking joking."

And with that, he disappeared into a grove of palm trees and was swallowed up by the jungle in moments. The man knew this island better than some others knew their own bedrooms.

Reverend Bartholomew stood there for a few more minutes, watching the spot where Cristos had disappeared. He wasn't coming back; that was a given. He'd moved as if pure evil had a grip on him, not a man of God. Finally, he shrugged and took one last look around, to make sure the beach was undisturbed and pristine once again.

"Time to be more careful," he said softly. "Very careful, and they will never know what hit them." He stood still and smiled, until he finally let the hysterical laughter bubble up and out of him that had wanted to explode since he read the hidden note. "Oh yes, Rafael," he said hoarsely. "When you least expect me, when you have finally forgotten me and everything I stand for, that's when I will be back, and I just figured out how I'm going to do it."

FIFTEEN

Rafael steered the 30-foot cabin cruiser out onto the lake and kept going for a good half hour, while Al sat up on the sundeck alternately squinting over the sparkling water and scribbling notes in a ratty black notebook he carried. Rafael thought he would give a small fortune to have a peek at those pages and then stopped himself. Maybe he wouldn't, curiosity killing the cat and all that.

For the first time in ages, he was enjoying himself, despite the nagging pressure in his gut that had been with him since the meeting with Tadeo.

"If this cannabis thing does not work out, you might have a future as a ferry captain," Al said all of a sudden. "I don't believe I have seen you so relaxed in ages."

Rafael looked up from the controls and grinned broadly at Al.

"I don't know why, but I haven't been out on this thing in forever. I quite enjoy it, always did, even though it was... Well, my wife wanted this boat."

"Alice. I heard she passed away recently. I never had a chance to express my condolences, Rafael. Let me do so now."

Rafael shrugged and swallowed hard, once, twice, until the lump in his throat was gone. "Ah, you know," he said when he had his voice under control again. "Cancer, when it gets you…"

"It could not have been easy, and this situation did not exactly make it any easier on you."

"This situation," Rafael quipped softly. "Is that what we are calling it now, a situation? Yes. It all happened just around the same time, and just when I thought it was all behind me and I was going to run my little construction company in peace until retirement—"

"My father steps up and pushes you into the role of CEO of PerCan." Rafael only nodded.

"Tell me one thing, Rafa. Why did you do it?"

"What? Say yes to this job?"

"Yes—why did you take it on, knowing that at best it would be a giant mess? At worst, an unsolvable puzzle. I know he tried to threaten you, but you had to have known I would help you get out of the situation."

"Your father didn't exactly leave me a lot of choice, true." Rafael shrugged again. "His veiled threats were perhaps more intimidating than if he had come out and said it. And true also, I could have told him to go to hell knowing you would have my back. I don't know for sure, but I believe the challenge tickled me. Maybe I was looking for something. Kayla thinks I took it because of Connor." He rolled his eyes. "I've done a lot of deals with Connor, and he was always in the driver's seat. Maybe, just maybe, all I wanted to do was see if I could do it myself, you know. Put the deal together and follow through the way I know it should be done."

"That's quite a tall order, and there would have been easier ways to do so."

"Yes. And with that, we are back to your father's unspoken threats. Why take that chance with my company and my son's lives?"

They had gone out into the lake far enough, and Rafael cut the engines, letting the little cruiser drift at anchor while he got comfortable in his seat.

"It always was a tall order, and it's about to get taller. I don't think I had any idea how deep the cesspool would be when I started out."

"If it's any comfort, none of us did."

"And if we're all honest here, Al, I don't know if we can still save PerCan the way we thought. We rely on your father for every dime at the moment, and failing a miracle, things are going to stay like that for a while. Quite a while. I don't know how much money he is willing to burn, but I am afraid one man's private fortune may not be enough to save a cannabis company of the size we are planning."

"You might be right." Al hunched over and folded his hands between his knees, letting his gaze wander out, way out over the endless horizon. "My father is looking for something as well, a new way of life perhaps. Something away from the clubs and dive bars. He made some ill-advised purchases, and he is getting frustrated. Which is where my original idea came in."

"A takeover?"

"A merger if you will," Al said slowly, still scanning the horizon. "Right this moment, you're having trouble raising funds because the company is in disarray, and the licensing process stalled."

"Correct."

"At the same time, there are numerous smaller producers out there without our resources and information network. They are struggling to service the customers they have, all while trying to achieve consistent, high-quality results and delivering them on time and responsibly. Many of them got into the business thinking growing cannabis couldn't be all that hard, and they are finding out just how difficult it can get."

"You've done your research."

Al nodded. "I have. And it makes sense, some type of fusion with one of these smaller producers."

"Merger—takeover—what?"

Al shook his head. "It's just an idea for now. Perhaps an equal merger would be better, friendlier. They bring an established small production facility and a license."

"And we bring—what? A grand-scale business plan, an empty building, the knowledge one of your brothers nicked off the other? Where's the value?"

Al managed a small smile and leaned back again in his deck chair. He took a few deep, cleansing breaths and let the wind ruffle his dark hair while birds screeched and wheeled overhead.

"Nice place to meet, a boat like this, you know."

"I know. Now help me figure this out."

"Your phrasing is brutal. Say what you will about Connor—he had a grand dream. Nobody else would have had the cojones to start something on this scale, never mind follow through."

"Some follow-through."

"Stay with me here, Rafael. I know you're down right now, but don't let it show. That's not helping. Say we hire this famous grower from Colorado Connor was keen on."

"I think I know the man you're talking about, yes. And?"

"Bring him up here, put him together with my brother."

"One of them."

"One of them." Al raised an eyebrow and didn't elaborate. "Give him carte blanche to design this thing. Go wild. Take what TC and Dan did and then take it one step further."

"TC is long gone, took a job elsewhere when things went south. But fine, I follow you this far."

"Then make Tadeo buy into it."

"It just comes off your tongue, doesn't it," Rafael said and rolled his eyes. "Easiest thing in the world, just convince your father."

"It is not." Al uncapped a bottle of water, took a long swig and rested his chin on his fist. "The old man is sly—and wily—but there's one thing that drives him, and that's making money. If this is what it takes to make a lot of money, then once you've got him fired up and convinced, he'll do anything."

"Leaving that aside for now. Let's say we do convince him, let's say he buys into it, and our grower is on board. We merge with the smaller outfit…"

"Bingo. Enormous grow facility, well-trained staff, decent financing…"

"License, distribution network," Rafael finished. "Life is good."

"Life is good."

"Christ, Al. I don't know if I can do this."

"Of course you can. And I'm still here too. There's a reason you brought me on. So, once we get to the part where you have to present to Tadeo…"

"Convince him to open his pockets. Beyond the pain threshold most likely."

"We work together. I know how he thinks. I know what he needs to hear and what his hot buttons are."

"Now he mentions this."

Rafael rose, checked on the drifting anchor, and took two bottles of beer out of a cooler in the cockpit.

"I know. We're not supposed to be doing this out here, but the hell with rules right now. Let's drink to this."

Al took the offered bottle and clinked its neck to Rafael's. "To the rebels."

"You really think we can pull this off?"

"I don't know, but we have to try. Because I sure see no other way to get us out of this mess Connor got us into, do you?"

"No."

SIXTEEN

Weeks started flying by like days. Tadeo grudgingly agreed to finance them 'a little while longer,' as long as Rafael managed to show him ongoing progress. The consequences were unspoken, and ongoing progress, meanwhile, was at best a vague concept, designed by and judged by Tadeo Ivers.

David worked like a man possessed getting their government filings up to date and, with that, the company back into the good graces of the SEC. It produced progress he could show to Tadeo.

Rafael managed to liberate a couple of construction crews from Roger Carmichael, and Dante spent his days at the building, supervising a construction process he only hoped would lead to a large Cannabis Growing Plant one day. One day.

In the meantime, it produced exactly what he needed: more progress for Tadeo.

Tadeo kept a tight leash on him. Every day, he expected Rafael to show up at the diner at seven p.m., to take his dinner in the diner while he sent a progress report to the back for Tadeo to study. If anything on it was unclear, or needed explanation, a note would appear with his bill and he had to present himself for discussion.

Rafael hated every moment of the process, but he knew it was the only way for now. That or close the doors for good and walk away.

Every now and then, when he had a particular lousy day, and every investor had showed him the door, more or less politely, when the constant succession of calls demanding money would not end, and problems piled on top of problems—in those moments, Rafael contemplated walking away.

Especially late at night, when he sat alone in his study, the ancient lamp on his desk the only light in the room, that's when he put the pen down sometimes, rested his chin on his fist, and wondered what it would be like.

What would happen if he just packed up a few things and left the country, like Connor had? What would happen if he showed up at the diner one day to say, *sorry, I'm not doing this any longer*? What would happen?

When Tadeo threw a 20-minute fit over the layout of the grow rooms—which his own son had designed—when he questioned David's invoices and flat-out refused to acknowledge them, or when he decided Rafael could damn well go without a salary while he wasn't bringing in investors… Those were the moments when he was half out of his chair, reaching for his jacket, and ready to say, *that's it.*

Yet, every time, he sat back down. A stubborn refusal to quit, a nagging concern about the fate of his construction company and that of his family, and a plan in the back of his head that refused to go away… Especially as he knew he could do this. He damn well could. If he and Al worked together and followed through, they could do it.

And dammit if he was going to let Tadeo Ivers and his childish temper tantrums stop him from succeeding.

He had too much work to do anyway. Every night when he got home after his exhausting sessions with Ivers, he cleaned up and sat down again to do his research, sometimes until late into the night. One after the other, he took a look at any small existing licensed cannabis manufacturers and studied them, their size, business practices, successes and failures. Every time he had only one question in mind: was this the takeover target he was looking for?

He dismissed the kooks right off the top, small time redneck-types who used the new legislation to make their own drug habit semi-legal, surprised at how many of these he discovered. They would not keep their license long, and if there was one thing Rafael did not need, it was yet another set of problems.

No, he was looking for a good fit, a company much like the one he was building, serious, business- and growth-oriented, and well managed. It would help if they had some experience and success, but not too much, or they would be unmanageable.

"Needle in a haystack," he muttered and sifted through a pile of papers on his desk. In essence he was looking for himself, as long as there was a license to grow involved.

At the same time, he cautiously reached out to Nick Ambrose, the federally licensed grower he had met in Denver. God, had it been really two years ago? Two years since the entire merry group had piled into a Dassault Falcon private jet and buzzed around Colorado and Oregon for the better part of a week, gathering information and knowledge, generally running through funds like they would never end?

The memory made him smile for the first time in ages. Connor had been so keen to hire Nick, and, say what you will about his horrendous spending habits, Connor had an excellent nose for people. He always knew who had the real goods and who was presenting a load of BS.

Nick Ambrose was the man who would give instant credibility to their facility, like hiring Steve Jobs to manage your IT department. But between Nick, Dante and the giant question mark that was Roberto Ivers, he faced a balancing act of gargantuan proportions. Labeling it 'handle with care' amounted to calling Godzilla a garden lizard.

Dare he even approach Nick unless he had cleaned up this mess?

Another day had come and gone. Rafael sat at his desk, staring into the yellow pool of light made by his desk lamp, and rubbed the bridge of his nose with two fingers. This, he thought, had to be the reason why men like Connor Beauregard lived in their own fantasy world.

There was no way in hell Connor would have been able to cope with this pace, this kind of detailed research or these kinds of questions. Not even if he tried, so he made the world up as he went along. Much easier that way.

SEVENTEEN

Dante had lost much of his attitude, Rafael thought, as the man strolled into his office a few days later. Gone was the swagger and the air of 'my father wants me here—live with it.' In its place, something vaguely recognizable as politeness and his own style had appeared. He'd abandoned Tadeo's usual car and driver and was suddenly known to show up with a cherry-red motorcycle. Go figure.

There was a good chance the wrath of Ivers Senior extended to other people besides Rafael Covin, he thought, allowing himself a little smirk. Considering Dante's extravagant lifestyle and dependence on Daddy's money, this would not be an easy or enjoyable thing to live with.

"Hey, Rafa," Dante said and plunked himself into a chair across from Rafael. "Your message said it was a little urgent."

"How are things progressing?"

Dante shrugged. "Not much happening right at the moment except for the construction and a lot of—planning."

"Looks like daydreaming some days, doesn't it?"

"Sometimes."

"And your father does not have a lot of patience for our flights of fancy, or our plans, no matter how good they are. I noticed that."

"He prefers facts and figures, things that can be proven, documented, and repeated as desired."

"There's no such thing in our business. Especially since there is no such thing as 'our business' yet, until we actually manage to build it."

Another mildly annoyed shrug.

"OK, Dan, I'm going to ask you something, and I'm going to need an honest answer. You ready?"

"Not if you're asking like that."

"I'll take my chances and ask anyway. Tell me…" Rafael twirled his pen between his fingers and watched it dance about for a moment before continuing. "What exactly is Roberto's status at the moment?"

"His—status?"

"Yes, status. Is your father planning to bring him into the company? Is he going to be part of Perfect Cannabis at some point?"

"I highly doubt it. Why do you even ask?"

"It should be self-explanatory why. From what I heard, Roberto is the unofficial expert on marijuana and the growing and distribution thereof. I have big plans for this company, but I want to know if your father intends to bring in Roberto one day. It—might change things a bit."

Outwardly, Dante merely shrugged, but Rafael could feel waves of resentment rolling off the man sitting across from him. His crossed arms, the scowl on his face, and the narrowed eyes kept the world at a distance. No welcoming mat being rolled out by Dante for his brother around here.

"Don't count on it."

"Care to elaborate?"

"Well, when your… Connor. When things went sour the first time around, Father went absolutely ballistic."

"No doubt."

"He was ready to throw Roberto back into jail, carry him there personally, if necessary, for dealing with Connor."

Rafael allowed himself a small grin.

I just bet, he thought. Junior had done a first-class job at basically ruining the senior Ivers's attempt at a serious, legal drug business and given him the proverbial finger in the process. If that wasn't cause for one of the fabled temper tantrums…

"I think he offered Rob a lot of money to go away and never set foot into his house again."

"I can picture the scene. And—did he go away?"

"Must have. Nobody has seen or heard from him since then. If I wanted to take a wild guess, I'd say he took off for Thailand, or some other South East Asian destination, Bali, maybe even."

"So, your father didn't know what Roberto was up to in the back room originally. He just used it as a convenient tool to unseat Connor, who had become a thorn in his side?"

"What Connor and Roberto were up to, together remember? They both cooked up this wild scheme."

"Six of one," Rafael said and shrugged.

The Ministry of Health, the police, and several other investigative bodies had spent months trying to figure out who knew what, when, and who had been working together with whom, only to come up with exactly nothing. Nada. Amazing how quickly evidence could disappear when needed.

But if Ivers had not put Roberto in place to discredit Connor, if Roberto had just taken a chance and squatted in their building to grow illegal marijuana for a while and potentially ruin his father, then the chances of seeing him return were decidedly slim. Ivers would not want him near the company, at any time. Dare he bet on that little fact? Rafael wondered.

"So, I'm going to make a suggestion here," he said. "But don't blow up at me right off. Think about it first."

"That don't sound good."

"Depends." Rafael put down his pen and folded his hands. "You ever heard of a guy by the name of Nick Ambrose?"

"Hell yes." Dante nodded. "There's no better grower. I met him at a grow expo one year. Really good man. Knows his stuff."

Grow expo! Rafael almost rolled his eyes. Who would have thought the growers of weed and manufacturers of assorted paraphernalia would set up their own expo? He'd have to get with the program here, if he stayed.

"That jives with what I heard. He's the best. And to tell you the truth—well, I'm kind of thinking of hiring him."

"Hiring him? Now wait just one minute. My father put me in charge of the grow operation here, and I can…"

"That's why I told you not to blow up at me." Rafael raised his hands. "Just an idea, OK? I know you know your stuff. But how about some help to make this a first rate, best-of-'em-all kind of facility?"

"I wasn't aware you had doubts."

"I just said I don't, Dante." Rafael sighed and dragged his fingers through his hair.

In the construction industry, he'd met his shares of these divas. The concrete guy who thought he was the only man in the world to pour a proper foundation, the roofer who had to have his way or the highway, divas each and every one of them, and he couldn't stand them.

"I'm not questioning your abilities. Believe me. I thought it might actually be, god-forbid, fun to learn something from a guy who has that kind of rep."

"Well…"

"Can we leave the 'do you know who I am' attitude on the shelf, please? I know your father owns most of this outfit, and I also know if he says 'go,' we're all expected to head in the indicated direction without question. If I could just have my way here for one damn minute."

"You want to hire this guy?"

"I want to hire Nick Ambrose." Rafael held his left hand and began ticking fingers off it. "One, he is a federally licensed grower. The feds don't license people unless they are ace. He is the best there is, and we could use that knowledge and credibility. Two, if you like this business, there is no one better to learn from. Three, I need all the help I can get raising funds, and his name is going to give me a leg up. Do I need to go further?"

"How long would he stay on for?"

"I don't know, Dan. However long we can use him. Not forever. His home is in Colorado. I doubt he wants to move, and he'd be a consultant. I just think it makes sense to pick this guy's brains for a while until we've learned what there is to learn."

Dante said nothing for a long time, and Rafael could see the emotions move across his face.

"That's why I asked you about Roberto a few minutes ago. The way I see it, with a little bit of guidance from Nick Ambrose, hell, Dan, you're going to be better than Roberto ever was. And it's all going to be legal."

"You don't have to try to play me against my brother."

"Fine, sorry. But promise me you'll think about it. Marijuana is just becoming legal in this country. You could become an authority in the field, if you want. In a few years—who the heck knows? You could tell all of us to go to hell and be a consultant for anybody who wants to get into this business. This could be your own thing."

That finally did it. Dante relaxed, and a slow smile spread on his face. Working for Good Old Dad wasn't all it was cut out to be. The idea of cutting him loose a few years down the road and having something of his own tipped the scales.

"It might not be a bad idea to get some outside advice."

"I don't think so, no. But I don't want to get into this without knowing you're on board."

"Sure. Why not? But Rafael?"

"I knew there was a but. What is it?"

"You're going to have to explain this to my father yourself. I'm not helping you there. And don't think it's going to be pretty."

"When has dealing with him ever been pretty huh? Leave it with me."

***

Rafael allowed himself to sit back in his chair, close his eyes and think of nothing at all.

"Endless game of whack-a-mole," he said when he heard Connie come in with a fresh cup of coffee. "Kill off one problem, and catch your breath. There's another one popping up behind you."

"Now that you mention it… But remember, I'm just the messenger."

"Christ, what is it this time?"

"Just more bills that need to be taken care of."

"What else is new?"

Rafael put out his hands for the latest stack and promised himself to get back to his research ASAP. This idea of a merger wasn't just interesting anymore. One might call it vital now.

***

"Imagine the funds I could raise," he said to Al a few weeks later. "The US's best federally licensed marijuana grower on board, a nice, at least partially renovated building and grow facility, and—and a license."

His hands spread as if he could draw a larger, more successful corporation in the air between them

"You've made progress. I haven't seen or heard from you in a while."

"I haven't had the time to breathe, Al. Sorry for going deep six on you. Have a look at this."

He spread a sheaf of papers on the little table between them. The weather had been a little unstable just of late, but they both liked the idea of their little meetings on Rafael's boat, out on the lake away from prying eyes and curious ears. It had a cozy and at the same time clandestine feel to it that appealed to both men.

"Mariposa?"

Rafael shrugged. "Sounds like somebody's wife's idea. No matter. Mariposa Inc. Decent little grow facility out in the middle of nowhere up north. They managed to put up a good size greenhouse operation and keep it going. Had their license for the better part of a year now, weathering the storms, more through sheer luck and hard work than anything else."

"Quality problems," Al said, speed reading through a few pages. "Infections, fungi. Not exactly what you want in a medical production facility."

"They've lost a few crops, heat-treating the marijuana to guard against fungi and the like…"

"Which gets them nothing but quantity problems and low quality." Al nodded. "I wouldn't want to be in their CEO's shoes."

"Essentially started as a family affair grown too big for their britches," Rafael said, turning his notes back around so he could read. "The beauty is their entire setup is very closely held. Less than a hundred people involved here, so you're not inviting a whole lot of unknowns into the boat."

"As the case may be."

"I wish you'd seen my research, Al. Do you have any idea how many weirdoes are hiding in and around this industry?"

"I would suspect the subject matter has something to do with it."

"Connor and I… we used to joke, you know, hey, we're going to be drug dealers, woo-hoo. It was funny then."

"And it's quit being funny."

"You have no idea. The thought of getting into business with some of these people gives me the creeps. That's why Mariposa Industries, notwithstanding the fact that they have branded everything with little orange butterflies, is an attractive target for this merger. Their share structure is clean, closely held. I don't know why they bothered to become a public company in the first place—probably somebody told them they should."

"Proximity advice," Al muttered and looked over the printed shareholder list.

"Pardon me?"

"Taking advice from somebody whose only qualification to offer it happens to be they are in close proximity to you at the time."

"I'll have to remember that."

"But you are right. What possessed these people to become a public company? It's usually connected to fundraising, but not in a hundred years would these people have grown big enough to need all the headaches of going public."

"And this is where we come in. Let's approach them, Al, carefully, just kinda testing the waters, see what they think."

"Good idea," Al said slowly. "Tell you what, I have a cousin, lives fairly close. He's a journalist."

He tapped his fingers on his thigh and scanned the horizon for a moment. "Let me send Paolo in first under the pretense of doing a story on the marijuana industry. They might tell him a few things they would never tell us, and by the time we come into the picture, we have a fair bit of relevant knowledge."

"You know, Al," Rafael said, shaking his head, "there's a pretty good reason why a lot of people are, oh, let's say, uncomfortable with the idea of dealing with your family."

"Because we are thorough?"

"But you can be sneaky. And you always have 'a guy' or 'a cousin' in every goddamn business there is."

"Gathering information is not sneaky. Most would consider it good business." Al shrugged. "And dealing with people you know just helps control the variables."

"That's what I thought," Rafael said darkly and shook his head. "OK, then, send in your cousin and let me know what they tell him."

"You got it."

Al offered a hand to shake, and Rafael hauled the anchor back in. Time to get serious, finally, and make a reality out of his and Connor's dream.

EIGHTEEN

The floor mats in the elevators of the Shangri-La Hotel in Singapore were always imprinted with the day of the week. Always, and it was always correct. Travelers had been known to lurk around just around midnight to see if they could catch the fellow who changed them from one day to the next, usually without much luck.

Shangri-Las in South East Asia were among the first ones doing so. Later on, every big cruise line and hotel chain had picked up the habit, and 20 years later, it was no longer much of a thing. But the guy changing them, that guy still remained elusive and hard to catch, as were the people who were trying to spot him.

A tanned young man pushed his shades up on the top of his head and grinned. Those mats came in handy sometimes. Living in paradise, doing not much of anything, a guy could lose track of the days quicker than anything.

Just another day in fucking paradise, he thought. He'd just about given up on anything exciting or outlandish ever happening again when he received a phone call.

A call he'd never in a million years thought he would get. A call he wouldn't have dreamt of taking a few short months ago, but now, with boredom not only having set in but grown to gargantuan proportions, any silly idea that promised diversion and excitement seemed like something to pursue.

And this idea was so silly you could not walk away from it, no matter what.

Huge, daring, stupid, and still kind of silly. Not skydiving kind of silly, not laugh your ass off kind of silly. More 'why the fuck would anyone want to do that?' kind of silly.

***

Prevailing winds swept the upper sundecks of the Shangri-La clear of debris and clear of people at this time of day, but privacy was exactly what his meeting partner was looking for.

He stopped short stepping off the elevator and scanned the few people sitting on the deck this afternoon, enjoying a coffee, an iced tea, or an early cocktail of some type. Simple tourists, he decided, chattering away and not paying any mind to the lone man who had just arrived. A waiter approached him, smiling, but he waved him away. He had spotted his target.

Sitting in a corner, away from the crowd, the man who had called him sat sipping his coffee, with his legs crossed as if he hadn't a care in the world.

Looking closely, though, his body exuded the tension of a spring. He didn't settle into the chair as much as perch on it. And the mirrored shades he wore were perfect to hide his face.

"Fancy meeting you here."

The man looked up and scanned the new arrival from head to toe. "You came."

"I have to admit—I was kinda surprised getting your call."

The young man signaled the waiter and ordered a drink in perfect Malay.

"You speak the language. Impressive."

"Helps." He shrugged. "If you're going to spend any kind of time here."

"I heard you'd been banned."

"Banned, sent on an extended exotic vacation. Same difference. I heard you ran to avoid jail. I have to say, Co—"

"Uh-uh, no names now."

"As you wish." The drink arrived, and the young man took a deep draft. "One thing they do know around here. Might want to be a bit careful with that—Reverend."

The man twitched for a moment and finally shrugged. "You've done your research."

"Always. Nothing else to do in this fucking place, I might add."

"Better than working for a living. I thought you'd enjoy that."

This time, the younger man laughed. "Right. Last time I saw you working was, let me think, never."

"Watch your mouth."

"Unless you count working a room for marks, which happens to be what you excel at."

They both grinned and finally shook hands.

"You're still a crook, you know that?"

"Said the person calling himself a reverend. I have to say your message intrigued me. I don't even know if there's a way to pull off what you want to do."

"There's always a way. And they are looking seriously right now." The reverend slid two paper coasters around like a slide puzzle.

"For investment funds?"

"For someone to partner with."

"Forgive me, dearest Reverend…"

"You can call me Barry."

"Barry. If they see either one of us coming, they'll be up in arms. And I do mean arms, my friend. Not the kind used for hugging either."

"That's the beauty of it now, isn't it?" Reverend Barry's smile turned into something so ugly and fierce for a moment it made the younger man shudder.

"They will never see it coming. Not until it's too late. And when they find out… Payback." His palm slapped on the table between them with a hard crack, his eyes blitzed with fury bordering on madness, and the energy of the moment flashed over to where the tourists sat. For a minute, their chatter subsided, and they shifted in their chairs a little to get a better look, but nothing happened. The holy man folded his hands again and brought them to his lips. "Nobody will know until it's too late. Now tell me, are you in?"

"Obviously, you have a plan."

"I have a plan. But I need a partner to help execute. Especially after, well, after you and I are in charge again, as we always planned to be."

"Oh, did we now, you and I? I don't remember that being the plan." The young man leaned back a little, putting some distance between himself and Barry.

"It was, and you know it. It would have been good; it would have been goddamn perfect. But you fucked it up. You let them buy you out and send you… here." His hand took in the luxury hotel, the roof deck, and the scurrying waiters with one huge sweep. "Was it worth it? Was getting bored out of your mind worth ruining everything?"

The other man shrugged. "It was good money. I'll say that. Still is, no matter where it comes from."

"That's two things I like about you," Barry said. "You'll do anything for a buck, and you always say what's on your mind."

Another shrug. "So? What's this all about then, revenge? Not really my thing."

"Revenge? Jesus. Revenge is for beginners and women. No, my friend, I had a vision, an excellent vision, and I am going to see it through. You and I can do this and finally get what is rightfully ours. Are you ready to leave the same old, same old of this here vacation and do something completely off the wall?" the reverend asked and offered a hand.

The other man took it, and they shook.

"Dammit if I can figure out how you're getting on the inside, but shit, I'm in. Anything's better than playing chess with the Malay drivers all day."

"What, don't tell me they got you beat already?"

"You kidding? I'm the boss. They wouldn't dare. Not a chance. But it bores the tears outta me. No challenge. Shit!"

The reverend who called himself Barry produced a short list written on the stationery of the Shangri-La Singapore.

"You're absolutely sure there won't be a problem when you are reentering the country?"

"Not that I know of, 'less they've done something really dumbass back there and put me on a no-fly list or something."

"They haven't."

"And you know this why?"

"Because I have my sources, and that's all you need to know for the moment."

"You have sources, and you have cash." The younger man cocked a thumb and circled it around to indicate the opulence around them. "Doesn't look like you're just getting by. I didn't know preaching paid that well… Reverend."

"Well enough, my friend, but I managed to sell an ass-load of shares to a man greedy enough to want them all without wondering where they came from."

"And who…?"

"Never mind the gossip for now. There's information you actually need to know without worrying about the details. This list," he flattened the folded paper out on the table between them, "it contains a number of companies…"

The young man studied them, quickly scanning the lines one by one as fast as he could. Then a slow grin spread on his face and stayed there. He whistled softly. "Marijuana producers back home, each and every one of them."

"They are," Barry confirmed. "I need you to memorize this list and go back and study these companies. Keep an eye on the corporate structure. I want to know what happens, when it happens, and who is involved. All of it without showing your face. Can you handle this?"

"I can handle it. Easy." A lazy shrug.

"Uncomplicated, maybe. Easy, no. Not a girlfriend, not a buddy, not an old business associate, nobody can know you are back in the country. Not even your—family."

The younger man answered with a dry laugh.

"I'm serious—nobody."

"Fine, Barry, nobody. I got it. What am I looking for?"

"One of these companies is about to be approached with an offer of a merger. I need to know which one it is, and I need to know when it's going to happen. Immediately."

The younger man whistled again. "I like it. This is getting interesting. How do you know all of this?"

"I told you. I have sources."

"And these sources, they cannot give you information you want me to grab?"

"Can you for once just accept something I say without arguing about it?"

"Probably, but why would I, Barry?"

Barry ground his teeth, and his face flashed from anger to irritation, back to fury again and, finally, calm. He growled, "I have paid a lot of people a lot of money to keep me updated on what's going on."

"More than that I would imagine, considering that a very interesting court case became a massive train wreck just recently. Kind of interesting, wouldn't you say?"

"Another thing you can safely let me worry about. The main thing is the time for watching and gathering information is past. Now I need somebody who is ready to jump into action when I say go, somebody who knows what's going on and what's been done before, somebody who doesn't need any kind of handholding when the action gets thick and heavy. Do you finally understand, or do I have to draw you a picture in fine details?"

"No, I'm good. But tell me—do you trust me?"

"I don't trust anybody, least of all you. And you ought to know that. But for once, for now, we actually have the same goal and the same target in mind." Barry gave a little half shrug and waited.

The younger man finally nodded, rose, and rapped his knuckles on the patio table a couple of times. "Let you know when I'm leaving."

And with that he was gone.

***

Barry sat there for a moment and enjoyed the iced tea the waiter brought. The piece of paper with five company names had long since been torn into tiny little pieces and disposed of in three different trash bins around the rooftop patio. Now he sat back, turned his face into the sun, and closed his eyes.

"Ladrão que rouba ladrão tem cem anos de perdão," he said so softly even the waiter hovering nearby could not hear him. "A thief who steals from a thief will have a hundred years of pardon." And this time he laughed out loud, a hoarse, cracking sound that brought two of the waiters to his side, checking to see if everything was all right with the odd, wealthy man.

NINETEEN

Rafael had become used to looking over his shoulder, trying to spot a stranger in a crowd of strangers. Perhaps it was his own paranoia or instinct or just plain old caveman behavior, but over the past few weeks, the conviction he was being watched had become stronger than ever.

He assumed Tadeo Ivers's people kept a close eye on him and reported back his every move. In the beginning, it annoyed him. A few weeks later, he was almost used to it.

Over time, he forced himself to forget about these incidents, until one day, he walked down the street by his office and realized something that stopped him dead in his tracks.

The feeling of being watched, annoying and familiar as it was, had all but disappeared.

Rafael stopped and pulled out his cell phone, pretending to read a message he had not received, all while scanning his surroundings without being obvious. Nothing.

He didn't know why he knew, but he was now 100 percent certain whoever had been watching him had quit—from one day to the next.

It made no sense. If the spy were Ivers's man, then he should have doubled his efforts. Not a day went by that Ivers did not give Rafael a hard time about funds, spending them, raising them, and allocating them. Not one day. He wanted to know what was being done when, how, by whom, and how much it was costing him—in minute detail. Rafael had given up arguing.

If Tadeo Ivers had people watching him, he would not quit.

Not now. Which meant what, exactly? The thought sent an icy shiver down his back, and he turned on his heel and disappeared into Montecito Publishing.

He still felt uneasy, even as he sat in his old beat-up chair, his hand gripping the edge of his desk.

"Get a hold of yourself, Covin," he said, only to hear the sound of his voice. He was talking to himself on a regular basis lately. Just further proof that he was going insane. First, he complained because he thought somebody was following him; now he complained because that someone had stopped following him.

He picked up the phone to call Hank down in Security and put it back down again. Shit, the dude would think he had gone totally off his rocker, and he likely had.

But Al, Al would know what to do...

He had just picked up the phone again when Kayla strolled into his office, beautiful, confident, and all smiles.

"Well, there, Rafael, you dashed by me in the lobby without looking. A girl could really take offense, you know."

"Did I? Sorry, just a lot on my mind, that's all."

"What's going on? You don't look happy."

"Kayla, happy is not a word I use to define my days lately."

"Maybe you should."

Kayla came close, uncomfortably close indeed, and Rafael tried to sit still without causing offense. She was Connor's former girlfriend—fiancé—had been—whatever. He did not really need this right now.

Her hand landed on his arm, and Rafael breathed in and out carefully Did. Not. Need. This.

"Relax. You're all tense, Rafa."

She stepped around behind him and began to massage his neck, which would have felt really nice if he hadn't been in an all-out panic.

"Thanks, but I really—I really need to... "

"I said relax, Rafael."

Her voice was far too close to his right ear. Heck, he could feel her breath there, and if he didn't pull himself together right now... He shifted in his chair and finally grabbed hold of both of her wrists.

"Look, Kayla, I appreciate your efforts, but..."

His phone rang. His blessed goddamn phone rang at that particular moment. Whoever wanted to talk to him right now to get money, to yell at him, or whatever—that person would get whatever he asked for.

"I have to get this," he said, reaching for the phone without looking at the display.

"Rafael. Are you interruptible at the moment? I have a few questions for you."

"No problem, just give me a minute..."

He covered the phone with his hand and smiled as brightly as he could.

"It's Al," he said. "Sorry, he's bound to go on for a bit. Was there something you needed from me right now?"

Kayla made a face. Damn straight there was something she wanted right now, or he was a complete idiot. She straightened up, tucked on her blazer, and smiled.

"Oh, it will hold until tonight. Dinner, at seven?"

Without waiting for an answer, she walked out, and Rafael barely managed to contain a curse.

"Well, now, that does not sound good."

"Al, sorry—I—I had forgotten. Thanks for calling."

"Did you leave a message for me?"

"Not unless it was a psychic message. You interrupted an—embarrassing moment, is all."

"I don't think I want to know what that is all about."

"You don't. Believe me, you don't. Now what's the news from your cousin or friend, or whatever? Did he go see the folks at Mariposa?"

"He did," Al confirmed. "And he was not truly impressed with what he found."

"I'm listening."

"For starters, you were right—the go-public transaction was too much for them. Bad advice. They thought it would be an easy way to raise cash without thinking about all of the regulatory headaches that come with it."

"And then some," Rafael muttered, thinking of all the corporate filings he still had to read, check out, and sign off on. "Go on."

"Secondly, they have extreme quality problems. They did not come right out and tell him so, but from what he could gather, they just had to destroy another harvest because of an infection."

"Ouch."

"And then some," Al echoed. "Seems like those cannabis plants are fickle little things that don't take well to being forced into anything."

"I heard that."

"In any case, they have more problems than they can handle over there. They are pushing an order backlog of several months, and their CEO stays behind half the night packaging product trying to get it to the customer before it spoils sitting in his own warehouse."

"Does that sound like they would be interested in partnering with a bigger company who would have the cash, the technology, and the know-how to do this thing right?" Rafael mused, tapping his fingers lightly on the desktop.

"It does indeed. But I neglected to tell you my cousin is a thorough man."

"Why does that not surprise me, Al?"

Al chuckled softly, and Rafael leaned back. He found himself enjoying their daily phone calls and update meetings. As much as Ivers Senior had not wanted Al in the company, had indeed tried to block him when he hired Al, Rafael thanked his stars every day he had thought of it.

He settled back and shifted the phone to his other ear.

"And what did he find out, your thorough cousin? Skeletons in somebody's closet? Somebody have their hand in the wrong cookie jar? It does happen in these kinds of companies."

Another soft chuckle. "You would know. No, Jaden was sufficiently intrigued by his research at Mariposa that he went to visit another company on your list."

"Oh?"

"Yes, he went to see Green Technologies after that."

"All right," Rafael said, perking up a little. "That was my number-two choice. Small outfit again, relatively well run, not public, but possibilities there. Another interesting target."

"Well, Rafael, shift them to number one. They have just about as many problems as Mariposa, but they are privately held, which makes for a lot less headaches in a merger rather than two public companies."

"True, but…"

"But one of their directors recently got killed in an accident out on the highway…"

"That big crash, I think I read about that. That's not good."

"Everybody read about it. But now what's happening is that his heirs are pulling out all the money the man invested into the company. Every dime he loaned Green Technologies, they want it back, and they want it back instantly."

"Ohh, talk about a nightmare."

"A big one. Looks like he loaned money out of his private funds without bothering to have a lawyer draw up contracts. Suddenly, the company is bleeding cash left, right, and center to keep the heirs happy and not go under."

"Two good targets." Rafael sighed. "Tell your cousin thanks for doing all this research for us. Not sure if I should offer him any cash or if indeed I can."

"Thank you, Rafael, but it's been taken care of."

"You see, that's the kind of thing I do worry about, Al, things being taken care of behind the scenes, off screen. That's never good news. And Jaden's story about Green Technologies ought to give you pause to think."

"No money changed hands, Rafa, relax. He owed me a favor, nothing else."

"And I don't take well to people telling me to relax. And you know what else I don't take well to?"

"I don't," Al replied. "But I'm absolutely certain you're about to tell me, so go ahead."

"Going to see your father and asking him for money to hire Nick Ambrose as our new head grower. The one thing these companies have in common is they need some damn good technical advice when it comes to growing marijuana, and we're going to be there to give it. Except..."

"Except for the small detail that Nick Ambrose is not going to come cheap."

"Not even close."

"I am about to make you angry again, Rafael."

"Uh-oh. What now?"

"I anticipated this very crossroads for us and our company, so I took the liberty of arranging a small meeting between you, him, Dante, and myself."

"Swell," Rafael said, "I'm positively glowing with excitement."

"It's set for tonight, seven o'clock."

"Seven?" Rafael laughed out loud. "That's the second time you've saved my butt today, Al. I ought to hug you—or something."

"Do I need to understand this?"

"No, you do not. Not at all," Rafael said, laughing again, while he wrote out a note to Connie to give his regrets to Kayla. Unfortunately, ever so unfortunately, he'd been called away to speak to Tadeo Ivers tonight.

Another bullet dodged nimbly.

***

Rafael left the building only a little while later. If he had looked up as he walked away, deeply tangled in his own thoughts, he would have seen a person standing at the picture window of the corner office, staring down at the retreating figure.

**

Kayla stared out that window, a steadying hand against the glass, her teeth set hard. *Look up,* she thought, *look up already,* trying to will Rafael to stop and turn. Wasn't that how it worked in the rom-coms on Netflix? Hero walked away, cue the violins and the rain, until the very last moment. Hero turned, their eyes met, he stopped walking, and the music swelled…

Rafael didn't turn. He didn't stop.

Kayla's hand on the glass slowly slid a little further down, and her breath fogged the window. Why should it matter, she thought, as she pushed herself off and sat back at her desk. If Rafael didn't care, if he'd rather hang out in dingy diners and at filthy construction sites than have dinner with her—why should she care?

With jerky, angry movements, she whipped her phone out of her purse and thumbed through her contact list, just to prove to herself that there were dozens of men who would drop everything for dinner with her. Dozens. Her finger flew down the list of names, and with a frustrated growl, she turned off the screen again.

No point. She didn't care for any of them. They were mostly interesting, wealthy, and they did not matter. Like her husband Hanson had been and, after his death, Connor. Powerful men who were only too happy to share that glow of power with her, long as she stood beside them.

Rafael mattered—a lot. She cared what he thought of her, she waited for that crooked little smile, and she felt that deep knot in her stomach when he didn't take her call or blew off dinner with her.

145

"Argh," she said through clenched teeth. Years of training herself not to cuss like a streetworker—and then there was Rafael, who cussed, wore serviceable, 'comfortable' clothes, and managed to throw off her carefully built persona with a single, 'Oh, hi there, doll.'

What on earth was she going to do about it?

TWENTY

The good reverend had changed hotels three times in the span of a week, for no good reason other than he found some perverse pleasure in this cat-and-mouse game. No one knew where he was, and no one knew what he was planning, and that was just the way he liked it.

No one truly cared where Reverend Bartholomew Wentworth chose to stay, and the brand-new passport deposited in the hotel safe proclaimed him to be exactly that, Reverend Bartholomew Jeremiah Wentworth. Glorious old cash. It just blasted open doors that stayed tightly shut to everyone else, didn't it?

Cristos might wonder for a few days where he had gone. He had become far too curious for his own good of late, asking too many questions about this sudden 'spiritual retreat' and pilgrimage Barry required. Cristos did not believe his bullshit excuses for one minute, and for a while, the reverend worried about the little Portuguese man left behind on Vaomar Island. He could imagine Cristos going through every shred of Reverend Bartholomew's possessions, with questing eyes and hands.

"Fuck it. Let him if he wants to," Barry thought. "Let him look for something until he drops dead."

There was nothing left to find back on that island, nothing that would identify him or give away his plans, nothing at all. He had made sure of that.

He wasn't planning to return to this hellhole of a Pacific paradise ever again. Goodbye, so long, forever.

He could get used to staying in Singapore, living the good life, not a care in the world, but he still considered himself too far away from the moment when a man thought about settling down and doing nothing for the rest of his life.

Before he could concentrate on that, he had one more score to settle.

Revenge was for beginners, he had told his new business partner, but late at night, when it was just him and the ceiling fan, sometimes, the anger would come. He would remember the people who had started the business with him, the people who had gone and betrayed him in the end, turned their back and taken his company away from him, and he would let the hatred take over.

He'd been cleared, innocent of all the charges they had brought against him, and still they had crucified him and driven him out of town like a thief in the night. For that they would pay. Then he could settle here and enjoy his life.

In the meantime, his new partner was doing excellent work and delivering results without the need for instructions or handholding.

He read the missive that had been delivered to his room in a plain courier envelope and frowned. Two excellent targets, two good choices. But which one? Damn, he had thought when the time came, he would simply know as if by osmosis. Suddenly, he drew a blank.

"Which one are you taking, Rafa?" he mumbled and held up two pieces of paper side by side. "Which one?"

Equal value, equal opportunities. How would the man in charge choose?

He closed his eyes and put himself into the position of the CEO of a large corporation, asking the same question. How would he choose?

When he opened his eyes, he dropped the sheet with the butterfly on it. He would never choose that one, just because of that silly orange butterfly.

Which meant only one thing…

Slowly, he picked the company description up again and covered the butterfly with his thumb.

It only meant that his former business partner would most likely pick this one, the sentimental fool!

Reverend Barry grinned and folded both pieces of paper into his pocket again.

This was too easy. All you had to do was know the players and imagine what they would do, then use it against them. Way too easy.

TWENTY-ONE

"When did I ask either one of you to look into mergers or acquisitions?" Tadeo Ivers's voice dripped with contempt and suspicion just then, and Rafael thought it might just be the worst mood he had ever seen him in.

The bluster, the yelling, posturing, and mean looks he was used to by now, and they did not bother him any longer, but at the moment, Tadeo resembled a large venomous snake, deadly, coiled, and ready to strike without prior warning.

"Refresh my mind, Al, if you would please. Have we ever discussed a merger of any kind?"

"We have not."

"And yet you drop this on me?" He flicked the company profiles with his finger so they sailed across the table to where his son and Rafael sat. "Really? Do you think I feel like giving half of my company away?"

"Of course not. That would be a foolish thing to do."

"Then why doesn't somebody—please—explain it to me."

The voice might have been soft, but the steel hid just under the surface. Rafael felt mesmerized by those dark, glittering eyes. Dammit, he should not have made the snake comparison. Now it would stick in his mind.

Instead, he folded his hands and forced himself to think of something pleasant, a large high-rise building under construction…

"May I?"

"I beg of you."

"Perfect Cannabis Corporation is in trouble," Rafael said. "I don't have to explain this to anyone."

"And we all know why."

"Right. But here is the problem, Tadeo. In order to deliver on our plan for the company, in order to follow through on our admittedly grand plans, we need money, lots and lots of money, or it is not going to happen."

"This is also not news. So now all of a sudden you can't do the job anymore?"

"Our capital expenditures are running away with us, and fast. In my opinion, we have only two choices. One, I am not entirely in favor of, I am only showing it to you. That choice would be to scale back our plans, sell our building, use the cash to pay off old bills, purchase something much smaller, and start over on a massively reduced scale."

"I don't think so," Tadeo snapped. "I did not spend all of this money to start small, now did I? Small I could have done by myself."

As if, Rafael thought, but he had promised himself to keep his temper in check. Tadeo Ivers never reacted well to being challenged, especially not when he was in a dangerous mood.

"Like I said, I'm not in favor of choice one either."

"So, what's choice two?"

"Choice two is we drive on with our original plan and change nothing. In order to execute here, we need a huge infusion of cash."

"Money you were supposed to raise from all these investors you said you were seeing, all these people who could not wait to put money into the marijuana industry. Tell me, how come you could fail at such a small task as raising money for a drug company?"

Because it is by no means a small task. Rafael bit the inside of his cheek and forced himself to nod.

"You see, Tadeo, all of my investors, they are indeed putting money into the marijuana industry."

"Come again?"

"Of course, they are. It is the hot investment property of the moment; they cannot wait to get into it. The problem is Perfect Cannabis has no license, a long list of unpaid bills, and a spot of bad history to overcome."

"You don't say."

"So, most of my investors opt for a—let's call it safer choice. Another company…"

"That is the wrong choice. And it was your job to prevent that," Tadeo thundered, and Rafael forced himself not to lean back from the anger. He wondered whether Tadeo actually stomped his feet under the desk. Sure looked like it.

"Of course it's the wrong choice, Tadeo. You know that, and I know that. We will be the most successful company in the medical marijuana business. There is no doubt in my mind."

"Then make it happen, instead of sitting here talking about it!"

"You know why they always paint a house before they sell it or show it to a new tenant?" Rafael asked and cocked his head to one side.

"Make it look better? Do I need this? What the…"

"Right, to make it look better. More attractive, and that's what I'm trying to do with PerCan. So, no investor will be able to resist it. In order to do that, I need two things."

"Money?"

"Money, yes. But I need a government license to grow marijuana— that is the most important thing. And I need something nobody else has, something incredibly attractive, irresistible even."

"Rafael, I like you, but I am losing patience with you. Don't give me an economics lesson here. Remember that I have made more money in my life than you will ever…"

"No offense." Rafael raised his hands and stood, gathering his thoughts for a moment. "Marijuana is in. Everybody is looking for marijuana stock, if only for the wow factor."

"Rafael…"

"I'm getting there." He pointed at the folder on the table between them, his research notes and analyses on the different companies he had looked at to prepare himself for this merger idea. "Unfortunately, it's like junior gold mining 20 years ago. There are just as many companies as there are acorns on an oak tree. And, for the most part, they don't have a snowflake's chance in hell of succeeding."

He took a moment and picked up the folder, opened it as if he were scanning the details, and dropped it on the table again. "That's where all of these came from. Somebody thought it would be cool to start a medical marijuana manufacturer the moment the legislation changed and just plowed right on into it. Most of these companies do not have the financial backing, the experience, or the knowledge to go further than the first ruined crop. It's a fact."

"And?"

"And… Investors have become careful. These people," he pointed at the folder, "these people are starting to realize it, and we are feeling the pinch as well. Have for a while now. When Connor pitched it, it was new, it was sexy, it was something nobody else was doing, and people threw money at him to be a part of it. Nowadays, your average investor is a lot smarter. They want to know that you're going to succeed, and they want to know exactly how and when you are going to do it. And the research into who we are and what we have done is just a click away."

"Still nothing new…"

"Patience, Tadeo, I am getting there. So here I am walking into an investor's office, wanting him to put money into our company—you know what he is going to say? He'll ask me just exactly why I think we are going to make it when nobody else will. And originally, I would say, 'Because I am not Connor Beauregard.' That worked a couple of times too, and it was funny, but enough time has gone by that savvy investors, the kind who have real money to put in, not just a few thousand, want to see something real, concrete and tangible. What makes you better than everybody else? Answer that question."

Tadeo spread his hands. "So, answer the question, Rafael."

Rafael smiled and allowed a couple of beats of silence. "Of course, Mr. Ivers. What makes us better than everybody else are exactly four things." He spread his fingers and began counting off on them. "We have a license from the Ministry of Health to grow marijuana, and we are inspected, audited, and certified on a regular basis. We have an experienced and consistent management team overseeing every step of the production, we have the largest and most modern production facilities in the country, and we have Nick Ambrose on permanent staff, one of the few federally licensed marijuana growers in the United States. He is completely loyal to us. Those four points, gentlemen." He held up four fingers, spread wide. "Those four points absolutely assure not only our success but market domination for a long time to come."

No one dared to speak. Al sat, not moving a muscle, although Rafael thought he detected the shadow of a smile on his friend's face, the ubiquitous bookends on Tadeo's left and right looked confused, and Dante fiddled with a thread on his shirt cuff.

"Dante." The name cracked like a whip, and the young man looked up from a daze.

"Father?"

"What do you think about all of this? Don't sit there like you need to take a dump."

"Um…" Dante looked helplessly at Al and Rafael, and Rafa nodded encouragement. They'd had this discussion before. Dan knew all the arguments.

"Um—I think it's a good idea, Father."

"A good idea? That's all you're going to contribute here, that it's a good idea?"

"We all know…" Dan swallowed once and pulled himself together. "You put me into this business to keep an eye on Connor Beauregard, and I've been catching up with the required reading and knowledge. But there is only so much I can learn from—from what others have written down. I would like to work with this expert, this Nick Ambrose, to learn all I can to make our business and myself the best we can be in our field."

He took a moment, straightened his shoulders, and nodded. "Father."

Tadeo said nothing. He liked to be in control of every situation, Al had warned him, so he was likely going to hate being ganged up on.

"Isn't it nice of you to have all of this all planned out and bringing me in at the very end? I am only the man who has to finance the lot."

"You don't have to," Rafael said mildly. "It's your choice. We just think it would be a good idea."

"If I want to know what you think…"

"You hired me to clean up this company, and I'm going to tell you what I think, whether you like it or not, Tadeo. The final decision is yours. Always has been, always will, but," he pointed at his folder, "this is a good solution. Instant license, instant credibility, funds raised."

"What about this Ambrose character?"

"We'd have to hire him. That will cost a bit of money."

"Will he come up here?"

"He lives in Colorado, nice area. It's going to have to be good money to make him come up here for a few years. By then, Dante will be the expert, ready to take over."

Why not throw a bit of family pride in there?

"Then all the newcomers will come to us to learn how it's done. They'll ask Dante to see why he does what he does and how he is so successful."

"You have this all planned out already…"

The anger hadn't quite gone away, but the temperature went down. He would of course never admit it, but even Tadeo Ivers could see that Al and Rafael had worked hard to solve the company's problems. Their reasoning was sound, their solution good. Now for the buy-in.

"Just think about it for a bit," Rafael said and took his jacket off the back of his chair. "No need to rush into something headfirst if you're not comfortable. I'll start chatting with Nick in the meantime, and you can always let me know later."

"You're walking a fine line, Covin."

"Yup, always have. Nothing new here."

"I could still…"

"I am sure you could, Tadeo. Damn sure. But you know what—I don't give a shit any longer. I am going to do the best I can with what I've got. And that's all anybody could ever ask of me. And if it all goes down the crapper…" He turned around and opened the door, even though Ivers had neither dismissed him nor ended the meeting. "If it all goes down the crapper, Tadeo, then on the last flush, I'll say, hey, guys, I did the best I could. Wasn't meant to be."

"Your business, your sons, I could still…"

Rafael walked out and down the hallway without hearing what Tadeo could 'still' do, and he felt his knees buckle just a bit out in the main diner.

Feigning sudden thirst, he sat in a booth and ordered a coffee until Al slipped in across from him.

"That was quite the floor show, Rafa."

He shrugged and stirred his coffee.

"I don't think anybody ever stood up to him like that or walked out on him."

"I might have to go home and change my underwear."

Al chuckled, and Rafael looked up, unused to the sound. "You think that's funny?"

"I think you're the only man he respects because of it. And it bothers him to no end."

Rafael shrugged again and stirred his coffee like a queer science experiment. "So, you think he'll go for it?"

"Who knows what he'll do. He could do the sensible thing or something stupid, just to get his own way."

"Grand."

"You said it, Rafa. Whatever happens, we'll do the best we can with what we've got and, if required, walk away knowing that."

"Yeah—I was just hoping…"

"Keep hoping, my friend. And most of all, let's go to Denver and talk to Nick Ambrose. The less we pay attention to what Tadeo is up to, the better we can do our job. He'll let us know when he's ready. He would have to be a fool to say no at this stage, and he knows it too. But he'll make us wait and wonder, and squirm, just for the hell of it."

"You got it." Rafael put his spoon down and looked at the light brown liquid in his cup with something akin to disgust. "I don't really want coffee any longer."

"Neither should you. Nobody drinks that stuff in here. No idea what's in it."

"Now he tells me."

Rafael abandoned the coffee and followed Al out of the diner.

Likely, Al was right. Tadeo never counted on someone like Rafael, someone he couldn't control or bend to his bidding, no matter the threat, and it bothered him.

Time to go to Colorado.

***

Back at his office, he asked Connie to make airline reservations for himself and Al, remembering the last time they had gone that way. Connor, the man who did everything in style, had rented a private jet for them all, and shuttled them around Colorado and Oregon for days. Oh, the memories…

For now, he had to put a number of good reasons together why a man like Nick Ambrose would possibly want to ditch a good job, solid income, and a nice workplace to come slave away at an uncertain startup in unknown conditions.

Nothing to it. Just convince him how much fun this would be…

TWENTY-TWO

"Are you ready to make your very own personal mark?" he asked Nick when they met a few days later in the lounge of the Denver Hilton. "I know you've already accomplished more than any one man could want to accomplish in this industry, but you're still working for someone else."

"I would be working for you, if I take your offer."

"Not necessarily." Rafael sat back and took a sip from his fifth coffee of the day. "We could set you up as a consultant, give you a place to live, a building, staff, and a company waiting for you. From then on, anything you say goes."

Nick chewed on his thumbnail and slowly shook his head.

"I've heard a lot about your company just recently—none of it great. I've done my research."

"Of course you have, and that's exactly why we need you. Totally free hand, Nick. Anything you want to do, as long as it comes out as the most modern, and largest, operation in the end."

"Hmm…"

"Come on, there must be things that you would like to do here, things that you know would work, and work perfectly, if somebody would just let you try."

"Well…"

"This is your chance to try them. This is your chance to show the cannabis world how it's really done, how Nick Ambrose does it."

"You say all the right things, Rafael. It sounds good. But I have a solid job here, good money…"

"Which I am offering you as well—really good money. And when we are all done with Perfect Cannabis, there isn't a company around that's not going to know your name and want to hire you to do for them what you did for us."

"Again, you sound good, Rafael. But how do I know you're not going to go bankrupt halfway through the process and leave me hanging there?"

"Do I have a guarantee, Nick? No, of course I don't." Rafael spread his arms and tried for his most charming smile. "Does anybody? I'm offering you better money than you're earning now, total freedom, and something that might be an interesting adventure. That's all I've got. You'll get cash, and you'll get shares in the company, and if it works out, we'll all make out like thieves. If it does not, well, don't you think we all have a hand in making sure that doesn't happen?"

"We have an investor who is extremely interested in making sure this company becomes a huge success," Al said, putting his hands around a glass of water. "If you are worried about your fees, don't be."

"That's all good and well for you to mention, Al, but you are asking me to give up everything, just on your say-so."

Al said nothing for a moment, and Rafael almost smiled, feeling a wave of irritation from Al. Possibly this was the first time anyone had questioned whether Al and his family really brought sufficient cash to the table.

"Nick, there are never any guarantees," he said quickly before Al had a chance. "None. Just a chance and a challenge, and those don't come with money-back guarantees."

"That's thin."

"Could be. But we, all of us," he moved his hand to indicate himself, Al, and Kayla, who had insisted at the last minute to be part of the group, "all of us put part of our lives on hold to rebuild this company properly and make it the best there is. I'm offering you a chance to be part of this group, part of something extraordinary. If that sounds like something you may want to try, here is your chance. If you're more comfortable being somebody's employee, then no harm done. I had nothing to lose by asking."

"I didn't say that," Nick said and ran his fingers through his hair. "It's a challenge, all right, and one I know I can excel at."

"That's why we are all sitting here."

"But I have a home here, friends, a base…"

"None of which you'll have to give up. I'm willing to throw in an extremely generous travelling budget if you'll come help us out. A couple of years from now, you'll be able to write your own ticket. Anywhere in the world."

"It sounds really good." Nick rose and offered his hand to Rafael. "But as you well know, I'm going to have to think about it some more."

"Wouldn't have expected anything else," Rafael rose as well and shook the younger man's hand. "Don't let money be the only consideration here. Al is right when he's telling you we have that end covered." *God, I hope so*, he thought and mentally crossed himself. "There are developments in this company that are going to make it an industry leader. If you want to be part of it, let me know."

They shook hands, and Rafael stood until Nick Ambrose had disappeared through the revolving doors.

"Hard to imagine that kid could make our operation or break it. He barely looks old enough to shave," he finally said and dropped back into his seat, picking up his coffee and putting it back down with mild disgust. "Jesus, I need something else. How do you think it went?"

"Not bad. Hard to tell." Al shrugged. "Thanks for having my back."

"Anytime." Rafael grinned. "First guy to suggest you might not have the kind of depth in your pockets that's required?"

"Something like that."

Something like that. And that was as close as Al Ivers would let himself get to getting angry.

"He is a really nice man," Kayla offered, and Rafael nodded.

"Nice, talented, famous. We need him. I just hope Tadeo doesn't make a liar out of us all if Nick decides to go for the deal."

Kayla went to powder her nose, and Rafael relaxed in his chair a little more.

"I can see it," he said to Al. "I can see the company we could build together. You, me, this kid, your brother… It's amazing. We could be the biggest, the best anywhere. All that has to happen is he says yes, and your father finances us for a little while longer, until I get a few more investors convinced."

"You're getting excited," Al said dryly.

"Yes, of course I'm getting excited. We have a one-of-a-kind chance here."

"I thought you didn't care, as long as you could walk away saying you did the best you could."

"Of course I don't—I do. Shit, I don't know, Al." Rafael laughed. "Connor used to get this way when he could see something nobody else saw. When he knew how he wanted things to work out and nobody else could yet. Now I know why he sometimes did stupid things, just to make it happen. He had it right here…" His fingers pointed to a vague area right before his eyes. "Right here, he knew what he wanted, what could happen, and all it took was this one little thing—this one little detail to be taken care of, and it would all happen."

"I hope you're not contemplating something stupid."

"No, of course not. I know when to let go—at least, I hope so. But you have to admit it is irritating, when everything depends on other people doing the right thing."

"Let it go, Rafa."

"I'm letting it go, I'm letting it go."

Rafael spread his hands and finally grinned. "Hey, we make an excellent team. Who would have thought?"

Kayla returned, sparing Al an answer, and she put her arm around Rafael's shoulder.

"Al, I hope you won't be cross with me, but I want to hijack this man and take him on a little shopping excursion. It's time we had some fun, and his wardrobe is in sore need of some updating."

"Hijack away," Al said, smiling. "I have some reading and emails to catch up on anyway."

"Thanks, bro," Rafael said, rolling his eyes.

The moment he had been least looking forward to: being left alone with Kayla. She'd been good company and fun, and useful as a PR officer, but the more he let her, the closer she tried to get to him, and with every passing day, it became harder to escape her attention. What did she want from him anyway? With her looks and her money, she could hardly think of Rafael as a catch. Both her former husband and Connor had been wealthy, charismatic businessmen—and here was Rafael. For the life of him, he couldn't figure her out.

"Well, at least it is decent of him to leave us alone," Kayla said and took the chair beside him, vacated by Al. "I wouldn't want this trip to be business only."

"That is kind of why we came out here," Rafael said, focusing on the cold coffee in front of him as if it held all of the answers. "Tell me, what do you think of this Nick—um…"

Her hand took his wrist, her thumb pressing into the inner part of his hand, and Rafael swallowed hard, staring straight ahead.

"We are in Colorado, Rafael."

"Rocky Mountain high," Rafael said, still not looking at her, and finally drank his cold coffee.

"Rafael, what's wrong?"

"Wrong? Nothing is wrong. Why would something be wrong?"

"You're not looking at me."

"Kayla, the last time we were here, the last time all of us were in Colorado, it really was—all of us."

"Connor was with us. Is that what your problem is?"

"Kind of. I'm sorry. Maybe, kind of, yes."

162

"Will you finally stop thinking about it, Rafael? Connor betrayed both of us—no, all of us. You, me, Al, Tadeo. Then he took off. So, from where I am sitting, we don't owe him anything. Please stop making excuses for Connor Beauregard. Unless there is some other reason you're making a face like you're about to be called up to tax court."

"No." Rafael managed a smile and made himself relax at least a little in the deep club chair. "Of course not. It's just—odd. A lot of memories, that's all."

It had better be all. Jesus Christ, Kayla of all people.

He managed to look up and this time didn't have to force the smile. Of all people... Not like Kayla didn't catch the attention of most of the males in any room, no matter where they went. Matter of fact, he should have slapped himself silly if it were not too late for such a thing.

A very beautiful, very smart, and obviously very wealthy woman tried to catch his attention, and all Rafael Covin could think about was how in blazes he could fight her off.

"So, what did you have in mind then?" he asked, pulling down on the hem of his old but clean and serviceable sports jacket. "And what's wrong with my wardrobe by the way? This is fine."

"This is fine if you are going to a construction project meeting. As the CEO of a large, successful corporation, you will need... Well, I can already see you will need my input. Come along then and pay attention."

Kayla all but took him by the hand and dragged him through several high-end menswear stores. She knew exactly what she was looking for and pulled items off the racks in every store, sending him off to the dressing rooms, no arguments allowed.

Rafael smiled, changed, changed again, waited for her verdict, and produced his credit card, store after store. After a couple of hours, the stores ran together in his mind, and all he could do was to follow Kayla from one store to the next and try to stay on his feet.

When he looked down at her feet and saw her high heels, all he could do was shake his head.

"How the hell do you stay on your feet all day, Kayla?"

"Practice. I've been doing this my whole life."

"I thought I had—on construction sites."

"In those boots you wear," Kayla scoffed. "No wonder. Now hurry up. They had no decent shirts at Nordstrom's. That is a crime if I ever heard of one."

"Crime. Indeed. Can I get a beer first?"

Kayla gave him a schoolteacher look and finally acquiesced. "One. Fine, then we need to keep looking."

One beer turned into three, and before he knew it, even Rafael discovered a modicum of fun in this shopping game.

"One day," Kayla giggled, "one day Connor and I, on our way to the South Pacific, we went shopping and bought all new stuff, including suitcases. Then we left everything we brought behind at the hotel."

"Everything?"

"Everything. You should have seen the bellboy when Connor told him 'you may dispose of these, young man. We have no need for any of it any longer.'"

Kayla collapsed with laughter against Rafael in the back of the taxi, producing a champagne bottle from somewhere, pouring two glasses.

"Are you sure you should…"

"Oh, relax. We're having a good time." She giggled again and waved the champagne at the cabbie. "No problem, right?"

"No problem, Señorita." The cabbie grinned from one ear to the other, and his eyes met Rafael's in the rearview mirror.

Lucky bastard, he seemed to think, and Rafael finally took the offered glass. What the hell anyway. He'd been working like a dog for the past few months, and after three or four beers and God knew how much champagne, he didn't care any longer. He plain and simple did not care any longer.

"Salut," he said waving his glass. "And fuck Tadeo anyway."

"No thanks, but you go right ahead."

Kayla giggled hysterically, and Rafael joined in. *Only live once,* he thought and turned the radio up. *Go make it count.*

They kept their cabbie for the rest of the evening, and at some point, the tour of menswear stores became a cocktail bar and a steak at Del Frisco's and, even later, a dance club. Colors, images, and tastes blended for Rafael at that point. Too much work, not enough fun—kid in a candy store. He knew his body tried to shut down at some point, but the hell if he even still cared.

***

Kayla had to admit she hadn't had this much fun in a long time. Perhaps since she and Connor had taken out that helicopter for the first time and Connor had...

Never mind. She linked her arm through Rafael's and toasted him with another champagne. Whatever she had thought Connor would do in her life, the person she had thought he was—it had all been a lie.

When he left, on top of dealing with the persistent rumors and gossip about her past, she then had to deal with another round: the woman who had lived with the famous Connor Beauregard and maybe even been a part of his deceptions and lies. Who knew? And didn't her husbands have an odd penchant for disappearing or dying? Strange, that.

Kayla had withdrawn even more, locked herself inside and concentrated on her magazine.

Back then, she'd thought of Rafael only as the slovenly construction worker who showed up with Connor and followed him around like a little puppy. Ever since Tadeo had made him CEO of PerCan, she had discovered a new side of Rafael, an honest, straightforward, no-compromises kind of man. A man who would most definitely never lie to her or take the kind of shortcuts she had seen Connor take.

No, it wasn't fair to compare the two men, but after their shopping trip, decked out in his new wardrobe, Rafael was the man most likely to win that comparison.

TWENTY-THREE

Early the next morning, Rafael dreamt his phone rang—again and again. This made no sense because nobody would phone him so early, so it had to be a dream. But a dream loud and intense enough to annoy him and make him sit up.

He quickly realized sitting up was a bad idea, a really bad idea. Every inch of his head, right to the tips of his hair, was a sea of hurt, and still the goddamn phone kept ringing. He fell back into the pillows and groped for it on the right side of the bed where he usually kept it, cursing softly when he failed to find the thing.

On it went, ringing with dogged insistence, reminding him that at some point, he'd been planning to change that annoying 'classic ring' ringtone to something a lot friendlier. Friendlier at least if you were going to wake up with a massive, teeth-grinding hangover.

Groaning, he sat up again, reaching for the annoying sound, when the covers on that side of the bed started moving, and a mass of blonde appeared slowly from under the sheets.

"Oh fuck," Rafael said softly, and despite the lore in common novels, he did not sober up instantly. The pain behind his right eye became blinding, and the phone finally stopped its noisy cacophony.

"That your phone, Rafa, or mine?"

"I think it was mine." To his own ears, he sounded like Roger Rabbit, and he pulled the sheets up a little. "I think."

Anywhere else, he thought. Right at this moment, that's where he wanted to be. Not here, not in this hotel room, not in this bed. Kayla appeared to be quite naked under those sheets and grinned like the cat who had tipped over the creamer.

"Why, don't you look roundly embarrassed just now, Rafael Covin. I think you might be blushing."

"I'm—I'm sorry. I'm sure. I'm not quite certain…"

"What happened?"

"Yes."

"Everything you think happened—did. Does that explain things?"

Rafael said nothing and swallowed, hard.

"And then some."

"Kayla…"

"If you tell me you're sorry one more time, Rafa, I will stab you personally."

Kayla reached over to the fruit plate on the night stand and precariously balanced a paring knife on her finger. In doing so, the sheet draped around her slipped just enough, and Rafael closed his eyes.

"I—won't. Promise. But I… Damn."

"Open your eyes, big man, and stop panicking. Nobody made any promises, and nobody has any expectations. This was supposed to be the fun part of the trip, remember?"

"I—do remember." Rafael opened his eyes again and managed a small grin. "And fun it was, right?"

"If you don't remember…" The paring knife dangled in front of his eyes again, and Rafael fell back into his pillows.

"I remember. No, I definitely remember. Kayla?"

"Yes?"

"We are—crazy. Certifiably crazy if you ask me. Downright nuts."

"And that is a problem? Not as far as I am concerned."

"Not a problem, not the way you're thinking." Rafael closed his eyes, and just there, past the headache and the pain in the tips of his hair, he did remember, the comfort and familiarity of the night, the companionship, the caring, the passion…

Rafael did not usually let others close to him. He kept a careful separation of business and private, and few people, if any, were invited into that private space. Connor had been. Invited—welcomed. And, later on, abused the privilege. Connor, the fiancé of the woman right here beside him. Former fiancé… whatever. Fact remained, when Connor came back and found out about this, Jesus.

"It's just very, very complicated," he said, his eyes still closed.

"No doubt about that. Rafael?" Cool gentle fingers massaged his eyebrows, and he allowed himself to smile, still without opening his eyes.

"We'll work it out. We always do. It's what you're good at, remember?"

"And then some." He finally did open his eyes, supported himself on his elbows, and rolled over, burying Kayla beneath him. "And then some, young lady."

His growl drowned out her giggle, and the complications were forgotten, along with the hangover, the phone call, Al, Tadeo, Nick and everybody they had left behind.

***

The little space of comfort and joy they were building, alas, did not last long. A few hours later, Rafael ordered room service breakfast, and he had hardly had a chance to step into the shower, with as little embarrassment as possible, as he heard his phone resume its noisy demand for his attention again.

Cursing softly, he wrapped the hotel's oversized bath towel around him and padded back into the sitting room to answer its insistent call.

"What?"

A moment of silence answered him before the caller recovered his composure. "This is not entirely the greeting I was hoping for, but good morning, Rafael."

"Al."

"Did you expect another caller?"

"No, never mind—what's up?"

"I should ask you the same thing. I came to pick you up for breakfast this morning and could not find you. Kudos to you for getting in an early morning workout."

"Workout. Kind of, rather—never mind. Were we going to meet for breakfast? Sorry, that totally slipped my mind, Al. I'm sorry."

"No need. We did not have an official engagement, no. I merely wanted to be the first one to give you the good news. I gather he has not called yet."

"Good news? Called? Slow down for a minute," Rafael said, trying to force his brain back into working mode, groping for coffee while trying to hold his towel in place at the same time. Not an easy task at the best of times, near impossible while being watched from the big bed in the main room by a giggling Kayla, clad at this point only in the corner of the white sheet. Rafael dragged his eyes and his mind away and back to the phone.

"Wait, what was that?"

"I get the distinct impression your mind is not entirely on this call, Rafael. Where are you anyway? I hear—noise."

That would be Kayla, stifling laughter under her sheets. Rafael grinned and signaled frantically for her to stop, which had of course the exact opposite effect.

"I was just about to step under the shower, Al. Can we meet in an hour, in the courtyard café? I think I'll be a bit sharper by then."

"That would be preferable. Let me just say Tadeo has greenlit everything. That ought to help speed up your brain process a little bit."

"Wow, oh wow. Yes, it does. Considerably. Don't go anywhere, Al. An hour, the courtyard café. I'll meet you there."

Without waiting for Al, he hung up the phone again and spun back around toward the room.

"You know you're being a brat just now, don't you?"

Kayla still rolled in the sheets with laughter. "Yes, but it's fun."

"Well, hear this, giggling princess on the pea. According to Al, Tadeo just greenlit everything."

"Everything, what does that mean?"

"I'm not exactly sure. I'm meeting him in an hour, and I better get a move on before then. I'm hoping it means the funds for us to keep going, and the funds committed to hiring Nick Ambrose and to make our grow facility the best in the entire country."

Rafael really liked the way those words sounded, and he grinned from ear to ear. "You hear that, Kayla, the best in the entire country. We are doing this. We're on our way. Hot damn!"

Her laughter followed him as he finally made his way into the shower, trailing his bath sheet, trying to hurry the process along as fast as he could.

***

Finally, he knew how Connor felt. When all the pieces fell into place, when bit by bit the thing you had only been imagining and building in your head came together and clicked into place, right in front of your eyes. That's when it hit you—you were doing it. You were making this goddamn deal work.

It was a feeling like no other, a rush, a hit, a high. He did not have the words to describe it, but he knew one thing: he never wanted to come down. And if this deal was done, he would just have to find another one and do it all over again.

TWENTY-FOUR

Rafael imagined he still looked a little worse for wear, flying into the courtyard café a good hour later, 10 minutes late, and ill-prepared.

Al sat in a corner, quietly sipping a cup of coffee, reading the morning newspaper.

"I'll say," he said without looking up. "Look what the cat dragged in. I'm thinking you went to celebrate ahead of schedule last night."

"I might have."

"Did you have fun then, you and Kayla?"

Al raised one eyebrow, the left one, as he was wont to do in moments of intense curiosity, and finally studied Rafael from head to toe.

"I dare say you did."

"Well…"

Rafael could feel the blood rushing to his cheeks, a failing he had never managed to get rid of entirely, and struggled to hang his jacket over the back of the chair.

"You said you had good news?"

"Oh, I do, not as good as yours, though, I would wager."

"Al…"

"Please. I'm quite enjoying this moment, Rafael. So don't leave a man hanging. Tell me why you look like—well, like Connor when he crawled out of one of my father's finer establishments at 3 a.m., a lady on each arm."

"Al, I swear to you, if you don't…"

"Yes?"

"Stop it."

"But I'm having fun. You and Kayla, anybody with a set of eyes in his head knew it was bound to happen. It was merely a question of when."

"Al, let's just change the subject."

"All right, all right." Al grinned from ear to ear, a strange expression on his normally composed face, and finally raised his hands, surrendering.

"I give. Just leave my imagination to fill in the finer details. Just so you know, this is a temporary reprieve. You will tell me eventually."

Rafael glared at him and folded his hands slowly.

"Now, your news?"

"My news, indeed. To the point."

"Please..."

He tried to ignore the grin on Al's face—no, actually it was a smirk, and he wanted to wipe it off his friend's face, really badly, but he found he was actually in a good mood, and he couldn't fault Al for smirking. Shit, he would have done the same thing in the same situation.

"You've spoken to Tadeo."

"Indeed. And after he blew up at everything and everyone around him..."

"The ubiquitous fit."

"The fit, yes, he realized that what we were talking about was actually not only a decent idea, but perhaps the only way to save this company while at the same time avoiding bankrupting him."

"Bet that went over well."

"It actually did. You know my father; he won't ever give anybody else around him any kind of credit."

"Not that I've ever seen."

"But he came as close to saying 'good job' as I've ever seen."

"So, after you marked this day in your calendar, with a red pen I would hope, what does our plan look like?"

"He has committed the funds to clear up all of the old bills that are still hanging around from Connor's reign, as much as you can determine they are reasonable in nature."

Rafael rolled his eyes. "Like I was just writing checks willy-nilly, but continue."

"You know him. After that, he wants us to attempt to hire the grower Nick Ambrose to give this company a much-needed boost in the image and reputation departments."

"Wow, what a good idea," Rafael said, letting the sarcasm drip from his words.

"But get this, Rafa, using any means necessary."

"Any means necessary? That's nice for a change. No hooks anywhere? No burning hoops to jump through or pits of piranhas to climb into?"

"I did not say that."

"Here it comes…"

"He does expect you and me to continue to forego salaries until this is all settled."

"Does he now?" Rafael shook his head and sighed. "Still the same old Tadeo, get in a bit of a right hook. Wait. Just you and me? What about Dan?"

"Nope."

"The favored son, Jesus. How do you feel about this?"

"Never mind, Rafael."

"Message received. Don't mention it. Fine. And after all of this?"

"After all of this, he wants you and me to concentrate on pursuing a merger with Green Technologies."

"Green Technologies." Rafael sat back and folded his arms for a moment. In his mind, he had always preferred Mariposa because of the company structure, the assets, the fact that they were a public company already, and a couple of other factors. Mostly, he simply got a better 'read' off this company, even just on paper. There was something about Green Technologies he did not like, without being able to define what exactly it was.

"Are we sure about that?"

"We do need to proceed with this merger," Al said and shrugged. "To tell you the truth, my preference would have been Mariposa."

"So was mine. We're on the same page."

"But Tadeo finally agreed on everything else, especially the financing."

"I realize that. There's just something here that makes me a wee bit uncomfortable, and I can't rightly tell you what it is."

He sat back without relaxing and tried to recall when he had first made up his mind between the companies, what it might have been that turned his attention one way or another, what might have turned him off or made him pay attention.

"I don't know, Al. Not my first choice. Hell if I know why."

"I understand, and I share the sentiment, Rafael, believe me. At the same time, we do need this merger, and sooner rather than later, as you yourself know better than anyone. The point I am trying to make is, to you, to the project, is the choice of merger partner at this stage worth an extended battle with Tadeo? Is the difference between GT and Mariposa so massive as to make it worth it?"

"Six of one, half a dozen…"

"That's one way of looking at it. If you want my honest opinion, I would try to avoid another fight with Tadeo over the choice of merger partner unless you have a particularly strong argument for one over the other in your back pocket."

"I don't. That's my problem."

"I don't either. So that's my advice."

"So, we just do it? We sweeten the pot for Nick until he gets too greedy to say anything but yes, and then we go approach GT and make this thing happen. That just about it?"

Al shrugged and sat back. *Your call*, his body language said.

Rafael massaged the bridge of his nose, wishing, not for the first time, he hadn't drunk quite as much last night.

Six of one, half a dozen of the other.

Had he not said the same thing to Al when they looked over the company profiles just a few weeks ago? Had he not thought the same thing, sitting at his lonely desk in the middle of the night trying to identify targets?

It didn't—it really didn't matter all that much. Except for that stubborn gut feeling, and that wasn't something he could take into a meeting and defend. Where did that leave him?

It left him being a CEO of the future biggest manufacturer of medical marijuana.

He'd make sure he was in charge after the merger. He could structure the company and operations exactly as he wanted them. No need to go thinking there would be things in this deal he couldn't live with. He was the guy in charge of making sure there were none. His would be the final call, so why the hell did he even hesitate? It did not matter; it plumb did not matter.

"It's going to be a brand-new company, Rafael. You can put policies and procedures in place to make sure things go exactly as you want them to go."

"Stop reading my mind, Al. It's not nice."

He flashed a quick grin at his friend. "It really isn't, especially since I was thinking just that a minute ago."

"So?"

"So, I have no bloody idea why I'm still hesitating. We just got everything we asked for, from a man who never gives up anything as far as I understand. The fact that I'm sitting here quibbling over having to give on one point, and I can't come up with a good reason why that should be a problem. Well, I'm thinking that makes me kind of a dick."

"It makes you a very careful man."

"That too."

"So, you can live with this? We go tell Tadeo good to go?"

"Why not." He spread his arms and shook his head to clear the rest of the doubts away like clingy old cobwebs. "Why not. Let's write up a good proposal, call a board meeting with Josh and Simon, get it all out on the table, have a proper vote, and take it from there."

"Take it from there."

Al smiled and signaled the waiter. "Bit early for a celebration, but you could probably use a fairly strong coffee right about now. Think Kayla will join us?"

That shit-eating grin was back, and Rafael chose to ignore it. "I don't know. Why don't you call up to her room and find out? I have to make a couple of phone calls."

***

He'd forgotten how much more fun it was making an offer to someone when budget constraints were not part of the picture. At least not the main part of the picture.

Nick Ambrose knew his worth to the company, and he knew how to get paid for that value. He negotiated for every penny worth of it. Once or twice, Rafael had to fight to contain his temper. Nick wanted this, and he wanted that, and he wanted more as the day wore on. He expected to be taken care of every step of the way. Every one of his needs had to be addressed.

Be a man, not a diva, Rafael thought, and smiled, and told the man, *No problem. We will find a way to make it all happen.* Every time another outrageous demand popped up, he found a way to swallow down the *you have got to be kidding me* that sat right in his throat and smiled again and promised it wouldn't be a big problem.

Given enough money, nothing needed to be a big problem, but his patience was waning after a few days of negotiating.

Finally, they were down to just talking about company-sponsored healthcare programs, and Rafael thought they good and well had him.

Everyone walked away happy after that first round of meetings, and Rafael called Dante and told him to get his rear down to Denver to meet this man, and make nice. They would be working together after all.

"So, he is really coming up and working with us, showing me everything I need to know?"

Somewhere, Rafael thought, somewhere he sounded relieved. Happy, that somebody else was going to help carry the burden of being in charge of the grow operation for a little while. He'd called it all right. Dan needed to learn, and what was more, he wanted to learn.

"Nick is really coming up there," he confirmed, and stretched deliciously on his enormous hotel bed, shifting Kayla's head just a little so her blonde mass of hair wouldn't tickle his nose. "Exciting, isn't it?"

"You did want a first-class operation."

"We all did. We're building something special here, Dante. And you are part of it."

"Yeah, it's nice…"

Rafael rolled his eyes. *Oh, go ahead,* he thought, *go ahead and say it. Jeez, you were right, Rafael. We needed somebody with the knowledge and the reputation. Thanks for setting it up, Rafa.*

Nothing came, of course. Dante was an Ivers after all. They didn't say thank you.

"So, get the next flight down here and meet him, will you? The two of you will be working side by side for the foreseeable future. The more you get along, the easier it will be for everybody."

"Now?"

"Now, Dante, like tomorrow…"

"OK. And Father…"

"Your father has greenlit this entire project, so move. Time to celebrate."

"Entire project? So, there's more?"

"There is more, Dante. And in time, I will explain it all to you, OK? For now, just worry about getting a plane ticket to Denver and meet us here as soon as you can."

Another eye roll. Why did the people around him move at a snail's pace all of a sudden? Was there a good reason, or just a reason?

"My apologies to you, Connor," he said to the ceiling, after he had hung up, and Kayla, beside him, stirred. "Sorry."

"What's going on?"

"People are dragging their feet instead of moving on this project at the same pace I am. I think I understand another piece of Connor. It used to drive him cray-cray. Sorry, didn't mean to stir up old memories."

"Don't be. Just don't turn into him."

"I'm not. I just want people to catch the excitement and move along at my pace. Is that too much to ask? It's not that I am asking a lot of…"

"Hush."

Kayla smiled and put her fingers across his cheeks. "Good God, you're already starting to sound like him."

"I am not."

"Yes, you are, and that's a good thing."

"It is?"

"It is. Remember the first couple of days when you were not sure you wanted to take over as CEO?"

"Things were in a bit of mess back then."

"Well guess what? They still are a mess. But you are straightening that mess out, one project at a time, one problem at a time. You're making this company the greatest there ever was."

"You bet I am. So why are we lying here in bed talking? Got an answer for that one?"

TWENTY-FIVE

Dante hung up the phone and opened his travel app, scarcely believing what Rafael had just told him

Nick Ambrose was hiring on with PerCan. The famous Nick Ambrose would be teaching him everything he needed to know about growing medical-grade cannabis. Even his brother Roberto said Nick's name with a bit of admiration, though he would never admit to it. 'The' Nick Ambrose…

He would have to get over being a fanboy, or it would turn entirely embarrassing, but his father couldn't have made a better choice.

Finally. If he paid attention, if he got into the growing business as much as he wanted to, he would outdo even Roberto.

Given your ability to pay for them, seats appeared on flights that had previously looked sold out, and it only took him the better part of a day to get to Denver.

Rafael waited to get him settled and introduce him to Nick, and finally, the time had come. They shook hands, exchanged a few pleasantries, and eventually left Rafael and Al behind at the Hyatt, to go 'talk shop.'

***

"Looks like they'll get along just fine," Rafael said to Al, scratching his head. "I was worried, seeing Nick seemingly turning into a massive diva, but Dante seems to like him, no?"

"Hmm…"

Al looked after the two men with a strange look on his face, and Rafael gave him a little nudge.

"What's up?"

"Nothing," Al said, still looking to where Dante and Nick had disappeared. "Nothing at all. The way those two just clicked. There is something—there. Forget it."

Rafael only shook his head and let it go. He had other worries just then; he had a merger to prepare.

***

"This is the time to tell you that I've never done this before," he said to Al on the plane back home, pushing aside the paperwork he'd been studying. "There are a lot of moving parts to a merger, and the more help and advice I can get, the better it will be. Honestly, I don't have a clue where to start."

"The lawyers will draft a big piece of it, all the agreements and who can do what documents. That's not something for you to worry about."

"But?"

"Don't put the cart before the horse. You haven't even approached the folks at Green Technologies yet. Go, meet them, see what their people are like, how they tick. Get a feel for the company. That's where you need to start."

"Good point. You're coming with me, are you not?"

"I don't know. Am I?"

"You are," Rafael confirmed. "I just told you I haven't done this before. I'm not going in there without backup."

"You've got Kayla, Simon, and Josh, people who are actually on the board of directors and have some sort of authority."

"All due respect, Al, but with the exception of Kayla, none of them has been as involved in this company as you have. They don't have the experience."

Al shrugged and tilted his head.

"Where is all this coming from now?" Rafael asked. "Am I not talking to the guy who has been talking me down off numerous ledges all along? The guy whose idea this merger was from the get-go? What do you think, yes, I need you there?"

"If you're sure."

"If you're sure," Rafael mimicked, waggling his head. "Of course, I'm sure. We will set something up next week. We'll go see these people, talk to their CEO…"

"Greg Turner."

"We'll talk to this guy, Greg. See how he thinks. His company is in big trouble…"

"As is yours."

"Exactly. Perhaps together, we can work our way out of this thing. If anybody remembers around here, we actually got into this business because we thought it would be fun."

TWENTY-SIX

"Fun," he said to Greg Turner a few weeks later. "For all intents and purposes, we are trying to make a living being drug dealers. If nothing else, this should be fun."

"It should be, Rafael. But you, more than anybody else, know that at our level, the headaches far outweigh the fun portion of the job."

"I don't believe that. I know if we do it right it can be a lot of fun. Somewhere along the line, you must have thought so, or you wouldn't be here."

He still wasn't quite sure what to think of GT's founder and CEO. The man walked in, all businesslike, dressed in a fancy suit and the kind of loafers you had to cover in your homeowner's insurance. A suspicious flash of gold crept out from under his shirt cuff now and then—and yet… And yet he had started a company to produce marijuana.

Not your average get-rich-quick scheme.

What drove the man then, if it wasn't money?

"I come out of the construction industry, you know that," he said lightly. "And we understand the headaches that come with the job, every job."

Greg nodded, not offering any of his own history. Some type of finance company, Rafael remembered from the corporate profile. Not exactly the kind of man who decided one day he wanted to be a drug dealer. Nor the man who wanted to have fun on the job. Fortunately, he didn't have to like the man to make this merger happen.

SABINE FRISCH

It would be a nice bonus, sure. But it wasn't a requirement.

He wished Al could have been there, but at the last moment, Al had had to beg off. Rafael suspected it had actually been his intention to let the two CEOs meet on their own for the first time. He still would have liked a wingman.

"I understand your company is open to offers," Greg finally said in that blunt way Rafael had noticed about him earlier, and Rafael smiled.

"We are open to making offers, as well as taking them. We have the start of a nice company here."

"You have a lot of problems, you don't have a license, your staff isn't really experienced…"

"We have a couple of things everybody in this industry wants."

"Oh?"

"Of course," Rafael laughed and settled back into the club chair. Say one thing for Green Technologies, he thought, their executive offices were comfortable and tasteful. He had yet to see the actual operation, but if their offices were anything to go by, he would have a hard sell ahead of him. "One, our financing is solid and committed."

"Committed for the long haul?"

"Committed for however long it takes," Rafael said, mentally crossing himself and hoping not for the first time Tadeo wouldn't make a liar out of him. "And two, we have just signed Nick Ambrose to our team for the next two years."

How like a sports analogy was that one then? Perfect Cannabis just signed the most famous quarterback in the game on for two years.

"News release will go out this afternoon, so I might as well tell you now. Yes, Nick Ambrose is going to oversee our growing operation."

"Wow, I didn't think anything would make him leave Colorado. You know how many operations have tried?"

"We just get things done."

"I am prepared to believe you on the financing after hearing that. You must have given him a small fortune."

Now Rafael shrugged. "Something like that," he said. Al's go-to phrase when he didn't want to reveal anything further. *Something like that.* Inwardly, he smiled. Who would have thought a couple of years ago, when he and Connor sat at a bar, thinking of a new business to get into, Rafael and Al would end up running it together, becoming friends in the process?

"Good thing. Because I'm sure I don't have to tell you financing is one of the biggest pieces in this crazy business."

"Tell me about it." Greg shrugged and brushed an imaginary speck off that $5,000 suit he was wearing.

"So, who is it whose pockets you have tapped so deeply you are able to go and sign Nick Ambrose to your operation?"

"A group of people. A family office, as a matter of fact."

"Somebody's family home office? Nice. Do I know them? Anything I should…"

"Greg, why don't we stop circling around each other like two heavyweights in a ring?" Rafael said and put his hands flat on the table in front of him. "We both know why we are here. The death of one of your key executives and financiers has put you in a tough spot."

"Could happen to anybody." Greg smiled without giving anything away.

"And the misdeeds of Connor Beauregard and his subsequent disappearance put you into an equally tough spot, I'd say."

"Indeed. But you and I both know the real reason why I'm here."

"Could be. Why don't you spell it out for me?"

Rafael thanked his luck he'd been watching Al for the past few months. Al could sit in any meeting, listen to any bullshit—anything at all—and his face never moved. He did not smile, he didn't frown, he didn't say, 'bullshit,' as Rafael was bound to do now and then. He just sat there and listened, with that bland, polite face.

So, Rafael simply sat and listened.

Something bothered him about Greg Turner. The man looked just a bit too slick, too polished, and too perfect for this business. He would have looked at home in a bank, top floor of one of the glass-and-steel towers downtown. You would expect him in that kind of setting. Why was he in this business then? It was like an ill-fitting shoe. And now, after the death of his business partner, he owned the majority of Green Technologies. Thus, he really was the guy to talk to.

Maybe people said the same about Rafael, he thought. 'Weird guy, looks more like he should be running construction downtown, not sitting in an office discussing mergers and acquisitions.' Rafael stretched his legs and hid a grin when one of his construction boots hit the leg of the table.

"I can't speak for you, but cards on the table, I'm here to see if there is compatibility for our two companies—working together," he said.

"In what capacity?"

"I have capital, I have a building ready to go, and I have Nick Ambrose."

"You don't have a license."

"I do not have a license, and I do not have the reputation that Green Technologies has. This is where you come in."

"So, what are we talking about, a full merger?"

"Could be. If we can see a scenario where we would put our two companies together. You could move out of that little greenhouse you have outside of town and move the production into our building."

"That colossus out by the airport?"

"The very one. As we speak, Nick Ambrose is working with my people on the final plans for build-out and retrofit. Won't take long. We will be able to put in the first growing pods and bring in clones. Personally, I think that's when it gets exciting."

Greg waved his hands in a 'been there, done that' gesture, and Rafael leaned forward a little.

"You know you can't sustain an operation like yours in the long run. You won't be able to keep up the quality and quantity your license requires, and sooner rather than later, you will be in deep, deep trouble."

"You're quite well informed."

"Better than you think, Greg. I know you've been battling the heirs of your former board member for all of the investments he made in this company. They want it back—every last dime, and they want it now."

"I'd like to know the name of your spy."

"No spies, just good information. Listen, I don't know much about cannabis myself. I have no green fingernail, never mind a green thumb. That's why I hire experts. And those very experts tell me that the way Nick is planning things is the only proper, successful way to grow marijuana, if you want to grow it for medical use, not just entertainment."

"Which does not happen to be legal in this country, yet. Never mind what your business partner…"

"Forget about Connor. He's yesterday's news." Rafael waved his hand in a massive gesture. "I'd rather not discuss him. Fact is, once we put in our grow pods, hermetically sealed, climate controlled, artificially lit, supplied with just the right amount of nutrients, light, and water, we will be playing God with these plants."

Playing God, that's what Connor had always called it. *You have to play God with the marijuana plant and be in exact charge of which plant is receiving what. That's the only way.* It was one of the phrases he had picked up on their first trip to Colorado, and the concept had appealed to him. Playing God, being the one in charge, the omnipotent one.

"I heard about all of it," Greg said and looked down for a moment. "Frankly, I didn't think technology had advanced that far, and the retrofit was expensive, but who knows?"

"Who knows, Greg? I will tell you who knows. My people know. So, think about this for a bit. Here's my offer. We put our companies, our resources, and our people together. We create one company, Perfect Cannabis. Perfect Green Cannabis, if we want to have the G in there. And we see just how far we can take this thing. We now have everything we need to become the biggest producer in the entire country. The entire country, Greg, and once everything is running, you and I can go and look at other markets, other countries. Who's to stop us?

Right at this moment, we just have this one hurdle to overcome. Both of us. I suggest we do it together."

He waited for a moment to make sure his words had sunk in with the other man and produced a nice bound presentation from his briefcase.

"Lawyers made this up, should explain all the details of how this transaction could look. I'm going to leave it right with you."

He dropped it on the table, and Greg snatched it up, leafing through the 30 or so pages.

"You're well prepared. I have to give you that. Nice."

"I am." Rafael shrugged. "But it's just paper. Above all, I like to know the people I'm going to work with. How their mind works and what their attitudes are. Anybody can read off a presentation, you see?"

He tried hard to overcome the bias of Green Technologies not being his first choice. But still, something about Greg Turner still struck him the wrong way. Rafael usually made up his mind about a person in the first 10 minutes or so when he met them. He had done it for as long as he remembered. Hiring construction workers, getting into partnership with a developer—heck, even getting his nerve up to ask his wife out, he had always known within 10 minutes of meeting the person in question whether this thing was going to fly or not. Done.

And he had never been wrong, either.

He and Connor had been friends for a long time, and right off the bat, he'd known that he needed to keep some sort of leash on him. He'd known to keep his eyes open so he wouldn't get dragged into something he wasn't comfortable in. And something in Connor's voice always alerted him that there was trouble ahead.

So, he'd watched his back and made sure Connor did not run too loose or too wild. Right to the end, he thought that was why he had doubts about Connor's involvement in the illegal growing operation.

Connor had certainly known about it and ignored it. He had tried to capitalize on it, sure. But had Connor really been the mastermind behind it? Rafael's gut said no.

So now here was Greg Turner, founder of Green Technologies Inc. And Rafael's gut was telling him something was off with this guy. What was he supposed to do now?

***

Rafael pushed his beer glass back and forth on the bar at The Lighthouse, staring at the beautiful vista of the inner yacht harbor through the picture window, trying to get his mind around his impressions from this first meeting.

Something off about the guy, no doubt about it. Something about Greg rubbed him the wrong way.

"Your message said it was urgent."

Al slid into a bar stool beside Rafael and ordered a plain mineral water.

"It is. You know this water habit of yours is no fun. Makes you look suspicious at a bar."

"No offense, Rafael, but the water thing, as you call it, is all about control. I let loose with the best of them, as you well know. You went to see Green Technologies; how did that go?"

"I wish I knew," Rafael said and shrugged, staring down at the bar, pushing his glass back and forth between his hands. "And if that sounds strange, that's because it is."

"In what way?"

You had to give him credit; Al didn't blink or frown at Rafa's statement, didn't say *what the heck are you talking about*. He simply asked, *in what way?*

"You and I would have preferred Mariposa," Rafael said. "Then your father chose GT. OK, not what we wanted, but he is footing the bill. There's no need for this to become an issue. That is the attitude I went in with, I swear."

"You and I spoke about it. We control this deal, and we do the best we can with the hand we're dealt. So?"

189

"In walks Greg Turner."

"Didn't go well?"

"No, it went fine, Al. We didn't dislike each other on sight, we didn't find any skeletons in the closets we opened, everything was fine."

"Except it wasn't, or you wouldn't have called me to talk about it."

"Except it wasn't." Rafael brought his folded hands to his face and thought for a moment. "I—I don't even know how to phrase it. There is something about him, something…"

"Something that makes you uncomfortable?"

"Extremely so. There is something about this man I don't trust. I can't say why. I can't tell you what ticked me off about him. I can't even tell you if I don't trust him, or if he just rubs me the wrong way. Damn."

He ran his hands through his hair and took a generous sip of beer.

"I wish I knew. It would make it easier."

"Your instincts are usually right," Al said slowly and frowned. "And if you say there is something about him that you don't trust, I would always err on the side of caution."

"But?"

"But you already mentioned it. Tadeo is footing the bill here, and we are a little limited in what we can do. Unless we provide him a good reason, of course."

"A reason I don't have," Rafael said darkly. "Nothing I haven't told myself for the past few hours. Even I'm not stupid enough to walk into your father's office, such as it is, and tell him not to do business with a guy just because."

"Tadeo has scuttled deals for less reason than that. But in our case, he has his back up big time. I can see him insist on this one point, just because we made him give on every last one of the others."

"Got it," Rafael said and rested his chin in his hand. "And I knew that was what was happening. I just needed to hear somebody else say it."

"That does not mean you just roll over and give up, Rafa," Al said and picked up his glass again. "Not at all. Forewarned is forearmed, so consider your instincts a warning."

"Where are you going with this?"

"I suggest we keep an eye on Mr. Turner. If he does or says anything that endangers our merger, anything at all, no matter how small, we act on it and kill the deal."

"You give me the creeps when you talk like that, you know that?"

"I do. But all we can do is watch him, carefully. Perhaps, in time, we will find out what it is that makes you uncomfortable. In the meantime, you and I will proceed with caution."

"I don't like it, Al. I didn't get into business so I would have to watch my back and my business partners 24-7."

"That's all we've got..."

"Damn." Rafael finished his beer in one big gulp. "He is stubborn, your old man. Let's hope his stubbornness does not get us into something we can't handle."

"It already has on a number of occasions," Al said lightly. "And the very fact that I'm still here means only one thing."

"Which is?"

"I handled it, period."

TWENTY-SEVEN

"I've been in contact with Greg Turner," he said to Tadeo Ivers a few days later. "We had a nice little chat. At this point, everything is set for our management teams to meet, exchange information, and get going on structuring this merger."

"You went to see Turner on your own? I don't like it, Rafael. You should have taken Dante," Tadeo said, drumming his fingers on the tabletop.

Not mentioning Al served as just another reminder what he thought of his sons in turn.

"Dante is happily working with Nick," he said instead. "At this point I don't think he can contribute much to the structuring of the…"

"And he will be at a meeting if I say he will. Keeping an eye on our interest, and on you if necessary."

Tadeo's hand struck the table, and Rafael barely stopped himself flinching.

"As you wish."

"Don't think because I let you drag Al everywhere you go I have in any way accepted this management partnership the two of you seem to have struck. I have no use for it. I want him gone."

Rafael nodded and said nothing. With Tadeo, he learned a while ago, sometimes silence got results, whilst arguing only landed you up to your neck in alligators. Not a place anyone wanted to be.

"Don't just sit there."

"What would you have me do, Tadeo? Argue with you? We both know that does no good, ever. Personally, I happen to think that Al is doing a first-rate job in the development of this company. I am even going to go so far to say I could not have done this without him."

"I hired you, not him."

"I'm well aware of that, Tadeo. Not only did you hire me, you also gave me a good idea of what was going to happen to my business and my family if I failed, or if I failed to comply with your—orders."

Rafael sat up a little straighter and squared his shoulders. *Fuck this shit*. The sentence sat right at the tip of his tongue, making him swallow once or twice to stay silent.

"At the same time, I told you more than once that I would make this company successful, and I would do it my way or not at all. You are always free to fire me, Tadeo. Ask Dante to run the corporation. Or better yet, Roberto, if you have no confidence in Al and you don't happen to have another son handy. Hey, I just bet Roberto would do an awesome job at it, really awesome."

"Shut your mouth, Covin, before I have them shut it for you."

"What, those two bookends that sit beside you all the time? You want to have them beat me up? Is that the game? Then have at it."

He stood up and spread his arms, baring his chest.

"Take a swing, fellas. What's it going to get you, Tadeo? What? Compliance? Fear? Results? None of those. I can guarantee you that."

"I can still…"

"You can still—you can still—what? Threaten my sons and my business? Been there, done that, Tadeo. You don't remember? I have nothing left to lose you haven't threatened yet. So why don't we finally and for the very last time stop playing these games around here?"

The bookends looked down, checking left and right, waiting for a command from their lord and master, while Tadeo simply sat staring, staring at Rafael openmouthed.

Moments ticked by. Rafael settled back into his chair and tucked his sports jacket back to where it should be.

He's all talk, Al's words.

"You have got some nerve, Covin."

"I think anybody who has ever had the pleasure of working with you, Ivers, has got to have some nerve. Otherwise, they would run— long and hard."

"Like your pal Connor did."

"Oh, let's leave Connor out of this. He had his own issues, and there is no actual benefit from going there. I have no idea what your issue is with Al, and if you don't want him on the board, then I'm going to have to respect that."

That one pained him. But at the end of the day, Ivers still owed the majority of outstanding shares, and no matter what he or Al or Dante did, he could shut them down as quickly as he had bought up the shares.

"But I feel the need to tell you that his advice and ideas have been invaluable to get the company to this stage. Out of the crapper, if I were to speak frankly. We would have shut doors months ago if it were not for him, and I fully intend to make use of Al's counsel on a going forward basis."

"You're walking a line, Covin. Watch that you don't go too far."

Rafael merely shrugged. Hell, he'd been told that before. Most recently by his wife before she passed away. That little memory made him smile, and Ivers, damn him, caught it, of course.

"What, you think this is funny, Covin?"

"Not one bit, believe me. It's exhausting is what it is. This job of saving this company is difficult enough on a daily basis without making it more so."

"Are you saying I…"

"Stop, just stop." Rafael raised his hands again, surrendering this time. "I'm not saying anything, implying anything, or accusing any-body of any damn thing. I just want to get it done. If possible before it kills or bankrupts one or all of us. When we get to that point, Tadeo, then you are welcome to fire my ass, and I will even help you with it. I will walk off on my own. But for God's sake, just let me do my job without hog-tying me."

The weariness that had been gnawing at the edges of his awareness for weeks now suddenly punched him in the gut straight on. He was right, he realized. Plain old tiredness had turned into exhaustion a while ago without anybody noticing it, least of all Rafael. He wanted the constant struggle over with. Never mind which merger partner Tadeo chose, never mind who he wanted on the board, or off. Never mind how much grief he wanted to cause him, just out of spite. Rafael just plain did not care any longer. He would get the company there, for no other reason than he had promised to do so.

After that, he would go. He would take his beat-up old chair and leave and probably do nothing for a good long while. Shit, he realized for the first time, that's what he was planning. The little madman across from him would only get him for a finite time, and that was a good thing.

"Fine then, hire Al if you must. But I'm telling you—the moment I get the slightest inkling that he is not up to the job…"

"He's gone," Rafael sighed. "I understand. And I agree."

"Long as you do."

Rafael sighed, but thought it better to keep his mouth shut—again. Number one, he had every confidence in Al. 'Not up to the job' just wasn't going to happen. And number two, he had just decided on the spot to take a powder, once the company was on safe grounds again.

He wasn't staying forever.

That alone made him feel not only good, but awesome, and he allowed himself another little smile, no matter what Tadeo might think.

And then there was Kayla. Jesus, he had no idea where this thing was leading that they had started in Denver. If indeed it even was a thing. Maybe they were just hanging out, having fun, giving comfort after a massive betrayal, whatever. It would be fun to explore the thing a bit further—once he was out of here.

"Perfectly, Tadeo. I understand you perfectly. Now if you don't mind, I have to get back to work. Our executives will have to meet and greet. I need to put together schedules and timelines. And, oh… If you don't mind my asking… Were you planning on any personal involvement in this merger?"

"What are you talking about?"

"It's at least customary if not required to identify the major players when a merger such as this one is being contemplated, never mind being seriously worked out. Just so everyone knows who they might or might not be involved with at some later point."

"So? Why do you ask a stupid question like this one?"

"So, I will tell them Tadeo Ivers is our major shareholder…"

"Majority stakeholder. There's a small difference."

"So there is." Rafael nodded. "I don't want to cause concern with anyone, and I will make sure these people are aware. They might want to know if you are planning any personal involvement."

"Then it's a stupid question. I already told you I would not get involved with PerCan. Dante will be my eyes and ears." He shuffled through his papers with angry motions. "And Al—I guess—if you truly insist on having him there, which I would counsel against, but what is the use? You won't listen anyway."

"Then you will forgive my having asked a stupid question," Rafael said and rose. "Gentlemen…" He rapped his knuckles on the table and turned to leave.

Nobody ever left before Tadeo said the meeting was over and they could do so. Nobody, but it had become Rafael's signature defiance move. Every. Single. Time. He'd get up, rap the table—and go.

The way Rafael looked at it, you could threaten a man's life and business, but he'd damn well walk out of the room whenever he wanted to.

So far, Tadeo chose to ignore his little power statements, and Al had told him he was just poking the bear. He still couldn't figure Tadeo out. The man had more money than he could spend in three lifetimes, he had his hands in every cookie jar God had put on the face of this earth, and he had three sons. One of them he had sent to jail once, and now exiled somewhere. The second one he treated like an errand boy, and the third one, oh the third one. The golden boy. Dante appeared to be the one chosen to make everything all right. For the moment, anyway. Until something else displeased Tadeo, and he chose to change it.

Jesus, what a hot mess.

***

Back in his office, he tore off his jacket and dropped into his old chair, dragging his hands through his hair.

"You keep doing that, you're going to go bald, you know."

He looked up and raised an eyebrow at Kayla.

"Hey, is there a motion detector at my office door, to let you know when I walk in?"

"Yes, and she's called Connie. My, you are in a bad mood today."

"Sorry." He shrugged, knowing he didn't sound sorry in the least. "Ivers," he added by way of explanation. "I just can't make sense of the man."

"That bad?"

"Worse. For some odd reason, he seems determined to keep Al out of PerCan. Same reason, perhaps, that makes me want to keep him in."

"Which is?"

"Which is I think Al is a straight shooter and has an extremely good head for business."

"I remember you used to call him that strange dude."

"True. Tadeo uses him as an errand boy to go keeping an eye on bars and clubs. It's a job any halfway talented security guard could do.

No wonder Al tried to remain anonymous. I think Tadeo might be just jealous of his talent. Al's extremely adept in business."

"You and he work well together. Almost like…"

"Almost like Connor and I used to. Go ahead and say it. Nothing I hadn't noticed myself." He sighed and leaned back. A move Kayla interpreted as an invitation to step behind him and massage his shoulders.

Rafael closed his eyes and let her work for a moment before he stopped her hands and nodded.

"You don't have to try to pamper me."

"I don't mind."

"I just never imagined a booby-trapped setup like this one when we originally started this company. Now I have Tadeo and his moods to deal with, and the constant need for money and this merger. I'm only just getting my head around joining PerCan with another company and another group of people."

"Where is that going, if you don't mind my asking?"

"I—really don't know. Al and I had originally envisioned joining with a specific company we checked out, Mariposa. In wanders Tadeo and changes the entire plan. Without a good reason to fight him, we just went along so far. But here's the thing. I don't have a good feeling about this man, Greg. There's something about him I don't like, and I can't tell you what it is. It's driving me insane."

"Where does this man see his role, then, when the merger is complete?"

"No idea, and I think the better question is am I going to have a role in the company when the merger is complete?"

"Whoa." She did sit down then, and Rafael realized it was the first time he had said it out loud.

"Sorry. Remember, when Tadeo told us he owned the majority of shares, I said I would try to get the company back on track and running again."

"Of course. And?"

"And when I was sitting in the meeting with him today, I realized that I really don't want to go any further with him than that. End of the line for Rafael Covin. I don't have any desire to be the CEO in charge of this cannabis company. It's all just too much. So, if this guy Greg wants to take over when we get there, that's fine and dandy with me."

"I never heard of you giving up. You don't give up."

"I'm not giving up. I haven't told anyone about this. It just occurred to me today. I'm tired, Kayla, really tired of Tadeo's games. I enjoy putting a deal together any day, even running a business, but not like this."

"I wish…"

"I know I should have warned you earlier. It just came up. That doesn't mean you have to walk away just because I do."

"It's not that easy. There's still something called loyalty and sticking with the people you care about."

"Don't." Rafael shook his head, pointing at Kayla. "Don't put that on me. You do whatever you feel is best for you and don't put it on my head."

"I'm not sure why I got into this business in the first place anyway. Except…"

"Except Connor created this dream, and he had a way of energizing everybody who got within shouting distance of him. If you think staying in charge of promotions and publicity will be fun, please do so, and don't worry about me."

"Much of it also depends on what happens with this merger. I don't much relish the thought of being on the board with the likes of Tadeo Ivers."

"What happens immediately is we exchange a lot of information between the companies. Financial statements, projections, business plans. All the stuff Connor used to call nonsense paper…"

Kayla smiled at that.

"Then, when all the lawyers are happy, we'll figure out who exactly gets what, who has to pay for what, who gets how many shares, and then we put a new company together."

"Again?"

"Yup, again. I'd be in favor calling it Perfect Cannabis, since PerCan is the larger entity and we kind of started the ball rolling, but who knows? Maybe we come up with another name. We reshuffle the deck, assign new roles and titles, and the game starts over."

"Are you sure you don't want to be part of this new company?"

"I don't want to be near anybody called Ivers once I've done my job here. I may do more business with Al. We may choose to stay friends, but that's about it. But please..."

"Don't follow you."

"Do not follow me, unless you are certain this is what you want."

"Sounds like you have it all figured out, Rafael."

"Pretty much." For some reason, she sounded sad, and Rafael straightened up a bit. *Jesus, Covin*, he scolded himself. *Sometimes you can be a real ass, you know that?*

He got up, walked to where Kayla was sitting, and took both of her hands into his.

"The business part of it, yes. That was the easy part. The rest of it, I have absolutely no clue. But—I am looking forward to finding out with you. Does that at least make you smile a little bit?"

"The rest of it?"

"Well, you and I," he said, suddenly feeling more self-conscious that he had since high school. Geez, wasn't this supposed to get easier when you got older?

At least Kayla was not only smiling now, but positively grinning from ear to ear.

"My dear Rafael, if you thought you would get away that easy, you are so, so wrong. What you call 'the rest of it' is not open to negotiation at all. I will let you know that right away, so don't give it another thought."

"I thought something like that," Rafael said and sat again, hiding the shit-eating grin on his face by digging through the files on his desk.

"Last bit of bad news for the day."

"More?"

"Depending on how you look at it. I'm going to have to move my offices over to the building. Dante and the boys have finished the office section in record time, and with Nick coming to join the company..."

"You should be on site. Your presence is important and understood. As long as you take that with you."

Her long, polished red fingernail pointed at Rafael's old chair. "It is truly a disgrace."

"What, this old thing? I like it."

"And I hear the cleaning staff will not go near it. They are worried it might harbor bugs!"

"Oh, it harbors a lot of things, but most of them are memories."

"Do not ever tell me women are the sentimental gender, Rafael—ever."

TWENTY-EIGHT

don't do paper; Rafael could still hear Connor Beauregard's voice in his head.

Most of the time Tessa Connor's PA would take pity and take care of things. She knew if she didn't, Connor might take a stab at it, which usually resulted in an ever-growing mess she would have to clean up anyway.

Rafael preferred a day at the construction site any day, but he had always assumed himself to be at least pretty competent in the office.

Then he started planning a merger. A merger, he found out faster than he cared to, a merger was an animal of an entirely different species.

The first time he took a quick glance at the dreaded 'due diligence list' sent by Greg Turner's lawyer, he was absolutely certain he'd been sent the wrong document. The thing was 30 pages long.

He asked himself what Connor would have done and called David to help him out.

He still needed the accountant, so he had grudgingly made peace with him, after finding out David had taken money from Tadeo Ivers to keep up their SEC filings and provide inside information while the company was in tatters, just waiting for Tadeo to take over.

David had known that Ivers was planning to take over PerCan or, if he didn't know, at least had a suspicion something like this may happen. He was savvy enough. And it would have been common decency to come to Rafael with the information.

Rafa had told him as much and put a decision to the accountant: either be loyal to Rafael and Rafael alone from now on, or throw in his lot with the Ivers clan for good. No hard feelings either way, but he was never going to play both sides again—ever.

Not surprisingly, David had chosen Rafael. He'd muttered some unintelligible excuse about gambling debts, not that Rafael cared, but he was at least reasonably sure the man would keep his word.

This business, he concluded every time he thought of the incident, could truly be likened to a huge game of whack-a-mole: kill off one problem, stumble over the next. How did one not go insane?

"This must be the wrong thing," he said to David, holding one end of the document he had just received, as if it were covered in excrement. "There are like 400 questions and areas of interest on this."

"That may be normal in a merger like this one."

David looked over it and pushed it back at Rafael.

"No, I'm afraid this is the correct list."

Rafael sat perfectly still and glanced at David over the rim of his reading glasses while picturing the mountain of paperwork headed his way. He won. David reached for the printed pages and pulled them back to his side of the desk.

"Much of it will probably be easy for me to answer, Rafael. Why don't I get started on it and leave you with the stuff that truly needs your input?"

"Much obliged."

"A lawyer's wet dream," he muttered. "Designed to keep them busy and reaching into your pocket, isn't it? Sorry for sounding like Connor. I try to run a tight ship, but this is just a tad excessive."

"It's a corporate merger, Rafael. It will always be complicated. Down to the dirty underwear."

"Thank you for that visual, David." Rafael rolled his eyes. "Get done what you can, I'll fill in a few blanks, and, shit, maybe I can rein in the lawyers on the rest."

He put his hands on the armrest of his chair and sat a little straighter. "We'll do what we can and hope for the best. OK?"

He grinned and shook David's hand, narrowly avoiding a grin at the vision of David struggling through this mountain of paper on his desk. Jesus. Again, he had to think of Connor.

"Let's get to it then. And thanks for helping out. I have to go now and see an investor, matter of fact. I think the guy has big-time money. So, if you don't mind."

"Sure—um—I mean…"

"Thanks—thanks, David."

Rafael all but propelled him out the door, feeling like he imagined his older son did every time he had rolled chores off on the younger one.

**

Although 'seeing an investor' had always served as a convenient excuse to leave the office while Connor was in charge, Rafael actually did have someone in mind this time.

He'd been thinking about it for weeks now and finally decided the time was ripe to convince Irving Moody of the benefits of investing. He'd met Irving at the bar at The Lighthouse of all places, and usually, he wouldn't dream about turning his bar acquaintances into investors, but this one had promise.

Truth be told, Rafael had been 'saving' Irving. He had no desire to speak to anyone about fronting some cash while the company fate was more uncertain than the daily weather report and he would have to give away the store for nothing.

Suddenly, things had changed, a glimpse of better times could be had, and Rafael felt the old hunting instincts kick in.

Now when he walked into a meeting, he had something to offer that made sense. He had a plan for the company, a merger on the go, and Nick Ambrose under contract. He could use his old line, "This investment is going to make you really serious money," and he could use it without having to cross himself and add, 'I hope,' silently. Rafael Covin didn't have to go begging any longer.

Irving Moody never did seem to be in a rush to get anywhere or attend to any kind of appointments, which had intrigued Rafael since the day he'd met him at the bar, so he had done a little research. What he found had just about made his mouth drop open.

Irving Moody, the man who strolled into The Lighthouse casually, sitting at the bar reading the paper while enjoying a couple of brews, would have been considered a 'whale' by Connor Beauregard's standards.

The man had what's commonly known as 'real money.'

A few years ago, Irving had invested in a small software company like many other investors. They managed well and made good money, and for a while, life was good—really good, so the story went. The partners couldn't spend the money as fast as they made it. That type of thing never lasted, as Rafael only knew too well, and true to form, some minor problem caused a quarrel among founders, and Irving asked to be bought out. Profits were still healthy, the stock soaring, the company in demand, and Rafael's buddy found himself walking away into the sunset with millions in his account.

Fast forward by a couple of years, and management still couldn't settle their quarrels, the software company folded, investors got burned, and nobody made money any longer. Nobody except Irv, that was.

Irving Moody had pulled the plug just in time to make sure he would never in his life have to do any kind of serious work unless he wished to do so. Nowadays, he could be found flying his little Cessna Skyhawk across the country for fun and giggles and, since he had moved to town a few months ago, reading the paper at The Lighthouse in the afternoon.

Connor would have chased the man, hard, the moment he discovered his identity.

Rafael, on the other hand, preferred a more soft-shoe approach. They bonded over an affinity for the same brand of beer, fired trivia questions at each other, and complained about the TV program at the bar, women, and single life in general.

Just two guys hanging out in their spare time.

Now the time had come, Rafael thought.

He would cautiously approach Irv to see if he could awaken the old stock promoter in him. Every investment publication out there wanted to run a story about a cannabis project, in every issue that hit the market. Good news, bad news, hot properties, and dogs. The stories chased each other on a daily basis.

PerCan slowly had everything going for it again, with Rafael Covin at the helm, and Irving—Irving had what they needed most. Cash. Lots of it and readily available. And, with it, perhaps a way to buy themselves free from the specter of Tadeo Ivers.

Rafael caught him, just as he had come back from a week-long flying adventure into Alaska.

"What's going on with you? You going for the wild man look?" he asked, nodding at Irving's full beard, signaling for a round of drinks at the same time.

"You got any idea how difficult it is to shave at minus 20 degrees in a tent?"

"I don't. And I have no idea why you do something like that," Rafael said, shaking his head. "I freeze half to death just thinking about it, and you're tooling around in a tin can with wings. Sounds bloody dangerous and it can't be cheap."

"Not hardly. Outfitting a Cessna to fly in that kind of weather, not for the weak of wallet, my friend."

"'Nuff said. Yet still you go…"

"And still I go," Irving said and peeled a couple of peanuts. "You ought to give flying a shot one day. Take you up any time. I told you before."

"Yeah, thanks. I've tinkered around with the idea of flying myself, but the older I get, I find the best kind of airplane is reasonably large and has several beautiful stewardesses serving highly alcoholic drinks. That's all I'm saying."

"You're missing out."

"Keep talking, my friend. One of these days… My former business partner flew around in this helicopter…" Rafael made a spinning motion in the air with his index finger. "Thing was a technological marvel."

"Helicopter." Irving whistled and peeled more peanuts. "Now the man is talking serious money. My little Cessna is next to nothing compared to one of those. What kind?"

"Do I look like I know these things?" Rafael spread his arms and rolled his eyes. "I do not. I heard him say it was the same kind Donald Trump has."

"Sikorsky," Irving nodded. "Nice. Really nice if it's well done."

"Oh, it was well done—believe me."

"Uh–huh. One question if you don't mind my asking."

"Fire away." Rafael took a small sip of his beer and secretly looked at his watch. Al was due to show up any minute, and perhaps together, they could convince Irv to have a look at PerCan. Perhaps…

"What the hell kind of business were you guys in? Flying a Sikorsky? That takes serious money, and I think I would have heard about it if anybody in town here had one of these beauties."

"Interesting you should ask," Rafael said, hiding a grin. "Connor, my former business partner, he—left for other opportunities. Isn't that the nice way of saying it?"

"The very nice way."

"He left the business in a bit of a mess, but I'm setting her right again, if I might say so myself. Ever heard of medical marijuana?"

By the time Al joined them half an hour later, Rafael had Irving's full attention.

***

"I have a couple of interesting stories from my teenage years involving weed."

"Everybody does, Irv, absolutely everybody. The thing here is— medical marijuana is nothing like the weed you remember from your college days. For one it's legal, and there are thousands of patients not just waiting, but clamoring for a safe, stable, and consistent supply."

"And you just seed the stuff?"

"God forbid! No seeds, no greenhouses. We clone them. Put them under grow lights in sterile conditions."

"High-tech." Irv's eyes became a little wider.

"Very much so. Oh hey, Al." Rafael signaled to Al as he walked in. "Irving Moody, our operations manager, Al Ivers."

Al sat down and shook Irving's hands. "Irving Moody—Dot-Scan Software? That Irving Moody?"

"The very one."

"You left the company in the nick of time, I heard. Good luck or good instincts, either one."

Irving shrugged and grinned broadly.

"You are fabulously well informed, Al."

Al shrugged. "I have a good memory. You're talking about the company."

"We are. Rafael is just telling me about your little operation. Say, are you the man with the Sikorsky by any chance?"

"Dear god." Al pointed down to the floor by his feet. "See? Feet on ground… I only fly if I have to, commercial and business class."

"For shame! Two guys who are in the drug business and neither one enjoys flying small planes? What is wrong with you people? Do I have to explain this to you?"

Amongst raucous laughter, more beer appeared. He and Al took turns explaining the medical marijuana business, and by the time the shadows got longer outside, the three men had become fast friends.

TWENTY-NINE

It had been a while since Rafael had seen the building. He had plans to move his office into the space sooner rather than later, but when he gave Irving the grand tour, the progress Dante and the construction crews had made in almost every section surprised even him and filled him with regret at the same time.

He missed wearing a hard hat, having his boots in dust or muck. Good old times!

He waved at a couple of construction laborers he did not recognize, although they wore spiffy 'Covin Construction' work suits, and led Al and Irving to the far wall, where the construction drawings had been tacked up. Some things never changed.

"Here we are, almost ready to put the grow pods in. 48 hermetically sealed, individually climate-controlled grow pods, my friends. The phrase our founder was fond of using is, *here is where we get to play God.*"

"God—you have to like the sound of that."

"Indeed. We are in charge of deciding how much light, how much heat, and how much nutrition a plant receives at any point during its lifetime. We grow in sterile grow medium, not dirt, so nothing is introduced to the plant that has not passed our muster and quality checks. Even the water it receives is controlled, filtered, analyzed, and enriched on a regular basis. We are—God. If I want it to grow, it grows. If I want it to die… Well."

Rafael shrugged and spread his arms.

"And what does all of this playing God get you?"

"The goods, my friend. A safe, consistent, pure and untainted supply of medical marijuana, custom-tailored in many cases to specific applications and conditions in the patient. Designed for an individual patient, if necessary, infused with a preferred taste if desired."

"You can do that?"

"We can do that. We have the technology. That's why Nick Ambrose is here. A little more of this in a specific group of plants, a little less of that. A specific concentration of substances, even a specific flavor, we can do it. All you need to do is decide what you want and need. We will grow the plant to give it to you. Natural, efficient, pure."

"Wow."

"You did not know cannabis had gone this high-tech now, did you?"

"Entirely new territory, Rafael. Although I have to admit it's exciting. I knew medicinal cannabis was the newest investment craze. A drug trade for investors, it's called, but I had this image of you guys running around a greenhouse, watering little plants."

"Many do." Rafael smiled and walked Irving over to the far wall, sweeping his hands over the construction plans.

"See this? $29 million worth of rebuilding, refitting, and renovating. Nick and Dante can explain the details better than I can, but let me tell you. There's no running around with a watering can around here—ever. No one who does not have a specific job with a specific set of plants will be in contact with them at any time. This is how we minimize the danger of contamination and impurities. We have to. We are, after all, not just growing weed, but making the medicine that will impact someone's health, and maybe their life."

Irving looked at the drawings, then at the enormous space around them and back at the drawings. Rafael had never seen the man so animated. One did not build a software empire and walk away again by showing one's emotions easily, and Irv too had mastered the art of the poker face. But today—today, he couldn't hide his enthusiasm.

"I am—wow, I am beyond impressed, Rafael. Whatever I expected, this was certainly not it. Thanks for giving me the grand tour."

"It was not just for kicks and giggles and entertainment I brought you here, you know."

"No, I did not think so."

"I believe in this company, Irving. I've spent the last few months eating, sleeping, and breathing nothing else but PerCan. I left Covin Construction to put this company back on the map, at the top."

"Your construction company, from what I read, is benefitting from the leadership it's under while you are doing this."

Rafael shrugged. He'd read the same article, and he couldn't help a little twinge of jealousy. Roger Carmichael indeed turned out to be the rainmaker everybody said he was. He did amazing things for Covin Construction Corp, and Rafael knew he should be happy to leave a great legacy for his sons.

He should be. What he missed was not the company or the work, but the laid-back days of hanging out at construction sites, chatting with the workmen, not worrying about Tadeo Ivers.

"Roger is doing a great job," he said. "I have to keep telling him all he is doing is keeping my seat warm for a little while, though."

"With all of this at your fingertips, you're going back to building things when the job here is done? Are you serious?"

"Look at me, Irv. I'm a slob, I do whatever work needs doing, my language is in need of cleaning up, and so is my wardrobe if the lady I am seeing is to be believed."

"Trust her, my friend, she is right on the money about that one."

"You see what I'm saying? In reality I'm just more at home on a construction site than in the corporate offices."

"Where you are doing a bang-up job from what I hear. Don't be so quick to walk away. A lot of people are calling you the miracle man."

"I see somebody has been busy checking us out. So, nothing I can show you should be news to you anyway."

SABINE FRISCH

"What do you think, Rafael? You think when you start chatting me up at The Lighthouse, and your friend Al joins us—accidentally." Irving made air quotes with his fingers. "I don't know you're trying to steer me toward a small investment? Huh? I am semi-retired, not an idiot."

"Sorry, Irv, I shouldn't have assumed…"

"That's all right. I did do my research, and I'm impressed with your work resurrecting all of this. Add the process and plant you showed me today and I'm even more impressed. You, my friend, worked miracles."

Now it was Rafael's turn to smile. He heard it from Kayla, he heard it from Al—but for some reason, hearing Irving Moody say he was doing a great job rehabilitating Perfect Cannabis meant a lot. A lot and then some.

"I appreciate it. It hasn't always been easy. And when you're up to your ass in alligators, it really helps to hear somebody saying good job, even if it does nothing to fight the alligators."

"And don't think I was living under a rock either while I was running Dot-Scan. Not hardly. Even on the other end of the country, we heard about Connor Beauregard and his amazing and entertaining escapades. Truly cinematic at times."

Rafael closed his eyes for a moment and sighed. Connor Beauregard, the shadow that wouldn't go away. Would they ever get out from under that?

"You need to understand that…"

"Oh, don't try, Rafael. From what I heard and read, adding my own experience, I can put together a pretty complete picture and make an educated guess at the missing parts."

"There are a number of skeletons."

"And I would imagine a few more that have not even seen the light of day yet. I'm guessing you two started the company, and he took it upon himself to run this thing from the start. Like his own little kingdom. Am I right, or am I right?"

"On the nose," Rafael said with a deep sigh and shook his head.

"Rafael, I know these stock promoters, these starters of things and blazers of trails. I've met my share of them over the last few years, and frankly, that was enough."

"Connor put a great concept together. His ideas were out of this world. You need to know that."

"I do know, Rafael. And I can appreciate his ideas and energy. But meanwhile, I've grown old enough to realize that the world needs both—the trailblazers like your friend and partner Connor, who will start anything because it sounds cool, and the people like you and me, who build, clean up behind them, and try to keep things from getting completely out of hand."

"I—thought I did."

"I'm sure you did, and I suspect there were others as well running around behind Mr. 'This Is My Company,' trying their darndest to keep him from doing something really stupid."

Rafael couldn't help but laugh. You simply had to when somebody stepped right up and proceeded to read your mind, turn out the things inside there you thought were well hidden.

"You've been there before. I might as well forget about the gentle soft-shoe then?"

"Why do you think I left Dot-Scan? One day, I couldn't do it any longer. Turns out that was the exact right decision to make at the perfect time, and here I am today, without a care in the world. I could not, not for one more day, work with someone who operated like that. End of story."

"Well…" Rafael looked down at his feet. "And yet you asked why I was planning to walk away when it's done."

"Yeah, when you're telling me you're done, Rafael, I totally understand. I've stood at those particular crossroads. It's too bad because I really think you're good for this company—but I understand."

"Anyway…" Rafael moved a little faster to cover up his disappointment and swept his arm in a circle to indicate the remainder of the building. "Before this gets maudlin. You want to see the rest of it? I mean, if nothing else, it's going to be interesting and entertaining. Who else at The Lighthouse except you and me has seen a cannabis producer from the inside?"

"You have a point there. Lead the way…"

An injection of capital from Irving could have done wonders for the company. He asked all the right questions, listened carefully and without interrupting, and made his judgments quickly and without changing his mind or backtracking. He might have enjoyed working with this man.

Now that he seemed free from the mildly embarrassing task of talking a friend into investing, though, he really had nothing to lose. He could tell the PerCan story without the kid gloves required in handling a potential investor.

***

After they had visited the future factory, he drove Irving back to The Lighthouse, and they enjoyed another couple of brews. Al hadn't shown up during their tour of the factory, and Rafael suspected he wanted to avoid any discussion about the Ivers family, so he had chosen to let Rafael fly solo on this investment trip.

"So," Irving said. "You getting to the good part yet?"

"Which good part?"

"The part where you have to crawl into bed with that crook Tadeo Ivers. You tried very hard to keep the bulk of his story out of the papers. That alone would be what makes it the good part. Coincidentally, I do see you are friends with his son Al. You hang out here regularly. There's another story here, or my name is not Silver Wings Moody."

"Not much of a story." Rafael shrugged. "Al is a good business-man, decent in his own way. I like working with him. It helps to have someone around who will call a spade a spade and take the time to tell you when you are full of it."

"You respect him. The couple of times I've met him in here, he seemed like a likeable fellow. His father, though. That's a different story. I don't know, Rafael. I'd be a little concerned having that character in my company somewhere, God forbid in a position to call the shots."

"Ivers Senior," Rafael sighed, playing with his coaster. He shook his head again. "Ivers Senior. None of us even pretends to know what the man is truly thinking."

"Not somebody I want to have across the table from me."

"He's made a lot of money along the way, and nowadays, the authorities take a keen interest in anything he does. As far as PerCan is concerned, I can't say I always agree with his choices. Al and I have done business in the past, always clean, always successful. Jesus, I was the one who originally brought him into the PerCan deal, knowing we needed money, knowing Al's father had it."

"Hoping..."

"Hoping it would not come to this—right. The man saw we had a good deal on the go and stepped in to buy the majority of shares when Connor... had to go away for a while."

"Jail or another country, you mean."

"Speaking of calling a spade a spade. None of us is ever going to figure out exactly what happened, so we've given up trying."

"Let's not. So Ivers Senior steps in..."

"Steps in, buys up most of the shares, and voila—the man is in charge all of a sudden. Except he can't be."

"Oh?"

"His reputation. The intense scrutiny he is under. Licenses to grow are not only hard to come by, they are worth their weight in gold. Nobody in their right mind in the Ministry of Health is going to hand one of those to a man like Tadeo Ivers."

"And our friend suddenly has a problem."

"A big one." Rafael nodded. "He owns a significant part of a company he can't run, probably shouldn't even own. This is when he cooked up the brilliant idea to hire me to do so, while he's in the background pulling the strings."

"I don't know." Irving Moody took a long draft from his beer and thought for a while. Finally, he shook his head. "And you went for it, Rafael? You must have known what was going to happen. You must have known he would go insane eventually and make your life a living hell. Help me out here. What's the deal?"

"I have two sons, Irv. After my wife died, they were all I had left."

"And?"

"And Tadeo Ivers knew it. And while he is too smart to come right out and threaten them, he also knew I intended to leave them a very large legacy in the form of Covin Construction Corp. And with all of this knowledge…"

"He knew exactly how to word his offer to make it one you would not be likely to refuse—got it in one." Irving nodded. "Shit."

"Shit," Rafael confirmed. "But hey, I'm getting used to it. Most of the time, Ivers does not bother me any longer. I've made a commitment to him that I would manage the company out of this hole it's in and see it right. After that, I am a free man. That time is coming closer faster than ever with this merger we are working on."

"So, freedom is in sight." Moody took another big sip of beer. "It takes pretty big ones to work with somebody like Ivers."

"I'll drink to that."

Rafael lifted his glass and, all of a sudden, as if he had waited for that particular moment, Al appeared at his side.

"Hello, Mr. Moody, I heard you saw our little operation today."

"Irv, please. Mr. Moody makes me feel like I should be wearing a suit." His face suggested exactly what he thought of that possibility. "I did—nice setup you guys have put together."

For a moment, no one said anything. Then Irv signaled for another round of beers and smiled directly at Al.

"No offense, but I was just telling Rafael here how I admire his guts for working with someone like your father."

"I believe the words you used were 'it takes pretty big ones,' Irv," Al said and pulled a stool closer. "Which does not only hit the nail on the head, it drives it through the board and into the one below it."

"Ouch."

"Ouch," Al confirmed. "I grew up with him. I ought to know. Most people who worked with him would call my father a difficult man. Some would say he's downright impossible."

"Heard that too."

"But you see, Irving, all of his life, my father has run one company, his own. He will eventually come to understand that is not the way things work in a public company."

"Oh, you must be dreaming."

"Dreaming, hoping—whatever. If the thought of Tadeo Ivers is the one thing stopping you from investing in the company, don't. Besides, Father respects Rafael. It's why he delights in giving him a hard time."

"Oh, thanks," Rafael said, taking a generous sip of his beer. "You think if I started screwing up on a daily basis, he'd go easy on me?"

"Likely not."

"Bugger that."

They laughed and clinked their glasses, and in the dim light of The Lighthouse bar, it was obvious only to the bartender how much admiration mixed with a little bit of envy showed in Irv Moody's face. He didn't think anyone was watching, so for once, he didn't bother with the famous poker face.

THIRTY

Guests came and went at the famous Shangri-La in Singapore. Moneyed guests, famous guests, important guests, and everyday tourists. Didn't really matter to the maids who set out in little groups every day pushing their service carts, cleaning up after all of them.

The tourists tended to be a messy but relatively well-behaved bunch. The important people tried to stay low, and the moneyed bunch rang the service desk with impatience every five minutes. That was the way life worked. And then there were the celebrities...

Spoiled, ill-mannered, and messy at worst—just demanding and snotty at best.

Mila, who had adopted her English-sounding name in hopes of getting better tips, opened Room 519 and stood open-mouthed for a moment.

Big celebrity for sure.

The unknown inhabitant had reduced the room to rubble. Every lamp lay on the floor, its foot shattered and its shade crumpled. The mirror was torn from the wall, reduced to a pile of shards on the floor, and the bedclothes had been slashed every which way. Even the mattress itself had fallen prey to the man's unchecked temper. The contents of the mini-bar lay broken and spilled all over the carpet, and the mirror in the washroom sported a giant spiderweb crack, as if someone had tried to put his fist through it.

Mila muttered a silent prayer of thanks that the occupant was gone and proceeded to dial her service manager. A trashed room always meant trouble—every time—and she didn't particularly relish the thought of having to clean the mess up either.

To her surprise, however, Guang Ho, who was in charge of service, and usually an unlikable and difficult-to-please fellow, told her not to worry about anything. The man had experienced a minor problem, he said, but he had left more than enough funds to cover any associated cost. Mila was to keep her mouth shut and clean up as fast as she could. Two men from house services were to help her with disposal of any large and dangerous items, and would she be up to handling the supervision?

She was sure she could, Mila said, but quietly, she shuddered to think about who could cause such destruction on the inside of a few hours, and she hoped she would never, ever have to meet him in person.

***

Reverend Bartholomew checked into another room in another hotel and proceeded to get rip-roaring drunk as fast as he could. If he managed to stay drunk for a few days—possibly even weeks—maybe it would go away. Maybe he wouldn't have to think about the fact that he had chosen wrong. A 50-50 chance, and he had picked the wrong option.

How could he have, he asked himself for the hundredth time? His reasoning had been sound, he knew how his friend thought, he had looked at the same numbers, the same analyses, and he had been sure. Not just sure—he had been 100 percent certain he knew which of the two companies Rafael would choose as a merger partner.

There had not been a single doubt in his mind, and yet—and yet he had chosen wrong. How could it have happened? How? And what was he to do now? Too late. Fuck, it was too goddamn late, and he owned majority shares in a company that was of no use to him. Whatsoever. Absolutely no use.

His fortune, squandered. His future, destroyed. His precious cash, gone to pay for a hotel room he had disassembled in a mad rage.

The reverend rubbed his bandaged hands where the mirror he had struck had given him thousands of painful little cuts and cursed under his breath again.

It had been a sure thing, Goddammit. Guaran-damn-teed. And yet...

A sound penetrated his drunken stupor, and it took him a few seconds to realize that it was his room telephone ringing.

What the hell now? Nobody knew he was here. Nobody even had the slightest idea who he was, so who the fuck called him? There was not one soul he wanted to talk to. The reverend was determined to let the damn phone be, and said phone was equally determined to drive him out of his mind with its persistent jangling.

The phone won.

"What?" he barked into it, tempted to throw the thing against the wall, cautioned only by the ingrained knowledge of his dwindling cash supplies.

"Aren't you Mr. Sunshine now?"

"What the fuck do you want now, Rob?"

"Oh, it's Rob now, is it? We're using clear names suddenly?"

"Ivers, I swear to you, I might be drunk, but I can still beat you to a pulp."

"Yeah. I'm trembling."

"What do you want?"

"To congratulate you on your brilliant plan of course, Connor."

"Shut the fuck up. I told you before."

"So now what?"

"I don't know, yet. I'll let you know just as soon as I figure it out."

Rob laughed. One of those deep, guttural, 'you have got to be freaking kidding me,' laughs, and the reverend lifted his arm again, one hand balled to a fist, ready to put it through the nearest mirror or glass the way he had earlier. Only the sharp memory of that pain stopped him in the nick of time from repeating the exercise.

"If I tell you I will let you know, then I will let you fucking know, in my own fucking time, is that clear?" he said instead, through clenched teeth, and balled his fist ever tighter, so the sharp pain in his cuts would stop him from doing something stupid.

Christ, when had he developed such a furious unchecked temper?

"Face it, you bet on the wrong horse," Rob said, and for the first time in two days, Barry laughed.

"Well, no shit, Sherlock. Say, do they pay you for sage advice like this, or does it just drop out of your ass? No wonder your father sent you away with an allowance, kid. Your advice is worth a great big zero."

"Connor, I am warning you…"

"What, Rob? From what? Your father? Get real. Without me, you're reduced to getting shitfaced at 10 a.m. every day or playing chess with your driver. You got nothing; you hear that? You're a child playing with Daddy's money. So why don't you sit down and wait until I figure this out? I'll let you know."

He was being needlessly cruel, and he enjoyed the deep and satisfying charge it gave him, almost like grinding something disgusting under the heel of his shoe and watching it squirm.

"And don't call me again, ever. If I need you—should I need you—I'll be in touch."

"Watch yourself," Rob said with barely concealed disgust. "You can call me names all day long, Beauregard, but you know as well as I do that, without me, you are as fucked today as you were a year ago."

The good reverend howled with rage, and this time, he did throw the phone against the wall. If he could have, he would have put his fist through it as well, but last night's episode had taught him at least a modicum of caution.

Not again. Do not lose it again, he told himself as he paced up and down in the small room. *Whatever you do, rein in your goddamned temper now.*

There is a solution here. There is always a solution inside every problem, but you're not going to find it if you lose your head now.

Up and down, he paced.

He needed to take over a company, one that had a very specific potential.

Insider trading—insider takeover. Goddammit, he had not been wrong; he couldn't have been wrong unless…

Again, he cursed and kicked over the little metal trash bin by the desk.

Ivers. He had failed to take Ivers Senior into account. Ivers must have thrown his weight around and made the wrong choice.

Goddamn it, goddamn it all. Now what?

There was a solution here, and by God, he was going to find it. There was a way; there was always a way.

He and his best friend had said the sentence a thousand times if they had said it once. There was always a way—every single time.

He knew he hadn't chosen wrong. He could read his best friend's mind like his own. He knew what he would have picked, meaning that someone else had got there and changed the game plan. Why? What was going on back there to screw up critical decisions in his company's life? Could he use this? Could he discredit the company in some way, could he…?

Around and around his mind went 100 miles an hour.

There was a way—he kept repeating it in his head until it became a mantra. There was a way, there was one surefire way, and if it was the last thing he did, he would find it.

Fueled by determination and sheer unbridled anger, he straightened up the chair he had toppled earlier, sat again, and carefully picked up the phone. He dialed the number he had memorized and did not bother to identify himself when the other party answered.

"There's a way out of this."

"It warms my heart to hear you say that, Con—"

"Shut up and listen."

"OK."

"I need information. Again. I need every shred of information you can get your hands on about this proposed company merger and all of the people who are involved in it."

"I'm not sure how much of it's going to be available publicly."

"Then get me the non-public stuff. Jesus, do I have to explain everything to you, really?"

"And just how far would you like me to go to get this information, Reverend?"

"I don't care how far you need to go. That's your problem. Just get me what I need, you understand? Our lives depend on it."

"Our lives, Connor? Aren't we getting just a tiny little bit dramatic?"

"Listen to me, you little…" *Hold on to your temper—do not lose it again now. You still need this little worm.*

He took a couple of breaths and pictured his revenge. It would be so sweet. So wonderfully sweet and just. But in order to get there, he needed this weasel. And in order to convince this weasel…

"You're right, Rob," he said in the calmest tone of voice he had been able to muster in about three days. "You are absolutely right. I am—irritated that this situation has gone off track. So let me start again."

"Wow."

"There is a solution here, but in order to find it, I need all the information you can possibly get your hands on. Everything. By any means possible. Do you think you can take care of this?"

"Well, well. Look who's changing his tune."

Do. Not. Lose. It.

"You know me. I get excited about things. Especially important things. Now what do you think? Can you take care of this task, or would you prefer I hire someone on site? Either way, does not really matter to me."

The other man snorted.

"Do I take this to mean yes?"

"What do you think, Reverend? Of course I can take care of it. My question is how do you propose to get out of this shithole we find ourselves in?"

"You let that be my problem."

"Oh, it's your problem all right. I can walk away any time I choose to, remember? You, on the other hand…"

Do. Not. Lose. It. Now.

He counted to 10—slowly—and thought of his revenge again.

"I will manage. Don't worry your little head on my behalf. Now…"

"All right. I'll fly back and get information. When do you want me to go?"

"Now?"

"Now it is. What about you?"

"I think I will take a little safari tour. Lie low, get away from everything for a bit. You know what I mean? Be in touch when you get back. And bring the goods. Understood?"

"Understood."

THIRTY-ONE

"You are disappointed."

It was a statement, not a question. And it needed no answer. The truth of it was written all over his face. Rafael sighed and shook his head.

"I really thought I had him when we toured the factory. He saw the potential; he was excited about it—for a little while."

"But…?"

Rafael only shrugged.

"Your silence speaks volumes, Rafael. I have a pretty good idea what happened. He balked when he realized how deep my father was involved. He didn't want to have anything to do with him, am I right?" Al took a sip of his beer. "For what it's worth, Rafa, I'm sorry if this screwed up your deal."

Rafa forced a chuckle he did not feel. "Come on. We're at a bar. We're having a good time. Don't go emo on me now."

"Rafael."

"I mean it."

"It's not working. I know you, remember."

"OK. What do you want me to say? Yes, I thought Irv Moody would invest for sure. He has the money, he is an extremely smart man, and I actually like him. So yes. I wanted him to invest. Didn't work out. Move on."

"Because he did not want to deal with my father."

225

"Your father, my aunt Mary, somebody's third cousin Joey. Who knows? Maybe he thought there was too much debt on the books, or he didn't like the colors, or he just doesn't want to do weed. Al, there is always a reason when a guy says no to a great deal. It does not have to have anything to do with your father. The company's history reads like a drama, starting with Connor and all of his escapades. C'est la vie. One down, next please."

"You're not fooling anyone with this very fake cool act, you know."

"I know. But I also know without your father and his money, the company wouldn't even be here today. May never have seen the light of day a couple of years ago when this whole thing started. So what? You want me to cry over spilled something?"

"No, but…"

"But nothing. Irv did not want to do the deal. Period. Had he felt the urge to invest, he might have asked a few questions, and come up with a different way to structure the deal. He would have asked if we could safeguard his funds somehow or made a suggestion, anything. He did not."

"Which means?"

"God, Al, it means he didn't want to do the deal. We move on."

"You good now?"

"Possibly. But you want to hear something else?"

"OK."

"There is a teensy tiny bit of me, just this much." Rafael held his thumb and forefinger about half an inch apart. "Just this much that is happy that Irv did not invest."

"Care to explain why?"

"This, this is why." Rafael swept his hands around in a big gesture indicating The Lighthouse restaurant and bar, and the patio just beyond, which had opened only days ago. "This is why. You, me, Irv—we come here to relax, to shoot the bull for a bit and let go. I like it. I like hanging out here as my sons would say. Part of me says, what would have happened if Irv had invested, big time? And furthermore, what would have happened if the deal had gone sour, and he had lost it all? It would have ruined a potentially great friendship."

"Way to put a spin on it."

"A positive spin. Now, I can still buy Irv a beer when he comes in here or hit him up for one if I'm feeling low. I can ask his advice, and I can make off-color jokes with him. Life is good, OK?"

Al nodded and went back to his beer. He did not believe one bit of what Rafael was saying, and Rafa knew it. Shit, it really was written all over his face, and yet... Rafael leaned back, took another sip of his beer, picked up the paper someone had left behind, and flung it back onto the bar.

"I'm pissed off as hell," he finally said, and Al nodded again.

"It's a great opportunity. No, it's an awesome opportunity. And I'm here working my ass off to make sure it happens."

Another nod from Al.

"And he walks in here... He walks in here..."

"And says no, just like that." Al finished the sentence and snapped his fingers, and Rafael folded his arms, feeling like a defiant child.

"Yeah, basically. So, excuse me, but I am pissed off."

"As you should be."

"And this merger... There's a ton of paperwork. I'm not kidding, I mean a ton. You can weigh the shit they send over to my office on a daily basis, and you're gonna need a pretty big scale to do it."

"Mergers are generally like that."

"And Greg? Greg? I'm potentially being politically incorrect, but I do believe Greg Turner is a huge ass."

"And there you have it."

The two men looked at each other and suddenly broke out in laughter loud enough to attract the attention of the other bar patrons.

"Shit," Rafael finally said, still laughing, and slapped Al on the shoulder. "Shit, shit, shit. I really thought we had it in the bag. Had the world by the tail. Got the merger on the go, Nick Ambrose signed up, a huge investor on the line. Get the money, buy out your father, and develop the company. Sky's the limit. It would have been fun."

"I thought you were thinking of leaving the company once it was out of trouble."

"I was, but a guy can dream. You, me, Irv, Nick, and even Dante. What a hell of a team. I mean—if we'd gotten that far."

"And if you could have bought out Tadeo."

"If we could have bought Tadeo's interest—hell, the picture changes. I might have been tempted…"

Al sighed and looked down into his glass.

"Don't take this the wrong way, Al, but every single time I have a problem in the company… Every single time…"

"Tadeo somehow contributes to it."

"He does. I'm grateful that he's financing us. We wouldn't be here if it were not for him. I know that, and you know that. But…"

"But he makes it harder than it has to be."

"That's about it, Al, right there."

"And you want to know something? That is the exact thing Tadeo used to say about Connor back when you started the company, and he and I were only investors. This company has all the potential in the world, if you could only get rid of Connor Beauregard and his capability of making a mess of everything."

Rafael tilted his head and lifted his glass in silent cheers.

"Takes one to know one, huh?"

***

His mojo, he thought, sitting over a fine dinner with Kayla, poking at his food, that's what was gone. He did what needed to be done, yes, but at the end of the day, he felt like the inmate who was marking another X on the calendar. Another day closer to freedom and to running his construction company again.

"Something wrong with your dinner?"

"No." He made himself smile at Kayla and poked at his food again, realizing that he neither knew nor cared what he had ordered or was eating. "Just distracted, that's all."

"I guess I don't have to ask if they are business problems that have you looking like you're dragging the weight of the world chained to your leg. They always are."

"They are," he confirmed and made an effort to eat another mouthful. "Good, isn't it?"

"I would agree if I thought you had tasted anything you ate in the last half hour. What's going on with you, Rafa? I thought, once you decided you were leaving, you were feeling so much better?"

"I guess I was wrong."

"Hear, hear. Can I mark that sentence down in my calendar?"

"I had that coming. I really did think walking away would fix all of my problems with Tadeo and the way he chooses to run things, or have things run."

"And?"

"And then I met the kind of investor that comes along once in a lifetime for our kind of project. Deep pockets, nice guy, brilliant mind, and, if that were not enough, clean, honest business ethics. The type of guy you bring into your company, and it can't help but skyrocket, you know, because he brings that X ingredient."

"Sounds a little too good to be true. However, it's your story. Carry on."

"Irving Moody, name tell you anything?"

"Vaguely," Kayla said, frowning. "Didn't he just inherit a whole bunch of money?"

"Close," Rafael said and took another mouthful of food, making a real effort this time to taste his steak. "They bought him out of his company, and he walked away with a small fortune. No, I think it's a big fortune."

"I think I remember now. But I don't see the problem."

"The possibility of Irving Moody investing got me thinking what that money could do for the company. We wouldn't rely on Tadeo any longer. We could run a nice, clean, efficient operation, Nick, you, me, Al—even Dante if he wanted to."

Kayla's face lit up all of a sudden. It could be because he had included her so naturally or because she could immediately see the advantages of buying out Tadeo Ivers, making him a mere shareholder. Her smile brightened the table to such an extent he felt his own disappointment crippling his spirits again. Sadly, he shook his head.

"Didn't happen. Irv took one look at the company history, Connor's disappearance, the mess he left, and then Ivers's involvement. And finally, he said thanks but no thanks."

"But didn't you explain to him? With his money you actually could work on—minimizing Tadeo's involvement? I don't necessarily mean get rid of him, but... make him an offer, so he would be a silent partner. A very silent partner. Surely as a businessman, he could see the potential in this group."

"Yeah." Rafael spread his hands and shook his head. "I did mention that there was a chance we might buy out some of the partners, restructure maybe. I mentioned that, but he didn't bite."

"You could have been more specific."

"I could have. Yes. Connor would have."

That one shut the argument down instantly. Yes, Rafael had told himself a hundred times he could have been a little more—explicit about his plans when he explained them to Irving. But Rafael did not generally trash his partners. He hadn't when he was working with Connor, he hadn't on any of the numerous construction projects when he had been saddled with a particularly difficult client or subcontractor, and he wouldn't now.

Idly, he picked up his wine glass and twirled it by the stem.

"I'll figure it out. How's the magazine business going meanwhile?"

"Fine."

"That's it? Fine?"

"Yes. Fine. We find the stories. We write about them. Just fine."

"Kayla, don't be like that."

"Like what?"

"Don't be mad at me because I mentioned Connor."

"Oh—I'm not angry, Rafael. I am utterly pissed. Because just like him, you think you and you alone know how things ought to be done. You set up your little plan and run with it. You don't tell me anything about it. I'm sure Al didn't know what was going on in your mad head."

"Well, no, actually."

"There you go. You just go and do what you think is right."

"Isn't that what I'm supposed to be doing? Saving the company by any means I think is right?"

"You're supposed to let the people who are your partners know what you're doing, Rafael Covin. Had you told me about this ahead of time…"

"You would have come in and insisted on charming Irving Moody. You would have done everything possible to make sure he knew why we wanted him in the company and how we were going to use a good portion of his funds."

"And what's wrong with that, pray tell?"

"I told you—I don't do business that way. If it happened, if Moody invested and we had the funds, I would have given it a shot. But not like this, OK? Not like this."

He had spoken a little more harshly than he intended to and made himself relax back into his chair.

"I'm sorry, OK? I didn't mean to yell."

Kayla put her fork aside and said nothing for a long, long moment.

"You really are different," she finally said, and below her exasperation, he spotted something different. Admiration maybe? Rafael frowned and put down his fork.

"You have—ironclad principles," she said, shaking her head.

"I do. And I try not to break them unless there's absolutely no other way. Isn't that why Tadeo hired me, my supposed reputation? And you, I was pretty sure you knew."

"Yes. But you're talking about loyalty to a man who shows absolutely none to you, and who is more of a hindrance in business than anything else. Besides the funds he is investing, that is."

Rafael shrugged. No answer he could give would make it any better. Not like he hadn't kicked himself a dozen times over for the same thing, right? But at the end of the day, he just couldn't blindside another guy. If that was a flaw, he had it.

***

That dinner had been their first quasi-argument, and for a couple of days, Kayla and Rafael went out of their way to be polite to one another. Kayla tried not to talk about PerCan unless it became unavoidable, and Rafael made a purchase at the flower shop for the first time in a good 10 years. He felt foolish as heck carrying the enormous bouquet of fresh flowers through the lobby at the publishing house and refused to meet any of the employees' eyes. What the heck. Let them gossip. Considering their main publication, they were probably good at it!

Irving had been out of town for the last week, which suited him just fine. Perhaps when they met again at a bar somewhere in town, bought each other a drink and told some jokes—perhaps by then, the awkwardness of their investment meeting would have passed. One could hope.

THIRTY-TWO

"This is," he said and spread his arms, looking down at the five-page spread of additional due diligence requests on his lap. "This is…"

"Thorough," Greg Turner said and gave him the polite and bland smile Rafael had come to resent grandly.

He had wanted to say, "This is bloody excessive," and stopped himself at the last minute.

"Thorough, right," he sighed. "Stripping down to our skivvies then."

Greg Turner made a face that offered a not-so-polite opinion of what he thought of Rafael Covin down to his skivvies and flipped a page.

"Anytime you're dealing with a character like Tadeo Ivers, caution is not only warranted but essential, Rafael. You must have extensive experience in that area, no?"

Rafael twitched for a moment. Of course he had told Turner that Tadeo Ivers was a major investor and provider of funds. Of course his involvement and that of Al and Dante had been disclosed. Disclosed, explained, and documented. But something in Greg's tone made him feel as if he were suddenly shuffling along a rope strung between two extremely tall buildings. Without the benefit of a net below.

"Tadeo Ivers, yes," he said softly, keeping his voice as neutral as possible. "His son Dante is on the board of directors and working to be a grower. Al Ivers acts a consultant to me."

"Correct. And Ivers Senior is there orchestrating things in the background. With his hands in absolutely everything."

He is there. The amount of venom in the word there would have been enough to kill a fully grown bull elephant if necessary, and it had come out of nowhere.

Rafael looked down at his hands for a moment. He had led this company for a while now, had had to deal with Tadeo and been exposed to his temper, his unreasonable demands, and his constant suspicions. He had identified Tadeo as a source of financing and a shareholder, but Turner's knowledge went a lot deeper suddenly.

"He's in the background," he said as casually as he could. "Not actively involved. Have you done business with him before?"

"Just peripherally. Now when do you think you could have financial statements to us? We've been quite patient up to now."

"My accountant is working on them," Rafael said, still forcing his voice to sound light and unconcerned.

Peripherally, what the hell did that even mean? And how on earth did one do business peripherally with Tadeo Ivers? You either did or you didn't.

Instinctively, he knew that asking more questions of Greg would not get him anywhere. On the contrary, it would put the man on the defensive and put him on guard, and that was not what he needed to start a merger. Mergers were supposed to be about cooperation, not suspicions.

Great, Rafael thought, between the two of them, they made the perfect pair, paranoid Rafael and suspicious Greg. He tried to shake that feeling off, much as he tried to ignore his own paranoia, but when he looked up, the look in Greg's eyes made him stop.

What he saw there wasn't dislike. It wasn't envy between businessmen or an opinionated, 'that guy's a blowhard.' For one precious moment, Rafael saw pure hatred in Greg Turner's face.

In a split second, Greg made an effort to smile again and bend down to retrieve a fallen paperclip, and, when he surfaced, his features were as careful and controlled as if he had practiced it.

"I spent some time in restaurant management," he said, smiling broadly, and just as fake. "You don't really work in the hospitality industry without having heard the name of Tadeo Ivers at one point. I'm sure you know that."

"I do," Rafael confirmed. "Sure. I just wasn't aware Ivers ever left that dingy family diner of his on Decantur Street. Jesus, what a place."

Again, the fire flickered in Turner's eyes, just for a second. And just as quickly, he had it under control again.

"Not really a place you would want to take your family to, now, is it?"

Rafael shrugged and turned another page in his lap. "Oh well, to each his own. In any case, Tadeo Ivers's active involvement is marginal at best. Other than providing some financing to the company."

"And owning the majority of shares."

"And owning quite a few shares. He is not involved in the day-to-day operations of Perfect Cannabis Corporation, he is not an officer, he is not a director, and he has no active role whatsoever. Now..."

Rafael couldn't wait to get off the subject of Tadeo. He'd already made a mental note to ask Al what the heck was up between Turner and Ivers. Until he knew what was up and where the pitfalls were, he could not let himself be tempted to make a statement. It was business. You had shareholders. Some of them you did not like. Period. That in no way had to affect the running of business.

Except it did, and he, Rafael, had bemoaned that fact longer than anyone. So how, pray tell, did Turner get his insider knowledge about Tadeo and his relationship to Rafael and PerCan? Where was the missing piece?

"David will have financials to you shortly," he finally said. "I'm chasing my directors for their information disclosure statements, but you know how directors are sometimes."

"In my company things run a little different."

"I am sure they do."

Asshole, Rafael thought, surprising himself with his hefty reaction. He barely managed to close his mouth on the word.

Indeed, Greg Turner was... One. Huge. Ass.

Soon, this would not be his problem any longer. He certainly wouldn't hire this blowhard here on a construction job, not even if he were desperate.

"I'll get it done," he said, smiling brightly. "My personal assistant, Connie, is worth her weight in gold when it comes to doing these things. Anything else you need from me then?"

Pound of flesh, detailed drawing of my underwear drawer at home, he thought, and grinned. *Humor will get you through this too.*

Turner took his smile for acquiescence and rose.

"No, I think we're getting close, Rafael. Very, very close. Personally, I'm looking very much forward to working with you and your team."

Sure, you are, my ass, he thought.

"As am I, Greg, as am I."

He shook the man's hand and all but forced himself not to wipe his hand on his pant legs as he walked out. Even as he waited for the elevator, he fired a text off to Al to meet him at The Lighthouse. He needed the goods on Turner, no matter where they came from or how they had been acquired. On second thought…

'Hey, love,' he texted Kayla. 'Hope you're having an amazing day. Can you do this old man a favor and see if your databank has anything good on Greg Turner? We'll be working with him before long, and I'd rather not find any surprises.'

No surprises. Dream on, Rafael Covin, he thought. His gut told him there was a huge surprise hiding in there somewhere, and not the good kind. He burned to find out why Turner hated Tadeo Ivers with such passion.

He rushed off to The Lighthouse, hoping he would find Al there, and parked himself in a corner of the bar, thumbing through his messages.

Kayla texted him back in short order, saying she would look into Greg and his history, but off the top of her head, nothing came to mind. Why did he want to know?

Rafael's finger hovered over the screen of his phone. 'Nothing in particular, just curious,' he typed and put his phone away again.

What were the first signs of true paranoia again? Now he couldn't even tell Kayla what was going on and what had him spooked where Greg was concerned? Really?

Rafael ran both his hands through his hair and tried to rein in his runaway thoughts. *List, Rafael, make a goddamn list. That's what you are good at.*

One, that creepy 'somebody-is-following-me' feeling is back. Two, Greg Turner acting exceedingly strange now. Three…?

Three? Nothing.

"God, you're an ass," he muttered. "Ivers has you on the run, doesn't he?"

"You look somewhat perturbed," Al said, sliding onto the stool beside him. "And why are you sitting back here amongst the cheap seats? Did you miss paying a few bar bills?"

"Good, you're here." Rafael took a big breath and let it out slowly. "I need to ask you something, and, once again, I'm going to have to ask you to be completely honest with me."

"Oh, goody, I so love a conversation that starts with those words."

"Al, this is not a joke."

"OK, shoot."

"Are you aware of any prior history between Mr. Greg Turner and your father, particularly one that would have led to some extremely hard feelings?"

Al thought for a moment. His brows drew tight, and he pinched his lower lip between his fingers for a while. Finally, he shook his head.

"Nothing that jumps to mind, Rafael. I assume you have a reason for asking?"

Rafael filled him in on Greg's exceedingly odd behavior and finally shook his head. "It's not normal, Al. And what's more, he tried to hide it. He did a damn good job most of the time, but when he thought I wasn't noticing… I'm telling you, I've never seen such pure, undiluted hatred in a human being before. Never."

"That's not good," Al said and folded his hands.

"No kidding, Al. That's the kind of thing that comes right before, 'then disaster happened.' I need to know what's going on, and if it will affect that merger in any way. This is not the time for another crisis to jump out and bite us. We've made a couple of good-faith payments to them. Your father has made those payments personally. If this merger explodes in our faces, well, I don't have to tell you what will happen."

Al said nothing, but he did order another round of drinks.

"Has Kayla…"

"I've asked her, but like you, she said nothing jumped out at her without doing more detailed research. I didn't tell her any more."

Al merely raised his left eyebrow, high enough that it gave his face a bit of a twist, but he kept his mouth shut.

"If you must know," Rafael finally said, looking down at his feet. "If you must know, I'm getting that feeling again. People going through my office that shouldn't, people looking for information."

"Because of the merger? But that's hardly…"

"Don't you think I know that?"

Rafael slapped his hand onto the bar hard and made a fist. "Sorry. I'm irritated and on edge. I know this merger isn't exactly stuff for industrial espionage and insider trading. Not our little merger, not PerCan. But lately—lately, I just get the feeling someone's been in my office."

"Connie?"

"She says she hasn't, and I trust her."

"Kayla?"

"I asked her, and she got all irritated and said no."

Al waited for a moment, and when nothing else followed, he only shook his head.

"Crissakes, Al, it's her building. If she wanted to go anywhere, she would have every right to, but she says she hasn't been in my office unless I've been there. Period."

"Yet another reason to move your offices over to our building."

"And I've been meaning to do that, Al, for the past couple of weeks. I just haven't had the goddamn time to do it, OK? Have you seen the paperwork lately?"

"Let's not panic here," Al said, leaning back in his seat a little. "Nothing has actually happened that we need to worry about, has it? I'll ask a few questions later on, discreetly of course. If Tadeo and Turner have had dealings before, somebody will remember, and that somebody will tell me."

"Thanks."

"Most likely, it's nothing, Rafael. Greg Turner might have done some research on my father and found a few things he isn't entirely comfortable with. It happens."

"Easy for you to say."

"I've run into it before. The name Tadeo Ivers means nothing to most people, and that's how he likes it, but if you dig just a little deeper, you are sure to find a few things that might give a man pause to think."

"Pause to think," Rafael echoed sarcastically. "Pause to think, that's putting it nicely."

"He can be a ruthless businessman, but…"

"But?"

"But that's all. I've told you before. That and his tax returns are the worst of his crimes, except in his own fantasies."

Rafael sighed and leaned back in his own chair and exhaled slowly.

"I know I'm getting paranoid, and I can't figure out why."

Al shrugged and pushed Rafael's glass a little closer. "Stress. A business deal from hell, cleaning up Connor's old mess, dealing with my father. Take your pick, Rafa. If anybody deserves a time-out, it's you."

"And again…" Rafael lifted his glass in a toast and drained it. "I can't wait to have this thing over with," he finally said. "Get my life back, go back to being a sloppy contractor with uncouth language and dirty clothes."

"And you think Kayla will appreciate this?"

"Kayla…" Rafael looked out over the bar and twisted his hand at the wrist, around and around. He'd been doing far too much office work lately and not enough 'real' work. "Kayla will adjust, I hope. We'll just have to figure it out. Otherwise…" He shrugged. "Hey…"

"Are you sure about that, Rafael?"

"Right now, I have too much on my plate to even consider thinking about that."

"And anyway, Mr. Rafael Covin has beautiful women chasing him around all the live-long day."

A hand appeared and knocked on the tabletop between the two men.

"Afternoon, gents, got room for one more?"

"Irv," Rafael said and blinked rapidly. Irving Moody was just about the last man he had wanted to meet right at the moment. "Where the hell have you been?"

"He means welcome, why don't you sit," Al said and pointed to the stool at his left. "And when he says, 'Where the hell have you been,' he's wondering what exotic locale your adventures took you to most recently."

"No, I mean where the hell has he been. Don't put fancy words into my mouth, Al Ivers. Sit, Moody, and tell me where you've been, 'cause I bet it is some place I would not go for money."

"Guatemala."

Rafael spread his hands and rolled his eyes toward the ceiling, as if he wanted to say, *See what I mean?*

Truth be told, Irv Moody's appearance made him stop thinking about Tadeo, about Perfect Cannabis, and about people who might or might not be following him.

Irv Moody usually had a number of entertaining and hugely embellished anecdotes about flying that tin can he called an airplane around the world, and that was just what he needed right now. Anything, anything at all, to stop thinking about his business problems for a while.

"Guatemala, just like that?"

"Just like that. Needed a little time to think."

"Well, next time you need time to think, save yourself some money. Don't fly all over the country in a tin can. Go to a bar like normal people."

Irv grinned, sat down, and signaled the bartender. Usually, he would have passed his phone around to show off some pictures of him with his plane. At a barely there landing strip, or tanned and clad in shorts, hanging out in some godforsaken place with a bunch of other pilots and their planes.

The pictures never really changed much—just the background and the tail numbers on the planes did—but Rafael envied Irving Moody for the never-ending freedom that unfolded in those pictures.

Today, the pictures did not appear. Today, he didn't laugh and say, 'Wait till you hear what happened at this airstrip in the middle of nowhere.' Rafael waited and finally cocked his head.

"What, you crash this time around?"

"Nope, all good."

"So? No landing-on-one-wheel stories? No running out of gas in midair, or finding strange animals in the tail section of the plane?"

"I never found a strange animal in the tail section of my plane."

"Then you will, someday. Just keep looking. So, no stories, that's not right. You don't come to a bar with no stories."

"Didn't say I had no stories, just no flying ones."

"O-K…"

Rafael dragged the word out a bit and looked to Al for help.

"There is something that's been going through my mind ever since you showed me your lovely little factory, Rafael."

Rafael froze in midair reaching for his glass and barely dared to breathe. Now what? He couldn't speculate; he didn't dare.

"And what would that be?" he asked, exchanging a look with Al.

Al shrugged.

"This—drug dealing has one hell of a potential."

241

"Yup." Rafael nodded. "That's kind of why we got into it—my original partner and me. Didn't quite work out the way we wanted it to… yet."

"But the concept was sound."

"Daring, massive, but sound," Al confirmed. "Probably one of the most daring new ventures in the past couple of years."

"Took some guts." Irving nodded. "That's one thing I admire—guts."

He said nothing for a long moment, and Al and Rafael exchanged looks again.

"You're probably wondering where all of this is leading."

"Would be nice to know," Rafael croaked and cleared his throat. "I mean—yes, that would be good."

"I am—toying with the idea of getting active again."

Niagara Falls rushed through his brain, Rafael thought. At least that's what it felt like. For a moment, he could neither think nor speak and sat still looking down at his hands on the bar. Thunderstruck, he thought, this was the definition of that word.

When he finally managed to speak again, only a single word managed to make it out of his mouth.

"Wow."

Irv chuckled. "Well—yes, wow. I've been flying around the country for a few years now, and sometimes, I think it is time to get involved somewhere again. Do something productive and creative."

Rafael opened his mouth and closed it again, still struggling to bend his mind around what he was hearing. Al, on the other hand, didn't even twitch.

"I'm sure when Rafael regains the ability to speak, Irv, he will tell you how pleased he is that you would even consider investing. That is what you are talking about, right?"

"Well, yes, putting in some money," Irv said, "perhaps do a little bit of consulting here and there. See if you boys could use some input. The business intrigues me, and it'd be nice to have something to do between flights."

"You would—actually get involved?"

"And so he speaks again. Rafael, I'm sure it pissed you off when I said no to you."

"Some—yes... OK, I thought it was pretty shortsighted of you."

"Kneejerk reaction. There's a lot of stuff in that deal I don't really like. Starting with the drama your former partner created."

"Connor, yes," Rafael sighed. "The story that will never go away."

"I've had my fill of drama with my own company. Didn't want to go down that road again—ever. But then I kind of kicked myself in the rear."

"Oh, one of us would have done it for you if you'd asked—no problem. Remember that next time. But carry on. Why kick yourself?"

"Because you, Rafael, have made the impossible possible. You took a totally messed-up company, something that had gone off the rails and into a deep, deep pile of manure—and somehow righted it up again. By yourself."

"Not all by myself, no. A lot of other hands did a lot of pulling getting this thing out of the hole."

"Maybe. But they sure would not have done so without your leadership and your guts. I admire that. Matter of fact, I could have used it back when Dot-Scan started to get into trouble. If there had been anybody standing at the helm saying, 'guys, let's just for a moment put away all the swords and all pull on the same rope to get things moving in the right direction,' it would have... Aaaah, never mind." He waved his hand through the air and shook his head. "Yesterday's news. It went down. But you, Rafael, you saved PerCan from exactly that fate. So, I'd—like to be a little part of it, if that's OK with you."

"OK with me?" Rafael grinned broadly. "Are you kidding me? Are you fricking kidding me? I'd be happy to have you on board. Just what kind of involvement were you thinking about?"

"Not to rock anybody's boat, but I'd want to make it worthwhile."

"Naturally."

Rafael almost held his breath. Yes, he'd been talking to a lot of investors recently. Yes, he'd signed on guys who had a lot of money and who could part with a quarter million without even batting an eyelash. All correct. But this one mattered. This one right here really mattered. If he breathed, if he said the wrong thing…

"10 mil be ok with you?"

Niagara Falls was back in his head. Big time. Surreptitiously, he grabbed the side of his bar stool to make sure he would not fall off it.

"Sounds good," he managed to say and met Al's eyes over the bar. Just how much had they had to drink today?

THIRTY-THREE

The reverend was back in Singapore a mere two weeks later. He'd indeed gone on a safari for a little while. Nothing worked out a temper and the bad taste of a business deal having gone south like handling a big gun for a few days. A really big gun. Made you forget the 'whys' and the 'wherefores' for a bit and allowed you to unload—literally.

He checked into yet a different hotel this time, the Weston in Marina Bay, and sent off a few messages to his contact back home. Then he settled in for a wait.

If the little shit knew what was good for him, he would a) not make him wait for an extended period of time before giving answers, and b) those answers had better be what he wanted to hear.

They had better be.

Two days later, a large package was delivered to his hotel, and Barry eagerly rifled through the contents, hoping his answers would be buried in there.

Finally, he dialed his brand-new phone.

"Paper," he barked when the other party answered. "You sent me a bunch of worthless paper? Is that your idea of a joke?"

"Hello to you too, Barry. You wanted to know everything about the merger."

"I wanted to know how to torpedo it, not how to lead it by the hand."

"Then you have everything there."

The temper flared again, and Barry consciously made a fist with his right hand and released it again. A few little scars reminded him what might happen if he lost it again.

"How about the Cliff Notes version, huh, Rob? Can you do that?"

"Turner, he has a weak spot."

"Yes?"

"His father has done business with the old man before."

"Is that so?"

"Not a big deal on my father's level of thinking, but the man got shafted royally. Lost everything, left town, abandoned his wife and kid. His name wasn't Turner. That's why nobody made the connection. He must have taken his mother's name after his old man left."

"Then what? That's not all, is it?"

"Of course there's more. It's an old deal, Beauregard, my dad and Turner's dad—whose name was actually Lambert. That's why nobody remembered it. I found it, though, and now Greg Turner knows everything about it too."

"That's it? That's all you have done?"

"That's all I needed to do. Just wait."

Wait. The one thing he hated worse than anything else in the world. Wait. Barry closed the phone connection without saying another word and forced himself to sit still. Wait… Goddamn it…

Whoever had come up with that line about revenge tasting better cold was full of shit. Full to the brim. Revenge tasted better like fire, hot, searing, and satisfying.

He flipped through the stack of papers Rob had had delivered to him and finally pushed them aside and into the wastebasket. Waste of time, fucking paper.

The other idea had merit. Turner could not stand Ivers. Good. Hate was something he could work with. He understood it and knew how to use its energy to his own ends. A man tended to remember getting shafted and would do a thing or two to get back at the bastard who had done so, right? And here was the best part—nobody could ever link this back to him. Ever.

Maybe that little punk Rob wasn't as useless as all that. Jail had an interesting way to teach a man a few things, he thought. Opening a drink, he stood by the window, looking down at the city by the sea.

"There's always a way," he muttered and silently toasted his reflection in the window. If the way through this consisted of poking through the ashes of an extremely old fire, looking for remaining embers, then that was just what he would do.

THIRTY-FOUR

Ten. Million. Dollars.

"Wow…"

Rafael fought the sudden choking in his throat. He'd known Irv was a 'heavy'—everybody did. But this heavy? Holy fucking shit. With that kind of money… He opened and closed his mouth like a fish on dry land.

"You're gonna say wow again, Rafa?"

"I might," he croaked and cleared his throat. "You don't do things in small measures, do you?"

"Small measures are for wimps," Irv said, tossing an invisible something over his shoulders. "But I don't want to piss off anybody, just be useful."

"Good to hear," Al finally said. "Because my father…"

"Has been financing this thing all along, I understand that. And there are a handful of shareholders who have been hanging in with the company since the very beginning. I don't want to come on in with an assload of cash and take over. I don't want to be the dick who throws money around and gets to be the hero in the last chapter. That's not who I am. Let's find a way to keep the integrity of the shareholders' equity as much as we can."

Rafael's mind clicked away a dozen miles a minute again.

"Could do a loan," he said, "or a number of loans, or create a subsidiary, put the funds in…"

"Three things I want, Rafael." Irv ticked them off on his thumb and first two fingers. "I want the company to succeed, I want to have a fun, little bit of involvement because the business is cool, and I want a piece of the action."

"Naturally, but…"

"So how about this. I invest some of the money outright, for shares. Not enough to dilute the original shareholders' equity much, though you can also ask them to invest more to maintain their holdings, some kind of rights offering, maybe. But enough to make it interesting for everybody and make life a little easier for you. The rest, a couple of special-purpose loans. Convertible to shares a little down the road if we all decide to stay together, or to be paid back if we don't. That work?"

"Convertible debentures." Al nodded. "That'll work, make everybody else happy too."

"This merger complicates things a little," Irv said. "I'm going to have to think through the structure on that carefully. What does that do to the company and my investment?"

"Do you even want to do the merger still?" Al asked, closing his eyes for a moment.

"The reasons why we decided to do a merger are still sound, investment or no. I think we should," Rafa said slowly. "Never mind. We need to. Don't forget about the license. If we don't do this merger, we'll be caught up in red tape for several more years, I'm afraid, while everybody tries to forget the name Connor Beauregard."

"That makes sense. So, we form one Newco, whatever it's going to be called, and I invest into it. That about sums it up." Irv nodded slowly.

"I like it," Al said. "Greg Turner, he can be a bit of a loose cannon, but everybody from PerCan will be happy. The company gains value, their share structure stays intact, and things get moving again. That's what everybody is waiting for."

"Even Greg Turner, odd bird that he is," Rafael said and tried to make himself forget about his dislike of the man.

Good things were happening today. He had Irving Moody investing big time without screwing everybody or leaving a bad taste in the deal, he had another sharp mind to bounce ideas off and to set him straight when needed. What more…

He raised his glass.

"Gentlemen, this is…"

"Don't say it, Rafael," Irv and Al spoke as one, until Irv finally grinned and took over. "I swear to you if you say the beginning of a beautiful…"

"I wasn't going to. What I was going to say was the same thing I said a few years ago. Gentlemen, here's to being drug dealers."

THIRTY-FIVE

Greg Turner surprisingly did not like it when he heard Irv Moody wanted to invest.

Rafael had known he wouldn't, and it shouldn't have come as a surprise, but when he let it slip that he had a big investor on the line, a really big investor, the man's eyes acquired that greedy, glittering look Rafael had seen before and disliked. And almost in the same breath, Greg started talking about completely reconfiguring the merger.

If he didn't have his own problems with Ivers, Rafael would have been tempted to feel sorry for the man. First thing on everyone's mind when there was money on the table? *Can we somehow get Ivers out of the deal?*

The man was a grandiose pain, but he'd stuck with this company and financed it when nobody else stepped up to the plate.

"Nothing about this potential investment will change the merger," he told Greg. "PerCan and Green Technologies are still going to come together as one company, just like we planned. With the one exception that right after we are done with the merger, we may have a big investor and a number of smaller loans coming in, that's all. It'll make life that much easier going forward." He snapped his fingers. "Expansion, hiring, the build-out. That is going to be one hell of a nice company we will end up with."

"We could still revisit and restructure this merger to a certain extent. I'm sure you know what I'm talking about, Covin."

Rafael leaned back and folded his hands behind his head, making his expression carefully bland.

"Have you lost interest in this deal, Greg? Because if that's the case, nothing has been signed and delivered yet. If you're uncomfortable…"

"Why, because you've got Moody offering you the big bucks all of a sudden, you want to deep-six our deal? Is that what I'm hearing?"

"Nobody is deep-sixing anything, least of all me. All I'm saying is if you are uncomfortable with anything inside this deal, anything at all, this would be the time to say it. Before any of the lawyers make more money."

"You got that right."

"Well then."

Greg leaned back as well, mirroring Rafael's relaxed stance, smiling thinly. Except, Rafael thought, the smile never quite moved beyond a grimace, the casual pose looked contrived and studied, and the eyes… The man's eyes had become hard and tiny. Black chips of ice. *More trouble on the way,* he thought.

Rafael sighed.

"No, Rafael, I am good. This is a good thing happening for all of us, this Moody character investing. I'd like to know where the heck you found him this quick."

"Acquaintance of mine." Rafael shrugged.

"You sure saved him to the last minute."

"You know how it goes. Guy decides to invest—or not. Doesn't always happen on our timetable, no matter how much we want it. There are no guarantees, any time. Just good chances." He paused for a minute and waited for Turner to say anything else. When it didn't happen, he rose and offered his hand.

"Personally, I have to say I'm really looking forward to putting this deal together and getting this company on the board, where it belongs. Our original investors are finally going to make money, and we'll shake up the marijuana industry. Our work is going to be fun again, for a change, for all of us."

"Yes. Fun." Greg shook his hand and smiled that weird grimace once again. "Of course. Straitlaced Covin, as he lives."

"Is that what they're calling me now?"

Greg only shrugged.

"Guess there could be worse things." He opened the door and nodded. "I just wanted you to know what was in the pipeline. We're all on track with the official merger paperwork. It will happen very soon. Take care."

"Yes, soon," Greg said, and this time, his grimace gave Rafael the creeps. Something dark was going on in that man's mind, and the hell if he knew what it was.

Straitlaced Covin. He had to chuckle at his own nickname. All right then. At least people knew where they were at.

***

"I'm excited about this deal again," he told Kayla over dinner. "One day you want to give up, in walks Irving Moody, and everything changes. Reset, start over, back to go. Unreal."

For the first time in ages, he attacked his food with gusto, tasted what he put into his mouth, and reveled in the enjoyment of a good steak dinner.

"This is fabulous. Something wrong with yours?"

"Not really." Kayla poked at her own food and managed to eat a few bites. "Are you sure this is what you want this time? First, you take on the CEO position, then you don't want it, then you want to quit once the company is out of trouble. Now you're back to wanting to run it again. What's it going to be, Rafa?"

"Well, things do change, you know," he said, a little off-guard by the venom in her voice. "You angry with me?"

"I'd like to know where I'm at, Rafael. Just where the hell does this business place in your life, and where do I? It's all good and well to play straitlaced Covin all the time and do right by everybody. That's great, Rafa, but stand for something, will you?"

"I thought I did."

"Do you, Rafael, really? Or do you just get to sit there and be that magnanimous guy everybody likes and who does right by everybody? That's not how business works."

"Don't tell me how business works, please," he said, hanging on to his manners by a thread. "I've run a few different companies, and I think I know by now, OK?"

"You know, all right, but maybe not on this scale, not these kinds of deals. Make the tough calls, make people follow your lead instead of changing your mind all the time. That's all I have to say to you. Make up your mind and leave it there, and it does not matter what Ivers wants, or Moody, or Al thinks. Just make up your mind."

She put down her napkin and finished her wine. "I think I'm going home now."

It wasn't a question; it wasn't even a request. As always, Kayla Montecito had a car and driver standing by to take her wherever she wanted to go, whenever she wanted to go. She rose, tucking her purse under her arm.

"Let me know when you decide, will you." And with that, she was gone, leaving Rafael to scratch his head in wonder.

Two fights in the space of a couple of weeks. That just didn't bode well. As much as he wanted to dismiss it as one of those women's things, he also knew he would be foolish to do so.

Was he really? He wondered as he finished his own wine and waited for the bill. Was he really just the guy trying to do right by everybody and never setting solid goals and direction for either himself or the company? He hated disagreements and conflict, true. He wanted everybody to feel comfortable and happy with every deal he started, and what the hell was wrong with that?

Except that attitude had make him go along with everything Connor Beauregard said and did, just so Connor would not get upset. Look at the mess that had made, and now he had Ivers Senior to deal with. He'd gone in short order from "I'm doing things my way or not at all" to "Whatever Ivers wants, as long as it's not a big deal and avoids a fight." He knew he didn't want to work with either Ivers or Turner, but somehow, he'd gotten stuck with both of them. Maybe he just had a habit of collecting the misfits of the business world because he pandered to them.

Dammit if that's my fault, he thought stubbornly and collected his stuff to go home. He knew nothing would really be waiting for him at home, so on second thought, he stopped by The Lighthouse for one last drink.

***

To his surprise and amazement, he found Al in the corner of the bar, reading something on his mini-tablet, looking for all the world as if he belonged there.

"Hey there, you got no place to go home to as well?" he asked, rapping his knuckles on the tabletop and indicating the seat beside Al.

"I might ask you the same thing, Rafael. I was under the impression you and the lovely Kayla were going to dine together."

"We did."

"Oh? The evening ended early then?"

"Small disagreement."

"Ouch. Nothing major to put a crimp into your plans for the future, I hope."

"Nothing but Kayla calling me a turncoat weakling who doesn't have the spine to stand for anything. And what plans for the future?"

"I was under the impression things were going splendidly for you and Kayla."

"They did, till just recently."

"And why is that, pray tell, or can I put a name to the issue? My father's name comes to mind, quite naturally."

"This time, it's not actually his fault." Rafael thanked the bartender bringing his favorite drink with a brief nod and settled back a bit. "Surprising as that is. Kayla thinks I should finally make up my mind about PerCan and leave it there."

"That might be a good idea."

"Things change, Al. First, the company is in the crapper. Then I'm supposed to pull it back out again. Then your father acts like a dick, saddles me with Greg Turner, and all of a sudden, Irv enters the picture. So, forgive me if some days I don't know where my head is at, or if I want to stay with the company when it's all said and done, or just move on. It's been a bit of a ride the past year."

"To say the least."

"And Kayla…"

"I suspect, Rafael, Kayla would simply like to know where she stands with you as well as with the company. And you changing your mind on a regular basis does not really make her as comfortable as all that."

Made sense, Rafael thought and took a long draft of his drink. He could have thought of it himself. Probably would have, if he wasn't busy these days looking over his shoulder for no reason at all.

"Well, she might have said that," he snapped as he put his glass back down. "Instead of giving me a hard time over nothing."

"Nothing, if you permit me the observation, has you quite on edge the past few weeks."

"And you know why." Rafael watched the big TV screen for a few minutes.

"There's Turner. Turner still gives me the creeps. That's not nothing. Something is up with that guy. I know it. I can feel it. I just can't for the damned life of me put my finger on it."

"I've asked a few people at the organization…"

The organization. Rafael grinned and barely bit back a smart-aleck response. To call Tadeo's various businesses an organization was more of a stretch than he cared to do. But to each his own.

"I've asked around, carefully, you understand. And nobody there seemed to remember."

"Mmmm," Rafael said. "That could say quite a lot."

"Could be he did business under a different name, company name, within a group or other organization. I didn't press the issue because sure and enough…"

"It would have gotten back to your father," Rafael finished. "And he would have asked questions. You think Tadeo himself would remember the man if anything had ever gone down between them."

"Not necessarily. Unless he's the wronged party, he doesn't really waste a lot of brain power remembering old business partners or grievances. Now, if he feels he got the short stick, that's another matter entirely."

"Then he'll remember 25 years and back."

"And you know he does."

"So, what the hell? The way I'm reading it, Turner truly hates Tadeo for some thing or other. Why?" Rafael rested his elbows on the table and his chin on his fists.

"Might I suggest you simply let it go, Rafa? Right at the moment, this suspicion of yours appears to be a huge distraction. If and when it becomes necessary to deal with something, we will."

"I don't know."

"Right now, we don't even know if there is a 'something,' and until we do…"

"Getting blindsided! I don't like it, Al."

"Nobody does. But you are wasting valuable resources worrying about something that might not have anything to do with the company. And in doing so, you are angering the lovely Kayla and damaging your relationship."

"Back up the horses there for a minute, Al… relationship?"

"Don't you want there to be?"

"I don't know. Geez, give me some time."

"Much like you don't know whether or not you wish to stay CEO of PerCan after the merger?"

"Yeah—like, I've been a little busy, living from one crisis to the next, all right."

"If you want my advice, Rafa…"

"Which you will give, whether or not I actually want it."

"Spend some time figuring these things out, sooner, rather than later. Nobody will fault you for being CEO or not, or for going out with Kayla or not. But changing your mind midstream does tend to piss people off big time."

"You know what I really want to know, while you are sitting there dispensing advice, I mean?" Rafael asked.

"I do not. So go ahead and tell me."

"Why can't things ever be easy? A nice little company run by decent people, everybody doing their job, and getting along… Why?"

"Because, my dear Rafa, if it were easy, everybody would be doing it."

THIRTY-SIX

Kayla's and Al's admonishments to make up his mind followed Rafael the next couple of days.

Every now and then, he would stop what he was doing and play through different scenarios in his head, just trying them out for size. Life had been easy and carefree running the construction company, and dabbling in the various startups Connor ran, that he had to admit.

It was no wonder they had all let Connor do as he wished. It allowed them to be involved in some exotic business deals without actually being involved in said business deals. The best of both worlds.

Now, he had the dubious pleasure of calling himself a drug dealer, running a cannabis company. Not something he had had on his life plan a few years ago.

If he could solve all of the company's problems, it might be fun to run it, yes. But therein lay the rub—if he could solve them.

And Kayla.

His best friend's ex-girlfriend. Ex-best friend's ex-girlfriend. Beyond complicated. But in this group, why should anything ever be easy and straightforward?

Al was right, indeed. He really did have to stop messing around and start figuring this stuff out, for his own good and the good of those around him.

Connor was not coming back. He wasn't keeping a seat warm for his former pal, or entertaining his girlfriend until such a time as Connor could step in again and do the talking. Nope. Connor Beauregard had made his choice.

There was nothing to wait for, no old friend to welcome back.

Rafael had read the letter personally, more than once. The prosecutor had dropped the case against Connor Beauregard in its entirety due to the lack of substantial evidence. Period. Whatever he may or may not have done, Teflon Beauregard had gotten away with it. And still he hadn't come back. Which meant only one thing: he never was.

Rafael put his hands flat on the table before him. Whatever he did or didn't do with this company they had started together was his own business and no one else's.

And Kayla…

"I'm not so sure about you," Al had finally told him. "Here's this beautiful woman, smart, charming, wealthy. And you are not entirely sure if you want to keep seeing her. You're not sure, Rafael? With all due respect, I know we're friends, but…"

He didn't have to wait for the rest; he knew it already. What Al was too polite to say was merely the truth: he was being a dumbass. A real dumbass.

Rafael sighed, pushed off the tabletop, and stood. Spreading his arms, he laced his hands behind his head and walked over to the window of his office, looking out over the busyness down on the street.

First things first, he needed to speak to Kayla and make things right. She usually understood and had his back. This time, she might want to do some of the rear kicking he had so generously promised Irv Moody.

Then on to the business of business.

Perfect Cannabis Corporation. Consolidated if you wanted to add something, but not GT. GT sounded like they were selling used cars, he thought. And he still wasn't sure if it stood for Green Technologies or Greg Turner.

Stop stalling, Covin, and call it. Yes or no? Are you or are you not committing to stay with this thing? At least a couple of years?

It sure as hell would be a bigger challenge than putting up high-rise buildings all over town.

It might be fun, he thought. *Plain old fun to build a thing like this from the beginning, to put it together and be there when it finally takes its first couple of steps.*

Forget about Ivers, who would tire of giving him a hard time soon enough, when he didn't need to ask for money every day. He'd be working with Al as his right-hand man—he had already decided that—and with Kayla. They'd make a fantastic team. And they'd find room for Turner, somewhere within the company structure.

He'd be the one guy nobody liked, who'd keep them all honest at the same time, make sure they didn't get too big for their own ideas.

He sighed and walked away from the window, standing by his desk, looking down at the old beat-up chair.

All right then.

He picked up his phone and dialed the extension for Connie.

"Hey, Connie? Are you still there for a while?"

"Certainly, Rafael, what do you need?"

"Well, I thought… If you don't mind—could you have the fellas in Security pick up my old chair in here and put it away somewhere where nobody can smell it? And when that's done… perhaps you can order me a new one from the office supply place you use."

"Oh, thank all the gods, the day has come."

"It's not that bad."

"Rafael, the thing smells horrid."

"Not that bad."

"Never mind—consider it done. Immediately."

"Don't be that eager now…"

Rafael laughed and finally felt his good mood returning. No turning back now. He was staying, and he was making this work. End of story. Chair or no chair.

Once his mind was made up, he could feel his energy returning, as if he had been in some sort of suspended animation while he waited for things to happen around him, as if by deciding to stay he had cleared a logjam, and all of a sudden, he knew what had to be done, how, when, and by whom.

He dialed Kayla's private extension and waited for her to answer. It took more than her usual two rings, which worried him just a tiny little bit.

"Hey there, beautiful," he said when she finally did pick up. "Are you up for taking lunch with a guy who is a complete idiot?"

"Dare I hope you are referring to yourself, Rafael Covin?"

"You dare. Thanks to you and Al."

"So, it finally sank in, did it," she said with a good measure of satisfaction. She was probably smiling. Matter of fact, he could hear it in her voice. She was smiling all right, but he didn't even care.

"Yes," he said with a sigh. "And for what it's worth, I am sorry."

"No need. I'm sure."

Rafael took a deep breath and let it out with a whoosh.

"I—well—I think it's time to man up, put my money where my mouth is…"

"Just spit it out, will you?"

"I made Connie throw out my old chair."

Kayla let that sink in for a moment and chuckled softly. "I guess you're hanging around in this business for a while then, are you?"

"I am," he simply said and paced around his office, scratching his head. "Although it does mean I'm finally going to have to move to our building, 'cause now I got nowhere to sit."

"I put a perfectly good chair in there for you."

"I kind of—might have given that away."

Her laughter made up for any doubts he might have had, and it made him chuckle himself.

"Some sort of idiot, huh?"

"That's all right. You came around to the right decision in the end. Didn't take you all that long."

"The right decision—yeah, well…"

"No changing your mind now. I am warning you."

"I won't—swear I won't."

"Good. I'm coming by your office in five minutes, with a new chair. And I'm picking you up for lunch."

It took her 10 minutes in any case, not that he minded, knowing she had probably taken the time to doll up in the private powder room off her office, and whatever apology he had to offer, it would not nearly be enough to make up for everything.

THIRTY-SEVEN

"What made you change your mind?" she asked when they had settled into a little British pub around the corner, where they served Rafa's favorite curry.

"You, Al…" Rafael shrugged. "No—mostly you."

"You sure?"

"And Al telling me I was being a colossal ass for making you mad by flip-flopping on every single decision."

"That man is brilliant."

"Don't let him hear that. I'll never hear the end of it."

"So now…?'

"Now…" Rafael played with his glass, pushing it here and there on the scarred tabletop. "The way I figure it, Connor's never coming back."

"I could have told you that."

"Took me a while to believe it. But I do. And whatever I do or don't do with this company, or do or don't do with… "

"With his former girlfriend," Kayla finished when he hesitated. "Yes?"

"It's really none of his business any longer, end of story. He's the one who drove this cart into a pile of you-know-what and left us behind to sort out his mess."

"That would be Connor."

"If it's OK with you, I mean. That is, hanging with somebody who might—who could be… Well, just as bad."

"Not unless I can teach you to speak in complete, easy-to-understand sentences, Rafael Covin. What on earth are you trying to ask me? If indeed you are asking something. It's kind of hard to tell the way you are stammering."

"You know, you and me…"

"No, I don't know, Rafael. You really are going to have to learn to speak."

"OK, you see…" He ran his fingers through his hair yet again, although it probably stood on end from all of his efforts, and sighed.

"I think we should…"

His cell phone tweeted to let him know a text just had arrived. Normally, Rafael frowned upon interrupting dinner or a conversation in mid-sentence to see what else might be going on. Normally, but this time he picked up his phone with a single swipe, running for the escape hatch of not having to explain their relationship in any way.

"Excuse me."

Kayla rolled her eyes with an amused smirk, all but telling him he wasn't getting away that easy. Not at all.

"Greg Turner? What does he want right now? The man's never texted me before."

And he hadn't. Instantly, all of his defenses came up, as if just now a gun-toting masked man had stepped into the pub. He squinted even as he fumbled in his jacket pocket for the little wire-rimmed readers he carried.

'Found a way to eliminate the chef. We leaders, our key personnel, and your investor ditch the companies, start over… clean newco.'

Rafael's fingers tightened on the phone. Damn Greg Turner. He'd known the man was headed there. The moment he smelled money, he came around like a shark when there was blood in the water.

"Rafael, what is it?"

He looked up into the concerned eyes of Kayla and realized that he was muttering under his breath.

"You look like you've just seen a ghost."

"Damn that man," he said.

"What man—Ivers?"

"Read. But keep it to yourself." He pushed the phone towards her and shook his head. "The moment he smelled Irv Moody's money, he wanted to find a way to get rid of Tadeo Ivers, by any means possible."

"Except this does not read like a buyout." Kayla pushed the phone back to his side of the table.

"No shit." Rafael looked one last time and put the phone back into his pocket. "Thank God we haven't ordered yet. I have to leave. I have to straighten him out. There's no way I'm letting this happen."

"What about this is freaking you out?"

"Don't you get it?" Rafael made an effort to lower his voice. "What he is suggesting? He wants to take Irv's money and the key people from his and our company and start over."

"Well, isn't that…?"

"Start over, Kayla. Clean Newco, ditch the existing companies and the investors, and the debt that's accumulated in both. Just walk away and start new. With Irv's money."

"But you can't do that. Your investors…"

"No, of course I can't do that."

"There are assets. You have commitments… There is the building, for God's sake."

"The building runs in the name of a separate company. An SPV. It's… It's not as straightforward as all that. I have to stop Turner from contacting all the other executives and causing a riot. I have to get to them before…"

Kayla's cell phone chirped at the same time, and Rafael sat back down again. Almost in slow motion, Kayla took the little device out of her pocket and checked the screen.

"Too late," she said without emotion. "Too late, Rafael."

Rafael looked and read an almost identical text, just a little more explicit, worded a little better.

"Whatever you do, don't reply please."

"Geez, Rafa—really?"

"Sorry." He stood there and ran his hands through his hair again and again, as if he were going to tear it out. "Did everybody get this, can you see?"

"Don't know, but…"

Rafael's phone rang, and he looked at the display again. Irv Moody.

"I would guess they did," he said and answered the call, already on his way to the car. "Irv, whatever you do, don't answer him."

"What the hell is this, Rafael?"

"I don't know, but I swear to you this did not come from me. I did not know until two minutes ago what Turner was doing, and I am trying to undo it as fast as I can."

"Is he fucking serious? This guy is suggesting we deep-six both companies and start over… with my money? With my money, Rafael? Is that what I'm reading?"

"Irv, I can't tell you any more than this is not something I would ever even think about. I had no idea…"

"And all the investors, and all the people who are owed money by either company? They're just going to have to suck it up? Yes? While the gentlemen from Perfect Cannabis and Green Technologies start out another company, The Perfect Green maybe. Not with my money, Covin. You can just stick that where the sun don't shine."

Rafael flew through the lobby at Montecito Publishing without stopping. Recognizing his panic-mode dead sprint, visitors, clerks, and messengers deftly sidestepped him and stayed out of his way. Everyone recognized a man on a mission.

"Irv, I am serious," Rafael said, fumbling in his pocket for the keys to his office. "I did not know anything about this. At all. Jesus, there is no way I would be part of anything like this—no way at all. Man, you have to know me better than this."

"Maybe…" Irving hesitated a little bit. "I just don't like it when I become party to an almost criminal act all of a sudden."

"This is not happening, Irv. I am telling you right here and now that this is not happening. I will not personally do any kind of business with Greg Turner ever again, that enough for you? If that's the way the man thinks, fuck what Tadeo wants—this merger is not happening."

"Breathe, man, you sound like you're having the big one in a minute."

"I am—I think—I have…"

Rafael dropped into his new chair and took a deep breath. *Don't have a goddamn heart attack now,* he admonished himself. *Not for Greg Turner.* He put a hand on his heart and started.

"I have to get my board together. And Tadeo Ivers, like it or not. We need to talk about this. I don't know who all got this so-called invitation, but we are not doing it. Not with me."

"That's more like the old Rafa…"

"Irv, this is not funny."

"I know that—I do. Sorry, when I got this thing, I hit the roof. I didn't really think you were in on it, but I had to be sure."

"You can be 100 percent goddamn guaranteed sure. That bastard Turner." He looked up and saw Kayla step through the door; she had finally caught up with him. "Irv, I gotta try and fix this. I'll call you back in a little while, OK?"

"You need a hand with anything?"

"I probably do, and thanks for offering, but I can't take you up on this right now. You're still an outsider, and this is—God, this is just a replay of the day we found out that Connor…"

"Go, Rafael, and just make sure there's no replay."

Rafael hung up and turned to Kayla with a sheepish look on his face.

"Sorry. I left you standing there at the restaurant. I can't believe it—I don't usually…"

"I'm good... What's our next move?"

"You heard me. I need to get the board together, and I need to find out who got this goddamn text—sorry for the language."

Kayla only waved him off. "Then?"

"Then we are going to have to talk to Ivers and weather that storm. I cannot in good conscience merge companies with a man like Turner. Even if Turner pulls back, even if he says—whatever he's going to say. We're not dealing with someone who make a suggestion like that."

"I don't imagine you could save that merger, no."

"Save it? Kayla, the man just suggested screwing millions of dollars' worth of investors and creditors. Let me tell you something that I'm never going back on. This merger is not happening. Not in this lifetime, not while I'm in charge at PerCan."

"I... well, good."

"Because it's assholes like Turner who ruin good business, and screw ethics, and whatever the hell else I do, I will make sure he does not get another chance at ruining this company."

His phone rang with an unknown number, and he picked it up.

"What?"

"Um, Rafael?"

"Yeah. Look, I'm in the middle..."

"It's Nick—Nick Ambrose."

"Nick, shit, I am sorry. I didn't recognize you. My apologies. Look, I'm in the middle of a bit of a crisis here and..."

"I imagine you are, if it has anything to do with the text Greg Turner just sent around."

"You too?"

If he had been standing up, Rafael would have lost ground under his feet. Nick Ambrose? Of course, Nick Ambrose, he thought after a second when the news finally had penetrated all the way to his brain. Of course, Nick Ambrose, the best grower the United States had to offer. Who else to make this deal really sweet, and round out the dream team Greg was trying to build, off the books? Who else?

"Look, Nick, I'm going to tell you what I told everybody else. I had no idea this was going down. I just found out a moment ago when I got that same text."

"Then you are not planning…"

"Oh, fuck no. I am not going to stand here and let that man take apart everything I've just spent years building and then repairing. There are a few dark spots in our corporate history, but Perfect Cannabis is a great company and a perfectly viable entity. We have shareholders, we have partners, and we are not deep-sixing any of them."

"He said it was because of the history and because of that finance fella—Ivers."

"You answered him." Rafael sighed. "Look, I can imagine what he told you." Rafael took a clearing breath and started again. "Sorry, Nick, yes, I can imagine what he said, and I know what he wants, but it is not happening. Not with this company, not with me at the helm."

"Then the merger is off?"

"This particular merger, yes."

"I don't have to tell you how much work we did to make the grows viable, to develop a program that works, policy, procedure…"

"I realize that."

"It is not specific to your current building, and current team, but darn close to it. I don't want to have to start over elsewhere and…"

"Nick! I know."

"Long as you do, Rafael." Nick sighed. "I'm telling you shit you don't need to know, but I've put my life in Colorado on hold for this thing, I've put a lot of effort into it, and I don't want it to come apart because some yahoo…"

"Thinks he can walk away with everything. Well, guess what, Nick, we're not going to let him."

Nick said nothing.

"I am not. We have a merger on the table and an LOI and documents that are about to be signed. About to be. We can still walk away."

"And then what, Rafael? You didn't start in on this merger because it was getting lonely up on the executive floor. You needed them for their name and their license, am I right?"

"You are right."

"And you still do. If you walk away now, you still don't have a license. You still depend on somebody to finance you. I don't want to work on something that might run out of steam sooner rather than later. I'm hearing a death knell here."

"Nothing's changed on financing, Nick. Financing might actually be one area where things are about to get a little easier."

"Why, because Ivers is going to reach deeper into his pocket?"

"No." Rafael thought for a moment and finally kicked back in his chair, his equivalent of throwing his hands up in the air. "There is a large investor who wants to come into the company. I suspect this investor is actually what is behind Turner's attempt to cut the companies loose."

"This is out of control, Rafael. I am not..."

"Nick, please. Turner smelled the money and tried to find a way to walk away from the debt in his company and the history and problems in ours."

"And from Ivers, I gather."

"And from Ivers. But that's not how we roll over here. I am not playing ball."

"Jesus, Rafael, if you walk away now, you're starting all over. Where does the license come from, or the money, merger or no merger...? It does not look all that..."

"Your contract and my commitment to you are not changing. So do me a favor please. Do not reply to Turner again in any way and keep doing your job. Just keep doing your job as if nothing had happened and let me worry about Turner and his *suggestion*. Can you do that?"

"A little while longer, yeah, sure, but I need some assurances. I don't envy your job right now, don't have to tell you that."

"No, you don't."

Rafael hung up the phone and exhaled in one big whoosh.

"Nick Ambrose," he said by way of explanation, and Kayla shook her head.

"I heard. He got that text too?"

"Yup, he's doing a solid job, our friend Turner. I can see what he wants."

"A whole new setup?"

"Shuffle the cards, pass by Go, collect your money, and start over. Screw everybody who put funds into PerCan. Screw the estate of his deceased director. Take the key people and the money that's left and, most importantly, Irv's money."

"And start over. Nice. Did he think you would go along?"

"Apparently, he thought we would all go along. He is wrong." He rested his wrist against his mouth for a moment and waited. "At least I hope he's wrong."

"What are you looking at me for? You think I would? Are you nuts?"

"I don't know what I am right now, Kayla. I feel like something just fell on my head. I can't even begin to process what just happened."

"Still, you would think that of me?"

"No. No, fuck. Of course not, sorry."

"Slow down, one step at a time, OK?"

Kayla rose and stepped around him, putting her hands on his neck, and started massaging his tight muscles. Rafael closed his eyes and exhaled again.

"Thanks."

"The last thing we need to do right now is fight amongst ourselves."

"Sorry."

"We need to have a meeting, deciding how to deal with Turner. I gather Tadeo knows nothing of this?"

"I... doubt it. Al hasn't... Shit, I don't know where Al is in this entire thing."

"Unaware, I would assume. Hope. If Turner wants to remove Tadeo Ivers from the deal, it would make sense…"

"It would make sense to keep all of the Ivers family out of the loop, and that includes Al."

"What about Dante?"

"Yes, what about Dante… Exactly." Rafael snapped upright again, put his feet square on the floor, and pushed her hands ever so gently off his neck. "Time to find out. I need to call a meeting. Think Tadeo will…"

His phone signaled the arrival of yet another text, and he picked it up like he would have a snake that had just fallen asleep. When he read the new arrival, his face split in an enormous grin, and he actually couldn't help laughing out loud.

"Go check your phone," he said to Kayla. "I think he actually copied you."

"On what, who?"

"Just read it."

Kayla looked down on her phone and smiled, shaking her head.

"Oh, so politically incorrect," she said, "but from the way you describe him, oh so Irving Moody. I cannot wait to meet the man."

Right there on the screen was the image of a middle finger, nicely extended from the remaining fingers curled back against the palm. Underneath it, a very brief and very terse message read, 'With all due respect, Greg, go fuck yourself.'

***

It took only moments to catch up Al on the latest crisis, and barely 10 minutes later, he stood in Rafael's office, eyes narrowed with suspicion, hands stuffed into his pockets, containing the restless energy. Sheer fury leached from every pore.

"Did the fool think my father would just sit back and let this happen? Shrug it off? Walk away? What?"

"I don't know what he thought, Al. I also don't have the time to worry about it right now. I need to get everyone on the same page."

"No doubt."

"You think your father will leave that diner for once and join the meeting?"

"Doubt it."

"Can you speak in complete sentences please, Al? I know you're pissed off, but I am trying to fix this, and I would rather not call a board meeting in the back room of the diner if I can avoid it. Your father should be there."

Al's eyes blazed anger at him, and for a moment, Rafael fought the impulse to take a step back. They were friends, but the fury still struck him like a punch. Don't ever get the Ivers clan mad. Good advice at any time.

"Then call it wherever, Rafael, and wait to see if he joins you. Don't ask me to be your errand boy. Might I remind you that neither he nor I are on said board? I'm not even officially involved in this company, so tell me why I should worry about it."

"Because I need your help right now, and I'm hoping you won't turn me down or leave us hanging, that's why."

Dark eyes held his for an uncomfortably long moment, and Rafael imagined he could feel it—the blaze of sheer anger right there, right behind that calm forehead and composed face. Al finally looked away, forced himself to calm by sheer willpower, and sat in Rafael's visitor's chair.

"And what would you be requiring my help with, Rafael? Calling a board meeting? Hardly. Your secretary can do that on the inside of two minutes."

"You know what I need. I need some—insight—in how to best handle your father so he doesn't blow up on us."

"Blow up?"

"Yes, and do something—ill-advised."

"Ill-advised," Al said sagely and raised his hands when Rafael blazed at him. "Cool it, Rafa."

"I'm not in a joking mood just at the moment. I know you are pissed. So am I. Let's just fix this thing and talk later."

"Talk later?" Al asked, and Rafael wanted to strangle him.

"Yes. Talk later, Al," he all but hissed. "You know I want you on my board. I always have. I never wanted your father to shut you out. That's not the issue here. The issue is how do I approach it so he will actually pull on the same rope with me, instead of putting blocks in my way, hampering my each and every move with nonsensical crap nobody cares about except him?"

"Best advice—go tell him what's happening right this minute, before he hears it from somebody else."

"OK."

"Whatever you do, do not tell him Turner's main motive is to get rid of him—or of Dante. That'll make him blow up in your face for sure."

"Might be hard to hide that. This whole episode screams it."

"Then let it scream, Rafa. Listen to me. Pretend the thought of Turner wanting to shut out my father never occurred to you. Pretend it's the furthest thing from your mind."

"And that'll work?"

"Maybe. But it will save face and has a better chance of working than anything else in this mess. Tadeo is a difficult business partner."

"No shit."

"But like everybody else, he does not want to hear that he is the reason the deal did not go down. It's just human nature, Rafa."

"OK, yeah. Makes sense."

"Then allow him to pretend. Let him come around by himself to the thought of cancelling the merger and going with Mariposa. Make him think you are standing with him."

"Turner has already cancelled the merger. I just need to formalize it and get all of my financial statements out of that ridiculous man's hands. And my good-faith payment," Rafael muttered and picked up his phone again. "You stay right here, Al. If only so you can kick me if I say the wrong thing. Hard if you please."

"You won't need me to kick, trust me."

THIRTY-EIGHT

In Singapore, the good reverend could hardly keep his joy contained. He'd been drinking steadily since he heard what Greg Turner had done, had actually read the text in question, and he had no intentions of quitting. Again and again, he read Greg Turner's message and slapped his leg.

"This is brilliant. This is just so absolutely brilliant!"

"Nice of you to mention it." Rob took a small sip from his own drink. "Better watch it with the drinking."

"I can hold my liquor just fine, thank you. And why not, pray tell? I am in the mood to celebrate."

"You are drawing attention to yourself, and to me. I don't like it. I would tell you that a reverend is not supposed to drink, but nobody is buying that act any longer. They haven't in a couple of weeks. So please…"

Barry waved his hand through the air, brushing away Rob's warning.

"Plus, we are not finished yet. They still have to formalize cancellation of their merger and look at the one you want. They haven't walked away yet."

"Mariposa, you can say it. And they will, don't you worry about it."

"There are a lot of moving parts to this thing. It's a little early to go celebrating quite yet."

"Then you can sit there and wait all you want, can't you," Barry said, balled up his room service ticket, and fired it at a wastebasket.

"You can damn well sit there and be that guy who says careful all the time. Rafael used to be that guy."

"He's not wrong. There are no guarantees."

"Well, I'm giving you one." Barry struck the tabletop, and Rob jumped a little, looking around.

"Christ, Con…"

"Barry."

"Barry. Do not freak out on me again. Do I have to remind you what happened last time you lost it?"

Barry took another long draft from his drink. "Yeah, Roberto, why don't you remember what happens when I lose it? Why don't you remember? Does that sound like a good idea, hmmm?"

Roberto said nothing and continued to chew on a toothpick. Only his eyes narrowed a little, and the muscles in his hand tensed. God, he disliked the man sitting across from him, hated him even at times. But he had nothing else on the go right now, and this man needed him desperately, so he hung in. Just for the feeling of being needed for a change, and he hated that, too.

"Do what you want, 'Barry,'" he finally said. "And call yourself whatever you want, no skin off my nose. All I'm saying is there's still a chance for this thing to go sideways if they get just a whiff something isn't what it appears to be. And when that happens, there won't be a merger… at all."

"You wouldn't be stupid enough to threaten me now, would you? Because I have to tell you, that would be a very bad move."

"What, me—threaten you? Whatever made you think that? I'm just telling you to hold your horses for a little while. Don't get piss-ass drunk, and don't do anything that will draw attention. I don't want to be the one whose fault it is when shit hits the fan."

"It won't. I can feel it."

Barry only nodded again.

"Brilliant—absolutely brilliant move, if I haven't told you before. What was it again they were involved in, a restaurant?"

Roberto rolled his eyes and rested his chin in his hand. "A club. One of those fancy nightclubs downtown. Used to belong to Turner's real father. I told you that."

"I know. I just like to hear the story. It is too good, way too good."

"He screwed it up, tried to gamble his way into money, borrowed money from the wrong people, and got ever deeper into a hole. You would know all about that, now, wouldn't you?"

"I never went gambling to double whatever I had, though," Barry said with a sly little grin, "nor did I lose my last dime doing so or leave gambling debts…"

"For Tadeo to buy up, I know," Rob said, rolling his eyes. "Aren't you the choir boy, now? My old man bought up all of the guy's markers. And then took the club from him. Pretty much destroyed Turner's father."

"Last time you said it ruined him."

"Kind of," Roberto said slowly. "He couldn't deal, left town because of it, and left Turner and his mother behind. From what I read, they fell on hard times after that. Your friend Turner didn't exactly have a pretty childhood and took his mother's maiden name, to forget, I would imagine."

"Which is why his last name is now Turner, and Tadeo Ivers never recognized him," Barry finished, rubbing his hands. "I so love it when fate is a bitch that plays right into my hands. I couldn't have set it up better. Years later, Greg Turner is seemingly in charge of the company financed by the man who ruined his father."

"I hear tell Turner's father actually killed himself later." Rob shrugged, and Barry rubbed his hands.

He never tired of hearing this particular story. Ever since Roberto had explained to him exactly why and how he was planning to use Greg Turner to torpedo the impending merger, ever since he had put together this plan and recognized the sheer simplicity and perfection of it, he had to stop himself from jumping with joy.

Perfect—better than perfect.

"How perfectly genius of you to remind Turner of that bit of history. Original Chef, my ass." He tossed back the remainder of his drink and shook his head. "Who is holding the strings now, pray tell me, who is the puppet master now?"

"Puppet master, you're out of your mind!" Roberto shook his head again and rose from his chair, pushing back. "And be careful. Jesus."

"Rob…"

Barry called after him, but the man had already covered the rooftop patio in giant strides, disappearing through a door at the far end. No problem. Barry could happily celebrate their victory by himself.

THIRTY-NINE

Rafael took a clearing breath and dialed Tadeo Ivers's number. Mentally, he had prepared himself for everything, except for the possibility that Tadeo should remain completely calm.

"This does indeed not bode well for a merger with this man and his company," he finally said, after Rafael had explained what had transpired in the past few hours.

"Not bode well? Did you hear what I said, Tadeo?" Rafael asked, struggling to regain his footing. "Greg Turner already cancelled this merger and tried to hijack key personnel from Perfect Cannabis as well as an investor."

"Nothing has been signed, has it?" Tadeo asked slowly. "No commitments made we cannot get out of?"

Rafael spread his hands helplessly and looked at Al, sitting across from him. Al could only make a circling motion with his hand. Keep going. They had agreed he should stay silent and merely listen to the conversation, so as not to infuriate Tadeo any further. Knowing Rafael had involved Al into what he considered 'his' company still irked him, and he never missed a chance to threaten Al and Rafael that he was gone if he screwed up.

"No, thank god. We were still mired in due diligence issues when…"

"Due diligence, just another way for lawyers to steal money right out of my pockets, for God's sake."

"Normally, I would agree with you, Tadeo. In this case, I'm glad all of this came up before we put our signatures on anything irreversible, saddling us with Turner. I want to make sure you understand this merger cannot proceed."

"Who the hell does he think he is? I spent good money on this. Gave him a good-faith payment of $1 million. I paid for those lawyers."

Rafael shivered a little at Tadeo's icy tone. Right now, he thought, at this very moment, he would hate to be in Greg Turner's shoes, having Tadeo Ivers's wrath directed at him. He shook his head again to clear the image and coughed discreetly.

"I need to call a meeting of the board of directors here, Tadeo, formally vote to cancel the agreements we had, assure everyone that we have no interest in Turner's proposition, that kind of thing. I just—wanted you to hear it from me."

"It is an outrage."

"You're not wrong. In any case, those of our executives who received that cursed text will need to be assured that this is not what is happening. Those who did not…"

"Those who did not," Tadeo laughed, and the hollow, dry sound, like crackling reeds, send a shiver down Rafael's spine again. "Yes—those who did not will go home and wonder why they were not similarly propositioned, will they not, Rafael? Perhaps they were not worthy of such betrayal, you think?"

"Right at this point, I only know that Kayla was approached, and Nick Ambrose. A major investor I had lined up, and myself."

"And when were you going to tell me about said major investor, Rafael? Is that something you planned to keep quiet, just to see if there was another way to structure this deal and this company? A similar way to what Greg Turner is suggesting perhaps?"

"Absolutely not," Rafael shot back. "If I have told you once, I have told you a dozen times. I'm committed to Perfect Cannabis and its success. I'm here for the duration until the company is where it should be."

"I hear your words, yes…"

"The reason I have not told you about this investor is that the man had not even decided to put money into the company until just recently. It was agreed that he wouldn't come in until after the merger was complete. It was agreed we would do the investment in such a way as to keep all the original shareholders' equity positions intact. That includes you. I was getting to giving you the good news when this happened."

"But you told Turner."

"Turner. Yes—Turner found out. Maybe a mistake on my part. A weak moment, I thought to reassure him that once the merger was completed, we could all look forward to a brighter future for the company."

"A brighter future…"

"I had no idea he would do something like this."

"Obviously you did not, Rafael Covin. Or it would have been a pretty stupid idea to entertain the thought of a company merger with such a man."

Well, you were the one who picked Turner and Green Technologies, Rafael wanted to say and barely bit the words back before they slipped out of his mouth. Al nodded slowly, and Rafael pushed on.

"I'm calling a board meeting shortly to update everyone. Did you wish to be present?"

"I am not on the board of directors."

"No, but you are the major shareholder. You're a man of considerable influence and say in this company, you authorized my paying one million to Turner, and as such I would think…"

"I don't need to sit in a room of self-important men to do what needs to be done. Remove every trace of this despicable Turner ever having had any contact with my company. And do it quickly. I want to see you in my office tomorrow."

"OK," Rafael said, before the words *yes, sir,* could slip out.

"I told you from the very beginning this merger was a bad idea. Something my son Al cooked up to disrupt the company. I told you in the beginning."

"The merger in principle was a good idea. We needed it then, and we need it now. It's just the execution…"

"We will discuss this tomorrow. I tire of this," Tadeo spat and slammed the phone down at his end.

Rafael sat back, dumbfounded, staring at the phone in his hand.

"I tire of this," he asked Al, shaking his head. "I tire of this? What the hell is going on with him? Has he gone completely insane?"

"He knows exactly why Turner cancelled the merger." Al shrugged. "He liked the deal but didn't like Tadeo. It's only because you didn't mention this that he went easy on you."

"Easy on me, I hadn't noticed," Rafael said darkly. "Still—he is acting strange, even for Tadeo Ivers. Sorry."

"No need."

"And he felt the need to bash you again, just for an added bonus. This is one strange family dynamic you have there."

"You'll get used to it eventually."

"I doubt it. Now I have to call this damned meeting and explain to everyone what is going on."

"Have fun with that."

"While you, my friend, help me figure out a way to convince your father that the idea of a merger is still valid, and we still need to go through with it or go under. Things haven't changed, only the players."

"Well, isn't Irving…"

"No, he is not. Irving was ready to invest in a viable company. With the current merger off the table for the moment, that is no longer the case. I can't in good conscience accept his funds without letting him know he may be throwing them down a large, deep hole."

"But wouldn't he…"

"No, he would not, Al. Irv wants to invest, OK, cool. But I will accept his investment if and when I can reasonably assure him that the company has a fighting chance. I need to be able to look him in the eye and tell him I will do my level best to make his investment work. Otherwise, he might as well take his money and start his own company."

"Yes, but…"

Al did not really understand, Rafael could see it on his face. Al wanted to say, *Let's just take Irv's money and run with it.*

If he'd been just a little uncomfortable about the friendship between him and Irv, the enormous amount of money involved and the risks inherent in the whole thing, if he had just had a bit of doubt before, now he didn't even want to touch Irv's money until everything was clear and in order again.

Clear and in order, whatever that meant in this business.

"He can always give us a loan, if we run into massive trouble." He softened the blow a little. "He wants into this business, and I would be stupid to stop him. I'm not cancelling his investment, just postponing it until I have this mess sorted out. Which includes getting a license. I'll not ask Irv to throw money out the window. That's just what Greg Turner was trying to do."

Al finally nodded. "OK, I hear you."

"Our problems are still here, Al. We have a bad rap with the licensing body and the Ministry of Health. The shadow of Connor Beauregard refuses to go away. It would be a mistake to give up on the merger at this point. Investment or no."

"OK, OK, I said I got it." Al raised his hands, surrendering. "But I have to tell you my father is going to give you the same argument. When he hears how much money Irv was ready to put in, he'll tell you to go see Irv for cash, quit bugging him, and drop the merger idea. Which, I might mention, he was against in the first place."

"Fine, then I'll tell him Irving Moody no longer wants to invest in this company, period, end of story."

"He'll want to talk to him."

"Let him. You can't make a guy put money into your company, just because he was interested at one point in time. Doesn't work that way."

"Again, I don't envy you."

"You don't have to, Al. I'm good. You want to know something? I learned a good bit from the whole thing. If I had stuck to my guns right away, gone with my instinct, insisted on the merger partner I had picked out and run this company the way I knew it needed to be run, then none of this would have happened."

"Maybe not none…"

"Maybe not none—you're being kind, and I thank you for that, but I did exactly what I said I wouldn't do. I let other people tell me how to do my job. And it is not going to happen again."

"A promise?"

"One you can take to the bank, buddy."

***

In a hurry, he had the workers from Covin Construction put a temporary conference room together, pulling furniture from other companies and rooms, rushing Roger and his people just to the point of being annoying. He needed to make his mark now, and he needed to make it here, in the future head office of Perfect Cannabis.

He walked in, dropped his briefcase on one of the mismatched chairs, and looked around. The room smelled strongly of the white paint they had used, probably just that morning. A few ceiling tiles were still missing, and wires hung out of several openings in the walls. Instead of an electrical outlet, he found a couple of extension cords snaking through a gap in the wallboards, and his feet hit bare painted concrete underfoot. Good enough. He had had meetings in worse places, and they were not trying to be on *Better Homes & Gardens* with their meeting space.

Kayla, who had come with him, looked around and crinkled her nose.

"I would say, 'love what you've done with the place,' but I really can't."

"It's coming along. Interior decorating was not at the top of our priority list over the last few months. This will do."

"Not like anybody will pay attention to the décor."

"Not like," Rafael confirmed and took a seat.

"I don't think we'll be long. All we have to do is confirm that we are no longer following through with the merger with Green Technologies, that we will take steps to recover our good-faith payments…"

"How much did you give him?"

"A million," Rafael said, making a face. "Wish Tadeo hadn't, but it's too late now. The moment I am out of this meeting, I'll send a lawyer with a bad reputation crawling up Turner's ass. He'll wish he had never messed with us."

"Too late now, isn't it? Then there is point three, another merger?" She pushed the agenda away from her and sought out his eyes. "Isn't it a little early?"

"Nope. Matter of fact, it's too late. I'm going to tell you the same thing I told Al earlier. We still need this merger done with another company. We still have problems we can't solve on our own, without delaying any kind of growing, harvesting, selling, or earning for several years. Several. I'm not kidding. The sooner we get to grow, the better it will be for this company and its shareholders. We cannot run out of money. And the fastest way to get there is still by merging with an existing company that lacks our resources and facilities, but has a license."

"Maybe with Irving's help…"

"Maybe with Irving's help, we could have done a lot of things, but Irving is out of the game, at least for now."

"He is?"

"He is. I would really rather wait until the others are here to explain it, but as of a short time ago, Irv pulled back his offer until such a time as we have our house in order."

Kayla searched his face, but Rafael had prepared himself. He gave nothing away. With a shrug, he looked down at his papers and gave his agenda one last scrutinizing look. The other board members were bound to ask the same question—*why not use Irving's money to get us out of the hole?* And here was the answer: *because that money is off the table.*

"Sorry."

"Sorry I'm late."

Simon almost ran into the room, with Josh on his heels. "Bit crazy out there with all the construction still going on."

"It is. I apologize for the state of our conference room, but I thought it would be better to start having all of our meetings here, in our own building from now on."

Dante wandered in from whatever portion of the building he had been working on, nodded at the men, and shook hands with Kayla.

"We're all here then?"

"We are," Rafael started. "You all have an idea why, and what happened over the last few days, so I don't have to spend all that much time on catching you up."

"Turner, what the hell got into him?" Simon asked. "I got his text, and I thought I was having a bad dream. I mean, the guy just…"

"I know, Simon, I know. We all got the same text. I don't think we need to waste any time going over why he did what he did."

"No, but I would still like to know what happened. Why did the guy go crazy all of a sudden when just days before everything was going along fine? A man doesn't change his mind just like that, so something must have happened, and I would like to know what, if it's all the same to you."

"Of course it is. But understand I have no way of reading the man's mind."

"Not asking you to."

"As near as I can figure, he got wind of a major investor who was toying with the idea of investing with us or, more precisely, the new company after the merger."

"That's nothing new. We're a public company. We sell shares all the time." Simon looked from Kayla to Rafael to Josh and back. "Well, don't we?"

"We do," Rafael confirmed. "This was going to be a slightly larger investment. Plus, the person who wanted to make it had an interest in getting involved in the company. All in all, it looked like a nice fit and a really good thing for the company."

"OK." Simon suddenly stopped. "Good, OK. But you're speaking in past tense. That's not good."

"No, and I am getting to that. Believe me, I'm getting to that. I can't read his mind, but as far as I can tell, Greg Turner smelled money, saw an opportunity, and decided perhaps it would be far more cost-efficient to drop the liabilities and baggage inherent in both companies—both companies. Take the new investor's money and start over."

"Whole lot of bullshit that is," Josh muttered. "We have investors, shareholders, people who've been here since day one. Did he think he could just ditch all of that and say, 'sucks to be you?' That's illegal."

"Again, I don't know what he thought, Josh, and I don't care to know the man's mind either. What is clear right off the top is that we no longer wish to do business with him."

"Business of any kind," Kayla said and raised her hand. "Agreed. When my magazine and I get through with him…"

"Never mind that now. There's no need, although the thought adds some levity here." Rafael smiled. "We're all officially agreed then on cancelling the merger plans with Green Technologies, invalidating the letter of intent, and officially severing any and all ties between the two companies, whatever they may be?"

General murmurs of agreement met him; Dante had actually raised his hand. Probably glad that the problem at hand had nothing to do with him, for once.

From what he heard, Rafael thought, Dante was shaping up to be a decent apprentice and assistant to Nick Ambrose. After years of doing nothing but being the middle son, Dante apparently had found his place in the world, and he didn't want to see it ruined by his father. There was another rumor going around about Dante and Nick being a lot closer than just mentor and mentee—but Rafael decided it was nobody's business.

He'd mentioned as such. If he had anything to do with it, Dante would see the day when he was head grower in charge of the biggest Medical Marijuana Corporation in the country, and this day would not be too far away.

For now, Rafael nodded at Dante with an encouraging smile.

"I notice a qualifier in that statement," Josh Novak said cautiously and looked down at the notes he had made.

"Your exact words were, 'the merger plans with Green Technologies.' I heard a little emphasis there."

"That's correct, Josh. Surely you don't want to suggest we even entertain the thought of a merger with this company?"

"God, no. What I'm suggesting is that we don't even entertain the thought of any kind of merger with any kind of company at this point in time. Live and learn, Rafael. This almost cost us the company. Don't you all agree?"

Josh looked around for support, and Rafael met Kayla's eyes. Almost imperceptibly, he shook his head.

"I thought I had explained that particular issue, Josh. We still need a merger partner with an active license if we want to be doing any kind of business before we're old and grey. There is another partner I have identified…"

"You mean because you did so well picking the first one? You felt comfortable enough to put our fate into this man's hands, and now you're just going to say, oh shoot, I missed on that one? Let's try again? Like this is a lottery game? Something is wrong here."

"Green Technologies was not my first choice," Rafael said carefully and couldn't bring himself to meet Dante's eyes.

Dante raised his head and straightened a little.

"My father chose Green Technologies," he said simply, and Rafael's head snapped up. His eyes met Dante's and held for a moment. "That's right," Dante said again. "Rafael had chosen a different company as the initial merger target because he was uncomfortable with GT, but my father—well, my father did what he always does. The exact opposite of what everyone expects."

"And you just sat there, Rafael? I have to say…"

"Josh, I understand where you are coming from, really. I hear your concerns. At the time, we decided a merger was our best course of action, and we went out to research potential targets…"

"Who's we, Rafael? Who exactly is we?"

"Al and myself."

"Al—yet another Ivers. These are the people who have our company's fate in their hands. I fail to understand why that does not concern you."

"Tadeo Ivers has financed the lion's share of expenses over the past several months. Please don't forget that, Josh."

"Far be it from me. I'm merely making an observation here. The Ivers family seems to want to own and run this company without actually doing so, if you don't mind the comment."

"Josh, this really is not Rafael's fault." Dante spoke up again, and Rafael felt a surge of admiration for the young man's newfound courage and backbone. He'd gone from a spoiled youth spending Daddy's money to… to a real man. That's what it was. Dante had turned into his own man.

"The merger target Rafael had initially identified had a lot of potential. They would have been my choice as well, for what it's worth. Then my father came in to throw his weight around."

"As he is wont to do, right or wrong, isn't that so?"

"Correct, but please let me finish, Josh."

Score one, Dante. Rafael almost grinned when he saw Josh blushing just a little. Josh had his reaction under control instantly, but Rafael had spotted the flash of embarrassment and got a childish kick out of it. Josh put way too much weight into his own opinions, given enough time to do so.

"As you perhaps know if you have followed our update circulars, we had just come out of difficult negotiations with Nick Ambrose—the world-famous grower who will put this company on the map once and for all."

"I thought you were supposed to do that."

"And I will, but in order to make that possible, I have to learn everything I can from Nick Ambrose. We needed him for the credit and reputation his name brings to this company. If you want to blame someone for that fact, go right ahead. Here I am."

"No—I—please continue."

"The financing to hire Nick wasn't there. It just wasn't there. Along with financing for a lot of expenses on the build-out and a stack of old unpaid bills that surfaced all of a sudden. So, Rafael fought a battle with my father over financing these items, and he won. I was there, so you can be sure when I call it a battle, it was one."

Rafael shrugged and raised his hands a bit. *Don't overdo it now, kid*, he wanted to say, but Dante was on a roll.

"So, you understand, having come out of a major disagreement like that one, when Rafael did not want to engage Tadeo again over something that looked like a minor issue."

"I thought you preferred—the other company, whatever the other merger partner was—as well."

"I did. But in the end, I came to the same conclusion as Rafael did. The differences looked marginal, and mostly rooted in the personnel side of things. If we could make it work, it would be worth it not to enrage Tadeo Ivers once again and risk cancellation of the entire financing package. That would have put an end to the whole company, let me assure you."

Dante paused and fixed Josh in his most penetrating Ivers stare, but for once, even Josh didn't have a smart comment to throw in.

"So yes, Josh, you are completely correct. We did go with the wrong merger partner. It was a risk we took to keep peace in the company, and no one could predict that Greg Turner would go rogue when he heard about a new investor. There was a vote of this board, and we all put our names to it, all of us."

Dante had talked himself into quite a steam, and Rafael raised both of his hands again.

"OK. Enough. Thank you, Dante, I appreciate you speaking up, especially since it concerns a sensitive, family issue. I made the decision, and it was the wrong one. I'm perfectly prepared to take the consequences for it. What I can't do is ensure this company's success if it remains mired in government red tape and waiting lists without a license. Gentlemen, we need a license to grow, period. We cannot survive for much longer without it, no matter how much money Ivers has."

He looked around the table and let that sink in for a moment.

"One man, no matter how large his private fortune, cannot save this company and carry it indefinitely. We need help."

"And that investor is definitely off the table?"

"That investor is off," Rafael confirmed, crossing himself mentally. "Until we have cleaned up our house, so to speak. So, we are at the exact same point where we were three months ago. We need this merger, and we need it now more than ever."

He sat back and folded his hands on the table before him, letting that statement sink in for a moment.

Irrationally, Connor Beauregard came to mind while he did. Connor and his mesmerizing way of speaking.

Dramatic pauses, Rafael, dramatic pauses are one of the most important and underestimated tools in a speaker's toolbox. Want to know why the preacher says amen? For the dramatic pause. Let it really penetrate and marinate. Amen.

Amen, he thought, and watched the thoughts race across the foreheads of his fellow board members. *Say nothing now, nothing at all. Wait and let them come around on their own.*

"OK, OK," Josh finally said. "I get it. We're sunk without a license, and we can't get a license unless we're willing to wait it out, potentially indefinitely."

"That's it in a nutshell," Rafael confirmed. "Which is why, in my opinion, we should still pursue the avenue of a merger. With another, more responsible company."

"All right." Josh shook his head and shuffled through the papers in front of him he had been using to make notes. "I still don't like it, Rafa. I understand it, but I don't like it."

Same here, Rafael thought. He didn't really like it either. It felt like losing a part of the company, but he knew it was absolutely necessary if PerCan were to survive. And survive it would. Not in its present form, no, but it would survive. He let the silence drag a little and finally put his hands flat on the table in front of him.

"I'm willing to live with anything you, the board, decide." He looked around from one to the next, trying to gauge their reaction.

No one dared meet his eyes, not even Kayla. Kayla, who he was so sure was in his corner. Even she looked down at her meeting notes and made an effort not to move a muscle. He knew her. Unless you held her hands down and taped her mouth shut, she was always moving, speaking gesticulating, expressing herself... Not this time.

Dante followed a fine line in the pattern of the tabletop with his finger back and forth, and Simon, Simon seemed to look down at his fingernails and appeared to have forgotten where he was at that particular moment.

"You tell me what you want me to do, gents—and lady. I am willing to throw in my hat to the best of my abilities and live with it. I've given you the options, such as I see them, and that's all I can do. One man can't—shouldn't—make all of the decisions for a company such as this one. That's why we have a board."

Again, he waited. He knew what they were thinking; there were risks. Risks in what he was proposing and risks in not doing what he was proposing.

"What about Ivers?" Josh asked. "He's a majority shareholder. Should he not be part of this decision process?"

"To a certain extent, he can give us direction, Josh, that is correct. But we here…" He spun his index finger in a circle to include everyone in their little group. "We here are the board of directors of Perfect Cannabis Corporation. Tadeo, as majority shareholder, can always vote a new board in, but while we are here, we make the decisions. We decide what direction the company is going to take. Now more than ever, we need to stand up and make use of that right, or forever be Tadeo Ivers's little group of yes-men. Sorry, Dante."

"That's all right. No offense taken. If you will allow me to speak…"

"Naturally, this is a closed meeting—speak freely, Dante. What's on your mind?"

"My father has a lot of experience in business, you know that. But public companies, not so much. He still tries to run everything like his own little kingdom."

Rafael nodded without speaking. *Does he ever,* he thought. *My way or the highway.*

"Rafael is right. We need to speak up now, as a board, or he will forever tell us what to do and what he wants."

"Wow, Dante, you've grown a pair," Simon said, his left eyebrow raised almost all the way to his hairline. "And here I thought you were just the number two son, put in here to keep an eye on us."

"I was, and you all knew that, and I'm embarrassed about it. But, working with Nick… I don't know. I found some—respect—for the job, and I really enjoy it."

"So, we have to show your father now who is boss, is that what you're saying?" Josh asked, and Dante nodded.

"That's about the extent of it. And I, for my part, am willing to stand up and say yes, Rafael. Go, identify another target for a merger, let us all look at it and decide as a board, and then we'll go tell Dad— Tadeo—our decision."

Rafael smiled. *Go, Dante*, he wanted to say again, if he could have without embarrassing the lad any more. Fine, another youth had found his place in the world. He couldn't have been more proud if it had been one of his own sons who had finally figured out what he wanted. That would come…

He looked around, and his gaze landed on Josh.

"Josh, you said you got it earlier."

"I did." The other man nodded. "I still do. I'm still uncomfortable considering what just happened to us, but I might just have to live with that discomfort for a bit."

"Up to you."

"OK. You got me. I'm in. I'm voting with young mister Dante here to tell you to go find us another merger partner."

"So am I." Kayla finally raised her hand. "You know I have every confidence in you, Rafael. You'll do the right thing, because you… Well…" Kayla blushed a little. "Well, you're good at it, that's all."

"Indeed." Rafael grinned. It would have taken a deaf and blind man not to see what was going on with him and Kayla, but much to their credit, none of the men around the table commented on it.

It would take some explaining going forward what exactly that 'something' was, and eventually, one of them might actually have to leave the board, but that was a while yet. For now, he could enjoy it, whatever 'it' actually was.

"Well, Simon, it's actually a formality to ask how you would vote, but I respect your presence and opinion, and I want to hear it."

"Like Josh, I'm uncomfortable with the idea, Rafa. And I also understand why we need to do it. I just wish there was another solution, that's all."

Rafael nodded and said nothing for a moment.

"I gather, from hearing all of you talk, that there is not. I too don't have the experience with public companies that I should." He sighed and spread his hands. "Be that as it may, here we are. We're damned if we don't and we might be damned if we do. You really think this is the best way, the only way to proceed, Rafael? Truly and honestly?"

"I do, Simon."

"Right-o. I thought I'd try. We might as well make it unanimous then. We are all voting for you to continue looking into alternate merger partners."

Rafael exhaled deeply a breath he didn't know he had been holding. What would have happened if they had all voted against him today? There was no one out there to save the company, no white knight in shining armor, no million-dollar bank bailout, as Irving Moody might have invested, but Rafael simply couldn't see himself taking his money, until…

"Thank you for your confidence, gentlemen—and lady."

"This time, we all want to be involved in what happens when you choose another partner, you hear," Josh warned. "There will be no more lone wolf actions."

"I hear you. And moreover, Tadeo Ivers will hear you as well, and he's going to have to live with the decision of this board."

And I'm looking forward to that moment, he thought. *I am really looking forward to telling that pompous so-and-so that the board of directors has decided something, and his choices are as follows: a) take it, b) leave it.*

"You're enjoying this, aren't you," Dante murmured close to him as they packed up and prepared to leave the makeshift conference room again.

Dante had brought a pack of loose-leaf notes, a clipboard, and several rolled-up diagrams with him. That boy was not only getting into his job; he was starting to live and breathe it.

"You bet I do." Rafael grinned. He nodded down at all the material in Dante's hands. "And it looks like you're getting to love the business of being a drug lord."

"Especially the part where it's all legal." Dante said and snapped his diagrams on his palm. "Who would have thought it, one of our family, getting into the legal drug business? If you had told me a year ago…"

"If you had told me a couple of years ago I would leave Covin Construction and be running a marijuana company, I would have asked you if you'd been smoking a tad too much of said product. C'est la vie. Here we are."

"Yup. You're going to explain this to my dad?"

"I will try."

"He's going to blow his stack."

"Just a little. He'll huff, and he'll puff." Rafael laughed and spread his arms. "And then he will actually have to admit that I do know what I'm doing and that this board has made a decision, and that's it."

"He might threaten you to walk away."

"Yup. He might do at that. And then he will lose everything he has put into this company thus far. If that's what he wants, I have some guys who will pick up PerCan for pennies on the dollar and kiss his hand on the way out."

"Jesus…"

"Dante." Rafael stopped and put his hand on the young man's shoulder. "You know—you and I have not always seen eye to eye on this project."

Dante shrugged one shoulder to say, 'you got that right.'

"But since Nick came on, and you've been working with him, you've really become the kind of guy I want to have on my team."

"Um—thanks."

Dante looked as if he had lost something vitally important down somewhere by his left shoe, and his life depended on locating it, so Rafael pushed on.

"Take it any way you want to, Dante. I don't hand out compliments just like that. But going forward, you're the guy I want on the grows, heading up the department. I want you to know that."

"Thanks, again."

"So, whatever happens when I go tell your dad, just keep that in mind, will you? I wouldn't even begin to guess the finer points of

Ivers family politics, but don't let him push you into a place you don't want to be."

Dante said nothing, and Rafael thought he might have leaned just a tad too far out the window. Knowing himself, he probably had, but some things needed to be said when they came to mind, or they would disappear forever.

"Anyway, who knows what's going to happen? Don't go taking an old man's rant all that serious. Go back to whatever you were doing with Nick before this meeting, and wish me luck."

"You got it."

FORTY

You got it.

Rafael drove to the meeting with Tadeo, his mind racing ten ways in every direction. His car could find the way by now on its own. Good thing, he thought, since he definitely could be considered driving distractedly. Shit—he wanted this company, he realized quite suddenly.

Almost as much as Connor had, he wanted Perfect Cannabis Corporation. He wanted it to succeed and thrive, he wanted it to be the best ever, and he wanted to be the guy standing there, pointing at it, and saying, *I did this.*

Ego, for sure.

But he wanted it, and the hell if he'd let Tadeo Ivers tell him how to run it and how to screw it up. This merger was good, this merger was what they needed, and one way or another he would talk Ivers into it.

He hoped.

He had already sold Ivers on the merger the first time around. Tadeo knew he would never get a license—never, period.

Connor had screwed up well enough to make sure it would be a long time before Perfect Cannabis received its own license to produce marijuana at all, and his business partner Ivers was, well, not grade-A licensable!

Rafael set his turn signal and grinned. God, he remembered Connor taking the Minister of Health for a jaunt on his famous helicopter to go to Martha's Vineyard for a sailing competition. On the surface, it was a clean and a nice little outing.

Nothing crass, just generating a bit of goodwill all around.

Except the thing went sour, there were drugs, there were underage prostitutes, there was a lot of press. A general, all-around fuck-up.

So here he was, Rafael Covin, construction company owner extraordinaire, trying to make the impossible possible, trying to get a company with a big black mark on the record, and a questionable business partner, a license to produce medical marijuana.

They damn well needed this merger.

***

"Greg Turner is a crook, no two ways about it," he said to Tadeo after he finally faced him, having gone through the now familiar, if boring ritual, of going to the diner, ordering a coffee, and waiting for Miss Dinah to allow him backstage.

Miss Dinah—sure. The lady had a set of muscles on her a professional athlete would be proud of, and she shuffled around that diner, but Rafael had seen her in an unguarded moment, and she had the grace of a cat.

She could cook too. Her pies were out of this world, as he had discovered waiting for Tadeo.

"Tadeo, we need to get back to work on this merger. If this company wants to survive, we need it. I know you don't like it."

"You are not wrong."

"I know there are risks in exposing our company to other partners."

"Now you come to me with this information."

"But I don't see another way."

"There has to be one."

"Tadeo…" Rafael rested his hand in his chin and shook his head. "I know it's none of my business, but what's the net value of your private fortune?"

"What makes you think I would share such information with you? Who do you think you are?"

"Never mind. You know I never lied to you. I do a lot of things, but I don't lie."

Ivers did not look impressed. Rafael ran his fingers through his hair and looked around himself. The dingy diner, the worn furniture, dim lights. Sure, the whole thing probably served as a cover as far as the tax department was concerned. Walk in here and see nothing.

It need not mean anything, but Rafael saw the man sitting across from him, a man who did not like to spend money, a man who knew the exact value of every penny, squeezed or not.

"You knew the history of this company when you bought the majority of shares, did you not?"

"Don't ask questions to which you already know the answer."

"You knew we were never going to get a license until every last company with a squeaky-clean record had one. And by then, well by then, the market would be good and saturated."

"You, Rafael, you are here to solve this problem. Not to lecture me, but to solve this problem. That's why I hired you. That's why I am…"

"Paying me? No, you're not, Tadeo, remember? You wanted me to forego any kind of payment when I asked you to hire Nick Ambrose."

Tadeo Ivers made a quick gesture like swiping a fly away from his face, and his eyes flashed that familiar dark fire, but underneath was something else.

He's worried, Rafael thought. *He might want you to think he is cool and in charge of everything and everyone, but he's worried.* Perfect Cannabis Corporation had likely grown over his head a long time ago. He didn't understand the dynamic in the corporation, if he ever had. He had no idea what was going on, and what it meant to the health of his company, and his sons weren't much help.

Dante suddenly enjoyed his work with the growers, made a real effort, and had probably distanced himself from his father. Al, the son he had all but dismissed, probably because he was jealous of him, had become Rafael's confidante and sounding board, and Roberto…

Well, Roberto, the black sheep of the family, the one son who could have been some real help to Tadeo now, he had been sent away on an extended vacation, so Tadeo wouldn't have to deal with him.

Rafael leaned back and met the cold eyes without flinching. He even crossed his legs to show how unconcerned he was and continued to hold Ivers's stare until the other man looked down at his hands on the table.

Holy shit, for the first time ever, Tadeo Ivers had looked away first. Rafael made a fist under the table and dug his nails in to stop the silly grin that wanted to spread on his face. Tadeo Ivers had looked away, holy shit.

"This is going to bankrupt you," he said simply. "Waiting to receive a license, continuing to finance a building, staff, utilities, it will bankrupt you. Sooner rather than later. And if you walk away now…" He shrugged and spread his hands.

"Then I will shut you down," Ivers spat with a defiant toss of his head. "Then where will you be?"

"Don't know. Build things," Rafael said and shrugged. "Unlike you, I do not actually care. It does not matter one iota to me if I'm running a construction company or a cannabis one. None. And if you want to ruin the company to get your revenge, then fine, I will start over elsewhere because I've done it before. Make no mistake—you shot all your powder when you threatened me to take this job."

"I can still ruin you. And your sons."

"Possibly, and then what? My sons are young. They'll start over too. We all will, but you, you are going to be broke. And I happen to know that you have enemies. What do you think they will do the moment they find out Tadeo Ivers can't pay for security guards any longer, huh? That there is nobody following you around keeping an eye behind and to all sides of you? Does that thought cross your mind late at night? Because if it were me, it sure would."

"Do not make an enemy of me, Rafael. I am warning you."

Rafael leaned forward and stared directly at the man across the table. "And I am warning you, Ivers—do not make an enemy out of me either. Because I can and I will make or break this company. All I have to do is this." He snapped his fingers and held the stare just a bit longer than directly necessary.

Then he leaned back again, let out a long breath, and spread his hands.

"But that's not why I am here, is it? I'm here because I want to save this company, build it up, and see it grow. For God's sake, I want all of us to make money here. Why is this so hard to understand?"

Ivers said nothing, as if Rafael's sudden defiance had taken him by complete surprise, and he was still three thoughts behind.

"I want Perfect Cannabis to be on the map, where it belongs. And in order to do this, we need to merge with a smaller company and take over an existing license to grow. The board happens to agree with me."

"Tell me how you are going to safeguard my company this time," Ivers asked, and Rafael decided to skip over the 'my company.' If he tried to explain public companies right now...

"Mariposa Products," he said slowly. "The company I had identified as the most promising merger partner when we started all of this."

"You and Al, you mean."

"Yes, Al was of tremendous help in researching and checking out this company, and don't try to get me to say otherwise. I won't. We looked into this company, we did our due diligence, and we decided they were the perfect target for what we were trying to do."

He spent another 15 minutes explaining to Ivers why they had thought Mariposa made the perfect partner, he picked apart the company structure and financing needs, he described in detail why he thought the two companies would mesh perfectly, and when he had talked until he felt he had no more words left, he sat back, suddenly exhausted.

"I want to do this, Tadeo. I want to do it because it makes sense, and because I think it will save this company. You made me CEO, even though you hogtie me at every turn. I'm asking that you let me proceed here and don't put any more stones into my path. We can succeed, please."

Ivers still didn't like it. Rafael could almost smell it. Every muscle in the man's face told him he hated the idea. And still, even Tadeo Ivers had to admit when he was sunk. No way out. No lifeline, except for the man sitting before him. He finally nodded.

"What's it going to take?" he asked, and Rafael sat up a little straighter.

"Not much. Al and I will approach them in the coming week and see if they're still interested in talking about a partnership. God willing nobody else has approached them in the meantime."

"I still don't like it."

"I know."

"But you are saying it has to be done, and there is no other way."

"There is no other way to save this company unless you have unlimited funds to wait out the Ministry of Health, and even then…"

***

He walked out of the meeting with his head spinning and the ground below his feet wobbling, although he was reasonably sure there wasn't an earthquake. Might as well have been one. Had he just won a major victory over the man everybody else in this world simply said yes to? Had he just bested Tadeo Ivers?

Rafael sat in his car and drove back to his own side of town, navigating on pure instinct and autopilot responses. He had finally done it.

Stopped at a red light, he threw back his head and roared with laughter until the motorists left and right of him started to stare. Who would have thought it? Straitlaced Covin had beat four-gun Tadeo Ivers. Unbelievable.

***

He had instructed a crew of five men to move his office and everything within it to the new building, and when he walked in, he almost felt at home there. There was construction going on all around him, smells, sights, and sounds, and for a moment, he thought the two worlds he loved the most had come together.

The guys had put his office back together almost the same way it had been at Kayla's building, and he dropped into his new chair. No picture window in this place, and unfortunately, he had had to leave Connie behind. At least until he could afford his own PA. He would miss her, yes, but he had a newfound determination driving him now.

Technically, he thought, flinging his laptop bag onto a spare chair, raising a cloud of dust, technically, it made no sense at all, this sudden renewed energy he felt. He had to quell the nasty rumors about this company, chase Greg Turner, for the cool million Tadeo had given him as a good-faith payment, approach Mariposa carefully, put together a major merger, finish construction on this building, and, if all of that didn't kill him, finally start producing.

He had enough on his plate to keep five guys busy for an extended period of time, never mind one. And all of it without getting paid.

If he had heard this story at The Lighthouse bar, he would have bought the poor unfortunate sod a beer, recommended he walk away, and commiserated extensively with him.

Extensively.

Instead, here he sat, the poor unfortunate sod, looking forward to tackling all of his tasks one after the other—or all at once, whichever. He couldn't wait to get in there and get going.

Made no sense at all, but maybe it was one of the side effects of winning one over Tadeo Ivers. Facing down the dragon and having the dragon blink first. Felt pretty good. He put his head back and laughed again, not caring for once if anyone passed by his office and went on gossiping that Covin had finally lost his mind. Let them.

He kicked back, put his feet on the table, and reached for his phone. One of the benefits of working in the middle of major construction, he thought. He didn't have to worry about putting his feet on his desk or making a general mess anywhere. The mess came pre-made, no worries.

"Al," he said when his friend answered. "Time to get our shit together to go see the folks at Mariposa. When can you be ready?"

Al said nothing for a moment, and Rafael heard him shuffling some papers in the background.

"You are in a suspiciously jovial mood, my friend," he finally answered. "Not the standard response I would have expected from anyone who just went to see Tadeo. If you don't mind my asking…"

"I do not. He looked away."

"Pardon me?"

"I asked him if he wanted to go bankrupt. We had to follow through with the merger or forget it. We had a staring contest, and he blinked first."

Another long pause.

"Al?"

"I'm still here, yes. I just don't believe what I'm hearing."

"Why, because your father finally saw reason?"

"No, because you are so cheerfully chatting about it as if you two had gone to have a drink together. And, permit the observation, you seem to be in a fine mood."

"I am."

Another long pause.

"Oh, come on, Al, I can't be the only one. As in—ever."

"Well…"

"OK, never mind, Al. Now get your ass down to the building and help me plan our approach to Mariposa. We can't miss on this one, and I need you. Unless you've got something better to do this afternoon of course."

"Something besides working with the only man in known history who ever got the best of my father? Heavens beware."

"Did I already tell you today you're being an ass?"

"No, but you did mention I should carry mine down there and help you work on a merger you are planning."

"Ass!"

Rafael hung up, flung the phone on his desk, and laughed out loud again. This time, he knew he attracted the attention of some construction workers passing by his doorless office, and still, he did not bother to care.

***

Al brought some decent ideas with him. It was likely, he mentioned, that the executives at Mariposa had heard at least a rumor of the merger that had been in the works with Green Technologies. Better to come right out and play with a set of open cards, he counseled. Without necessarily bashing Greg Turner.

That last part made sense, even if it rankled. No need to go causing more hard feelings or really kick a guy who was sure to go down. Greg Turner had hand-shoveled Green Technology's grave with his actions. Still, Rafael fought the urge to kick something every time the man's name came up, even in casual conversation. He'd told Kayla to leave it be, but for some reason, Green Technologies and its mercurial founder were mentioned rather frequently in the gossip column of her paper, not usually in a favorable light.

Rafael had an image of one of her photographers following Greg around everywhere he went and made a mental note not to get Kayla or anyone on her staff mad without a good reason.

Prudence demanded they mention the merger and the vote against pursuing it. Perhaps one could use the standard 'personality conflicts within management' phrase, though even that did not sit well with Al.

"Say nothing," he counseled Rafael. "Just say nothing. You decided not to do it, period, end of statement."

"But won't they…"

"They will. And they will ask, but at least you will be the guy who wouldn't go badmouthing a former business partner. Difficult as that may be."

"I'd like to stay away from the entire subject if it's at all possible. If anyone over there brings it up, fine, but I don't want to volunteer anything I don't have to. This time, it has to work out, Al. We're running out of time."

"Our shareholders have all the confidence in the world in you."

"Awesome. No pressure at all. Thanks, Al."

Al shrugged. "You asked."

"I know." Rafael drummed his fingers on his desk pad and finally looked up. "If you don't mind, I'd like to have you copiloting on this one."

"Me? But wouldn't they…"

"Everybody who is anybody in this industry knows your father has a majority stake here. You being there with me just makes sense. Plus, in your own inimitable way, perhaps you can keep me from saying something stupid."

Al only raised one eyebrow again and said nothing, but Rafael knew he had scored. He might try to hide it, but he could spot the pleased smirk on Al's face a mile off.

***

They pooled their efforts after their meeting, carefully approaching the management at Mariposa Industries, first for some casual chats, exploratory meetings, and countless dinners and social events. Feelers were stretched out and casually explored the general idea. Could they do it? Could it work?

The same questions were asked on either side. There had to be some chatter on the executive floor at Mariposa, about the failed merger with GT, probably rumors and stories.

But they came prepared. Both Al and Rafael had a few simple explanations they trotted out every time the subject came up, which was fortunately not often.

This time, Rafael swore, this time he would make darn sure he knew who he was dealing with. Kayla would joke and tell him he watched Thomas Donnelly, CEO of Mariposa Industries, as if he were about to propose to him, and Rafael would joke about buying a ring. Some days, he felt as if it were not a joke.

Screw due diligence. This time he would find any and all skeletons, no matter what dank closets they hid in. He would drag them out, examine them, and have Al take them apart and make darn sure there was nothing gross underneath.

Meeting after meeting passed, and Rafael found nothing. Mariposa appeared to be just what he expected—a nice, clean, midsize company manufacturing marijuana. They had no idea how to optimize their grow process, they lost too many harvests to diseases and fungi, their management was inexperienced and ineffective, and everybody spent way too much time cleaning up messes instead of moving forward. In short, they knew they were in trouble.

They needed help, funds, information, resources, and training. And Perfect Cannabis Corporation had all of that.

Rafael approached the subject as carefully as he could, mentioning Nick Ambrose and his 'team,' and all the wonderful work they were doing, the ongoing research into protecting the cannabis plants and the construction on the building. This beautiful factory they were creating in the most perfect spot just outside town, with direct railway connections and a road out to the airport that was close enough to double as an emergency runway if anyone ever needed it.

He realized that he had become the storyteller. Whenever he slipped into story mode and proceeded to paint a picture for an investor, business partner, or, in this case, merger partner, he remembered Connor Beauregard and his 'prime story mode.'

Connor had countless faults, and Rafael could name them all—but Connor could also build castles in the air, right before the listener's eyes. He could make anything sound perfect, desirable, fabulous, and divine down to the last detail. No chance of failure, no potential for loss. He knew what you wanted and told you there was a surefire way to get it. And all you had to do was believe him.

Nobody told a story like Connor, nobody.

Except, Rafael thought, he seemed to have picked up the talent. When he got excited about the project—as he was right now—he could feel it too, that knowledge that he could move mountains with no more effort than a single thought.

***

"You spoke exceedingly well," Al mentioned, as they sat over a beer at The Lighthouse, celebrating another successful exploration meeting with the upper-level executives from Mariposa. It had become late enough that the crowds had thinned out, the bartender cleaned up, dreaming of quitting time, and beyond the window front, the lights over the town had not only come on, but were slowly extinguishing again one at a time.

Rafael knew he should be exhausted, bone-weary after another day of convincing, sidestepping, explaining and proving, telling and retelling. By all rights, he should have dropped dead a few hours ago and be sound asleep on his couch at home, but an inexhaustible internal fire kept him going.

"Did well, did I?" he asked and smirked. "I kind of thought they were buying it, but you never know."

"Buying it? By the time the evening came to an end, their CEO wanted you to adopt him if there wasn't going to be a merger."

"You're exaggerating just a little."

"I wish I were, my friend. You've grown into this talent without batting an eyelash. If I were not afraid to offend you, I might suggest you were channeling Connor Beauregard."

"You hush up your mouth before I do it for you. And I don't bat eyelashes. That's Kayla's territory."

"I mean it. You speak as convincingly as I've ever heard him speak. And he was good—very, very good."

"That he was," Rafael took a deep swallow of beer and looked out over the city. "And the only reason I'm not slugging you is because I was thinking the same thing just now."

"Do you ever wonder what happened to him?" Al asked, and Rafael folded his fingers before his mouth.

"Yes—no—maybe—I don't know. You said it. The one thing Connor did best was talk and convince. So, unless something drastic happened, I would assume he's somewhere in a country far, far away without an extradition agreement, selling something. Like self-improvement tapes, or courses on how to double your selling rates, religion, or booze…"

Al laughed and took a swig himself. "And that is a never mind on the extradition agreement. We both know the case was dropped."

"Yup, he could have come back if he wanted to."

"Any time, and nobody could do a thing about it."

FORTY-ONE

Sitting in a hotel room in Singapore, far above the city, he ordered his second bottle of champagne, in a lonely celebration, all while packing his suitcase, getting ready to leave.

Goodbye, Singapore. The time had finally come to step up to his revenge, to see *his* dream realized, and his enemies vanquished.

Wait a minute, he thought. That last bit was brilliant, his enemies vanquished. Yeah, that was brilliant, worthy of the good reverend and his fiery sermons, indeed. He'd remember this one.

Maybe he'd write a book one day. Or maybe he'd just follow through on his plan, get his revenge, get the corporation and the position he'd been dreaming of, and leave well enough alone. So close to having everything he wanted right in his hand.

His right hand still bore the scars of a temper tantrum from what seemed like a lifetime ago, and he had come into the habit of rubbing those scars. Two red welts along the back of his hand, to remind him that he still had a task to complete. But he was close.

Another swig of champagne. So close to grinding into the dirt all those who had opposed him way back when, leaving him to flee through a bathroom, running away like a thief in the night.

He could see their faces before him, one by one, and he wanted them gone. Gone for good. He would win. Nothing else mattered.

His cell phone rang, and he took one look at the display, frowned, and flung it back onto the bed. Roberto was beginning to be a nuisance.

He always wanted to have his hands in everything, got involved where he should not, and he knew things. Things nobody should know but the master himself.

How to deal with the little sneak? Dammit if he didn't need him, for the moment at least. Roberto had done good work for him. He'd ferreted out information where no one else could and been a first-class spy. He couldn't have done it better himself. And later, when he had his company back, he might even need him more than he did right now, for his knowledge and his connections.

He sat on the bed, picked up his phone again, and tossed it from one hand to the other. But here was the best part about the whole thing: no one could connect him to anything. Not now, not ever. No one would know or suspect until he was ready to show his cards.

He smiled when he thought of that moment, an ugly, cold sneer that would have struck fear into other men's hearts if any had been there to see it. No mirth or joviality lived in that smile; it spoke of revenge and pure hatred.

He couldn't help it. Every time he thought of the moment when he would open the door to a conference room somewhere, knowing they all sat inside discussing some nonsense, knowing they didn't suspect a thing, until the door opened, and he walked in, and they realized…

What would they say, he wondered? His former friend, his woman, oh yes. She who had come closer to him than anyone, close enough to stab him in the back. He would step in, smiling.

The others, the others would likely sit there, open-mouthed.

He allowed himself only a few minutes of daydreaming every day, but it was good. It had become his drug of choice, his driving force, getting a hold of that feeling.

Roberto knew it. He'd seen the gleam in his eyes, and the satisfied little groan that sometimes escaped his lips when the fantasy became too real. That made him clench his fists every time.

Patience, he thought, *just a little more patience, and Roberto, too, would be an extra, ready to be cut loose.*

He stared down at his phone again and curled his fingers around the edges. Patience. Where else would he get a business partner who was not only useful and knowledgeable, but also perfectly set to take the blame for almost everything? Where?

Roberto could look back on a long and distinguished criminal record, which made him the perfect business partner in this case. And his connections in the murkier parts of the drug business? Worth their weight in gold.

As much as the man annoyed him at times, regularly of late, he had to keep him around.

Sighing, he turned on his phone and called the number back.

"Yes."

"Oh, hey there, Conn—Barry. Did I catch you in the loo?"

"What's happening?" he asked in clipped tones, unwilling to give anything away, least of all his earlier train of thought.

"They're getting ready, so you better do the same."

"Already working on it."

"Yeah?"

"Bags are packed. I head out a few days from now."

"A few days?"

"I need to make sure everything is perfect before I come back. What's it to you?"

"Nothing, just making conversation. Let me know when you get into town."

Barry hung up without confirming the request and stood by the window. He needed a few more documents and letters of confirmation, and then the good Reverend Barry could legally immigrate to his old country. And by the time anyone realized what was going on, by that time, it would be too late to do anything about it.

FORTY-TWO

"There are a couple of silent partners," Rafael said, pushing a tightly stapled document across the table towards Al. He had highlighted in yellow the relevant sections. "That worry you in any way?"

"I don't know. I'm not happy about it," Al said, flipping back and forth by a couple of pages. "I'd rather put a name and a face to these ownership percentages, to make sure they're clean."

"Thomas mentioned it was a private corporation, registered in Europe. They put in their money, but passive investors." Rafael shrugged, "Thomas wasn't concerned."

"OK." Al seemed hesitant.

"Hey, we've investigated this from every conceivable angle."

"And Thomas has done the same with our information. He is a prudent, careful guy as well."

"Does it worry you that he did?"

Al shook his head. "Not in the slightest. I know exactly what comes up when you do exhaustive research on me. Mostly because I put all of the information there myself."

"Jesus. These are the moments I'm glad you're on my side, you know that?"

"There are no sides here, Rafael."

"Yeah, yeah, this is me you're talking to, remember. Now back to these entries for the silent partners. A couple of basically offshore corporations? Is anything about that worrisome?"

Al pulled the document back to his side of the table and tapped the highlighted lines with his fingers.

"I can't say, and that troubles me a little."

"In what way?"

"Last time something seemed off, the merger blew up. We can't afford the same thing to happen again. We need this merger to go off perfectly this time."

"And so far, it's doing just that," Rafael said.

"I don't need to remind you this is our last line of defense. We can't afford there to be the slightest hair in this soup. That usually means there is…"

"So, what are you saying?"

"I feel I should do a little more research into these people—these corporations—who collectively own quite a bit of Mariposa."

"Collectively? Wait. They're scattered all over the world, it looks like." Rafael pulled the document back. "I've never thought of this as collective anything."

"I might be getting paranoid, Rafael. I really might."

"Paranoia can be a good thing, Al. Especially given the experience we just went through. Don't hold back, please."

Al sat back and closed his eyes for a moment. When he spoke again, his words came out with a frustrated sigh.

"I don't know, Rafa. If it were any other situation, any other company, any other set of circumstances…"

"It's not. Speak."

"Then you and I both would say, 'Hey, everything looks relatively good. Let's do this,' don't you think?"

"Correct."

"But because of everything we've just gone through with my father…"

"And with Greg Asshole Turner."

"And with Mr. Turner, we're sitting waffling, worrying about keeping our panties clean."

"I don't know about you, Al, but I usually don't wear…"

A stern look from his friend shut him up, just as both their faces split into wide grins.

"You're right. We wouldn't usually be this exhaustive in our research and due diligence, but if something here gives you pause to think, then stop and let's do some more—investigations."

Al sighed again and shook his head. "It's not unusual for big investors to use offshore companies to make an investment. And there are always a couple of skeletons in every company. So no, I don't think we should freak out…"

"Where's the *but*?"

"But perhaps one of my guys should… make a couple of quiet phone calls, see if he can figure out who's in the driver's seat with those companies. All we need is a quick look. If everything is clean—no harm done."

"No harm done." Rafael slapped his palms flat down onto his desk, raising a little puff of dust. "OK, let's do it. Now that wasn't too hard, was it?"

"Not really, and caution is…"

"Is the better part of putting together a public company. Or something like that."

"Indeed. So, let's look at getting a cleaning service in here, at least now and then. The dust devils are big enough to pick you up and carry you outside, if they so chose."

"Devils, yes—dust, never mind. It serves as an excuse to get out and have a beer. Speaking of which, let's do that."

***

They settled into their accustomed barstools, waving away the bartender's tired jokes about their moving in, bringing their suitcases, and sleeping in the janitor's closet.

"He'll never get tired of it," Rafael said, sighing, "and in a way, this whole thing is his fault."

"His fault? In what way?"

"Right here, right at this bar." Rafael patted the marble bar top lightly. "Right here, the idea for Perfect Cannabis was born. And that fella over there...." he nodded toward the bartender, "had a relative or friend or whatnot who had to take medicinal marijuana and complained to Connor about it. That's how the whole thing got started."

"Could have done worse. You're lucky he didn't suffer from anything requiring leech therapies, now."

"Always Mr. Bright Side, aren't you, Al?"

"I have heard that raising leeches for medical purposes is quite the business nowadays."

"Lovely image. Just for that, I ought to stick you with the bar tab for a few months."

"Don't you usually?"

"Wouldn't have to if your father paid me like every other CEO."

"That's going to stop soon as the merger is all arranged. Can't have our CEO running around begging for spare change."

"Speaking of which," Rafael said and became serious in an instant. "You'll reach out to a few people, find out what these offshore companies are all about?"

"Already done."

"Huh? How...?"

"I made a few phone calls while you gave the workmen instructions they did not really need. It appears to me they've done their jobs before."

"Sure, they have." Then he clued in. "You used my phone, the one on my desk."

"Yup."

"You still don't carry your own cell phone?"

"Never have, never will."

"You just show up whenever and wherever you please?"

"Yup. I'm aware people ascribe it to some sort of mystique I apparently have, or paranoia about being traced."

"But?"

"But it simply allows me to stay out of range, doing what I please whenever I please. That's all."

"Nowadays I would call that…"

"Smart?"

"Wily, is what I would say—wily. So how are they getting back to you?"

Al made a show of checking his old-fashioned wristwatch and comparing to the modern chrome-and-glass clock on the wall.

"This time of the day? Here, I would presume. At some point, you and I will have to arrange for a new place to unwind. People are starting to notice."

He nodded toward the entrance, where a bicycle messenger wended his way through the maze of tables, only to catch the bartender with a question. Their bartender nodded toward them sitting at the end of the bar and went on doing what he was doing.

"You see?"

Al reached his hand out for the proffered envelope and put a small bill into the messenger's hand. He slit the envelope with one long, graceful index finger and pulled out a single, handwritten sheet.

"Uh-huh…"

"So, what's it say?"

"It explains a couple of things, I would say."

"What?"

"Matter of fact, it almost makes sense, now that I look at it, and given our earlier conversation."

"What does it say, Al?"

"Yes, I would say…"

"Counting to three here." Rafael held up his fingers. "One…"

"Now don't get all huffy on me." Al raised an eyebrow and shook his head. "God, the impatience. Give a man a chance to read the thing first. Now…"

"Two…"

"It appears the face behind at least one of these offshore corporations is one Reverend Bartholomew Wentworth."

"There's a mouthful."

"Runs some Church of the Redeemer on Vaomar Island, South Pacific."

"Never heard of the place."

"You and 99 percent of the population, I gather." Al turned the sheet of paper around and dramatically adjusted his reading glasses. "According to this, it's a fly speck of an island in the South Pacific somewhere."

"Vaomar, South Pacific," Rafael said once and then repeated it. For some reason the words had a quasi-familiarity. "Have I heard this before?"

"I doubt it." Al studied a hurriedly drawn map.

"A reverend," Rafael said. "Guess the collection plates are looking healthy down there."

"Maybe."

"And you're right—it makes sense. A man of the cloth may not wish to be known for investing in a drug company. It does make sense."

"Unless someone were running from the law," Al said slowly and studied the description of Vaomar Island again. "This could be one of these—havens."

"For a man of God? So, it seems this reverend owns offshore companies to hold his shares because his flock should not know about the types of investment their leader makes."

"But Mariposa Industries? This is not Pepsi or Coca-Cola. You have to know about this stock. You have to be pretty well informed."

"You'd be surprised how well-informed reverends are nowadays. Take Connor's father. Man made a fortune off a simple phrase, 'Sunday's coming.'" Rafael raised his hands and spoke with a dramatic fake accent, rolling his eyes toward the ceiling.

"Yes, I remember Reverend Matthias Beauregard's church. I investigated it before getting into business with you. Did well. Raised funds like there was no tomorrow out of that nothing church in Dunnville."

"You looked into him—no shit?"

"Of course I did. I like to know who I'm getting into bed with. You ought to be aware of that. In some ways, the Reverend Matthias would have made a formidable businessman. Some say he is."

"So, it's not too farfetched this Reverend Bartholomew would be as well, no?"

"I suppose." Al slowly wagged his head side to side. "It's just a very, very odd coincidence, two men of the cloth in the same type of business."

"You are grasping, Al. Two different companies, PerCan and Mariposa, two different reverends, one a shareholder, one the father of the founder."

"And you may be making the same mistake 90 percent of the population make. You implicitly trust a man of the cloth."

"And you are an incurable cynic. If you truly think there is something sinister there, by all means, investigate a little more. This does not have to be settled tonight. I'm once again flabbergasted at your getting answers at the speed of light."

Rafael shrugged and took a sip of beer, putting his head back and swallowing with great satisfaction.

"I'm quite happy to make this your call, Al. If you think there's something there, do some more digging. If not…"

Al put two fingers over his mouth and sat still for a very long time, letting his gaze wander over the patrons of The Lighthouse, from one table to the next, one person to the next. Rafael had seen this with him before, this quiet form of caution, awareness, and paranoia. As if he were listing and evaluating these people in his mind. What was he worried about?

He didn't envy Al his family and the reputation that came with it, and the constant looking over his shoulder it appeared to require. Rafael didn't want to know why it might be necessary. It had to weigh on a man if he couldn't sit down in his favorite pub to enjoy a quitting-time beer without being on guard. One day perhaps he would ask Al. One day perhaps he would know where the caution came from.

Deep in thought, he almost missed it when Al spoke.

"Pardon? Mind wandering."

"I can see that. I said it's fine. We're all overreacting a little. Most likely scenario would be we have a reverend from an island that harbors some very wealthy people. He's likely hiding what fell off the collection plate."

"Fell off, huh?"

"If you would like my insights into how some of these people operate. Some say it's one of the best rackets going. Especially in a place known to attract sinners with deep pockets. Offer salvation, take money. The church built an empire on this simple but effective principle."

"You, my friend, are a hopeless cynic."

"Sure." Al nodded. "Tell me I'm wrong."

Rafael chuckled and shook his head. "So, we're good then, no more research, no more background checks?"

"No, we could do this for months and not be any further ahead than we are right now." Al shrugged, letting his eyes roam over the guests again. Still not entirely comfortable or relaxed. Still watching and looking over his back.

"We're getting too old for this. Seeing an enemy behind every rock or chair. Why not just go ahead with the merger?"

"You know I want to. I just needed your insight. Between the two of us, you're the more cautious one."

"The more paranoid one is more like it. Tomorrow. One last meeting with Tadeo. Then I say we go ahead."

"Got it." Rafael clinked glasses with Al and took a deep, cleansing sip. "Now I feel better. I can finally see the end of this thing. But tell me something if you will. And you don't have to answer if you don't want to."

"Oh—here we go again."

"You ever call Tadeo Dad?"

"What?"

"Every now and then, you get comfortable, and you say 'my father,' but usually it's just 'Tadeo.' You ever call him 'Dad?'"

"Not likely."

"You ever did? In your life, I mean, when you were little."

Shutters came down over Al's eyes. It wasn't just that he looked away or made a face. It wasn't just that his look expressed the cynicism and general dismay Rafael had come to know and appreciate. Something literally pulled the shutters on Al's eyes. Rafael suddenly faced a mask, a carefully constructed and planned mask, put there for the benefit of the people around him. He had seen Al like this—before they became friends, just as he began investing in the company and still didn't know them that well.

This particular Al wasn't friendly, jovial, and smart. This particular Al was guarded, careful, and most certainly poised to defend himself at a moment's notice. This Al showed only little doses of himself, carefully measured and accounted-for doses—nothing else.

Shit, Rafael thought, now what? He didn't know if he should say something or avoid the whole thing entirely and change the subject. But Al relaxed again.

"I don't think anybody calls him anything but Mr. Ivers, except for his sons, and the few select who have been invited, like you for example."

"Lucky me."

"You got it. Besides, he would likely have a fit if anyone called him Dad. The implied softness in the mere phrase would…"

"Piss him off?"

"And then some."

Al relaxed his shoulders a bit, although Rafael noticed that it took a deliberate effort to do so, and shook his head.

"You ask the most peculiar questions, Rafael Covin. You do know that, right?"

FORTY-THREE

They did go to see Tadeo Ivers the next morning, marching into his little diner office side by side, as if it had always been this way, showing him what had been done on this new merger to date. Much of it, Rafael suspected, went right over the man's head, although like most, he would never admit any such thing. Rafael quite simply did not feel like explaining.

He laid out the facts, the documentation they had gathered, and sat back in his chair, arms folded before him. Out of the corner of his eye, he caught Al's glance, a mixture of incredulity and amazement. *You've got one set of big ones on you.* The thought all but stood in the room, and Rafael almost grinned because he realized he no longer cared.

Or, more precisely, he cared, but no matter what Ivers decided, he knew it would not have the power to affect him in any way. If Ivers became reasonable and said, *OK, go, do what you know needs to be done,* fine. If, on the other hand, he insisted on being stubborn and going broke, also fine.

The thought did make him smile, and he worked to hide it, before Tadeo caught it—barely.

"Something amusing, Rafael?"

"Not a thing, Tadeo. Just thinking how much fun it will be when we get this thing finally off the ground and running the way it can run."

"Fun?"

"Of course it will be fun. Tadeo. We have a great team, talented, enthusiastic people on board…" He looked sideways to catch Al's glance and raised eyebrow. "Of course, this will be fun. There's something about running one of these startups that is—like nothing else."

"I don't see where you've ever run one of these."

"Not at the helm, no," Rafael admitted. "But I've been there often enough with other—people."

"Connor Beauregard!"

"Amongst others. But let me tell you something—it's exciting like nothing else when you get it humming."

Ivers made a sound that could have been a cough, a yawn, or sheer dismissal of Rafael's thoughts. Maybe he was just saying 'hmf.' Rafael shrugged one shoulder and folded his hands.

Decision imminent, he thought. Right about now, Ivers would have to admit that they had done a great job and send them out to complete it. *Do it already,* he thought, and Ivers cleared his throat.

"You ever hear anything about him?"

"Him who?"

"Don't play stupid, Covin. Of course I'm talking about Beauregard."

"Oh, him." He caught another glance from Al that warned him not to take the game too far. Flippancy would get him nowhere, least of all the company he wanted.

"Not one word, not since the day he left," he finally said as politely as he could manage. "I think he's disappeared somewhere safe and is enjoying the proceeds of his ill-gotten shares."

"He should never have had those. What's wrong with the regulators?"

"He never had them. Number of ratholes he used. That's a term for people who are holding…"

"I know what a rathole is."

"Of course. Sorry."

Rafael shut up and rested his folded hands in his lap, so he wouldn't fidget. *Just make the damned decision already and let us do our job.*

He'd been thinking about Europe. There was an entire market over there, as of yet untapped and underserved. They could go there; they could have subsidiaries. He wanted to spend a lot of time in Oregon and Colorado, really learn what was working for these guys down there, and not just on a growing level. That was Nick Ambrose's field, but in marketing, in software, in selling. Jesus, there was so much he still needed to know, so much he needed to learn, and he couldn't wait for it all to happen.

Now if Tadeo Ivers would just up and make his final decision so they could move ahead with this merger.

"You're just going to sit there, not moving until I say yes to this merger, are you not?"

Rafael shrugged. "Pretty much so, Tadeo. I've given you all my good reasons for doing so and then some. I've pointed it out to you as well as I can. Now all I can do is wait. Until you come around to see that this really is the only way to move forward without bankrupting you. Or you can throw me out of your office. Your choice."

"I guess you leave me no other choice then…"

Silence spread in the little room around them, and Rafael blinked. Once, twice… Had he heard right? Was Ivers changing his mind? Was he making this hard on him?

"We go forward, then?"

"Move ahead, merge, do whatever. But do not—I repeat, do not—screw up my company again. If you do, the gates of hell won't open far enough for you to…"

"I won't. We won't."

Rafael heard himself babbling on and finally laughed. Despite his casual attitude, he'd been holding his breath so hard it all but exploded out of him.

"You will not regret this," he heard himself say. "I promise you; you will not regret this. Al and I will build this company into the biggest and best the market has ever seen. Nothing will stop us."

"Just make sure the damn thing makes money. That's all I want. And might I ask what you are talking about, Al and I…"

"Well, we've planned this merger together, Tadeo. I naturally thought…"

"You're taking all of Dante's time with this silly growing operation. Suddenly, all he wants to do is learn how to grow drugs. And you are to blame for it. Al has been decidedly distracted the last few months because of all the time he's been spending with you at Perfect Cannabis. Do you mind leaving me one son to run our own business back here?"

Ivers spread his arms and looked from Rafael to Al and back.

"I need somebody to look after the day-to-day operations around here, as you well know, Al. You cannot just up and leave for better pastures. So, what's it going to be?"

"What's it going to be, Tadeo?" Al said impossibly gently, almost as if he were speaking to a stubborn child. "What it is going to be is I will hire a smart, competent business manager to help me run this business."

"I don't want any strangers in here."

"Whom I will naturally supervise 100 percent at all times. Surely you don't need me to run little errands during the day while our biggest business opportunity is left wanting."

"You know how I feel about strangers."

"There won't be any strangers. Relax. I've asked my cousin Federico to step in on a few things, at least the simpler ones. I'm sure he meets with your approval."

"Federico is a smart kid," Tadeo grudgingly admitted. "Not half bad a choice, Al. Although you might have asked me before you went to him."

"No point in doing so until I knew you would agree to the merger and to our continuing work there," Al said, and Rafael was once again struck by how patiently he spoke to his father. He himself would have…

"What, does everybody around here think I'm an idiot? Do you not trust me to make the most basic of decisions for this business and its continued survival? This gives me grave doubts as to leaving the two of you in charge. Of course I would say yes. Not to think what would happen…"

Rafael tuned him out and looked at Al. His grin was met by a raised eyebrow and a secret thumbs up under the table. Gotcha! Al wanted this just as much as he did; he had caught the fever just as bad. From here on in, there was no limit to how far they could go.

Rafael cleared his throat and rose.

"I knew you would understand," he said briefly and nodded at Al. "Now, we'd better get going. There's a lot of work waiting for us."

***

Thomas Donnelly responded with a huge relieved sigh when Rafael called him with the good news. Who could blame the man? For the past few months, he had been investigated more thorough than many a criminal had been.

His business had been taken apart, examined in pieces and as a whole and put back together, his records had been removed, thumbed through, scanned, copied, and brought back, and his staff questioned separately and in groups.

Some days, Rafael thought, Thomas probably didn't know if he were in the middle of merger talks or a securities investigation, or indeed which one he preferred. He could hardly blame the man for crossing himself with relief when Rafael called him to tell him the funding necessary for the merger had been greenlit.

"I never thought this day would come," he said, not bothering to hide the relief and satisfaction. "Any more investigations or due diligence from your side, I would have had to show your fellow David my underwear drawer. Trust me. It ain't pretty."

"That bad?" Rafael asked and leaned back in his chair.

He remembered the same feeling dealing with Turner. Yes, it had been an ordeal over the past few months. It had been twice as difficult as it needed to be, and everyone had been dancing around on eggshells. It felt good to be done, finally.

"What do you think, Rafael? Is there anything you don't know about us?"

"I guess not. Welcome to Perfect Cannabis."

"Thanks, I think. Now for the task of signing what is sure to be a rough tonnage of paperwork and merging our both operations? Man…"

"Yes—man…" Rafael hesitated for a minute. "Mind if I tell you something?"

"Tell away, Rafael."

"This is my first merger. So, I'm not even sure where we go from here."

He reflexively pulled the phone away from his ear, while Thomas's resounding laughter almost burst his eardrums.

"Well, Rafa, you're my first as well. So, you're in good company. I don't know. Maybe you and I should come up with a plan. Being the two CEOs and all. Does that sound reasonable?"

It did sound reasonable. Except the phrase, 'being the two CEOs and all,' grated a little. Two CEOs meant one of them had to go. One of them.

Instantly, Rafael knew he wanted 'one of them' to be Thomas. He, Rafael, who had packed his bags more than once over the last few months, ready to walk away the moment he could, who had started a huge fight with Kayla over the subject—he had this burning desire to be the man in charge, the one whose name came up first in connection with Perfect Cannabis Corporation.

"Rafael? Something wrong?"

"Not wrong, no…"

"Hits a bit close to home all of a sudden, does it not? Now it's time to make nails with actual heads, as my dad would say."

"Nails with heads, strange phrase."

"Well, they're not much good without them, are they?"

"Guess not," Rafael said and sat up a little straighter to gather his thoughts. "But you're right, time to get serious around here and put all this theory we've been chewing away at into practice. It's just—all new, that's all."

"Permission to speak frankly, Rafael?"

"Sure," Rafael said, and cocked a finger at Al, who had wandered into Rafael's little office and made a show of pulling his finger through dust, looking for a place to sit.

"If I don't miss my guess, you're a bit attached to the CEO seat at Perfect Cannabis. How am I scoring here, close on target?"

"You're not wrong, Thomas. You're not wrong. My fault—I should have given some thought to the final corporate structure before this. We've had our hands full."

More roaring laughter, and Rafael thought if he kept working with this man, he would have to invest in a good speakerphone or suffer from tinnitus most days of the week. The man had a way to laugh that could bring down the house.

"Well, I'm in the same position here. I've been CEO of Mariposa for what feels like forever, and I kinda like it."

"I'm sure we will find a solution."

"But I also know, Rafael, that without Perfect Cannabis, your financing, your know-how, and your state-of-the-art facilities, this gig would be over one way or another anyway. And not in a good way."

Suddenly, there wasn't a trace of laughter left in Thomas's voice. "We've been raising funds desperately, trying to keep from drowning, selling shares to anyone who would have 'em."

Even offshore corporations, Rafael thought, but said nothing.

"And still I know that none of it would have done me any good if it were not for you and PerCan, even if I have to put up with Tadeo Ivers in turn."

"His bark is far worse than his bite, I assure you," Rafael said, distracted.

"What I'm saying here in the long roundabout way, Rafael, is that I am more of a hands-on guy anyway. I've been standing down on the production floor packaging product, doing menial labor, even cleaning the floors to save my company. So, if COO is it, then so be it."

"Get a good CFO to help us all out…"

"Get a good CFO and work will be fun again. I just don't know about your man Al. What's his plan with the company?"

"Oh, Al is going to stay on as a consultant. He's not looking for a seat on the board."

"That's a little odd, if you permit me the observation."

Rafael laughed again and looked across the room at Al, perched on the edge of a chair, flipping through some documentation and regarding Rafael with his customary raised eyebrow.

"Everything about the Ivers family is a little odd, and I don't mind the observation. I have that end of things under control. Let's you and I meet, I'll bring in Al to advise, and we'll put together a workable company structure. Look, I want everybody to be happy where they're at, and using their talents in the best way for the company. If not—we will do something about it. Sound good? Are there any loose ends at Mariposa, anybody on your list of shareholders who might have issues?"

"Well… OK."

Rafael sensed just the tiniest bit of hesitation—just that one heart-beat too long before the man said OK. It could be nothing, it could be something, but it bothered him. Right there, the hair on the back of his neck stood up, and he squared his shoulders almost automatically. Had Al caught it?

He looked across the room at Al and saw the eyebrow race up to his hair line. Yup, he had noticed it too. Paranoia? Real or imagined? Deserved or not?

"Thomas?"

"You were saying?"

"You were not saying, Thomas. I asked if there is going to be anyone on your shareholder list who you've already highlighted as, 'this guy could oppose the merger or make trouble.' If there are any, I need to know. And I need to know now so we can clear it up ahead of time. The majority of our shareholders have to agree."

"I know. And there are no issues. I really don't think so."

"You—really—don't—think—so," Rafael said, enunciating every single word as if reading a foreign language. "You don't think so… Thomas, what have we been talking about for the past couple of months? Communication. Making sure there are no surprises. And now you come around, three minutes to 12, you want to tell me, oh yeah, there might be somebody who could oppose the merger? And by the way, does he or she own enough shares to make a hash out of our deal? What is going on?"

"Take it easy, Rafael. That's not what I'm saying at all. I don't expect any issues."

"But there might be. You are concerned?"

"No—it's just… Jesus Christ, Covin, do you know each and every one of your shareholders personally?"

Rafael forced himself to breathe in and out deeply through his nose and closed his eyes. No, of course he didn't, and it was not reasonable to expect the CEO to do so. They sold shares every other goddamned day to some guy with enough money, they had guys getting groups together to raise funds, they had…

"No, of course not."

"There you go. I don't either, and it's no big deal. There's this one fellow who owns quite a bit, and I have no clue who he is, or where his head is at as far as this merger here is concerned."

"That reverend guy from overseas?"

"I'm not even going to ask why or how you know about one of my investors already. You might have simply asked me." Thomas laughed dryly and sighed. "Look, the subscription agreement came in out of the blue, just when we needed money in the worst way. It all looked good. Then when we issued the shares, he requested for them to be issued in these offshore corporations. Not unheard of. One of my guys checked. He's a man of the cloth, for Christ's sakes."

"Apparently we use the same information system," Rafael said and shot a dirty look over to where Al sat, leaning forward, elbows resting on his knees, listening to Thomas's voice on speakerphone.

"Maybe. Anyway, didn't look like a big deal, and like I said, the money came like water to a dying man, so we took his cash."

"And why shouldn't you? It's just shares." Rafael worried his lower lip.

"Right. Just a bunch of shares."

"Except then he did it again, and again. And then he started using a different offshore company. But it all looks like the same guy. And I do get a bit of a—creepy feel, where he's concerned."

"Fuck," Rafael said simply.

At that moment, it was merely the most eloquent word he could think of to express what he was feeling. Not another merger going sideways, not another one to go to his board and tell them, *sorry, guys, we screwed up, again. Redo from start... again!*

If that happened, he was gone. Goodbye, Perfect Cannabis. Not only was he gone, they were all gone. Tadeo would shut them down in the time it took to say get out of here, no matter how much money he had invested. He wouldn't do it. Wouldn't risk the company again. He had made Rafael promise, swear an oath for crying out loud, that this very thing was not going to happen again.

Damn you, Greg Turner.

"It does not need to mean anything," Al said softly, but Thomas heard him nevertheless.

"That's right, Al. It really doesn't have to mean anything. All it is is an unknown quantity, and that's what you asked me. I gave you an answer. Not a reason to panic."

"Is there any way to get in touch with this investor?" Rafael asked, mind racing 15 ways to Christmas. "Reach out, speak to him, explain in person what's happening and why, and make sure he's on-side. Before we take even one more step?"

"Tried it," Thomas said. "Believe me, if I had the cash, I would have sent a man down there to Vaomar Island personally to knock on each and every church door until I found him."

Vaomar Island. Such an unusual name, and yet…

Kayla. Suddenly he wished he had asked Kayla. For some reason, it never occurred to him, but if it were a hideout for people running from the law, or debts, or something, she might have heard the name.

He would just have to work with the information they had.

Kayla had been out of town, and unreachable, on some sort of research project, or he would have fired off a text to her.

"OK, let's not go looking for trouble before it actually shows up," he made himself say, which failed to make either Al or Thomas feel better. "We'll find him, talk to him, and alleviate any concerns he might have. What does everybody who buys shares want in the end?"

"Make money?" Thomas asked, and Rafael nodded.

"Right, make money. So, this is what we'll do. Al, you have the best connections in the group, find a way to locate our good reverend."

"Consider it done." Al rose as if he were leaving to take care of it right then and there.

"Thomas, you and I will get together tomorrow, go over our shareholder lists, our employee lists, our board lists. Just check everybody who might oppose this merger or cause trouble."

"Sounds good."

"And if they don't own enough shares to give us a hard time, never mind. If they do, you and I will see them personally. Personally, you understand?"

"Is that necessary?"

"Yes, it's necessary. There is no way, Thomas, that we will let this merger go belly up at this stage. We are gone—both gone if that happens."

"I hear you."

"Good. Then everybody knows what they need to do."

"Understood," Al and Thomas said as one, and Rafael allowed himself a small smile. Didn't he have a great crew now? This was not going to get screwed up. Not this time, not now. He had good people.

***

Late that night, he sat in his office instead of going to The Lighthouse as he usually would have and pored over his shareholder lists. Many of the investors he knew personally, having met them in the initial drive to raise funds.

Some of them were original investors from the time when he and Connor Beauregard had started the company. It became something of a walk down memory lane as he ran his finger down his most recent list. Thinking of the excitement of their idea and their original investment pitches made him remember why he sat here again, why he put himself through all of this. When it was all said and done, it was still the most exciting things he knew—starting a new company and seeing it grow.

None of 'his' people would stir up trouble. He finally sat back and made that statement with a fair amount of confidence. He need not worry about any issues from that side.

He checked the big clock on the far wall of his office and compared it with his wristwatch. Al had left hours ago. Usually, his information network was quicker than this. What on earth was going on? Al should already have called him with information on the reverend.

Rafael cursed softly and began to pace the length of his office. When that did not help, he went out into the hallway, and from there into the big manufacturing hall, and paced the length of it. That took a bit longer, at least, though it still didn't relieve any of the tension he felt.

Round and round he went, stopping at the freshly painted western wall. This was where it had been, where Roberto Ivers had boldly cut off a good 20 feet of the building, put in a false wall and used the remainder for his own purpose. Which happened to be growing marijuana. Illegally.

Simple and brilliant. Connor had called it a stroke of absolute genius, hiding an illegal grow op right inside a legal one.

Connor had literally stumbled over it, or so he said. Right up to the end, he claimed all he had done was discover the installation, not create it. He never wavered from that, even when Roberto Ivers stood there and claimed the whole operation had been Connor's brainchild in the first place. Was it? Or was Roberto covering, or had he been paid to say what he did? Who the hell knew?

Rafael stood and stared at the wall. Up to the day Connor disappeared, he had believed him, had been ready to stand beside him and work to make everything right—until Roberto appeared on the television news with a tape that showed Connor inspecting his grow op, even shaking hands on a deal.

What was a guy to believe? God, he knew Connor well enough, and Connor always did as he pleased. Legal, illegal, the line was decidedly blurred where Connor Beauregard was concerned. Connor had one law—you did what was best for Connor Beauregard, you looked out for number one, and then you looked out for number one again, and if there was still any time left in the day...

Rafael put his hand against the wall the way he had over a year ago. This time, it felt cool and rough, just as it should—not warm from the heating elements behind. Everything was as it should be. He allowed himself to close his eyes for a moment and let the feeling of the cold solid wall and the hard ground beneath his feet ground him to reality.

Everything was fine, goddammit.

Al had to be right. That reverend was just spending donations. Unwisely for sure, but nothing else. He'd be mortified when Al's people came to speak to him. Whoever they were, Al's people.

Rafael shivered and forced his mind back to a calm space.

"Dammit, Al, call," he muttered.

Al had left the office almost immediately after the phone conversation with Thomas, without another word, without explanation. He would show up when he had news. He always did, and until then, all one could do was hope, and pray.

How hard could it be to locate the man? How hard could it be to pick up the goddamn phone and speak to this priest, or whatever he was? There had to be a church and a church office somewhere.

Connor would have used a line like this one. *Look, we know you picked up a lot of shares, and we have big plans with the company. Really big plans, and here is why you are going to make more money off it than you ever dreamed possible.*

Connor always spoke about making money, more money than anyone had ever dreamed of. No matter what it took to get there, no matter who got ground up in the wheels of the machinery.

Even Rafael himself, his supposed best friend, and Kayla, the woman he had been living with.

Kayla… On impulse, Rafael pulled his phone from his pocket and dialed Kayla's number for the fifth time in the last two hours. Nothing. Still her messaging service telling him she was busy.

Dammit, he didn't like it.

He needed her right now. He needed her knowledge and her memory. He needed somebody to talk him out of remembering Connor.

Rafael headed back toward his office, only to barely avoid colliding with Al, who came striding down the hallway like a general in battle.

"Tell me you got something," Rafael said and sat heavily in his chair.

"Nothing," Al said and shook his head, straddling a visitor's chair. "He's gone."

"Gone, what do you mean he's gone, Al?"

"Hey, it's taken me this long just to get a guy on the ground on this—this island.

"The church is still there. There's a guy squatting in it now. Portuguese con man by the name of Cristos."

"So, what the heck is going on here?"

"You know how much I hate saying I don't know, but this fellow Cristos has not seen the good reverend in months. Took off from his church and the island one day and didn't come back."

"I don't like it."

"On the other hand…"

"On the other hand what, Al?"

"On the other hand—it could be what we were thinking all along. He's a con. Collected as much as he could and took off."

"A crook," Rafael said and rested his chin in his hand. For some irrational reason, the image of Connor came to mind again. Taking money off regular well-meaning people and taking off when he'd had his fill.

"If that's the case, Rafa—maybe we don't have anything to worry about."

"And what makes you say that, pray tell?"

"What does a crook want, after he pulls off some racket? That's right, cash. Nothing else. Cash. And what we are doing?"

"What we are doing is going to make him more money than he ever dreamed of," Rafael repeated, still in a state. "Maybe."

Al raised his hands and let them drop into his lap.

Helpless—he had never seen Al look helpless before, and it raised goosebumps on Rafael's neck.

Al Ivers always had a way out, a backdoor or a failsafe. And if that didn't work, his famous 'guys' were standing by to lend a hand. Al Ivers did not ever appear helpless.

"All we can do is wait, Rafa. As much as you and I might not like it. We have to wait for this man to surface—if he even chooses to do so. He might just cash out and disappear."

"And in the meantime?"

"In the meantime? I don't see why we don't just proceed."

"You're comfortable with that?"

"Comfortable?"

Al made a snorting sound that might well have been laughter, had it not been devoid of any mirth.

"The man owns too many shares for comfort. But what's our alternative? Call the whole thing off? That doesn't make any sense, Rafa."

"I agree. It doesn't. But to have this hanging there…"

"To have this hanging over our heads at a critical time in the company's life is the worst of all scenarios. You think I don't know that?"

Rafael looked up because Al had spoken in a sharp tone and struck the armrest of his chair. He'd never addressed Rafael as anything but a friend. He'd never hit anything. Where on earth had they got to?

Al ran his hands through his hair with frustration, another gesture Rafael had never seen from him.

"Rafael? Believe me when I tell you, if my guys can't find someone, then he cannot be found."

"But…"

"But nothing. Eventually, he will do something that will leave traces, and we will find him. Until then…"

Rafael leaned back in his chair, closed his eyes, and sighed.

"Until then, we keep going," he finally said and nodded, eyes still closed. "I don't have to like it, though."

"You do not."

Rafael opened his eyes again and found that Al was still looking at him. Except now his look had become friendly again, their moment of tension disappeared.

"You have access to every single resource at my disposal, Rafael. This man can't hide forever, even if he tries. But let's not push too hard right now, OK?"

Rafael nodded. He had no other choice, and if there was one thing he hated, it was having his back to a wall. A very solid wall, and no way to fight his way out. No control. God, he hated it. 'Every resource' at Al's disposal only served to improve his mood marginally.

***

He met with Thomas a number of times over the next few days and examined the list of involved persons one by one. Employees, executives, shareholders—he wanted to know who everyone was and what their role in this company might be. To his great relief, the good reverend appeared to be the only one they could not pin down.

***

A week later, he found himself with two things to plan, a board meeting finalizing completion of the merger and assignment of new roles and tasks, and Kayla's stubborn insistence on hosting yet another lavish grand opening celebration.

"What's the deal, anyway, with women and grand opening celebrations?" he complained to Al a few nights later. "I mean, I still remember the first grand opening Perfect Cannabis celebrated, and not in a good way."

"Women do appear to relish these things," Al replied, brushing an invisible speck off his pants. "But the original PerCan opening was a spectacular affair, if I recall correctly. People spoke of it for weeks."

"Oh, you man of understatement, Al... Spectacular does not begin to describe it." Rafael snorted. "I might want to say stupendous, and then some. Remember that damned helicopter?"

Al smiled and folded his hands on top of his head. "Jesus, yes, the helicopter. Beautiful machine. And Mirko..."

"Mirko the loan shark Connor 'forgot' to pay—I'd almost forgotten about him."

"You argued with him. Stood shoulder to shoulder with Connor who was committing probably the dumbest mistake in history, not paying a ruthless loan shark like Mirko, then pretending it was just one of those things that slipped the mind. And you, you just stood with him backing him up. I couldn't decide if you were as insane as he was or tired of living, to tell you the truth."

"He was my friend." Rafael shrugged. "I felt I should. Maybe even needed to. We started PerCan together, and he did what he had to do in order to move us forward. Who was I…"

"Connor did a lot of dumb things, Rafa, a lot of them. Let's just stop right there. But that night, he tried to write a check to Mirko—a check—to a loan shark. Really? He thought he would walk out of there alive?"

"Mmmm, and then you walked in," Rafael remembered with a chuckle. "You paid him off, with that monumental wad of cash you just happened to have in your pocket. You sure saved his ass."

"Not because of anything Connor did or said, I assure you that."

"Then why?"

"Same reason you stood beside him. We didn't need a war that night. We didn't need Mirko doing something stupid, endangering hundreds of guests who had come for a grand opening celebration. He had his hands on the main electrical power. At the very least, he would have caused tremendous panic. At worst? Connor…?"

Al shrugged and made Rafael shiver once more. It just sounded so casual.

"Wouldn't have walked out of there the same way he came in, would he?"

"Not a chance."

"God, how naïve we really were, Connor and I. We never thought something like that could happen."

"Connor sure did not, no."

"And your bundle of cash. That was the first time I realized I was officially in the drug business. I always wondered where the money came from or why you just happened to carry it with you that night."

"Best that you don't. And don't ask about it again either."

"Hey…" Rafael shook the memory away with an effort and pressed the button on that fancy espresso machine Kayla had installed on his desk. "Why are we talking about this anyway? Do we not have better things to do than reminiscing about Connor and his escapades?"

"He is the single biggest reason why we are here, Rafael—in trouble."

Al suddenly raised his head very slowly, as if he had seen a ghost. Something had sparked a memory or given him an idea. And, from the look on his face, that idea was not pretty. A steep line appeared between his eyes, and he had a faraway look that said he wasn't listening to a word Rafa had just said.

"Al?"

"Pardon me?"

"Kayla's new grand opening party? Where is your head at? I asked you what you thought about it—in principle. Should we even entertain the thought?"

"We were remembering Connor."

"We were."

"Rafael. It was something you just said. Made me think of something. Give me a second. It'll come back."

"Hello, my two favorite men. How are both of you this evening?"

Rafael looked up and smiled at Kayla, who breezed into his office like a refreshing spring wind, as always on a cloud of some expensive and delicious scent, trailing brightly colored chiffon scarves, sporting the biggest smile. He couldn't help it. Looking at her made him grin like a dimwit as she walked up to his seat and pecked him on the cheek.

"Hello, my love, Mr. Big Shot Executive, how are the plans for the company coming?"

If Al raised an eyebrow to Kayla calling him 'love,' he didn't say one word, just the ubiquitous eyebrow.

"Indeed, we are working on it. We're trying to put together a decent, working board of executives here."

"Oh, dear, I'm sorry. If I am interrupting, I'll go and work on my grand opening plans for a while again."

"Of course you're not interrupting," Al said, rose, and offered his chair to Kayla. "My apologies. Your wonderful man here does not keep enough chairs in his office."

"And he does not keep it very clean either. Thank you, Al, you are a perfect gentleman."

Another raised eyebrow in Rafael's direction and a barely suppressed grin.

"I know it. I've been trying to interest him in a good, reliable cleaning service for this place. It's horrendous how he lets it go to seed."

"Horrendous." Kayla nodded. "Have you given any thought to our grand celebration at all? Once the merger is all done? I want to have an affair the entire country is going to remember."

"Well as they should, my dear. Rafael here is about to be the head of the biggest producer in the country."

"If the two of you are done then…" Rafael tapped his pen on the wooden table in front of him. "Number one, Rafael is sitting right here, so don't talk about him like he's out in the parking lot, and, number two, he still does not have a board. And he needs one, remember? Or nothing is going to get done. Al, for the eighth or ninth time, your input—please."

He tried to sound stern, missing it by a mile. Truth be told, the relief at Kayla walking in and getting Al off the unpleasant subject of Connor and whatever memory he had triggered was enough to make him want to celebrate. Enough dark thoughts for now. There was a company being created here, and it was a good one!

Al made a big show of carrying in a wooden crate so he would have a place to sit.

As to the new board, Simon Graff and Josh Novak had been there at the very beginning of the company, they had put money into it, and they had suffered through all of the ups and downs that came after… They hadn't exactly worked themselves to the bone, nor given any creative input as far as day-to-day management was concerned, but he thought he might want them back on. Just to be fair, and for the old times.

Kayla would be there again. Al didn't want a seat, and he could actually understand him. If he were Tadeo's son, surely he wouldn't want to be on the board of a company his father all but owned.

FORTY-FOUR

Flight 915 from Singapore, travelling via Hong Kong and Alaska, landed with a mere 90-minute delay. Not bad, considering the distance they had covered and the bad weather they had encountered somewhere over the pacific. But there always had to be a few passengers who made complete fools of themselves, loudly complaining about everything.

The flight attendants had seen it all and deflected the comments with a smile and gentle greeting but, secretly, even they couldn't wait until the last passenger had left the airplane.

The man seated in Seat One-A, however, surprised them all. He'd been nervous, fidgeting, and more impatient than most to reach their destination. He'd spent dinner glued to the flight progression map, checked his watch and the onboard timer every chance he got, leaning forward as if he could somehow push the plane faster. Even when most of the other passengers fell asleep, some part of him stayed in perpetual motion, impatient to get where he wanted to go.

Until about two hours out from their final destination. Suddenly, a switch in his head went off, and he sat back, smiled, folded his hands in his lap and generally appeared to be at peace.

Drunk? No, the head purser couldn't remember having given him enough to change his attitude so drastically, but something surely had happened. The man had turned into a different person.

On the way out, he smiled serenely, shook the purser's hand, and wished them all a pleasant flight back home.

***

A cab took him downtown, and Barry Wentworth settled into his next hotel room, opened a bottle of champagne, and looked out over the city, quiet at this late hour of night.

"It's open," he called out when gentle knock on the door summoned him. He already knew who would walk in at this hour, unannounced.

"Took you long enough."

"Your flight was late," Roberto said casually. "Didn't want to hang around at the airport. You found your hotel without me."

"That I did."

"So?"

"So—what, Roberto? Is there something you wish to ask me?"

"What's our next move? You're here… I mean…"

"Yes, I am here." The man smiled and took a deep breath. "Home again."

"How much alcohol did they serve on this flight?"

"Ah, but Roberto…this is not alcohol. This is—completion," he said, in a hushed voice, turning away from his visitor to look out over the city once again. "Out there—out there is the culmination of a plan too many years in the making. To be this close…"

He put down the champagne glass and folded his arms tight to his body as if he were shivering. "To be this close to having everything I want."

"We want."

"Pardon me?" A flash of irritation, a quick movement, and he had himself under control again. He'd worked on it, the temper that flared at the most inopportune moments. He almost had it—almost.

347

"You know," Roberto said casually, plopping his long body into one of the straight-backed chairs at the desk and stretching his legs. "Everything 'we' want. You and I are in this together, remember? Partners, amigo, 50-50, all the way."

It boiled and bubbled. The temper almost broke loose. Almost… Roberto sat perfectly still, watching the spectacle.

"We will both have a place in the company," Barry finally said, his hand clenching the neck of the champagne bottle hard enough to make the knuckles turn snow white. Snow white with fine red scar lines crossing them.

Now Roberto did shift in his seat a little and finally squared his shoulders.

"Don't forget that my father…"

"I'm not forgetting anything, Roberto. And don't you forget that your father sent you to jail once, and off to Southeast Asia the other time, so you could rot far away out of sight? Sucker for punishment, are you?"

"He had his reasons."

"Good reasons, I am sure," Barry scoffed and shook his head. "And now you're ready to go in for round three? Is that what I'm hearing? Why don't you let me handle it—and Tadeo? I've done it before. When the time comes, you and I will be the men running this company, is that enough for you?"

"Nobody handles Tadeo. He owns a huge chunk of the company, if you remember. He won't like you coming in trying to take over."

"I said don't worry about it," he interrupted with a quick hand gesture that might as well have brushed aside an insect. "I said I would deal with him, and that is what I am going to do. Deal with him. Leave me to figure out the how."

"Which means you have no idea how you're going to do it yet, doesn't it? I've warned you—Tadeo is not the kind of man who will take this sitting down."

"Roberto? Shut the fuck up, OK? I run this thing. There's no reason for you to get involved, or to know every little detail about what's going to happen. Now why don't you tell me when this board meeting is going to take place?"

Roberto sat back and folded his hands again.

"Don't fuck this up by being arrogant and not listening to advice, Connor."

"Barry."

"Whatever. Don't you fuck this up. Not for the second time, not with me involved."

"Involved? How exactly are you involved? Want to tell me that?"

"I gave you every shred of information you have. Without me, you'd be rotting on an island in the South Pacific."

"You've done some research for me, big deal."

"And I fed Greg Turner the information he needed to go ballistic and torpedo the first merger."

"Really? You think that makes you involved, entitled to something?" He advanced on Roberto with such speed, he was no more than a moving shadow. He stood before him, his impressive six-foot-four frame shadowing Roberto, lounging in his chair. "You are a wheel in this machinery, Roberto. You are here because I want you to be. Nothing else."

Roberto did not even flinch. He looked down and picked on a piece of skin by his thumbnail. Finally, he shrugged and smiled broadly.

"OK then, have it your way. I guess you won't be needing any more information." He rose slowly, rolled a kink out of his shoulder, and smiled. "Best of luck. I would say see you around, but it's not necessary. Much as it would be fun to stick around to watch you crash and burn. I really have more important things to do."

Barry's hand flew out and clamped around Roberto's bicep, just hard enough to show he meant it, without starting a brawl right in his hotel room.

"Tell me when and where this board meeting is taking place."

"You hear something?" Roberto tapped his ear. "I don't know—maybe it's these damned headphones I'm always wearing, but ever since some fool told me to go shut up because they didn't need me any longer, I can't hear one thing." He shrugged and made a big production looking for his phone and keys. "Gotta go see the ear doc about that someday. Mother always said…"

"The meeting, Roberto? When and where?"

"Mother always said I'd go deaf wearing those damned earphones. What?"

Barry let go of Roberto's arm, folded his hands in prayer, and took a few deep, slow breaths, much like venting pressure out of a giant steam boiler. Every bit of self-control he possessed seemed to go into his next sentence, slowly and deliberately.

"Roberto, I would really like information about the board meeting of the proposed merged company if you have it."

"Along with my notes on the company structure and newly created positions and task fields." He grinned and actually batted his eyelashes. "Really, Connor, why didn't you say so right away—polite-like? Jeez."

When the other man did not speak, he spread his arms.

"Well? We got a deal now or what?"

"We have a deal, and you know how it works. You will be part of the new company once it is formed. Do I have to write this down now, or will my word do?"

"Well, I'd prefer a nice ol' contract. But seeing you steam like that… It was almost a treat. All right. Here is what I know…"

FORTY-FIVE

"Do you suffer from a split personality, Rafael? First, you push like hell to get this merger done. Now suddenly everybody is twiddling their thumbs while you delay the whole thing for I don't know how long? What is it I'm not getting here?"

"Three weeks, no more, Al, just three weeks. I want to start this company with a giant bang. To do that, I need a bit of time."

"I wish you wouldn't talk about explosives in this context. It makes me nervous."

Al was having trouble keeping up with Rafael dashing down the hallways of the PerCan building. Every day, it started looking more like the pharmaceutical company that would be headquartered here soon. So very soon.

All the walls had been painted a bright shade of white, kept from being blinding with a barely noticeable hint of green, compliments of Kayla and her input. Stainless steel doors and railings gave the appearance of a private clinic and the just-polished shine of the white vinyl floors made a man want to drop a gum wrapper, just to break up the perfect surface. Things were ready—or almost ready if Rafael were to be believed.

He pushed open the double doors into the growing area and stopped short, in a room that could have doubled as a jail, had one been filming a B-rate adventure movie in here.

"The grow pods," Al said and whistled. "I didn't know they had been installed already. That is way ahead of schedule."

"45 perfect little rooms. Grow pods—climate and light-controlled, security monitored 24-7, Al. All ready to receive our first shipment of marijuana plant clones, produced specifically for Perfect Cannabis in Amsterdam."

Rafael spread his arms and spun in a circle, grinning like a proud new parent. "I want the clones in, Al. In the growing medium, doing whatever it is they do while we wait for the harvest. I want to bring the board down here and show them our first potential harvest, you get it? I want them to see why we are doing this, why we are working our asses off."

"I've seen this before," Al said softly. "Back…"

"Yes. Back when your brother was up to his shenanigans behind the double wall. I remember. I saw it too, and I was blown away. I know we can do this. Just imagine for a moment…"

He took Al's elbow and swept his outstretched hand before him like a magician might. "First thing in the morning, we're bringing the newly formed executive committee down here for a tour of the plant before our first meeting. To get everybody into the mood. They open this door, walk in—bam."

"They won't know what to expect, much like I didn't just now. OK."

"There will be plants, green plants, lush, healthy. Almost ready to harvest."

"And you can do this, in that short a time?"

"Nick said he could. And Nick Ambrose is God, as far as marijuana plants are concerned."

"So, we will have a few plants in here," Al said, still not convinced. "Surprise element, I get it. But then what?"

"Then what? Al, I remember it. The first time I saw the grow room that Roberto built. It was amazing. Everything we had been planning and scheming and drawing up on paper for months, now years. Right there in front of us. I remember thinking—yeah, we can do this. It works."

"Of course it works. Marijuana plants have been growing for a lot of years all over the world."

"But there's a difference, Al. This is it; this is our vision coming true. Don't you feel it? The wow factor?"

Finally, Al smiled and took a few steps closer to the grow rooms, opened one, then the next stainless-steel door, and peeked in into grow trays ready and polished, lights suspended above them, electronic metering and surveillance panels on the walls.

"OK, OK. Maybe it's just me. I'm hard to impress. Your executives will think it's amazing."

"Amazing, Al? Amazing? It will be cool."

"Cool?"

"Yes, cool, definitely. I'm going to have live camera feeds into every single grow pod. I want statistics and calculations how the plants are coming along and how our profits are growing. All on a heads-up real-time display. I want this new board to be completely blown away by how far we've come. I want open mouths and dropped jaws. Come on. I'll show you something else."

Rafael laughed out loud and dragged Al along down the hall and deeper into the manufacturing area.

The sheer excitement of having his dream take shape piece by solid piece had been driving him at an insane pace for the last two weeks. He jumped out of bed at 5 a.m. after a mere three hours of sleep and drove down to the plant, every single day, including Saturdays and Sundays. Kayla hardly saw him anymore, and she had mentioned that little fact more than once. But for once, Rafael felt unstoppable and unbeatable.

Everything he touched magically turned out exactly the way he wanted it to, the way he had seen it in his mind, years ago, when

Connor Beauregard came to him and asked him if Rafael wanted to start a medical marijuana company with him.

It was happening exactly the way they had planned it, all coming together, and Rafael felt the excitement bubble inside him, as he watched it grow. The company—his company.

He dragged Al down the hall now, pointing out everything they had done in the past couple of weeks, pretending not to see Al's amused grin or the growing admiration in his friend's eyes.

He couldn't pinpoint the exact moment when it had happened, but just after they had finally put their signatures on the final documents to make the merger official, he had woken up with the distinct sense that a spell had been broken. Some stars had aligned, some magic formula spoken, and things were finally going his way.

He secured interim financing without having to sell his soul to do so. He discovered solutions where he had stared at problems before. Suddenly, he was introduced to the right people who knew what needed to be done and how to do it, and even while it was all happening, he felt as if he only had to point at something, and it was done, magically, mysteriously, and to perfection.

He had crested the hill and finally got the ball rolling. Maybe that was the magic behind it all. Whatever it was, Rafael loved every moment of it. That's when the thought started to take shape in his mind. He wanted his executives to be part of this incredible moment of transformation. He wanted them to see and feel when an idea became real. Only then would they all work together like one well-oiled machine, all working on the same dream.

He wanted them to be part of the magic, so he had made the decision to delay the board meeting he had been pushing for, just until he could walk them into the operation, as he had done with Al just now, and completely blow them away.

***

The city still slept the next morning, as Rafael turned the key in the lock, punched in his security code, and swiped his hand over the slide panel by the door that would bring up the lights in the whole building—section by section.

His company… It made him smile to think it. How often—just how often had he listened to Connor Beauregard talk about 'his company?' Every time, either Rafael, or David, or Al would correct him. *Connor, it is a public company. It's not yours.* And every time Connor would brush away the comment. His company, he started it, he thought of it, it was his!

"Mine," Rafael said softly, listening to the echo of his voice in the still-empty building. "My company."

He had helped found it, watched it go down the drain, and fished it out again, and got it back where it belonged.

Investors started to get interested again. His phone had been ringing with cautious inquiries. Soon, he would hit the road to raise funds again.

And this time, he would not need to go begging. This time, he would have results to show. He'd walk in there with pride and lay it all out.

Rafael couldn't wait…

He'd developed a little routine. Every morning, in the early hours of dawn before the sun was even over the horizon, just after he turned on all the lights, he walked around the entire building. Along all the walls, he paced, and into every corner he looked.

He saw everything. His mind checked off every bit of progress that had been made since the day before, and somewhere in a back corner of his brain, he always measured the interior dimensions of his building.

That too made him smile.

Unlikely anyone would try to hide another illegal grow op here. It had just become his superstition.

No illegal grow op hiding in the building today? No? Then we are all good to go.

And so he paced it off, every morning. It meant that by now, Rafael Covin knew every nook and cranny, every desk chair and metal shelving unit they owned. He knew every individual plant, and he knew if it had grown in the last few days or not. He memorized the environmental settings for all the grow pods, and he would have known if something was off. It didn't happen, but if it had, Rafael would have seen it.

He knew every person who worked in his building, from Dante and Nick, to the laborers who kept the plants pruned and the grow pods clean, those who worked on the loading dock, who swept the warehouse aisles, who still assembled packing machinery and installed the telephone and computer systems.

He had hired a group of young specialists who installed what he thought of as his humongous kickass server—HKS—on the first floor, so their future orders could be taken, paid for, and handed off to one of the courier companies on the same day. All of those workers had to, at one point or another, step into his office, tell him what they did and why, and Rafael memorized their names.

If anyone who had never been there stepped foot into his building, Rafael wanted to know who they were and what their business at PerCan might be. He drove Simon and his people nuts with his endless questions. Simon Graff and his crew worked installing their new, completely impenetrable security system. Rafael thought he would see about that.

Al had already told him he knew some guys who took great pride in breaking any security system on the planet. They would be allowed to test Simon's magic as soon as he determined it to be ready.

He had finally moved out of his temporary office space down by the main doors, into a cavernous room that had a glass-front wall overlooking the manufacturing floor from two stories up. Rafael had immediately decided it was far too pretentious for the man everyone knew as 'Rafa' and split the area in two, the larger portion for himself and the newly rehired Connie, the smaller one as an office for Al.

Al didn't like it right off the bat. He didn't want to have an office anywhere. It made him feel as if he should be present during set times of the day, he complained to Rafa, and he really wasn't an office-hours kind of guy.

Rafael ignored his protests and taped a sticky note to his desk: 'deal with it.' Of course, Al would come and go as he pleased. Consultant or not, he needed Al, and he would drag him into his working group kicking and screaming if necessary.

His talents, Rafael knew, his talents were decidedly wasted running errands for Tadeo Ivers and keeping an eye on nightclubs and bordellos, collecting cash.

Al had some sort of smart-aleck response to that one and walked away. Rafael refused to listen to his grousing for even a moment because he had seen something. Just before Al turned away, grumbling and muttering, pretending to search for something inside his portfolio, Rafael had seen the pleased and proud smile when he had said *I need you*.

They felt the same way about this company, like a proud father who was about to witness the most amazing thing in his life. Scratch that. Maybe more like a father who survived the teenage years and watched his son take an oath of office.

Kayla stopped by frequently and told them they literally 'sparkled' with enthusiasm, good cheer, and humor.

She had spun her index finger by her forehead, laughed, and walked away to chat with Connie.

Connie herself had given him the biggest hug when he brought her back on at PerCan and showed her to their new office. Rafael still didn't think he absolutely needed a personal assistant. He hadn't changed that much, but it was kind of nice to have her around again, keeping his chaos under control. Plus, she knew what needed to be done, and she knew how he worked. Big bonus.

5 a.m. Rafael put down the paper cup of coffee he had brought with him and stood by the glass wall, looking down on his manufacturing and growing area. This was the day when the clones finally arrived. Nick would check them—one plant at a time—and install them in

their trays of gelatinous grow medium. Then he would lock them up in their pods and… And? Pray, presumably, Rafael thought.

He still only knew the basics about the process whereby a little green plant turned into a precious pharmaceutical substance, but he had given up trying to know and understand everything a while ago. A good leader hired good people and let them do their thing.

You've done well with your team, Covin, he thought and rested his hand on a vertical steel support. Nick Ambrose and Dante Ivers for growing and biology, Al for business development, and Kayla for promotions and publicity.

"We are going to rock this thing," he said softly. "Hard. Because I've got the best people right here, working for me."

Being alone in his building reminded him of Connor again, and he still wished he could have shared this moment with his friend. The day the first plants finally went in, and the clock started on growing, harvesting, and selling. Soon the bay doors would open, and they would wheel in the crates with the clones. How long had he waited for this moment? No longer were they a company in preparation. When he went home tonight, they would be a bona fide manufacturer.

And it was good.

He turned around and sat at his desk, pushing his hands left and right through the piled-up paper like Moses parting the Red Sea. Jesus, even during due diligence, there hadn't been this much paper. When would it end?

If it hadn't been for Connie, he would have run screaming and never come back. Under her guidance, the chaos had assumed some sort of order and organization.

Without her, he'd still be trying to figure out if the compressors for the climate control machines had been delivered or not, and he'd likely be running down the stairs hollering at different people to find out. It was kind of how he'd been running his construction company.

Things were at his fingertips suddenly, and it felt odd.

Information had its place, and it was a place that made sense. Kicking and screaming, Rafael Covin had actually learned how to run a pharmaceutical company. Who would have thought it?

His sons still thought he had gone a bit lulu, though they admitted to the 'cool factor' of medical marijuana.

"Let's go be drug dealers. How hard could it be?" Connor's voice echoed in his head.

How hard could it be? If he had known two years ago, if he had even had the slightest inkling what was coming his way, he would have bought more drinks and told Connor to go fly a kite.

He hadn't. And thus, he had become a drug dealer.

He picked up the running task sheet for the day that Connie had prepared, scanned through the first 50 or so items, and sighed. He would definitely need more help, and quickly too. Thank God, she had made a note in the margins to look through the applications she had prepared for him. Suitable candidates for a number of positions in the company, starting with another business manager to help Thomas when he took up office here.

Thomas ran just as hard as Rafael did. He was still supervising the transfer of equipment and people from Mariposa to PerCan.

Thomas had caught the spark of excitement and matched Rafael's enthusiastic work ethics. Every now and then, they passed in the hall, exchanging a quick and exhausted greeting. Rafael had seen Thomas driving the forklift to and from the giant trucks that delivered materials, and he knew he had to step in sooner rather than later.

Thomas needed to step up and be his COO, not drive the forklift around the plant, as much as he got a kick out of doing so. Thomas had been bang-on describing himself a hands-on kind of guy. Rafael hoped he would make the transition, up into the management floor where all the activity happened on the phones and in people's heads.

Time would tell. Hadn't he himself had to learn how to let go, just after Roger Carmichael took over the construction company? He did, and he had. Nowadays, he only thought of Covin Construction when someone brought up the fact of how completely he had changed industries. Looking back, he thought it hardly made a difference whether you were building houses or building companies, as long as you put your mind to it.

He really hadn't thought of anything he had done over the last 30 or so years as his 'life's work,' certainly not construction. It had been just a job, picking up construction jobs here and there when he was young, getting good at it along the way, and opening his own company.

Originally, he had done it because he hated somebody telling him what to do and what to think every single day of the week. Youthful ignorance figured he knew what had to be done and when and where, and he would do it—without a boss breathing down his neck.

He'd fallen on his ass often enough, finishing jobs on a Saturday night while his buddies partied, because he'd dawdled or mixed up a delivery or plain miscalculated. That's how you learned. Eventually, Covin Construction went from a guy with a truck driving around town offering basement renos to a corporation. Yeah, he'd been good at it. Life at a construction site suited him, along with the swearing, the mess, and the dirt.

He had never given it a second thought until… Well, basically until the day Tadeo Ivers asked him if he would step in as CEO and pick what was left of Perfect Cannabis Corp out of the garbage disposal and fix it. Just fix it. Suddenly, he figured he knew the definition of the phrase *his life's work*—and he liked it.

***

A few hours later, he stood in Tadeo's little back room and felt he had the upper hand for the first time during this project. The more Rafael had made the task his own, the more it slipped away from Tadeo and his sons. It was his company now—public or not.

"They're bringing the clones in today to be put into the grow medium," he said, realizing his voice trembled a little. "It is a momentous day. Nick and Dante sent me here to update you, but really, I think they're worried I'll get in their way. We are there—heck, we are finally there, Tadeo. Very shortly now, we will have our first executive meeting as a new board and a newly formed company."

He tried and failed miserably to hide his pride. It did more than show. It shone out of every pore. "I know they'll be pleased when I show them how far we've come."

"Is all that really necessary?" Tadeo griped, much like Al, to have something to say on the subject. "To have the plants ready, I mean? For a meeting? Did you have to wait that long? You could have had your meeting weeks ago and let everybody have his say and move on. There is much work to be done, and you'll be doing little more than look at the little plants."

"Oh, Tadeo, believe me, I know how long and difficult the road ahead of us is. We have about this much to do…" He held his hands a foot and a half away from each other, "and this many resources left." Now his index fingers almost touched. "That is why I believe it is important to get everybody excited about the project. It is going to be tough."

Tadeo waved him away with a swipe of his hand as he so often did. "No lectures, Covin. Facts, remember? I don't want to hear anything I don't absolutely need."

Facts, then. Rafael sat back and straightened his shoulders.

"Facts, Tadeo. This is going to be a difficult task. It will take all we've got to give. I want to show them why we are doing it."

"To make money?"

Tadeo raised an eyebrow, and for a second, Rafael wanted to tell him how much he looked like Al, before he thought better of it.

"Well, yes, but if we just wanted to make money, we could just—I don't know—make widgets or invest in the next biggest internet fad, whatever that is. We are building something important here. I want to get that point across."

Tadeo glowered at him for a long moment and looked left and right to the men who sat there, as they always did, doing nothing, as they always did. Rafael had long ago named them the 'bookends' because that's all they were good for, as far as he was concerned. Who knew? Maybe Tadeo kept them sitting there because he was afraid somebody would come in with a gun. Or, more likely, he wanted people to think he was the kind of man who needed to hire a couple of goons to sit beside him at all times because his life was in constant danger. One day soon, he would tire of them and send them away, Rafael always thought.

In all of his meetings with Tadeo, he had never seen anything more dangerous than the day-old coffee they served in the diner out front. Once, they had taught Connor a rather painful lesson about asking too many questions, and there did seem to be an inexhaustible supply of cash around here, cash from undefined sources, but that was all.

Don't get careless now, Covin. That's how shit happens. What was Ivers going on about now?

"You think an awful lot of yourself, you know that?"

"Yes, I do. I've taken a defunct, decrepit company and put it back on the map. Our first harvest is going into the tanks as we speak. God, Tadeo, this is…"

"You're CEO for one single reason, and that's because I wanted you to be. I've checked. You don't own all that many shares, Rafael. You've never been CEO of a company like this before. You were never meant to hold this position long term, and the time has come to make a change."

That one hit him unprepared, and Rafael folded his hands immediately and held them hard, just to keep his anger from making him say something foolish without thinking. The pride, the joy at his accomplishments with the company, went out of him as if someone had stuck a large needle into a tire.

"I suppose you could," he finally managed to get out, sounding almost calm. If he let go his hands would shake, he knew that. But he damned well would not let his voice shake. Not unless someone came up with something a lot bigger. "But why would you do that? We are on a good road right now."

"I own the majority of shares; I can do anything I want."

"Can we just work together, Tadeo? Build a company? Create something you can be proud of, something that is good?"

Tadeo said nothing.

"If you want me gone, you want me gone, I suppose. But if you want to make money…"

"If I want to make money?"

"If you want to make money, you leave good people in a place where they can accomplish that for you. I don't know—it just sounds like good advice to me, Tadeo. You can take it or leave it. Regardless, I know I've done the best I could with what you gave me, and I know I did a damn good job."

His anger showed. He knew it and actually did not care. Damn Tadeo for catching him unprepared. He'd been so caught up in his success at Perfect Cannabis. He had forgotten that Ivers had made him 'interim CEO' when he took over. Just long enough to get the company out of the dumps and up and running again.

At some point during that journey, he had started to like it and identified with it. He was good at it, he was successful at it, and people liked his style, his leadership. They followed him. Along the way, he'd forgotten that it was only temporary, that it would all be over one day.

Dammit, Ivers, you want to try doing what I did, he wanted to ask. *Do you want to see how far you get, given all the handicaps I had and stones you put into my road? Really, you want to see how you would fare? You have got to be kidding me.*

Out loud, he said none of these things. He sat still and waited for Ivers to show his hand.

"My sons—my sons are perfectly capable of taking over now."

Rafael bit down on the inside of his cheek to avoid laughing out loud. Tadeo's sons, right. Would that be Dante, the kid he had sent to PerCan to spy on him and Connor, or Al, the man he was jealous of and tried to keep out of PerCan? Or perhaps he meant Roberto, the jailbird who most definitely had something to do with the illegal grow op found in the back? None of these men could do what he did. *My sons can take over*—what a joke.

Still, he said nothing. Experience had taught him over the past few months that with Tadeo, saying nothing at all and letting him run out of steam could be far more satisfying and beneficial in the end than arguing with him.

Especially not arguing with him. Connor had tried that—once. So, he shrugged.

"Probably, yes."

"What do you mean probably, Covin? Of course they can. Dante would be able to do your job without needing a moment of coaching."

"Dante? Dante is one smart kid, and he's turning into one of the best growers I've ever seen. Nick is teaching him everything he knows. He's a huge asset to the company."

"Then don't give me that 'probably' bullshit. And he's not a kid."

"Just making conversation, Tadeo, nothing else. Do you want to make Dante CEO then? And should I do so before the merger is all finalized and the first board meeting and grand opening, or a little while later?"

Rafael folded his arms over his chest, trying to hold in the sheer fury that would have made him slap Tadeo Ivers otherwise. Dante? CEO? The man would not only be unhappy and miserable; he would resent it if Rafael made him CEO. He would follow orders from Dad, yes, but since when was leading a company all about following orders?

He wasn't best pals with Dante, but he knew one thing about him: having to be a CEO would kill Dante. Under Nick's tutelage, he had turned into that guy, the one who lived with his plants, knew them, talked to them, understood them, even. That guy didn't relish the management side of things. Whatever it was that went down between Nick and him, they were happy as two men could be working together without needing a special license and a rainbow-colored banner.

But one thing he was sure of: if you took Dante out of that environment and into the upper floors where all he got to see every day was paperwork and share issuances and investors and financial talk, disaster would follow.

How could you not know your son? How the hell could you miss your own son's interest and gifts by a mile and still have the same last name?

"I expect you to be there for him and guide him."

"I can do that. Whatever help Dante wants and needs from me, I will..."

"Never mind what Dante wants or needs. I'm telling you to make him CEO. Is that clear?"

Rafael felt his arms tighten even a little more around his middle until he almost cut off his own breath. *Hold on to your temper, Rafa!* Of course, it was entirely likely that Ivers here had failed to ask Dante before he came up with this latest harebrained idea. Dante would have something to say about that. Oh, it would be more than something. Of that, Rafael was certain, and the thought of the explosion in the Ivers household almost made him smile. Almost. Another thing he had learned from his dealings with Tadeo: *keep your facial muscles in check.* If Ivers thought he was as much as grinning at him—

"Perfectly clear, Tadeo. Let me rephrase my question a little then. When did you want Dante to take over?"

"As soon as possible. Tomorrow would be my choice, but..."

The old man's eyes became tight little slits as he thought.

"I assume it might be too much of a stretch for the nitwits you put on the board to ratify the merger, all of the new positions, and a new CEO all in one sitting."

"It might be just a little much to digest."

Nitwits, were they? Simon and Josh hadn't done much, but they had helped hold this company together when it was in tatters, helped with cash and advice and equipment, and Kayla? Kayla had gone all out. Rafael forced himself to ignore the stab in his chest and to sit perfectly still. Perfectly cold and still.

"Well, all right then. Give it six months. No, give it a couple of months."

"A couple, are you sure? Wouldn't want to have a misunderstanding here now."

"A couple, two. Two months. Then you will all step down, and I will tell you who is going to sit on the new board."

Oh, a complete replacement! Rafael couldn't wait. Such fun. To take the time to explain to Ivers that he could not simply exchange one executive board for another, especially not in a public company, would have taken more energy than he could muster just at that moment. Heavy with fatigue and weariness, he nodded.

"All right then, Tadeo. Anything else?"

"No. Don't screw up my company in the meantime."

Rafael stalked straight out to his car, slammed the door, started it, and put it into gear, burning rubber on his way out of the dingy parking lot. Most of what went on around him passed by like a movie rolling just beyond his windshield. He let habit and familiarity take over and get him home.

Not back to the building to make his last walk around and check-in, not to say hello and see you tomorrow to the workers, but home. Home, the house he had built a good 20 years ago with the proceeds from his first commercial construction job, and which he had barely seen during the last year or so.

He saw Kayla's Mercedes in the driveway and parked behind it. No doubt she would be bubbling with some sort of news about her grand opening and her invitation list and some other nonsense for his to-do list. Did he care? He sat in the driveway for a minute and tried to decide. Well, did he?

Not really. OK, maybe a little—damn straight he did. This company was like a child to him. It was his work that had brought them out of the hole and to this point, his efforts that made it happen, and this damned grand opening should have been the most satisfying moment of his career. Instead, it would be his swan song, his final goodbye. Damn straight he cared. He wanted to go back there and rip Tadeo Ivers's throat out of his...

"You ever going to come in, or are you just going to sit in the driveway woolgathering?"

Kayla stood beside his car, a vision in white and gold, the gold bangles on her wrist tinkling a pleasant tune with every one of her movements, and he made himself smile.

"In a minute, love."

He still stared straight ahead through the windshield, his hands grasping the steering wheel for dear life.

"Rafa, what is going on?"

She knew him well enough. So, he got out of the car, hugged her awkwardly, and marched straight on into his front room.

"I think," he said, putting down his portfolio and kicking off the damned uncomfortable dress shoes he had to wear with a suit, "I think I just got fired."

"What are you talking about, you think you got fired?"

"I've never been fired before, so forgive me if I'm not all too familiar with the exact procedure and terminology."

"Rafael, you look like... Well, you look bad. So just tell me, who fired you and why? You're CEO. Nobody can fire you. What are you even talking about?"

He raised his hands to stem the torrent of her voice. "Mercy, Kayla. Mercy. You are precisely wrong. There is one man who can fire me, although it's more appropriately called a change in leadership, and that is Tadeo Ivers."

"Tadeo? What is going on in his head? Does he think he can even run PerCan Consolidated? Not by a country mile, not as well as you can. Look at what you've done. You've brought the thing back to glory again, built it up. You have brought in investors, talent, and smart people to help out."

Again, he raised his hands, and this time, his smile was a little more genuine. "I know, I know all of that, and I'm madder than a wet hen, believe me. But realistically, Ivers owns the majority of outstanding shares. He can do whatever he wants."

"And who will run it—him?"

"No, not him. He wants one of his sons to step in. Dante specifically."

"Dante? Dante Ivers?" Kayla threw her head back and laughed. "Good one, Tadeo." She marched straight over to the sideboard where Rafael kept the rare bottles of liquor he owned and poured two scotches, straight up, handing one of the glasses to Rafael.

"Dante," she scoffed. "Number one, Dante does not have an ounce of leadership inside him. He is not even remotely the kind of personality men will follow."

"My thoughts exactly."

"Number two, and more importantly, Dante has no aspirations to the executive level what-so-ever. Whatsoever, Rafa. Dante is happy down there on the manufacturing floor babying those plants, together with Nick. It's all he ever talks about."

"Like I was saying…"

"You know what he told me, Rafa? He wants to write a book about the cannabis plant. What it likes and doesn't like, how it grows, how you can adapt its characteristics to different diseases and their cures. He came to me with this, wanting to know if I could find a coauthor for him."

"I think that's a good idea."

"And you think he's going to say, 'Oh, why, grand, never mind. I'll do mergers and acquisitions instead. No worries.'"

"I don't think that's going to happen."

"It will not."

Kayla swallowed most of her scotch in one large swig and paced up and down in Rafael's small living room. Her eyes blazed a blue kind of fire he had seen before, and usually, things didn't end well for the person on the receiving end of that fire. Finally, she stopped and stared at him for a long moment. Also a look Rafael had seen before, on a snake at the zoo, just before it ended the life of an unsuspecting mouse.

"And you just stood there and shrugged? You just let this happen without a word?"

"I didn't exactly just let it happen, no, but I found out only a few hours ago that Ivers wants to replace me, and not just me, but apparently the entire board. Give me a chance."

"He can't do that."

"Trying to explain to Ivers what he can and cannot do feels like herding cats, Kayla."

"Stop putting on a brave face, Rafa. It's not even remotely funny, and it is not right. We have to stop this madness. We have to find a way to make him see reason. We have to. It can't happen again."

Not again. Words that struck like a physical blow. *Not again.* Yes, they had been here before, hadn't they? Trying to save the company, trying to stop impending disaster when Connor's little grow op behind the main wall had been discovered. Not again. He spread his hands and shook his head.

"I don't want to sit there and let him rip everything away either, Kayla, but my hands are tied. He is our majority shareholder."

"What about Irv Moody? He could still come in. He could still…"

"Irv can't bail us out at this point. I haven't spoken to him in ages, not since the GT disaster. And even if he did invest, even if, Ivers would never agree to a large enough buy-in that it would dilute his ownership position. Never. You know that."

"Then you will just have to make Ivers see reason. If anyone can, it's you."

Determined, strong, always on his side—why on earth did Connor leave a woman like Kayla behind, even if he was on the run, Rafael thought, and made himself focus again.

"Thanks," he said dryly. "I will most assuredly try. If it is possible…"

"Al, Al will be able to help."

"I don't actually know where Al stands in all of this, and I haven't asked. Perhaps he would be more comfortable to stay out of it, if you know what I mean."

"Screw what he's comfortable with, dammit." The words came out so quickly and with such uncensored passion, Rafael instinctively recoiled and raised his hands before he could stop himself.

"Do you think he's in on this, maybe had his eye on the CEO seat himself?" Kayla asked and turned away from him again, and Rafael sighed.

"I don't know. I haven't had the time to think, never mind figure out who is in on what."

"Then find out right now. And after that, we will have to speak to Dante."

"We?"

"You will. And I will get the rest of the board together and talk strategy. We are not going to let him get away with it and dismiss this entire board like a set of lackeys. We are not. He is not taking our company, Rafael."

"It's not actually…"

"Oh, shut up already. I know it is not actually our company, OK?" She put the highball down on the bar top hard enough to make a hard, cold noise. "I know that. Don't stand there sounding like a god-damned professor. You and I were there at the company's inception. You were the one who had the idea. Who the heck does Ivers think he is, waltzing into the room and taking it away from us? Who the hell does he think he is?"

"He's the guy who owns most of the shares, Kayla. That's who he is. That's the golden rule of finance. He who has the gold makes the rules." He put down his own glass, hard, and turned his back on her. "Don't you think I'm just as angry as you are? But one vote—one vote is all he needs to get what he wants. Anything he wants."

"He can't run this company."

"Again, don't you think I know that? Is any of this new to me? No, it is not. But my hands are tied, Kayla."

"And you are just giving up then, is that it?"

"None of this is new."

"Then straighten up and make Ivers listen. We can get the board together and object."

"Not against the majority shareholder."

"Then we are goddamn going to try. And what if Dante says no? What if he won't be CEO? Goddammit, Rafa, there is always a way out, always."

"You think so? Was there a way when Connor ran the company into the ground and ran off somewhere?"

"Yes, there was. And you just proved it. You were the guy who pulled it out of the hole. And again, you're giving up? I thought you were past that."

"I've had enough of this bullshit. I am done."

Rafael picked up his glass again, downed the remaining whiskey in one shot, and slammed the glass back down.

"I'm going for a run now. Close the door behind you when you leave and leave me the hell alone, will you?"

He slammed his bedroom door, changed into athletic gear with jerky, angry movements, put on his headphones, and stormed out of the house. Down the street and into the nearby park, dodging and weaving around couples out for a relaxing stroll and people walking their dogs or children.

He selected a particularly loud track of music and refused to see anything except the four or five feet of the path before him. The world around him didn't matter, the people didn't matter, the weather didn't matter—nothing mattered as long as he kept moving forward.

FORTY-SIX

The track dipped down toward the lake in the center of the park and around the perimeter. Normally, Rafael would have been done. He actually hated running with a passion. He had picked up the habit right around the time he started seeing Kayla, originally to lose a few pounds, then to clear his head and for the feeling of accomplished tiredness it gave him.

Damn Kayla anyway.

As if he didn't know she had a point. He'd been so cocky and so full of piss and vinegar because of everything he had accomplished, he had neglected to keep an eye on Ivers. That's what really bothered him, taking his eye off the ball.

Not seeing it, he stepped on a branch and landed wrong on his left foot. With another curse, he stopped and leaned with his hands on his thighs.

Fuck, he shouldn't have run this far. Now he would have to walk back, and his left foot stung like a son of a bitch.

He chose a few shortcut paths, finally arriving back at his house again, dirty, sore, angry, and in a pissy mood to boot.

The Mercedes was still there.

And he still was in no mood to argue.

So, he stood outside of his house, wondering whether he should go in, have a shower and an argument with a damn fine woman who had stuck with him through a lot of crap over the last year, or just stand out here.

If there's one thing I know, he thought, pushing off the trash bin box and taking a few steps, *it's that she has a lot more patience than I do. I could be standing here for months.*

So, he let himself in through the front door, dropped his keys into a ceramic bowl, making maximum noise to announce his arrival, and toed out of his running shoes. A large bottle of water appeared in his field of vision.

"Took you a while out there."

"Yeah. I went too far."

He took a swig, re-capped the bottle, and sat on the bottom of the stairs leading up to his and his sons' rooms.

"Be damn sore tomorrow."

"So, are you ready to listen now?"

This was the part he hated. The part where she would suggest a dozen things to try to get out of the situation. None of them had a snowball's chance in hell, and if he told her so, she would get pissed off right alongside him.

"OK."

The go-to phrase for every adult male who didn't know what to say. OK.

"The only chance we have at saving this company is with Al and Dante on our side. Maybe even that other son, the one who was around when Connor—when he got into trouble."

"Roberto?"

"That's him. If all of his sons are on-side with us, what is Ivers going to do, run the thing himself?"

"He might try. He can always get a few hired guns as executives and just own the company and—basta."

"Basta, you're talking like Connor now. But that is not what Ivers wants."

"How do you know what he wants, Kayla? You've hardly ever spoken to him."

"Hear me out. Ivers has been running dozens of businesses right on the edge of legality for years now. A lot of the strip clubs, nightclubs, and bars in this town belong to him. And if they don't belong to him, he owns a large portion of them. I did check him out, thoroughly, but he's changed. I think he wants to get out of the skin trade and into something a little more—serious."

"Serious? Tadeo Ivers? We're talking about a man who runs his seedy empire out of the back of a dirty diner. A diner that never seems to see any customers, and yet their cash take is enormous. What does that tell you?"

"It tells me he's getting old. His competitors are sniffing around, and his sons don't want to work in that kind of business. Al doesn't have any desire to work with him. He'd rather be a consultant for you. Dante and Nick talk plants and biology all day long, and half the night, and who knows what Roberto is up to or where? The way I'm thinking, Tadeo is going to use Perfect Cannabis Consolidated as leverage."

"And use it as a bargaining chip with his kids? Whoever does what he says gets to run the company. That's kind of sick if you ask me. And it won't work with Dante anyway."

Kayla shrugged and sat on the stairs beside him. "Family dynamics. Play one against the other, get what you want. It's complicated, especially if you throw in a lot of money. You were an only child, weren't you?"

"Sort of. My parents split when we were young, and everybody took one son. Me with my dad, Cole with my mother."

"That's kind of sick too, but not my point. Jesus, these stairs are uncomfortable. I hate to interrupt a good pout, but won't you come into the living room where one does not sit on an uncomfortable hard stair tread?"

Hard to argue with pure logic. Rafael took another sip of water and finally rose. She was right to boot. Every joint creaked and ached as he stretched, but he'd still rather have bitten off his tongue than complain about it.

"Sore?"

"Nothing a hot shower won't fix."

This time, she laughed and shook her head.

"You can admit it, Rafael Covin. You like running PerCan, and you care about the company. It pisses you off like hell that Ivers is trying to take it away from you."

"He's doing more than trying—he's doing a pretty dang good job at it, and you don't usually use words like 'piss off.'"

"Unusual circumstances." Kayla held out her hand and allowed him to help her rise to her feet. "I know you hate talking about Connor, but here is where you are different from him. He wanted the company for the prestige it gave him, for the CEO title and for the power. You care."

"Well, don't let it get out, will you? Who knows? Before soon, I might have to be the tough guy around a construction site again."

"You won't."

"OK."

"If Ivers wants the company so he can keep his kids in line and close, then all we have to do is work together with said kids—and our problem is solved."

"I really don't think it's going to be as easy as all that, Kayla. Not even for you and your—superior powers of persuasion."

Kayla smiled again, bad mood from a couple of hours ago all but forgotten.

"Maybe, and so what if it doesn't work? Nothing will change, but at least we can say we went down fighting."

A fact of life he could hardly argue with. Always go down fighting if you're going down at all. Fighting Ivers would take deception, manipulation, secrets, going back on agreements. All the stuff he was no good at.

"I don't have a problem with solving issues in business—serious issues even. I always get it done. But it's dealing with snakes that gets to me every single time."

"Can't say I blame you. Fortunately, I have a bit of experience dealing with them."

The bitter way in which she said it—was she talking about the magazine business now or something else? Someone else? Connor perhaps?

Kayla shook her head as if to clear away that particular train of thought and moved on before he could say anything.

"So, this is what we will do. You will have a shower and get halfway presentable again. I'll phone Al and Dante."

"Now?"

"Right now. I'm going to ask them to meet us at that Greek restaurant down the road, and we will find out."

"Bit of a joint. I've never eaten there."

"Exactly the point, my love, exactly the point. So go." She actually pushed him toward the stairs again. "Get cleaned up while I make some calls. I will not go out with you looking and smelling like this."

"You're pretty pushy, you know—for a girl," he laughed.

"Comes with the territory. You think the magazine trade is easy? Jesus. Now go before I realize you said 'for a girl' and get really offended."

FORTY-SEVEN

Dante and Al showed up almost immediately, as if they had dropped everything on the spot. Kayla could convey urgency in a way that made people drop everything and rush to help.

When Kayla and Rafael arrived, the men were already seated at one of the scarred Formica tables in a quiet corner. Al had his hands folded on the table in front of him and looked as if someone had died, and Dante idly shredded a coaster in his restless fingers.

They knew something was up, and they knew it was not good. Rafael had not called a meeting like this one in—well, he had never called a meeting of just the four of them. Al's face told him all he needed to know. Tadeo had already outlined his grand plans to them.

"Rafael, Kayla," Al said, and rose a bit off his chair, and they slipped into the booth. "I wish I could say always a pleasure, but…"

"So Tadeo told you."

"Yes, earlier this afternoon. He made a big show of outlining his plans for the company to Dante and me. I am—stunned, albeit not surprised. I… I don't know what to say, Rafael."

He looked at Dante, but Dante carved precise parallel lines into the cardboard coaster with the edge of his thumbnail. He didn't raise his head, didn't acknowledge either of them, and in general pretended the whole thing had nothing to do with him. Except it did. His father meant for him to be the key player in this miserable drama. He was to be CEO of this publicly traded company, and, at that moment, he looked as if he wanted to be sick.

"Dante, believe me. I had no idea this was coming," Rafael said gently. "Hell, I—I still can't even grasp why he would do something so, so…"

"Stupid," Dante suggested. "Because as far as I'm concerned, it is so goddamn stupid, I don't have the words for it either."

"I assume your father wants to…"

"Screw what he wants, Rafael." Dante flung the coaster away and squared his shoulders. "He always went on about how you were on borrowed time, how he wanted the Ivers family to be in charge. And we always knew there was a chance he would do something rash eventually, but we kept our mouths shut. So, I say screw what he wants. He doesn't care what any of us in this room want, so why should we care? If he wants to force me to be his CEO, he is going to get the worst damn CEO the world has ever seen, you got that?"

"Easy, Dan," Al said and shook his head gently. "None of this is carved in stone yet."

"And you're so sure about that? Have you ever seen him change his mind? And what does he want you to do, brother? Come on out with it now, if we are all being honest. He wants you to stay away from PerCan, where you would actually be happy, effective, and he wants you to 'wrap up his business dealings in the club sector.' Wrap up his business dealings—don't make me gag. Clean up his mess after he just takes off is more like it. Didn't he tell you 10 years ago the job as his assistant was temporary, only until he found someone trustworthy?"

"Well, yes, but…"

"And you're still driving all over town, collecting money, threatening to beat up assholes who dare to skim off Tadeo Ivers and keeping the riffraff in check. You get your hands dirty while he sits in his diner. Wrap things up—what does that even mean, man? Give me a fucking break."

Al looked down at his hands and said nothing. Rafael bit the inside of his cheek so he wouldn't open his mouth and embarrass them both.

He'd never asked just what exactly it was Al did for his father, and Al had never offered. It didn't sound like a great job, and certainly not one that suited the intelligent, creative Al. Their friendship didn't require an explanation, and none was offered.

Finally, Rafael raised his hand and silenced the next tirade from Dante.

"I get it, Dante, OK? None of us around this table are OK with what your father is doing with the company. I just came here to get a feeling how all of you think about it, and I think I just got my answer."

"The question is how do we stop it?" Kayla picked up the thread. "Because I'm not sitting down and letting it happen, and neither is Rafa."

"You might not have any choice. He owns majority shares, remember?"

"Fact is you cannot simply replace the entire board in one fell swoop, Al. It's not done. Investors will go insane, the regulators will get real touchy…"

"So, he'll pick you off one at a time. Do you feel like waiting around for your turn? Sounds like a wonderful working environment. Yeah, I can go for that!"

"You haven't heard the entire story either, have you?" Al asked, and Rafael shook his head.

"The way you say it I already know I'm not going to like it, so go ahead. Have at it. What is it I don't know?"

"Remember Tessa?"

"I do—and not in a good way. Connor's personal assistant. She was the one who sold out to your father in the first place and gave him all the information he needed when we were—no shit!"

"No shit," Al confirmed with a nod. "He's bringing her back. She is supposed to run the entire company together with Dante."

"Tessa is a great administrative assistant, but she doesn't know dick about running a company. Sorry, Kayla."

Kayla shook her head and brushed off his apology. "That Goth girl who always had her face in a computer? She is supposed to run the company. Good luck to them."

"And David."

"Not David," Rafael said and slapped his hand on the table. "Not David. Damned little accountant took Tadeo's money once and worked behind my back when our filings were late."

"He needs David for his business knowledge and knowledge of the company."

"And I'm telling you that David won't do it, Al. After the first time I figured it out, he swore to me he would never do anything like this again—never. He swore it, and he won't go there again."

"Maybe. But did he swear on the half million-dollar gambling marker Tadeo just bought up?"

"Fuck this."

Rafael forked his hands through his hair, and Kayla waved away the apology before it had left his mouth.

"What else is he going to do?"

"Whatever it takes, Rafael. He knows no boundaries. Frankly, right now, he even worries me."

"But why—why does he want PerCan so badly? Up to now, he was perfectly happy to sit in his little old diner, run strip joints and escort services, and leave the rest of us to do business. Why now, why this company?"

"No one ever tries to figure out Tadeo's reasons, Rafa. For what it's worth, I think he sees himself as something of a drug czar for the whole country."

"Medical marijuana. He does not even know the definition of that. How it works, how it's produced, or how it's marketed. He has no clue about the rules and regulations."

"The clubs and escort services were a good business for the last 30 years, but it's become a tough business, and times are changing. The things he got away with years ago—they are illegal now, there is a new and younger crowd pushing in from Asia, and Tadeo wants out, whatever it takes. And he figures he will learn what he needs to know about the business."

"And what better business to get into than this? Tell me, does he have any idea of the governmental scrutiny he will be under? He won't be able to sneeze without somebody taping it."

"I know that, and you know that, and he probably suspects it—but right now, he does not care. He thinks he will deal with everything if and when it happens."

"Stupid idea," Dante muttered and picked up another coaster to maim just like the first one.

"I'd have to agree with you there, Dan." Rafael shook his head. "When my sons were 10, they acted like this. See something they want and make a grab for it."

"Well, how is this then…" Dante straightened up to his considerable height, even sitting down, and flung the next coaster away. "I'm not doing it. I'm just not going to do it. I'm just gonna tell him to fuck off."

"You will do no such thing," Al said and grabbed a hold of Dante's wrist. "Remember what he did to Roberto?"

"So what? I've learned enough from Nick; I can make money anywhere marijuana is legal. Companies need growers like me, desperately. He can't hold me by force. And you—you ought to be ashamed."

Kayla raised her hands, both index fingers pointed, and hushed the men.

"Wait, wait, guys, don't start arguing within this group now. Not now. This is exactly what I was asking Rafael earlier. What if both of you refuse to do what Tadeo wants? Then what? Is he just going to surround himself with strangers and let others run his company? Is that his plan? From what I know about Tadeo Ivers, he does not trust anyone. Not even his own kids, apparently."

That one was said with a hard sideways look at Al, and Al actually had to look away. He took a deep breath and let it out slowly.

"He—might," he said, with deliberate caution.

"Do you know something we don't?" Rafael asked and searched Al's blank eyes.

Secrets? Had they not come far enough together to be honest with one another?

But Al did know something. That was clear as day in his evasive look. Something was up, and it was not good.

"Al?"

Al sighed again and made a fist, putting it before his mouth.

"I'm the last guy who wants to pick sides, Al. You know that. But if something is going on that affects the company and our running of it, then I need to know. Loyalty to your father or not."

"That's not it, Rafael."

"Then what is? I can't promise you I won't use the information, but…"

"These Asian gangs who are moving into the club territory in this town, the people I spoke of earlier, they are not—overly burdened by morals. And I have a feeling that terrifies him more than anything."

Dante looked as if someone had struck him, Kayla blinked quickly and shook her head, uncomprehending, and Rafa followed the little red thread for a moment.

"They are trying to take over?"

"Yes."

"And your father…"

"He's been fighting them off thus far, but he's losing. These people are organized, they have money, and they are very, very well connected. A few threats have been made, and—he is taking them seriously."

"Shit."

Rafael nodded slowly, as a couple of missing pieces suddenly appeared in the story, completed the picture, and made it make sense where it had not earlier. The way Tadeo had become more and more erratic lately, the tired look in his face, the absence of any kind of business activity at the diner…

That place had never been busy in the traditional sense of the word, but people had been coming and going. Business partners making drop-offs, picking up something… Just lately, every time Rafael showed up, he was the only one.

And the bookends… He'd always made fun of the two sitting left and right of Tadeo, but if he didn't miss his guess, they had changed just recently. These weren't the usual type of doofuses he was used to. These were new guys, meaner, fitter—armed, perhaps? No doubt, and with this new piece of information it made sense.

"He's been fighting a war," Rafael said slowly, nodding.

"I believe so. That's why he has left us alone mostly to run PerCan any way we saw fit."

"But…"

"But, Rafael, he doesn't think he can win this war any longer."

"So, you think…"

"Isn't it obvious?"

When Rafael didn't reply, Al put both of his hands on the table palm up.

"Tadeo knows he can't win. Ergo, he knows he's going to be out of business fairly soon. By his own choice, if not by someone else's."

"He could just retire," Al said after a moment. "And many of us have suggested it on more than one occasion. But that's not a scenario he enjoys contemplating."

"But…"

"Being forced out of a business he has run for well over 30 years and going home to retire as an old man who cannot cut it any longer? Rafael, as much as you and Tadeo have butted heads at times, I would hope you understand how difficult that would be for him?"

"I do, Al, but that's life sometimes."

"That's life. And he has funded us for months and let us do our thing. Sure, he could be reasonable and suggest some type of cooperation, but he is Tadeo Ivers. What sounds reasonable to you and me is not necessarily the most acceptable conclusion to him."

"I get it," Rafael said slowly, trying to catch up with what he was hearing. "I get it. So now PerCan becomes his alibi business? His proof that he's still got it? 'I'm not quitting. I'm just doing something else.' Is anybody actually going to believe that?"

"It hardly matters what anybody believes or not, Rafael. It matters what Tadeo believes, and what's going to allow him to go home at night and hold his head up high, that's all."

Rafael sat back and folded his arms before his body. Tadeo wanting to save face made sense, which did not make it any easier for him. He had worked for PerCan, founded it, managed it, and got it out of the gutter. No matter what, he had no intention of giving it up any time soon.

"I'm not making excuses, Rafael, only explaining."

"Well…"

"I don't buy it, brother," Dante said, having moved on to a napkin to disassemble now. "I just don't buy it. If he wants to get out of the skin trade, fine, do it. But don't make me be CEO and shuffle paper all day long. I won't do it. And you? What about you? Are you even thinking about getting involved with the Chinese? Sounds like he wants you to clean up for them."

"Vietnamese."

"Whatever, Al. That job comes with a T-shirt that has a target on the back. He can't do it any longer, so he leaves you to clean up his mess? And, oh, by the way—there's zero chance you're getting out of this whole? Sorry about your luck."

"It's not that bad."

"Are you listening to yourself? You're supposed to wrap up and close out his previous business affairs. Shit that somebody else is fighting like hell to take over at this very moment. How did you put it, without being burdened by morals? That does not sound like a few polite negotiations, a handshake, and a signed contract agreement."

"Dante is right," Kayla said softly. "We ran a few stories in the mag about these gangs." She shuddered and shook her head. "All due respect, but please don't go anywhere near them."

"Well, you see, but I..."

Rafael raised both his hands to stop Al, and for once, his friend obeyed. Another bit of helplessness on his side there, perhaps? He had no desire to do as his father bode him to do, but no way to say no? For once Rafael could help him out there—it was quite easy. No. N-O. No. No way.

"Kayla's right, Al. If I were you, I would not go anywhere near this 'wrap up his deals' thing—whatever he has envisioned by that. But I'm not you. So, all I'm going to tell you is I wouldn't do it. At the end of the day, that's your choice. My original question tonight was what are we as a group going to do about all of this?"

He spun his forefinger once around their little circle, encompassing Al, Dante, Kayla, and himself.

"What can we do about this? Admittedly, we've been having a pretty sweet ride just of late..."

"Because of your hard work, Rafa."

"Thanks, Kayla, but each and every one of you had a hand in this. We've all worked our as—tails off to get PerCan to this point, and we are all steamed that Tadeo wants to dismantle it and take over. Agreed. Next stop, what are we going to do about it?"

"I am not going to be CEO. That's my next stop," Dante said petulantly and glowered at his brother. "I don't care what he had in mind, but I'm not doing it."

"What did you want to do instead, then, Dan?" Rafael asked sweetly because all of a sudden, the germ of an idea began rearing its head in the back of his brain. A tiny little idea... He couldn't quite grab a hold of it yet, but it was there, it was cooking, and when he grabbed it by its little idea-tail...

"Dunno. Grow marijuana. It's the first thing I've done I enjoy doing. It's what I'm now extremely good at. There are opportunities for a guy like me out there, and I'm going to take 'em."

"Good."

"And another thing, I'm pretty sure if I leave, and you leave, Nick is not going to stay on for very long."

"Oh?"

"He's had a couple of run-ins with my father, and he did not like them. Not even a little."

"When did your father start issuing orders to my employees and contractors? Damn. OK. Anybody else?"

"I've got a magazine to run." Kayla shrugged. "If I'm being pushed out of PerCan, then that's what I'm going to do. Why do I get the feeling you have something in mind, and you're leading us somewhere?"

"I might… Just wait. Al?"

Al rested his chin against his fist and said nothing. Rafael thought he could see just a tiny shake of his head. Understandable, perhaps. Al had been Tadeo Ivers's proxy for an awful long time. Doing what Tadeo said to do and when to do it. And here stood Rafael Covin, a man he'd known peripherally for a few years, and whom he had been a friend to for the past few months. All of a sudden, he stepped up and asked him to do—what? Oppose his father, throw away everything that had been his life for the past 30 or so years and… and do what?

Al shook his head again, the faraway look in his eyes seeing speaking volumes he couldn't, or wouldn't, speak just yet.

"You don't have to make up your mind just yet," Kayla said gently, "but Rafael and I mean it—and so does Dan. Do not get into dealings with these gangs on behalf of your father. Be safe. Tell him you won't do it. There is always work at the magazine."

"Or Covin Construction, for that matter."

Al finally smiled gently and sat up a little straighter. "That is very sweet of you to offer, Kayla, but I'm quite certain the magazine business is not ready for a character like myself."

"But…"

"Neither would the construction business be, Rafael. But thank you—both of you—for thinking of me and wanting to keep me out of trouble as it were. Friends like you… Well…"

He brushed away the rest of his sentence with a hand. "You know what I'm saying. Indeed, I have no desire to lead a territorial war against the Vietnamese. Your—intense reaction merely proves me right. Perhaps it is, after all, time to retire."

"Retire," Kayla asked as if he had said something rather obscene. "Look who's talking. You're hardly old enough to spend your days going down to the senior center to play bridge, you know."

"Neither do I have any talent for games of chance whatsoever, dear Kayla."

"So?"

"So, if I'm going to get involved into another project—well, a beach bar on some Thai beach is sounding really good right about now. Whatever it is, it will most definitely be something I enjoy, not something I must do."

"My point," Rafa said, raising an index finger. "My damned point exactly."

All eyes went to him, and he drummed the tips of his fingers together rapidly, trying to grasp said idea a little harder, teasing from it the thought, the core he had just felt like a beating heart. Dammit, it had been like this when he and Connor had the original idea—exactly like this. There was something there, if he could just…

"I'm working on an idea, gang," he said softly and made a fist. Still, the thought remained elusive…

"It's not quite gelling yet, but I know it's there."

"And is it going to help us with my father?" Dante asked, clearly unconvinced at the veracity of any idea Rafael Covin might have, no matter how good or how outrageous.

"Possibly, Dante—possibly. Let me work on it a little more. So…"

He looked around the table and spun his finger around one more time.

"Here's what we're going to do, if you're all on board with me. We are absolutely not buying into this whatever-it-is Tadeo wants to do with PerCan. If he wants to run the company, he has to do it without any of us, agreed?"

"Agreed. Damn straight agreed."

Dante. Eager as ever. Tadeo had no idea what had happened to the lazy, uninterested, biddable son he had sent to spy at PerCan. What Rafael and Nick Ambrose had done to him. Rafael almost smiled.

"Good. Then we are going back to work as if nothing had happened."

"Wait, I thought…"

"You thought we were going to march in there and quit as one man. Exactly not what we want, Dante. If and when he lays out his grand plan about replacing the entire board, making you CEO and bringing in a group of strangers to run the rest—we'll tell him we won't do it. You will quit. Don't worry. We'll have your back."

Dante only nodded.

"You, Al—well, I hope you will tell him where he can stick his Vietnamese gangs…"

"In less strong words, but essentially—yes."

"Kayla and I will lay low. He's basically already told me he's firing me. Fine. I'm going to pretend I am good with it and move on with life. You, my love," he smiled at Kayla, "can tell him you're more at home in the magazine business anyway."

"And what will this accomplish, Rafa?"

"It will buy us time. Time for this idea of mine to come to fruition."

"Time he can use to ruin the company—again."

Rafael sighed and shrugged. "Dante, he may do that anyway, and there's unfortunately nothing we can do about it. He is the majority shareholder for now, and unfortunately, what he says goes. We may not have a choice but leaving the company to him, much as that pisses me off. But what we don't have to do is play his game. OK, gang?"

They shook hands and walked off again, each back to their own homes, and their own memories of Perfect Cannabis. Back when it was just an idea in Connor and Rafael's head, back when they had all called their closest friends and moneyed associates to give them the great news—*there's this cool cannabis company I'm working with. How would you like to invest in it?*

Connor's voice echoed in his head as if it had been only yesterday. *We are going to be drug dealers, Rafa. There is going to be more money than you've ever seen in your entire life. Next stop—the big time.*

FORTY-EIGHT

He was close—he was so close. At the Mandarin Oriental Hotel, he clenched his fists hard enough to make his knuckles crack and turn white. So damned close. Days now, only days and what had been his would belong to him once again. He was so damned close.

He raised a glass of scotch and toasted the young man slumped in a deep club chair across from him.

"We are there."

"Almost. There's still the final board meeting."

"Details." The man swished his hands through the air as if chasing mosquitoes. "Mere details. It is ours again, only a matter of days."

"You know, you are one crazy fuck," the younger man said and took a healthy swig of scotch himself. "Most people I know of go out of their way to avoid having to do business with Tadeo."

"Or check their pockets when they're done. Isn't that what you're trying to say?"

"But you—you don't care, do you?"

The man who had been a reverend, and, before that, a slightly sleazy stock promoter, grinned and shook his head.

"I'm going to ignore the fact that you called me a crazy fuck and no, I don't care. Why should I?"

"Because Tadeo owns most of PerCan, or PerCan Consolidated as they call it now, so he's going to own half of your company."

"Wrong, kiddo." The man rolled his eyes. "He owns half of half of the new company. That's kind of a quarter by my math, but suit yourself. I own almost everything of Mariposa by now and a big chunk of PerCan still."

"Confusing, but so?"

"I excel in mathematics. I made sure I will have a majority share position. You just don't worry your head about this one, Rob. I am going to be fine, my friend." He had that faraway look in his eyes that worried Roberto now and then. That look that said he saw something only he could see, way down there in the recesses of his mind, and it usually meant bad news for everybody else. Just saying.

The man could be a dreamer, a builder of great castles in the air. But a lot of the time, he seemed more like a plain old crazy fool as far as Roberto was concerned. Roberto had no room in his life for crazy. Crazy got you in trouble.

Look at him now, with that silly grin on his face, and all the work he had done and the money he had spent to make sure he would be in this position. In this very position, about to finalize the merger between a company he now all but owned and a company he had owned once. And for what? For what exactly? Not to make money, certainly, because he had enough of that already. To take revenge perhaps. But if you were going to bankrupt yourself and your entire future in the name of revenge, then you were more than crazy—you were insane.

Aside from that, he even looked certifiable, sitting there, sipping scotch, planning...

Planning what exactly?

'We'll figure it out' had turned into his go-to line when Roberto asked him anything about the business.

"Who are you going to put on the board?" he asked instead, and the man who called himself Barry now shook his head absentmindedly.

"What? Oh. Well, you—and me, for sure. There's a capable guy at Mariposa who can run things, Thomas something."

"And?"

"And what? You just let that be my business."

"I would if it made sense, Con…"

"And stop calling me that. This is the last, the very absolute last time I am going to tell you this. Got it?"

"Fine." Roberto rolled his eyes again, knowing it would irritate the man—Barry.

"Barry. Fine. But you're going to need a lot of people to run this thing. And I mean a lot. Have you looked lately…"

"We will figure it out, Roberto, in due time. There are capable people there. Your brother for one, Dante."

"Dante," Roberto scoffed. "Dante. You have got to be shitting me. Dante knows nothing he hasn't stolen from me, Barry."

"I heard he's learning. Information you conveniently forgot to include in the package you gave me, Rob. Anything I need to know there?"

"Nothing. Nothing you need to know other than I'm going to run the growing side of things. I don't need any help, nada. And most certainly nothing from my snot-nosed younger brother who got everything he ever asked for from our dear father. Never had to work for anything, the little shit."

"Well, well, well, why don't you not hold back and tell me how you really feel. You know what? I don't really care. Go ahead. You want to fire Dante, fire Dante. Hire who you need and let's go run this thing."

"I think you are going to need an operations manager."

"Possibly."

"What about that guy you ran with back then, Rafael?"

"Rafael…" The faraway look was now definitely gone from his face, replaced by something cold and hard. He slammed the glass on the marble sideboard hard enough to splash the remaining whiskey onto his hand.

"Rafael. My former friend and current asshole. Now there have to be 3 billion people I would hire ahead of him to run my company, if you get my drift."

"But he…"

"But he… This is a deal-breaker, Rob. Rafael Covin will only set foot into my company as a janitor or as a customer. In no other capacity will he ever see the inside of PerCan Consolidated, do you understand?"

"But…"

"Do you understand? Only one answer is possible."

"Yes."

"Good. The asshole stood by while everyone crucified me for your mistake—your mistake, Roberto."

The younger man shrugged and drained the rest of his whiskey. "Remember what I told you about my father. Most people will stay away from him, far away. He gave me a lot of money to go on TV and say what I said—that it was you who put the grow op behind the wall, that it was your idea."

Barry brushed his hand through the air, wiping away anything Roberto said.

"Never mind that now. But Rafael… Rafael should have known better. He and I were friends, friends, Rob. I looked him in the eye and told him I had nothing to do with it. He should have believed me."

"Maybe he did. Maybe everybody else voted against him."

"And then what does he do? Then what does he do, might I ask? He takes up with my girlfriend—my girlfriend. No, the day Rafael can call me anything but an enemy is never coming. Never, you understand?"

"Never, got it."

The younger man put down his glass and rose carefully. When Barry was in that kind of a mood, it was better to be careful.

"From what I hear, the old man wanted to fire him anyway. So, either way, seems he is gone."

"Why would he fire him right now? That doesn't make any sense. Rafa might be a conceited ass, and he is gone the moment I own the company, but he pulled it out of the hole nicely—for us. Your old man doesn't know what he's doing."

"He wants what you had."

"Huh?" Barry frowned and poured more whiskey. "Bullshit."

"Not if you're Tadeo Ivers."

"What I had—what? What the fuck kind of answer is that?"

"You and Rafael, the way you ran the company at the very beginning, when he first met you…"

"Ancient past. And?"

"You ran this thing together—you and him. Frick and Frack, he called you, two guys against the rest of the world."

"Correction, I ran it, Roberto. I ran it—and write that down if you can't remember it. Rafael fucked off most of the time and told some of his moneyed friends where to find me. That's all he ever did. And if anybody starts telling a different story…"

"Have it your way." Roberto shrugged and rose. "Way I see it, he has this mental image of him and Dante running this thing together. Ivers and Son."

"How Norman Rockwell of him. Don't make me gag. That's not how business works, and if Tadeo doesn't know that—fuck, why should I even care."

The whiskey was doing its thing, slowly but surely. Rob had lost count how many Barry had downed by now, but he sank deeper into his chair with every glass. Time to go, his instincts told him. Time to go, before something set off the man across from him and he had one of his famous fits.

"I have to run."

"Your father needs to stick to what he does best, run strip clubs and provide prostitutes to the people who have the money to pay for them. That's what he's good at. Stay out of the pharmaceutical business."

"Probably would if he could."

The words were out before Roberto could stop them, and Barry sat up a little straighter. He might be drunk, but a piece of information you tried to keep from him always found his ear, every time. Barry froze the younger man in a laser-like stare and cocked his head, trying to hear something that had never been intended for his ears.

"What are you talking about?"

"I have to go."

"Never mind have to go. You stay right in this room until you explain to me what the fuck this is all about."

Barry rose to his feet and towered over Roberto. Give him one thing: the crazy fucker was taller than almost anyone Rob knew, and he used his size whenever he needed to.

"What, Roberto?"

"From what I hear, there's some competition moving into the business…"

"Competition, that's it?" Barry scoffed and sat down again. "If he can't handle a little competition, he's getting old, your old man. What he needs to do is knuckle down, run his business right, and stay out of mine. And since when does Tadeo Ivers not know how to show a competitor the door? Taking lessons from Rafael, is he? Whining, complaining, not willing to make the hard decisions?"

This time Roberto only nodded and kept his mouth shut. No skin off his nose if the old man went down or Barry right behind because neither would listen. Damn, he didn't owe a thing to either of them. Them or his thieving little brother Dante.

Dante! Now there was a guy with a wakeup call about to happen. Little shit thought he could just make off with all of Roberto's notes and pretend he was the big man in town, the one who knew all about growing weed. They'd see about that now, wouldn't they? Dante better not even think about staying in town once Roberto was in charge.

He punched his hands into his pockets a little deeper and shrugged.

"None of my business anyway, B... I have to go."

Before Barry could launch into another tirade against his family or come with the latest 'aren't I great' sermon, he jumped to his feet and nodded the briefest of goodbyes. He narrowly avoided running down a room-service waiter, skipped the elevator in favor of the stairs, and didn't pause to take a breath until the hotel was a block behind him.

Crazy idiots, the lot of them. The mere thought of having to climb into bed with them for a couple of years, pretending to partner with these fools, would have made him gag as little as a few years back. Fortunately, prison had made him smarter than any of them. Partnerships came and went and for a little while. One could put up with anything. Anything.

Besides, he still had his own plans where PerCan was concerned, beautiful plans—but none of them were any of Barry J. Wentworth's business.

Barry J. Wentworth. Even the name was bullshit, and as fake as his reverend's license, somber black outfit, and preacher voice. *Better watch your back there, Reverend Bartholomew, because you got more devils than angels on your team. Just sayin'.*

FORTY-NINE

So, this was going to be it—the day.

Rafael shook his head to clear it and pushed the button on his fancy espresso machine. When had that appeared in his kitchen? Must have been Kayla. Kayla right now carefully opening her eyes, squinting into the morning sun that always flooded his bedroom because he couldn't be bothered to close the curtains.

Rafael liked the wee hours of the morning. They allowed him to get stuff done before people had a chance to realize he was available and start to bug him with the daily minutiae of running a business. He didn't mind rising before the sun did, but slowly, he was learning that mornings and Kayla usually didn't get along all that well.

They would eventually find a middle ground that worked for both of them, wouldn't they?

Rafael took a sip from his hot espresso and sighed. Would they? After this day, after Tadeo Ivers's grandly announced meeting of the executive board, nothing would be the way it had been for the past years—ever again.

They'd reshuffle the deck and start over. But no matter what else was decided, Rafael Covin would no longer be CEO of Perfect Cannabis Consolidated. After today, all the knowledge he had acquired, the contacts he made, the plans he had put together, would all be useless and for naught, unless someone bothered to ask his opinion.

He'd have to have an uncomfortable conversation with Roger Carmichael to get his company back. Roger, he heard, had quite a ball with Covin Construction, and he liked it. His staff liked him too, and probably wouldn't be too happy with another change. Heck, maybe it was smarter to leave it be and let him do his thing. He and Kayla could retire if they wanted to. Travel, have fun. There was always that.

Unless somebody asked his opinion…

The precious little espresso cup almost slipped from his fingers. Not because it was hot, not because his fingers had a hard time hanging on to the delicate darn thing—but because it was back.

It was back! That nugget of an idea that had teased the edges of his awareness earlier. There it was.

Unless somebody asked his opinion…

Well, why the hell not? Why not take that brain trust they had between the four of them, five if they managed to enlist Nick Ambrose, and make it available to interested parties? Interested parties like, oh, let's say, anyone eager to gain a foothold in this up-and-coming industry?

Why the hell not?

Sneaky, damn straight it was. Illegal? Nope. At no point had Tadeo Ivers ever bothered to make any of them sign noncompetition agreements, and the hell they would now. There was no need. They were all in this thing until Ivers chose to tear it apart.

Ivers just assumed he could run his company without them. Nick and Dante, he needed, he realized that, but the rest of them he considered expendable, numbers on a board, figures to be exchanged. Why not let him try?

Rafael grinned and downed the rest of the puny espresso in one gulp and fired up his old-fashioned coffee maker. This one required more than a tablespoon of coffee; this one required a whole pot. Now he knew where he was headed.

He checked his watch and made a beeline for his excuse of a home office. 7 a.m. now. Tadeo had set their first board meeting for 2 p.m. When Rafael got fired and everybody got the sweet news about the new face of PerCan Consolidated. Before then, he had just time to put together a concept for Cannabis Consulting—which needed a better name—a quick conference call with the rest of the gang, and anchors aweigh.

Ha, he almost laughed out loud. Well, why the heck not? He was in his own home after all. He kicked his overflowing garbage can and laughed as it wobbled.

"What say you to that, Ivers? We are going to go on our own and screw you and your damn pettiness. Screw you."

He drummed his fingers on the table top while his laptop started up and slipped into his chair. First coffee of the day down.

"Executive summary, Consulting Co, Medical Marijuana…"

Today's date.

Key Personnel: Rafael Covin, Management; Kayla Montecito, Promotion and Publicity; Al Ivers, Management and Operations; Nick Ambrose, Horticulture and Experimental Biology; Dante Ivers ????

Space, space.

We have the knowledge, the experience, and the drive to turn your operation into a successful, fully compliant, turnkey medical marijuana manufacturer.

Yes.

"Yes, we do," he said and stared at the blinking cursor on the screen. "We most certainly do."

Best of all worlds. *Do what we do best—sell our knowledge, set up companies, make them run well.* That was exactly what they had been doing for the past few months, and they had done one hell of a job.

Damn if it wasn't the most brilliant thing he had thought of in the last few years.

There it was, that feeling he remembered so well. The excitement, the heart beating a little faster, the furious rush when they put something together, it all came back as one. This was how it felt when he and Connor put together a new company, a new concept. For the space of a heartbeat, he allowed himself to miss Connor, yearned for the friendship and the good times, then brought his mind come back to the task at hand.

"You're in an exceedingly good mood for a guy who is about to lose his job."

Kayla wandered into his little office, hair messy, eyes still tired, feet in fuzzy slippers, and he realized he had been at his summary and description for several hours now.

"No coffee for me this morning?"

"I am sorry. I know I neglected to bring it to your bed as usual. But come here…" He extended his arm so she could slip into his embrace and nodded at the screen. "Know what this is?"

"Not really." Kayla squinted at the screen, too vain to wear readers, as usual. "Do I need to know?"

"This, my dear, this is the idea that I've been chasing for the last day."

"The idea, capital I, as you called it?"

"Precisely."

"All right. Let's hear it."

Kayla drank his coffee now and looked around for anything in the room not too dirty or messy for her to sit on. Shrugging, she finally picked a stack of file boxes and perched precariously on the corner.

"Well?"

"OK, here goes…" Rafael fisted his hands and spread them again, almost as if he were trying to catch a ball right at chest level. "OK…"

Dammit, what was he, a first-timer pitching an idea? He wanted her to like this, he needed her to like this, and—never mind like, she had to love it, or he wasn't taking it any further. Right now, she just sat there, one eyebrow raised, waiting for the grand revelation he had promised.

"What are we really good at?"

"Pardon me?"

The eyebrow shot up a little further, and the smirk on her face meant business was the last thing on her mind.

"Not that, business. We, as a group. You, me, Al, Dante—you know what I'm talking about, right?"

"Sort of."

"OK, so what are we really good at?"

"I don't know. Getting things done at PerCan? Rafa, what are you getting at? I'm not very good at puzzles. And it's too early to boot."

"Right, perfect. You are an expert at puzzles. We, as a group…" He spun his index finger around as if the rest of them sat right there in his home office. "We excel at setting up and running a 'marijuana for medical purposes' company. Dante and Nick, best growers there are. Al and I, operations and management, and you, my dear, best promotions officer I've ever met."

"Aw. Do go on."

Kayla smiled that broad 500-watt charmer that melted his heart every single time. Every single time. There was a reason he tried so darn hard…

"So, what you're saying is Ivers is an idiot for firing you—and thus me in the process—for getting rid of Al…"

"He most definitely is."

"And we've gone there before. What I am missing is the idea."

"This is the hottest new business there is, love. This is the one everybody wants. A drug trade for investors, that's what one of those business writers called it. There are dozens of new MMP companies popping up everywhere, every single day, and only a small fraction of them will actually make it."

"Like the dot-com of the nineties. Most of them don't do the research as exhaustively as they ought to and lack the know-how and talent. Oh…"

Realization dawned, and Rafael spread his arms, waiting for it to sink in.

"Right."

"A consulting company."

"Bingo. We know what we're doing, and we have the track record to prove it."

"But…"

"All we need to do is put together a decent proposal and hang out our shingle."

"But Rafa—Ivers is never going to let all of us go in one fell swoop. He is too smart for that. He will lock us up in agreements…"

"Agreements that have not even been written yet. And they never will be signed. Nobody thought it would come this far. We were going to take care of contracts after the merger."

"Oh."

"Oh." Rafael nodded. "He can try, but hell if I'm signing anything. As far as I am concerned, all I am is a shareholder now, a shareholder with a bit of insider knowledge, and so are you. Ivers didn't know what he was doing, and I was too busy saving the company from ruin to worry about noncompetition."

"Holy crap, Rafa, this could actually work."

"Of course it could," he said smugly, one, because he enjoyed the brilliant, adoring smile on her face, and two, because she had said 'crap,' which was a word reserved for the most severe of surprises and situations.

"This is…"

"Awesome?"

"Won't he try to sue us?"

"Probably. It's a chance we have to take. It'll allow all of us to keep working together at something we really enjoy."

"Agreed. This could be the answer, Rafa."

"And?"

"And you are a genius."

He was probably blushing; he could feel the heat rising in his cheeks. Still, her words made him grin even more. This, this was exactly what he had been looking for, perhaps since the day Tadeo had put him in charge and he had groped desperately to put a team together. A team he could work with, a team that would have his back, a team he would stand up for and fight for. A team that was his.

Without a word, he pumped his fist and rubbed his hands.

"Then let's do it. Get dressed, love, and make coffee, lots of coffee. We have about seven hours worth of work to do in the four before Tadeo's meeting."

"Are you really sure you want to do this?"

"Why wouldn't I be?"

His hand, reaching for the telephone already, froze in midair. Why wouldn't he? Was there something he hadn't considered, a wrinkle in his perfect plan that hadn't occurred to him? No. He shook his head and focused on Kayla.

"Why wouldn't I be, Kayla? If I'm missing the obvious, I'd prefer if you told me now rather than later."

"Rafael?"

"I mean it. What?"

"Tadeo."

"Tadeo what? Spit it out."

"You're abandoning Tadeo and Perfect Cannabis Consolidated. You don't do that. You're the guy who always sticks to his promises and sticks up for the people he works with. So I am just—a little surprised."

Rafael dropped into his chair heavily and turned left and right for a moment, as if he were shaking his head.

"Right. I stick up for the people I work with, Kayla. Work with. If only for one moment I had the impression that Tadeo Ivers wanted to work with me, with me and with his sons, then I would move heaven and earth to make his company successful. I would find a way. Instead, he just tells me, 'Thanks, but you can go now, and don't let the door hit you in the ass on the way out.' That right there is not the way I work, so he ought not to be surprised."

"Still, it's not your style."

"My style." Rafael laughed bitterly. "No. It is totally not my style, but right now, this is the best I can do for the five of us. And that is something I can stick up for. You just said it yourself. Right or wrong, I always stick up for the people I work with."

"Fair enough."

"I can't promise you this is going to be easy. I can absolutely not promise you there won't be nights you will find me awake, pacing, asking why you didn't stop me. But what I can promise you is that if we don't try, we will always regret it."

He didn't wait for an answer, just went upstairs and stood under the hot shower for an imagined eternity, letting the water scald him and take away guilt and worry and regret. Kayla would be calling Al, Nick, and Dante, knowing that once he made it up, his mind would stay there.

***

Kayla called another rushed meeting at another coffee shop, this time down the road from Rafael's house. Did it really matter any longer if anyone saw them together? Probably not. In a few hours, each one of them would be persona non grata at Perfect Cannabis Consolidated anyway.

Rafael sipped a coffee that covered up lack of taste by being far too hot to actually taste it and passed around a few photocopied sheets.

Al and Dante sat across from him, side by side, while Kayla and Nick had chosen a seat to the left and right. A sign? Quit that, he scolded himself. He'd tell them his idea, and they could make up their own minds. They were grown men. If they did not want to join him, so be it.

"Thanks for coming, guys," he said quickly. "I'm sure all of you had other things you would want to be doing this morning."

"Kayla said it was urgent," Dante said, his long, wiry body restless and fidgeting. "You've figured it out then? You know how to stop my father from ruining the company—again?"

"Not entirely."

Al's eyebrow shot up all the way to his hairline, although he still said nothing, and Dante stopped moving, as if energy and air went out of him all at once.

"Then what…"

"I've had an idea, guys. A plan that might be good for all of us and allow us to work together the way we have up until now. But before I explain it to you, I need you to promise me something."

"Whatever. Anything. Let's hear it."

"Hang on to that thought, Dante. Once you hear me out, you might not want to be part of it." More surprise on Al's face, and even Nick stirred a little uncomfortably beside him. "I need you to promise me that if you experience even the slightest bit of discomfort with what I'm about to suggest, you will get up and walk out of here and forget you ever heard anything."

"This is starting to sound intriguing." Al finally came to life across the table. "I for one can't wait to hear it, and trust me, I will walk away if it's a harebrained, stupid idea."

Kayla nodded, so did Nick, and Rafael picked up the copy of his new company profile. "You, Nick, will have to be most careful of all of us. You were hired as a consultant. I don't foresee a huge problem, but best to be safe. Have a look at this profile."

He spoke for about 15 minutes, laying out the basics, the background, and his own projections. Details could wait until later. One by one, he saw understanding dawning in their faces. If they did this, if they really did this, they had an enormous chance of success. And Tadeo Ivers had an enormous chance of failure, possibly even a guarantee at the same time.

"Wow," Al finally said. The first one of the group to speak. "That's quite an ambitious plan you have there, but…"

"Before you say it, yes, I know I'm throwing your father under the bus."

Nick picked up the executive summary, carefully smoothed the pages with his hands, and put it back down again.

"I'm an independent contractor, Rafael. I've always done my own thing. I promised you loyalty when you hired me, but from what I heard, you'll be gone by tonight, so I don't see a personal conflict. Now you two." He looked up and let his gaze rest on Al and Dante for a moment. "You two are the people who are going to have a moral issue to wrestle. Tadeo is a jerk most of the time, but he is still your father."

"A father who wants to stuff me into a job I neither want nor am any good at whatsoever. Nick, come on. This here is exactly what we want. We've even talked about it, you and me. I say let's…"

"Dan, take a minute to think before you jump in, just because you are sore with him right now," Nick said. "I, for one, would be honored to work with a great bunch like you four. I think we would make one hell of a consulting company together. Rafael, I have no doubts at all."

Al sat quietly, looking at his folded hands on the table top before him. What might be going on inside his head, no one knew. As always, nothing showed he didn't want to show, a careful, bland façade. Dante looked at him, waiting for an answer, and Kayla pretended to be leafing through Rafael's executive presentation.

"It is an ambitious plan, and one heck of an idea," he finally said. "You are quite correct when you say the five of us have everything it takes to put together a successful company. And your forecasts are on the low side. I'm sure you know that."

"Deliberately."

"No doubt." Al nodded. "And Nick is equally correct saying Dante and I have a big choice to make."

"Didn't expect it to happen right this minute, Al. I'm just proposing…"

"I am honored that you would include me in this plan, without the slightest bit of hesitation."

Rafael had no answer to that and looked down at his hands himself. He and Al had not always seen eye to eye, that was true. And Connor only had one plan there for a while: get rid of Al and his family, end of story. It had become his obsession. Rafael and Al both valued loyalty above everything, and yet…

"Then let's do this, brother," Dante urged. "What are you waiting for? Jesus, do you really want to be the one dealing with the Vietnamese gangs, putting your life on the line, just because he doesn't feel like doing it? How long do you think you're going to last?"

"Thanks for the vote of confidence—brother."

"Get serious. This could be your death warrant. Let's say I do what he says. I become CEO. I really knuckle down and give it the best shot I can. How long do you think it will be before I foul up royally? And he'll hire somebody to fix it quietly, again and again and again. Then how long before I'm a joke in the industry, the guy who doesn't know what he's doing running Daddy's company? This is not my life; this is not what I want. I would have to quit just so I don't go insane. And the rest of my life would be wrecked. But you, Jesus, don't even go there. This project of Rafael's is just a shortcut to the life we want, man."

"You are 100 percent correct, Dante. I'm still having a small problem abandoning our father to his own foolishness. That's all."

"Then you make him see reason."

"I don't know if I can, or if indeed anyone can."

"Then that's it, bro. I'm not going to do it. I'm not going to commit myself to a life of years of mediocrity at a job I never wanted. I deserve better—we all deserve better."

His eyes glowed with fervor, and his voice had risen considerably during his long tirade. "I know I've never come out and said so. Maybe I was waiting for you to notice on your own, but Nick and I…" He looked over to his friend, only to find Nick's hand, and they both smiled. "Well—Father would hate it, and likely force his own standards on me. Again. What do you think…?"

Kayla reached across and gently put a hand onto Dante's wildly gesticulating ones.

"It's OK, Dan. We here, all of us, get it. We get it. And still, your brother is right too. Abandoning your father…"

Al rested his palms flat against one another and rested his chin on them.

"I wish I could decide as easily as you can, little brother. I really do. Listen, if it were Connor Beauregard we were talking about, I'd up and leave without another thought. He screwed everyone he ever made a deal with—and a few people he didn't."

Rafael cleared his throat quietly, and Al shrugged.

"You know it's so, Rafa. You of all people. But Connor is gone, this company belongs, to a large extent, to our father now, and there are just a few—allowances—we are going to have to make."

"Allowances. Don't make me laugh."

"It's not funny. And it's not going to be easy, and it might even be impossible. But here's the thing, Dan. I have to try. I have to go in there and let him run things for a bit, and when he finds out he can't, then we try and make him see things the way they ought to be."

"Goddammit, Al, do you have to be so bloody noble?"

"Far from being noble," Al said softly and took a sip of his long-cold coffee. "Far from it. I have to deal with the Vietnamese, remember."

"If that doesn't kill you first."

"Your concern is touching."

"Call it whatever you like. I don't even want to think about it, OK? What if I say no? And if I say no, I'm not going to be CEO? Is he going to pick you to do it?"

"To do it." Al chuckled. "Listen to you. This is not a task like taking out the garbage we're talking about here."

"You know what I mean. You'd be good at it. You'd make an excellent CEO. Or you." He pointed at Rafael and spread his arms.

"If I know your father," Rafael said carefully, "he would not do the one thing you expected him to do. Just out of obstinacy."

Al raised his hands to stop all discussion at the table, and for a moment, they all looked at him, waiting for the pronouncement, the final one. Because every inch of his body, of the way he held himself and acted, told them that this would be it. No talking, no discussing, nothing else.

"You all." He nodded at Nick, Kayla and Rafael. "You all are free to do as you wish. You have no connection to Tadeo, and you owe him nothing. I, on the other hand, will have to abide by his wishes, at least for the moment."

No one spoke for a moment. Kayla made a fist before her mouth, Nick fussed with his tablet, and Rafael sat as if carved in stone, staring down at his coffee cup.

"Well, that totally sucks, brother."

"You are correct. It does indeed—suck. But for my own personal conscience, it's the only choice available to me."

Al quickly gathered the thin portfolio he carried and nodded at Rafael.

"I should—go and prepare for this afternoon's meeting. Gents, Kayla…" He smiled a little sadly, nodded at Kayla, and disappeared as quickly as he could. Through the center of the coffee shop and out through the front door, before either of them could as much as say a word.

Rafael looked up and saw something sitting on the table, where Al had been. Dante reached for it and held it in his hand.

"Hey, Al forgot his phone. Maybe I should…"

"Never mind, Dante. Never mind."

Rafael shook his head. That was the phone he had given to Al when they started to work together, when he decided he could no longer work with a partner who was never available. They had had more than one fight over the carrying and answering of this particular phone.

Rafael swallowed hard, took the phone from Dan, and gently put it into his own portfolio.

"I'll take care of it. Go—the two of you," he said to Dante and Nick. "Go and give some thought to everything we discussed here. Don't make any decisions for now. Just think about it. And best of luck to both of you."

Dante and Nick disappeared next, and for a moment, Rafael and Kayla sat at the empty table, staring at the just-vacated seats.

"He didn't forget that phone, did he," Kayla asked softly.

"Nope." Rafael tried to look anywhere but the door where they had all disappeared. "No, he did not."

"Want to talk about it?"

"No—yes—I don't know. Al never carried a phone or a computer. It was part of his personal style."

"When he was working for his father."

"All that changed when we started working together on PerCan and PerCan Consolidated. He's the one came up with the original idea for the merger. He's the one who showed me how to push it through and get it done. He's the one I asked when I didn't know what to do next. Now..."

Now... Rafael sat back and blinked furiously past the choking in his throat.

"End of an era, that's all," he finally said. "When it's time to move on, it's time to move on and all that shit. You've heard it all. So, what do you say—you still feel like hanging around with an unemployed construction guy?"

"You know it, Covin. Who else is going to build me my dream home?"

"Sounds good, lady. Start drawing up plans."

"That's it then—we're just giving up here and walking away?"

"Hey, if Ivers wants to keep you on the board, I'll say go for it, if that's what you want and if you feel you'd enjoy it. I've been walking around with this little pink slip in my back pocket for a little while now, so it shouldn't surprise me. I'd just forgotten..."

"I know—I was just..."

"Hoping it would turn out differently in the end? Hoping I would somehow by some magic throw a hail Mary pass that connected."

"I guess—yes, I did."

"Well, I always sucked at football anyway."

Rafael called for the bill and gathered his things. Tablet, notes, his phone. He slipped it into the portfolio right next to Al's phone and tried not to think about it. He'd figure out what to do with it—eventually. He paid their tab without saying another word and rose from the table.

Mechanically, they walked back to his house, glad they had not chosen to bring a car. The exercise in the fresh air and sun and the silence between them helped restore a small bit of normalcy.

One bit at a time, Rafael thought, one bit at a time, things would return to normal again. He'd managed his life just fine before PerCan, and he would manage it again after. Maybe he'd go back to Covin Construction, or maybe he would let Roger Carmichael manage it and semi-retire.

Maybe he'd really build Kayla's dream home, and they would…

Anyway, he'd gained a few good things. He managed a little smile as he took Kayla's jacket and hung it in the wardrobe in the hall. He'd gained a few really good things. And they might still have their consulting company anyway.

FIFTY

The day was here. A day a few years in the making. A day he had dreamed about so often he sometimes couldn't tell whether it was a dream or already reality, whether he was recalling something that had already happened, or making it up as he went along.

Years of planning and scheming, months of sitting back, pretending to be patient, waiting for the right moment to come—it all came down to this day. Millions of dollars hidden, and brought back just at the right moment. Oh yes, he had basically bankrupted himself to see this day.

Roberto, fool that he was, had hit it quite right. Had he taken all of his money, he could live from now until the end of days on a lush island in the Caribbean. Scratch that. He had tried that on Vaomar Island in the South Pacific, and it had almost killed him.

This, this was what he needed, craved like a junkie, his next fix—the deal.

Chasing the deal, putting it together and making it work. The real juice. This one he'd actually have to run for a while, since none of the morons at the helm had the foggiest clue on how to run a company of this size and not trip over their own feet. But he could handle it.

He rubbed his hands together to warm them, although he was certain the temperature in this well-appointed hotel room would be at a perfect comfort setting. It always was, but the mere thought of the next few hours made him shiver.

It would be his, once again. Never count out Connor Beauregard, aka Barry J. Wentworth.

It had a ring to it, didn't it? Maybe he would have somebody design a badass logo for him. Something corporate, awe-inspiring. He couldn't wait. Couldn't wait to be at that meeting. He could taste it now, having them sitting there, around a conference table, then him reaching for the door and stepping in. He could hear Kayla's gasp and Rafael's silent curse. Another two hours left. Two more hours and it would all be his again. Why, oh why, could time not move any faster?

He tried pacing, he tried going over his introductory speech, and he tried reading the paper—nothing worked. He eyed the mini bar and turned away as quickly as he had looked at it. Not today. Today, he wanted to be sober all the way. He wanted to hear and feel and know what was going on. Today, he was not going to drink a single drop that might spoil the moment he had been waiting for. Silently, he sat back down, folded his hands in his lap, and played the situation out in his mind again, exactly the way he wanted it to go.

FIFTY-ONE

Once again, they had taken extra special care to spruce up the building today, Rafael noticed, wondering who had given the orders to sweep and clean the aisles as if they were going to perform surgery there, wash all the windows, and repaint the front entrance area. Repaint the entrance? Dang, had they not done so just recently? Rafael shook his head.

He didn't bother to step into his office, which wouldn't be his office any longer after today, and instead headed straight for the big meeting room. M1, the one with the retractable panels that opened to a glass wall overlooking the production floor. Genius design, really, and one Rafael was especially proud of. It tended to impress the heck out of the investors when the meeting was over and you opened the panels to let them look at the hive of activity they had just bought into.

Yes, he had accomplished an awful lot here.

And yes, it bothered him to have to walk away from it.

Kayla, walking beside him silently, took his hand and attempted to smile.

"Hurts to get fired just like that, doesn't it," she asked quietly, and he shook his head.

"It's irritating, that's all. It was starting to feel like—home."

"Yup, hurts like hell."

Rafael opened his mouth to argue and closed it again. No point in trying. She was right, and she knew it.

He met a few of the workers in the hall, who nodded and greeted him warmly. They liked him, and likely would hate it when he was gone.

Of course they liked him. He had made a point of getting to know them all, finding out what their job entailed and how to make it easier for them. When they asked why, he said he merely wanted to make the company run smoother and better. In reality he did so because quite often he didn't have the foggiest idea what these people actually did and why. What better way to find out than to ask them how to make it easier for them? He'd battled through all right, against everyone who told him a construction man couldn't run a pharmaceutical company. He could. It just wasn't easy.

Josh Novak and Simon Graff stood in the hall just outside the large meeting room, talking in hushed tones, quitting when they saw him come toward.

"Afternoon, fellas," he said more cheerfully than he felt. "Everything all right in your part of the world?"

"Not bad." Josh shrugged. "You know how real estate works—up and down and up and down."

"Long as you're more up than down, I always say."

Rafael opened the door for them, and they entered as a group. "So, what's this meeting all about then, Rafa? Again, we did not get a detailed agenda. Sometimes, I really wonder about the processes within this company."

"Let's just say it's Tadeo's meeting, Simon. And he does things in an—unconventional manner."

"Unconventional." The man who owned Graff Security rolled his eyes and shook his head. "More like disastrous. What's his business calling a meeting if I might ask? And when is he going to tell us what it is all about? The last time he called us down here like this…"

Rafael tuned him out and pulled out the chair at the head of the table. The hell with it if he wasn't going to take that particular seat one last time. And there she was too, the dark lady, as he called her. Tessa,

Connor's former assistant transformed into Tadeo Ivers's sometime employee, helper and purveyor of any and all information required. Legal or illegal. Great. The woman showed up every time something disastrous happened to them, didn't she?

This time, she didn't set up elaborate AV equipment or fiddle with laptop computers or screens. She merely organized a pad of paper and pens in front of her and nodded a brief greeting at him. Perhaps that meant the big man was going to show up personally. He usually didn't leave his hovel of a diner, ever, but stranger things had happened.

"Rafael, Kayla. Hello."

"Good afternoon, Tessa."

Kayla took a seat at his right and narrowed her eyes at the black-haired young woman. She looked like there was more than one thing she wanted to say to Tessa, but Rafael shook his head gently. Not now, not today. It likely didn't matter any longer anyway.

Dante and Nick showed up five minutes later and took seats at the left and right of the table quickly and without looking at Rafael. Even Simon noticed the heavy silence around the table and quit babbling, and quite suddenly, the only sound in the room became the hiss from the overhead air vent.

As irritating as that noise was, they simply could not get a handle on it or dampen it in any way, no matter what they tried. Rafael made a fist to hide a sudden grin. There had been this one investor he had entertained in here. The man just wouldn't shut up about that irritating noise, until Rafael told him it was white noise, designed to make sure no one walking by the conference room could overhear what was being discussed inside.

Memories... Amongst other things, he had also shoveled a few loads of bullshit in here.

Kayla noticed his silly grin and raised an eyebrow at him, just as the conference room door opened again and Tadeo Ivers strolled in, flanked as always left and right by the two bookends, who had actually donned some type of uniform for the day, which Tadeo undoubtedly thought made them look more threatening.

For a fraction of a second, Ivers stopped, stared at Rafael at the head of the table as if to decide whether he should make him vacate the chair or not, and finally shrugged and took a seat at the opposite end. His two guards actually remained standing behind him. God, the drama. Where on earth was he going to find this kind of drama in the rest of his life?

This time, Rafael did not smile.

"Well, you might all wonder about the purpose of this meeting," Tadeo said, and Simon sat up a little straighter.

"Indeed, Mr. Ivers, considering you are not actually on the executive board of this company, we are wondering, yes."

"Correct, Mr. Graff, I am not. I'm merely the majority shareholder of this fine company begging your indulgence for half an hour. After that…" He wagged his head back and forth for a moment. "Half an hour is all we will need today."

"Half an hour it is," Josh Novak said, desperately looking from Rafael to Ivers and back again. "But since we are indulging curiosity today, might we find out what the purpose of this meeting might be then? Just to put us into the right frame of mind if you will."

"Well then…"

Tadeo Ivers, unwilling to wait any longer, it appeared, folded his hands on the table before him.

"I do appreciate all of the time and effort all of you have given to rehabilitating this company after Connor Beauregard almost succeeded in ruining it."

"But?"

"Pardon me?"

"There's a but at the end of that sentence, it appears," Josh said, sitting up a little straighter now, alarmed as much by Rafael's continued silence as by the broad grin on Tadeo Ivers's face. "But?"

"But it is time now, gentlemen, to introduce a more permanent executive board as we move into ongoing operations."

Rafael still said nothing, though everyone in the room suddenly looked at him. Heck if he was going to make it easy on Ivers.

"Rafael?"

He nodded at Ivers and spread his hands just a little as if to say, *well, why don't you carry on, if you will?*

"I should thank Rafael Covin for everything he has done as interim CEO of Perfect Cannabis Corporation. Now that the corporation is moving into the next stage of growth, I propose to appoint Dante A. Ivers to CEO and president of the company."

10 seconds stretched in perfect silence, as if someone had hit the pause button. Then Josh rose to his feet and pointed his index finger at Rafael, his face a landscape of confusion.

"Rafael? Hello? Open your mouth, man. Did you know about this? Are you OK with this? Did you sign off on this?"

"Yes and no, Josh."

"Yes and no what? Christ, has this company not had enough ups and downs? Do we need to add drama and guessing games, and an ever-changing executive board? Do we need a revolving door on the conference room? Is this wise?"

"Yes, I did know that Mr. Tadeo Ivers, majority shareholder of Perfect Cannabis Corporation, wanted to introduce a new CEO of the corporation today. No, I cannot honestly say I am OK with it, but he is quite correct. I was appointed as interim CEO when Connor left. With the majority of shares, he can certainly appoint whomever he wishes. I have no other choice than to bow to accept his selection."

It all came out as one long run-on sentence, and Rafael was glad it did. Less chance of stumbling or saying something he would rather not say. He folded his hands again and stared defiantly at Tadeo.

"I have plans for this company," Ivers said, locking eyes with Rafael. "Ambitious plans. And my sons will be here to help me realize them."

"Wait, wait, wait just a minute." Simon looked back and forth as if there were a giant tennis game playing out between the two head ends of the table and shook his head. "I don't get it. You're firing Rafael? Why would you do a—something like that? He's the one who came up with the idea, the one who put the company together. He arranged the mergers. He… he…"

Rafael locked eyes with Tadeo Ivers, daring him to take over at that point, to say what was on his mind.

His stubborn streak and carefully hidden temper were getting the better of him again, Rafael knew it, and he didn't care. Shit, how much worse than firing him could Tadeo really do?

Matter of fact, his sense of drama urged him to stand up straight, right there in front of everyone in this fancy and way over-the-top boardroom and toss all of his notes and files and whatnots right there onto the table in front of Ivers and say, *Here you go. Have at it. Fail for all I care. Just don't ever ask me another thing—ever again.*

And when you've ruined your company, when everything we've built is in the crapper—don't come crying to me that it didn't work.

Those were the words he really wanted to use.

Stubbornly, some built-in Miss Manners kept him from doing so.

"Tadeo appointed me interim Chief Executive Officer of this company, if you remember, Simon," he said, using every ounce of willpower he still possessed to make it sound casual and perfectly normal. "It was always understood that at the point in time when the company was back on its feet, I would have to step aside."

"All due respect, Rafael, that just doesn't make any sense. You do a great job running the company—no, a fantastic job. You've put a first-rate team together. Look around you. People who really know what they are doing, people who get the job done. Why on earth do we need to make these changes now? We finally have the company where we want it to be. We are gaining some traction. What's the purpose of this change, can you tell me that?"

Simon spread his hands and challenged Ivers. "I don't doubt you have your reason, sir. As majority shareholder I mean. I—as a board member—would merely like to know what they are. Sir."

Oh, Simon, the sarcasm, Rafael thought.

Ivers would strike back and strike back hard, just to show everyone that you didn't speak to "the Original Chef" in this manner.

'The Original Chef.' He almost grinned at the nickname Ivers had used when he came into the company, just when he met Connor Beauregard for the first time. God, Connor had been furious having to meet the man in the back of a diner, incensed at what he considered a dumb game of codenames and hide-and-seek. He probably would not sit here and let himself be fired quietly either.

Not a chance. There he would be, rising ever so slowly and dramatically, all fire and brimstone, and without even thinking about it, he would find the words that convinced every single one of the men and women present that to dispose of Connor Beauregard in such a manner meant imminent and certain death for the company. In fact, the one and only way to avoid such imminent death was to give him even greater powers of decision-making and more freedom to do whatever he wanted. Failing which, they would all be doomed, lose all of their money, and face a life of shame and failure. Fortunately, he would say, fortunately, they all knew better and would vote to avoid such a grim fate.

And hands would go up, and Connor would get what he wanted.

Connor Beauregard… Heck, why not grin at the memory? What could Ivers do to him any longer? Fire him? Right. Rafael chuckled softly. He could almost see him there, standing in the open door, smiling broadly at the assembled board of directors—almost. What the…

He wasn't sure he had spoken that out loud, but suddenly, Kayla, beside him, gasped, and Dante Ivers said what all of them were thinking.

"What the fuck?"

Indeed, the door to the boardroom—that fancy, black-and-white, broadly lit boardroom—stood open, and an apparition had appeared.

Rafael rose to his feet slowly.

"Connor," he said, hearing his own voice tremble and a pitch too high. "Connor?"

Kayla reached for his hand, Simon and Josh sat frozen, and Ivers—Ivers turned to the two bodyguards behind him, a command on his lips. Surely a command that meant *remove this interruption this instant.*

"Good afternoon, gentlemen and lady." The man nodded at Kayla. "Nice to see all of you again. Forgive my tardiness. I had plumb forgotten about the horrific traffic in this city."

"This is a closed board meeting," Tadeo said icily and nodded for his two guards to close in on Connor. "And you, sir, are most certainly not a member of the board of executives of this corporation."

Connor took a chair, got comfortable, and folded his hands.

"No more than you are, Tadeo Ivers, or do you prefer to be called 'Chef?'"

Rafael burst out laughing at that name, and for the first time, Connor looked at him fully.

"Rafael Covin, what have you done to my company?"

"Well, Connor. I dare say I've kept it rather well in your—absence."

The man smiled again, and Rafael was reminded of a rather large and lazy snake. Lazy only because it wasn't hungry at that particular moment. Later on... who knew?

"Well, well. For the benefit of the executives of Mariposa Corporation, soon to be Perfect Cannabis Consolidated, my name is Barry J. Wentworth, and I do indeed..."

Rafael couldn't help laughing. "Barry? You're not serious, right? Connor, what the..."

Without ever missing a beat, the man reached into the inner part of his suit jacket and withdrew a passport, flipping it casually to land on the conference table right where Rafael stood. Rafael couldn't help it. He knew he was part of an enormous game or joke, but he simply couldn't help it. He picked up the passport and read...

"Bartholomew J. Wentworth," he said, shaking his head. "Reverend Bartholomew Wentworth…"

The passport dropped from his fingers, and a few things suddenly lined up in his mind with perfect clarity. Mariposa, a reverend—a reverend who owned a huge chunk of shares.

He remembered a conversation he'd had with Al, so long ago it was almost forgotten. They were trying to convince each other there was nothing to worry about, 'probably just a backwater pastor somewhere who is hiding the money he snuck out of the collection plate, no cause for alarm.' And Al's casual shrug.

"Connor—Reverend—Barry…" he said, trying to string them together like pearls on a string. Then he dropped into his seat again. Heavily, slowly, letting his hands drop by his side.

"Well then…"

"Well then," Barry said cheerfully. And that little muscle that always twitched along his jawline when he was having a really good time… it was doing a veritable dance there now. "Well then, for those of you who don't know—I do all but own Mariposa Marijuana Corporation at this point. Which means I am the new man in charge. But don't worry…"

"Wait, wait—wait just one goddamn minute," Ivers roared. "I still own PerCan."

"Oh, dear Tadeo. Once again, and slowly. PerCan is a publicly traded company, as my advisors so often reminded me. And I—I gave myself a generous portion of founder's shares when I thought of the original concept. After all, what is the purpose in coming up with a concept if you can't own it?"

Somewhere, a door slammed. The conference room had become so completely silent, so utterly still, every sound in the building became amplified a hundred times and more. 15 men and women around the great conference table tried to wrestle with what their eyes were showing them clear as day, trying to do the math in their heads as to who might own what, and, lastly, trying to figure out what it all might mean for them. Connor—Barry merely sat there grinning, and Rafael felt a giant hole opening up right there in front of him.

Dammit, I'm glad I got fired not 10 minutes ago, he thought.

Connor Beauregard was back.

"Don't ever count me out until you see my dead body before you. And even then, you would do well checking for a pulse, Covin."

Yes, Connor Beauregard was back.

Tessa squirmed uncomfortably in her chair, and Barry zeroed in on her in a second.

"You may leave now."

"You stay right where you are," Ivers countered. "Wentworth—Beauregard—whoever you want to be, you will not give orders to my staff."

"Your personal staff, no. So, go take her on as your own private secretary if you wish. Just remember that she's betrayed me to you, and you—to me."

"I did not."

Barry merely smiled again, and Ivers rose to his feet, planting his hands on the table before him.

Just then, the door to the conference room opened again, and another man stepped in. This time, Ivers Senior, Dante, and Al froze in shock, and Tessa let out a little yelp.

"Ladies and gentlemen, meet Mr. Roberto Ivers. I see you remember him, Tessa. Did you not share some pretty vital information about this company during your—pillow talk with him?"

Ivers fired something that sounded like rapid-fire cursing, but his wayward son Roberto merely shrugged and took a seat beside Barry.

"Afternoon, all, don't get yourself tied up in knots, Dad. It's not as bad as you think."

"Now then," Barry continued. "I think the lady's reaction says it all."

Tessa stammered something barely intelligible, and Roberto shrugged. "Sorry, babe."

"You dare walk into my company, Beauregard, disrupting every-thing, threatening me—to do what? What, Beauregard?"

"Oh, forgive me, Ivers. I thought that was obvious. In all of the confusion, perhaps I didn't make myself clear. I'm here to take my company back."

Everybody started talking at once. Rafael felt as if a great big wave had suddenly washed over him, and all the sounds and sights from the great conference room he had built to Kayla's specifications came to him through this layer of water.

He opened his mouth to say something and closed it again. Con-nor—Bartholomew. Then Connor looked at him and smiled slowly, that reptilian smile he used to find so comical in the old days.

"Mr. Covin, I believe you were let go from the company as well if I recall correctly, so if you will please…"

Barry Wentworth indicated the door with one wave of his hand, and still, Rafael couldn't say one word.

Calmly, carefully, he packed his pad of paper and pens into his portfolio. On second glance, the pens all were PerCan-branded issues, so he took them back out and left them on the table. He shrugged into his jacket, nodded an unseen greeting at Simon and Josh, who were arguing with Roberto over one thing or another, and left the room for the last time.

Down the hall, first right, through the cavernous reception hall. He made sure to nod a final greeting to the ladies who sat there and stepped through the front doors.

Walking into the parking lot felt like emergence of some sort. The sun on his face, the fresh air. *Dammit, I should have brought Kayla*, he thought, and pulled his phone out to text her. She would follow him. But even as his thumb hovered over the home button, he stopped and put the phone away again. Kayla and Connor—Connor and Kayla. What you would call an item once upon a time. And now?

"Who the hell knows," he said to himself just to hear his own voice and started the car.

For the moment, there was only one thing he could think of, and that was to get away from here.

FIFTY-TWO

He still hated running... Rafael tried to convince himself every now and then that if he gave it a chance, if he just put on the sneakers and ran every single morning, he would grow to like it. But looking in the mirror, he knew he was lying to himself. Deep down inside, Rafael Covin was a slob who drank too much and really hated running.

Then there were those occasions where nothing else helped but getting on the track in the park close to his house and letting his feet pound the path until he got tired of his own thoughts and, finally, just plain tired.

Lately, he thought as he ran around the little artificial pond for the third time, lately, it had started happening on a regular basis.

Just like that, his stint in the marijuana business was all but over. Damn! Just as he was getting used to answering with, 'Why, I am a drug dealer,' to the question, 'What is it you do?'

Nothing wrong with the construction business. It was what he had done for the past 30 years, and it was what he knew. So perhaps there was a way he and Roger Carmichael could run it together. Why not come to an understanding with the man? It was doing great, and, between his salary and bonuses, Carmichael had a good thing on the go.

Rafael stopped, took a swig from his water bottle, rested for a moment until he wasn't wheezing like a geriatric steam engine, and picked up his run again.

The answer was no. No, no, no, and no again if anyone wanted to know in detail. No way was he getting involved in anything that had a hint of Connor in it. Barry. Whatever. Didn't matter what the man called himself, how often he changed his name, legally or not, Rafael refused to deal with him ever again. Not after the mess he had just cleaned up.

Left the consulting business he had been contemplating—what, this morning? He checked his watch. Seven hours ago? Damn, life changed fast in this business.

Hobbling because of a searing pain in his knee, he decided to abandon any pretense of running and headed home at a more leisurely pace. This consulting business, could he still pull it off? That was the question. Without the others, or were they coming along?

Connor—dammit—the image of Connor right there in the middle of that board meeting still shook him. Like a fist to the gut and then some.

After more than two years, Connor Beauregard, or Barry J. Wentworth, Reverend, holier than thou, resurrected from the dead. *God, you really are an idiot, Rafa,* he scolded himself. *Running out of that meeting because Connor said you can go now.*

Connor, the man who had driven this thing into the ground by putting an illegal grow op into it. Right to the end… right to the end, he had sworn to Rafael he didn't do it. But there was evidence. There was a video. He had seen it.

There had been that goddamn video right on the TV news, and every reporter in the world running down his door, wanting to know what was going on, and Connor—Connor had gone to the washroom and disappeared through the connecting door into nothingness.

What the hell was he supposed to believe? That an innocent man would do such a thing? That someone who had nothing to worry about would just leave his entire life behind and run, taking nothing with him but the carry-on bag he'd happened to have with him?

And a bunch of shares in Switzerland, Rafael had later found out, but he couldn't rightly figure out how they'd got there, or how Connor would ever touch them again, so he had forgotten about them. He had just assumed that one day, he would get the time and the chance to figure out how to fix this nasty little problem.

Bad move.

He had never connected the dots to those Swiss shares with the Mariposa holdings. Damn, he couldn't have. He couldn't have known. Or should he have? What a mess.

And now, the man was back.

The man who had been his best friend, the man who had set this company into the sand, and the man who had been—well—almost engaged to the woman Rafael was now living with.

Talk about a real hot mess.

Rafael banged in through his front door and slammed it behind him. He never locked his door. Nothing to steal there anyway.

He took no more than three steps, and he knew she was there. She just had that—something—that made you know she was in the room without knowing why. Rafael turned the corner to peek into the living room, and sure enough, there Kayla lounged on his old leather couch, sipping from a highball glass.

If he didn't miss his guess, the clear liquid within contained a large portion of vodka.

"Running away from something, or just running?" she asked without looking at him.

Rafael stepped all the way into the room and plunked himself into the overstuffed chair.

"Don't rightly know. All I know is I had to get out of there before my head exploded, or I punched him in the face, whichever came first. Sorry. Sorry for leaving you behind—for…"

"Never mind." Kayla waved her hand and picked up the glass again. "He all but threw you out."

"So—Connor…"

"Connor."

"Or Bartholomew. Bullshit name that is."

"I didn't even realize you could change it just like that, but if any-body was up on that type of thing…"

"Then it was Connor." Kayla laughed, but her voice sounded more like broken glass tinkling. "Name any dirty trick in anybody's book, and he either knew about or had done it to somebody. Connor, God-dammit! You want to talk about it?"

"Not really—guess I have to. What happened after I left?"

"One word? Pandemonium. Everybody was yelling at everybody. The two goons wanted to beat up somebody, but no takers. "

"Tadeo's guards… Didn't see that coming, did they?"

"Nope. Roberto told them to get lost and never come back. And then there's Tadeo, screaming at Roberto in some language I didn't quite catch."

"What did Al think of all of it?"

"Al? Rafa, I thought Al was going to pass out right then and there. He was just about as white as the pad of paper he still carries."

"He never could stand Connor."

"And his brother—his brother Roberto up there on Wentworth's side as if they had been pals for years."

"Lovely family reunion. Too bad I missed it."

"And then Al, he turns right at me, and you know what he said?"

Rafael only shook his head.

"In our meeting, before I left, I said to Rafael it would be different if Connor were still around. And here…"

"And here…"

Rafael nodded, walked over to the bar cabinet, made himself a stiff drink, and all but dropped back into the deep armchair. Finally, after a couple of drinks, he could speak again.

"I am stunned. My brain is frozen, I think."

"I resigned—right after you left."

Rafael shrugged. "Don't blame you there. God—I can't get over it. All of us sitting there and that door opens… The last person I thought would walk through. He must have planned this for years, dammit."

"The moment he left."

"That would be Connor—revenge even if it kills you. He thought we took something that was his, so he would have moved heaven and earth to get it back. He would have bankrupted himself and walked over—well, over dead bodies to get his revenge. And all he had to do…"

"All he had to do was sit back and enjoy the money he had stashed away."

"Instead," Rafael said, standing up to make himself another drink, "instead, he hid away on a damned island in the South Pacific."

"Rafael? Back up for a minute. South Pacific? That's where he was hiding out?"

"Does it matter? First thing I saw, out of the ordinary, there was someone on some fly speck in the South Pacific called Vaomar Island, owning a ton of shares. I didn't…"

"Vaomar? Rafael, look at me. Did you say Vaomar Island?"

"Yeah. What do you know about it?"

"Rafael. Connor and I went there for our little getaway. He met a couple of characters there, men with lots of money, and something to hide. I thought he was too drunk to see any of it, but I guess he did. And remembered."

"And made a plan. Doesn't matter much now, does it?"

"But why go through all of it, just to own a company together with Tadeo Ivers, whom he hates more than anyone else in this world?"

"Get in line. A lot of people hate Tadeo Ivers, and that's just the lucky ones who have done business with him."

Kayla wanted to say something, but just then, someone knocked on Rafael's front door—hard. Rafael sighed and pinched the bridge of his nose, trying to decide whether he should answer or not, whether the vodka had put him over the edge yet, or whether he even wanted to see anyone right now. The person on the other side of the door, however, knocked with dogged determination until Rafael rose, muttering and grumbling, and went to see.

"I can tell you one thing, whoever you are, I have absolutely no—oh, Al."

"No comment—not expecting one." Al brushed past him into the hallway, tossed his coat over a chair, and strode into the living room without bothering to take off his shoes. Nobody had ever taken their shoes off at Rafael's house, except for Al, who insisted on doing so every single time. Until now.

"Kayla." He nodded and sat heavily in the chair Rafael had just vacated.

"You're welcome. Why don't you come in—sit," Rafael said sarcastically. "Can I offer you a drink now?"

"Not yet."

Al buried his head in his hands for a minute and finally looked up again. "What just happened?"

"Connor came back."

"Connor—Barry J. Wentworth."

"Barry…"

Rafael cast about for another place to sit and finally kicked a footstool into a convenient place and sat on it. They sat without speaking, Rafael and Kayla staring into their drinks, Al resting a fist against his face.

"What about Dante?" Rafael finally said. "Forget all that bullshit about abandoning your father. This is going to get hot over there. Dan is just going to get chewed up and spat out if he stays."

"I don't know what he's thinking. Roberto challenged him and Nick first chance he got. If I don't miss my guess, he'll have fired both of them by now." Al glanced at his watch and shook his head.

"What a hot mess."

"Welcome to PerCan Consolidated, run by three people who utterly hate each other—your father, brother, and Connor, plus a couple of execs from Mariposa who probably think the sky just fell on their heads. God help this company because we sure can't."

"Connor and my father will most certainly turn every executive meeting into a war zone, sniping at one another."

"So will Roberto and your father, although I sure would like to know how Connor brought him over to his side."

"You guys, can you not call him Connor?" Kayla said and rose to refill her glass yet again. Rafael had lost count, and didn't care any longer either. He'd probably had just as many.

"Barry, whatever. Sorry, love. It must bring back—memories."

"Not any good ones, I assure you."

"Forgive me," Al said with a nod. "I failed to realize."

"It's all right, Al. Just don't call him Connor. Don't remind me of the time…"

"When we started this," Rafael said, raising his glass. "The three of us—plus you, Al. And you just walked in and handed him half a million dollars."

"Worst thing I ever did."

"Be that as it may, to our departure from the marijuana industry."

Al looked around and finally took a bottle of water off the sideboard, raising it.

"You were all fired up about a consulting company this morning."

"I was."

Another visitor interrupted them, and from the sound of it, they had to be leaning on the doorbell with their finger. Rafael didn't bother, and Al rose to get the door, only to let in Nick Ambrose.

"Have you guys seen Dante?" Nick asked, a little breathless, as if he had been running all the way from the factory, which might even be the case, since he did not own a car.

"No. Didn't he come with you? What happened at the meeting?"

"Dante." Nick shook his head and spread his arms. "I tried to hold him back, but then he stood up and yelled that Tadeo had just made him CEO, so he was making the rules. Your father told him he was a no-good nitwit who needed an army of support workers to keep from ruining the company. Your brother called him a thief, and Barry—well, Barry didn't wait and fired him."

Rafael laughed and threw up his hands. "Yup, his favorite thing to do in the whole world. Fire people. I bet you he stands in front of the mirror and practices, you know. You're fired."

He turned to the bar cabinet again only to find Al blocking it, gently shaking his head.

"Enough now. We've got to sort out this mess. First priority is to find Dante before he does something really stupid. Any ideas, Nick?"

"He took off on his motorcycle. I checked every place I could think of," Nick said, shaking his head. "He just—screamed at your father, said he was dead to him, and stormed out before I could do anything."

"And you?"

"Me? I resigned before Roberto could fire me. He knows his stuff, true, but his methods—his methods aren't always clean, if you know what I mean."

"I don't," Al interrupted, "and I don't care. I need to find my youngest brother before he does something unwise. He's a hothead, much like Roberto, much like our father himself."

"And what would you suggest? Walking the streets, in pairs? Checking every bar he might have ducked into?"

Nick nodded at Rafael.

"Guys, guys, let's not argue. Not us, not this group."

Kayla stood, raising her hands just as the doorbell rang, again.

"Goddammit." Rafael stormed to the front door and opened it in one giant swing. "Grand Central Station, walk right in. Oh, hi, Irv, fancy seeing you in this place."

Irving Moody pushed past Rafael and closed the door behind both of them.

"Guess I don't have to ask what kind of mood you guys are in."

"Bad news travels real fast, Irv. How'd you find out?"

"About Mr. Barry J. Wentworth? Probably only slightly slower than you did. You don't think I would keep an eye on a company I had every intention of putting millions into?"

"Guess that's off the table," Rafael said and mentally calculated the distance between his liquor cabinet and Al, who still stood like a sentinel. "So, what, you've come to commiserate here? Because I have to tell you, you're in the right place for a wake."

"Contrary to what you might believe, Rafa, I am still your friend. I've come to see if you needed any support after Ivers fired you. Then Wentworth showed up. And since all of you are here," he trailed a finger around the room, "I gather his entrance was as per his usual. Flashy, unexpected, and accompanied by chaos."

"Sorry, Irv, wrong tone..." Rafael ran his fingers through his hair. "I guess I don't have to tell you we're all a bit—frazzled."

"Frazzled? This is..."

"This is utter chaos, and still, I need to go and find my brother," Al interrupted. "Dante's been in a sour mood ever since our father decided he wanted him to be CEO. I don't dare imagine what he's up to now."

"At his house?" Irv asked, and Nick shook his head.

"Went by, all dark."

"His office is out, I gather."

"None of the staff at PerCan have seen him, and entry card readout says he left shortly after Connor—Barry showed up, and he didn't return."

"Favorite hangouts?"

"A couple—I checked. I went to every bar and coffee house he likes," Nick said and plopped into one of Rafael's chairs. "I have no idea where else to look."

"Isn't it a bit too soon to be worried?" Kayla handed a large glass of water to Nick. "He needs to cool off a bit. It was a shock for all of us to see Connor there."

"Barry," Rafael and Al said in tandem, and Rafa managed a little smile.

"But that doesn't necessarily mean something is seriously wrong, now does it? For all we know, he's just gone for a drive or a walk or something."

"It means PerCan is f… in serious trouble," Irv said. "That's why I'm here. I checked into the business deals this guy's made before—and it's a mess."

"Some," Rafa admitted with a nod.

"Some? Rafael, I was going to invest in this company. Beauregard—Wentworth ran this company like his own personal little fiefdom, doing what he pleased, when he pleased, asking no one and taking what he wanted. Did he at any point consider his responsibility to the shareholders? No. Did he even once worry…?"

"Look, Irv, Connor founded PerCan, brought it to the stock market, and gave rise to something great. Did he screw it up royally in the end? Yes. Of course he did, and we also know that. But let's not stand here beating on the man a couple of years later. It's done. It is over. Other than that, why are you here?"

He squared off to Irv Moody and shook his head.

"Picking through the dead body? Hoping to pick up something of value? That is so not your style, Irv. I know that. So what is it?"

"Nothing."

"Out with it!"

"This—consulting company you were thinking of starting…"

"Where did you hear this one now?" Rafael glanced at Kayla and shook his head. "Nothing's a secret around here, is it?"

"No, and you know I wanted to get involved in the marijuana industry, so this—this sounded good."

"In what way?"

"In the money kind of way, of course, but also from a 'being active' point of view. Being a part of this—silent, perhaps, but a part. If I can't be a part of PerCan, maybe this would be an even better project."

"That's actually—kind of decent of you," Rafael muttered. "This morning, I would have taken my company outline and written 'financing already arranged' on it."

"And now?"

"Now, who the hell knows what's going to happen?" Rafael snarled. "Connor—Barry is back, probably to make our lives hell. Dante is nowhere to be found. Al… I don't even have an idea what Al is thinking, and—and I can't think straight right now."

"So, what do you think will happen?"

"What am I, a Magic 8 ball? Barry will come in as he always does, throwing his weight around, wanting to be the king of the hill. So, he will insist and, with the amount of shares he reportedly owns, successfully insist on being CEO."

"And Ivers?"

"I don't know about Ivers. Neither do I care right now. He wanted Dante to be CEO, so that's not happening. Matter of fact, I don't think brother Roberto is going to let Dante go anywhere near the company. Which makes Dante footloose."

"Good for us."

"In a way. What gave Dante his confidence was his cooperation with Nick. Nick just resigned from PerCan…"

Al stepped forward between Irv and Rafael. He took great pains not to show what was going on inside him, but today anyone with a pair of eyes could read it plainly on his face. Concern for Dante, worry over PerCan, maybe even guilt over saying no to Rafael and Kayla—it all sat there in his dark eyes.

"I might be the culprit here, Irv. I said I wouldn't get involved."

"That wasn't exactly a smart thing to do."

"Maybe not. I thought I owed it to my father. Then…"

"Then Barry showed up," Kayla said. "That usually ruins every plan. Can we just start over, please?"

"Not easily," Rafael said and finally herded everyone into his rarely used dining room. "Sit, everybody. I'm tired of playing musical chairs with the three seats I have in the living room."

For once, they all obeyed, taking their seats. Nick wanted badly to get up and look for Dante again, but Kayla put a hand on his arm and shook her head.

"Not tonight, Nick. He'll call, I'm sure. When he's had a chance to cool off. I promise you that."

Rafael passed around cans of soda and glasses. "Don't you all look at me with this 'what now' look on your faces," he groused, taking a hefty sip. "Do I look like I have all the answers?"

"More than any of us do. You know Connor."

"Barry. And so does Kayla. I told you what I expect him to do. He will take over and staff the board with people he can control. Roberto, probably Simon and Josh. Not you, Kayla."

"Not a chance even if he tried."

"And not me either. That's why he fired me, for the second time, after Tadeo... never been fired before, let alone twice in one day! Barry will do anything possible to get rid of Tadeo Ivers. That's what he wanted from the day he met him. Either that or kill him. Whichever comes first."

"Whoa..."

"It sounds like a joke, Irv, but those two hate each other with a passion. Ivers had Connor beat up at some point—some stupid story. But one thing is clear: they can never be in the same room together, never mind the same company."

"Then why did he go through such great lengths to take over Mariposa and subsequently PerCan? The research alone... And right up to the last minute, it could have gone wrong."

"Almost did. And if Greg Turner hadn't insisted on making an indecent offer to the board—and to you, Irv—Mr. Barry Wentworth would have owned a marijuana company that was of absolutely no use to him. Why did he do it? Same reason Connor does anything: because he felt like it. He wanted it."

"He must have half bankrupted himself to get here."

"Likely."

"And Roberto—he managed to track down Roberto."

"That part I haven't figured out myself yet," Rafael admitted. "Whether it was by design or sheer pure luck and evil coincidence, those two ended up in bed together once again. Like they had planned it the first time around, with that illegal grow op in the back of the building."

"Connor always said he had nothing to do with that," Kayla said wistfully.

"If you believe that, I have a time share in Florida to sell you."

"I don't know, Rafa. Right now, I am too numb to know what to believe and what not."

"I'm also sure Tessa had something to do with it," Rafael said and shrugged. "Connor's former personal assistant," he said for Irv's benefit. "Little rat gave all sorts of proprietary information to Ivers way back when, handed him Connor's head on a platter, and the company as a little bonus. From that little exchange in the boardroom today, I gather Roberto slept with her in order to get information for Barry and bring about an end to Ivers's reign."

Irv Moody laughed, sat back, and folded his hands behind his head.

"Rafael Covin, and you wonder why I can't wait to be part of a company such as this one? Man, the entertainment value alone is worth it. If we can, we have got to run this consulting company. Watch Ivers and Wentworth chew each other up, and when the company is in the dumps, again, pick out what we want and who we want and start over."

"That's pretty cold."

"It is, Kayla, but that's also how business moves, and don't tell me for a minute the publishing industry does not, because I'm going to start laughing if you do."

"No, you're right."

"So, what I am suggesting, folks, is this. Find the presentation Rafael gave you this morning. Kayla gave me a copy, and it is really well done. Find it, read it again, and mentally mark 'financing all arranged' on it. Then, if that sounds like something that would be cool to get involved in, we all meet here again tomorrow morning. Rafael, I'm afraid until this company acquires an actual boardroom, your dining room will have to do."

"You really still want to do this?"

"Yes."

"Why?"

"Don't know, don't care. Maybe for the same reason Connor bought Mariposa, so he could end up owning a company together with the man he hates most in this life. I feel like it just now."

"You're nuts, Moody, you know that?"

"Yup. And the worst kind too—nuts with the money to pull it off. So?"

Rafael sighed. "I guess we can try to pull it together one more time. After everything that happened today, I'm not sure I remember my name, never mind a cockamamie business concept I wrote 10 hours ago."

"That's why we are all going home, looking at it one last time, and coming back here tomorrow. Say 9 a.m.? That work for everybody?"

Kayla nodded, and Al spread his hands, acquiescing. No one argued. No one had the strength to argue or come up with one good reason why Irv Moody might be wrong. This day had done a number on all of them. Connor Beauregard was back. That seemed to be the day's recurring theme.

Nick dashed off as soon as he could politely do so, probably still hoping to find Dante somewhere, working off his anger. Al followed almost on his heels, awkwardly shaking Irv's hand and slapping Rafael's back. The man who never showed what he really thought or felt looked as if he had been struck by lightning a few hours ago.

Kayla stood in the doorway for an undecided moment, and Rafael forked his fingers through his hair.

"Better go home, Kayla. If there's one thing I know we all need tonight, it's one solid night of sleep."

"If you're sure…"

"I am. I'm not sure any of us will actually get any sleep, but hey…"

"As long as you promise not to sit there fretting half the night. It'll all work out, Rafa. One way or another."

Rafael cocked his finger and tipped his ear. "Your mouth to God's ear, my love. See you tomorrow morning. If you still…"

"Hush. I don't want to talk about Connor Beauregard ever again."

"I just…"

"Ever."

Kayla left behind a cloud of Chanel, and Rafael closed the door behind her with a sigh.

Irv had relocated to the living room again in the meantime, and Rafael dropped heavily into a chair beside him.

"Tough day at the office?"

"Shit," he managed to say and shook his head. "Picture it. Door opens, Connor walks in. I thought that was the moment the men in the white lab coats walk in and take me away."

"Don't blame you… But you know what's odd?"

"Odder than Connor/Barry showing up again? Pray tell! This one has to be good."

Irv chewed his thumbnail and said nothing, long enough that he might have actually lost his train of thought, but eventually, he came back.

"What is odd is something you said earlier. If Greg Turner had not insisted on making an indecent offer to me and to the members of the executive board, Connor would have owned a company he had no use for."

"Lucky—for him, I guess."

"And a little strange, don't you think? Call me paranoid, but I don't believe in coincidence. Connor buys the wrong company, and the offending merger deal blows up… "

"You're paranoid, Irv. The whole deal with Green Technologies was hush-hush. Only a handful of people actually knew what we were doing. So how would Connor have managed to get to Turner? And to influence him to blow up his own deal."

"Not saying I have the answers, Rafael. It's a little too slick for me, just a little too perfect. I have a feeling there's another rat buried there somewhere, and I'm rarely wrong. Think about it."

Rafael stood and rolled the kinks out of his shoulders. He didn't even bother to hide his yawn with a hand.

"Irv… No offense, but I don't think my little brain can handle any more conspiracy theories tonight. What I've heard and seen today—technically, I would call that enough for a whole month. So, if you don't mind…"

"You want me to get out of here."

"No offense, buddy."

"None taken. We'll resume tomorrow. Nine o'clock."

"Nine." Rafael yawned again, and with every yawn, a little more energy drained out of him, and he moved a little more slowly.

He closed the door behind Irv Moody and looked around his living room, lost for a few minutes. The hell with everything—absolutely everything.

He killed the lights and, despite predictions to the contrary, dropped off as if someone had punched him hard.

FIFTY-THREE

Somewhere across town, Barry J. Wentworth stood at the 40th-floor window in his hotel room and toasted the entire city with a healthy whiskey.

He had won.

Against all odds, against everyone who insisted on reforming and rehabilitating him—he had still won.

"Congratulations, Perfect Cannabis Corporation," he said lifting his glass. "Your king is back."

And he would get his helicopter back too—one day in the not-too-distant future, he would get that damned helicopter back. He wanted it, and he would get it, same way he had taken his company back.

That left only Ivers to be eliminated in some fashion. Tadeo Ivers could not be allowed to stay, and, since he had come back into his company, the ideas just kept coming almost without any effort. Roberto, the little fool, had accidentally given him everything he needed to get rid of the unwanted competition for the head chair. Vietnamese gangs were moving into the skin trade previously dominated by Ivers and his many sleazy little companies, so...

There had to be something there—something he could work with, something to sink his teeth into and slowly work into his favor. Certainly, there was. Then Ivers would be gone, and PerCan his, and his alone.

When he had finished his whiskey, he fired up his little laptop and did a bit of research, writing out some phone numbers, and two or three quick thoughts on what could be done. None of it meant anything, he assured himself. He could still change his mind. He need not follow through on any of it. Ivers himself might eventually get tired of being in the same company with him anyway. If he had any brains at all, he would retire quietly and leave the running of the company to Barry.

He'd still make money. Shit, the man should be in Florida sitting on the beach drinking rum drinks all day, watching the money roll in. Nobody could run PerCan like its creator could—and Ivers would learn that.

Barry carefully folded his notes into the back of his portfolio and smiled at his reflection in the window glass. He need not follow through on any of it and get his hands dirty, but he could use it as leverage. He could show it to Ivers. *This is what I could do. Unless you do as I say, of course.*

Another evil grin. Perhaps he'd even tell him about Greg Turner and his sad little tale—perhaps. Now that would make Tadeo Ivers sweat a bit, wouldn't it? And PerCan would belong to the one man who deserved it: Barry J. Wentworth.

"Cheers to that."

He leaned back, letting the whiskey burn a fiery trail down his throat. Probably drinking too much again, but who the hell cared?

For a while, he stared out over the town, the empty whiskey glass in his hand.

Tomorrow, he would move into the large office at the PerCan building, the one that overlooked the manufacturing floor, the one that allowed him to keep an eye on his entire kingdom all at once.

And Rafael and Kayla...

Barry's hands clenched so hard around the highball glass he felt the rim dig deep into the palm of his hand, and he put it down on the sideboard with slow and carefully controlled motions. No point in setting the anger free now.

***

He changed into a jogging suit and running shoes and made his way down to street level. He and Rafael used to joke about neither of them enjoying jogging, but at least it let out the excess energy. Running burned off the sheer fury that threatened to choke him at times, and tonight, that was exactly what he needed right then.

FIFTY-FOUR

Rafael hadn't expected to sleep well or long. When he turned in the night before, he thought he'd be tossing and turning, haunted by every minute of that day. A day he would never forget.

Instead, he had dropped off almost immediately and woken again with the first rays of the sun, as was his habit.

He shaved with careful precision, and when he met his own eyes in the mirror, he was reminded of a line from a TV interview in a show he didn't remember with a person who had become irrelevant in the meantime. His brain had only filed away this one line: 'sometimes, we are part of history without knowing it at the time, and generations will look back at that moment and wonder how we could fail to see it.'

Had he really been part of history then? Perhaps. Certainly, he had played a role in the creation of what he had come to think of as the country's largest manufacturer of medical marijuana.

Perhaps, 25 years from now, the name PerCan would come as easily to the common man as aspirin, Kleenex, or Coke did now. But the man who had picked the company out of the trash, painted over the rusted and ruined bits, put it back to working condition, that man would likely be forgotten.

Whoa there, Covin, time to quit your bitching and whining and get back to work, he reminded himself, and shook his head to clear it.

What was he looking for anyway, a monument to himself? Not necessary. How many buildings on the city had he personally designed, planned, and put there on the skyline? He really didn't need another reminder that he had done well.

But PerCan, PerCan had been special, and the biggest thing they had ever started, he and Connor. Connor just didn't know how to quit. Bigger, better, faster. Stock market leader, world leader, the world was not enough, right?

Rafael took a little step back and finally went into his kitchen to put on the coffee. Given enough time and resources, he could have made PerCan all that and then some.

"Whatever. Will you just stop moping around?" he said softly to himself just to hear his own voice. "Damn, next thing you're going to explain how this hurt your feelings."

He grumbled a bit more and slammed the cupboard doors with just a tad more force than they needed to close well. Manliness and all that.

For once, he wished Kayla were around at this time of day, to listen to his griping, and to reassure him that indeed he had a point and wasn't merely complaining.

Dawn crept over the city, and, slowly but surely, rush hour had started to build. Like many cities in North America, rush hour never really went away completely. It just slowed a little bit overnight.

Kayla showed up early, at what she would have called an ungodly hour, followed by a yellow cab discharging an extremely disgruntled and disheveled Al.

"Morning, beautiful lady. Hey, Al. No disrespect, man, but you look like sh—not extremely well to put it mildly."

"Neither would you," Al groused, brushing dirt off an extremely wrinkled and rumpled suit. "If you had spent most of the night at the police station."

"The police station. Christ, Al," Rafael said, and his head snapped up immediately. "Is it Dante? Is he OK?"

"Oh, Dante is perfectly fine. He finally did call me, said he went for a motorcycle ride around the countryside to cool off. My youngest brother appears to subscribe to the idea that clear thinking and logic can be found on the wide-open road, breaking the speed limit many times over."

"Go figure," Rafael said, maneuvering them both into the dining room. "So, what about the cops then?"

"Thank you so kindly for your touching inquiry into my physical well-being, my dear friend. If you must know, I was rear-ended last night shortly after leaving your place, and since the moron—the fellow human being driving the other car—happened to be a fair ways from being sober, we spent a very uncomfortable night giving statements. Which indeed would have been done considerably faster if he had not insisted on hurling insults at everyone in the room every time he came up for breath."

"Sounds like you had a ton of fun, brother. Wish I had been there. Why didn't you call? I would have helped if needed."

"Wasn't necessary. Besides, a police station is an extremely uncomfortable place when your last name happens to be Ivers."

"I guess it would be, sorry." Rafael immediately stopped grinning and pointed toward the table and chairs.

"Take a load off. You can go upstairs and take a shower if it'll make you feel any better. Just don't use the pink towels. Those are Kayla's."

"Not that I wouldn't have guessed. Thank you anyway. I'll be fine. I don't think this will be a long meeting."

"Might be, you never know. The industry is hot right now. I think if we can get this consulting company off on the right foot…"

His doorbell announced Nick and Dante, arguing about one thing or another to do with grow cycles and LED lighting, and the moment Rafael closed the door, it summoned him again to announce Irv.

Kayla had prepared some fancy coffee beverage with a name longer than Rafael's street address and handed out cups, while Al recounted his story again in great detail. Rafael turned away, hiding a grin at the way Al said 'rear-ended,' and fetched his own drink—coffee, black.

Somebody laughed heartily, and Al threw his hands into the air and cursed in some ancient language, starting a new wave of laughs and giggles. They could do it, Rafael thought. The five people in this room, plus Irv for financial support—they could actually pull this off.

"The marijuana industry," he said, slipping into his accustomed seat at the head of the table, "is hot. All of us here at the table know this. Heck, when Al and I did the research on potential merger partners..." He rolled his eyes dramatically. "You wouldn't believe how many of them are out there. Most of them, unfortunately—most of them don't have a clue what they're doing. Maybe they're a bunch of guys who were growing when they were teenagers, or they hired somebody who really couldn't handle things, but there are a lot of companies out there in trouble. A lot of them still think greenhouse growing is the way to go."

Nick snorted and turned his eyes heavenward, folding his hands.

"Or they can't get quality and consistency right. That's where it usually starts. But growing—growing is only one end of the spectrum, ladies and gentlemen. We could grow the most beautiful healthy weed plants on the planet. If we are not in compliance with licensing regulations, if quality and consistency aren't there, if the business is managed poorly, customers aren't serviced properly, any or all of those things, these businesses will fail."

He put his palms together and rested them against his chin for a moment, letting what he had just said sink in.

"I remember when we started the business," he finally said, very softly. "We were thinking the same thing—how could you screw up being a drug dealer? Not possible. I am here to tell you it is. And it's as easy as falling off a log. Medical marijuana might be the industry of the future, and the profits might be enormous, but the road to success is a rally from hell. Things went wrong in ways I didn't even know they could go wrong."

Dante looked up and opened his mouth to speak, but Rafael shook his head.

"Oh, I know. I had partners who were—difficult to say the least, and that had a lot to do with it, but even after all that... After all that BS was done, I have to tell you, we just didn't have a clue. And we wasted time and effort trying to find people who did have a clue, and more than that. People who really knew what they were doing."

He spread his arms and looked around the room, at each of them in turn.

"Ladies and gentlemen, Cannabis Corp Consulting. We made all the mistakes, we know where they are and what they look like, and, more than that, we have solutions that work in the real world and in the long run. Horticulture, business development, administration, leadership and promotion—we have the answers you need. And if necessary," he looked at Irv with a wily little grin, "if necessary, we have the capability to introduce you to readily available bridge financing. The only questions are... do we really want this, and how far can we take it?"

"Hell yes, all the way."

Dante. His young-puppy eagerness could make you smile in the worst of circumstances. But he was so right. If they did not go into this thing saying 'hell yes,' then they might as well go back to putting up strip plazas and high-rises, printing gossip in magazines and—whatever it was Dante and Al had as far as backup plans were concerned.

"I remember using those words when we founded Perfect Cannabis Corporation, Dante, hell yes. And I think you and Nick could do this without the rest of us."

"Not the business kind of stuff."

"Well, my friend, what you call the business kind of stuff is a large part of what keeps all of us in vittles. Together, as a group, I believe we are a force to behold. Just depends how large a force this is going to be."

"You know my answer," Irv said, grinning. "I'm in all the way, ready to help out where needed."

"I'm with you, Rafa."

Kayla. That left Al—the man looking down at his hands just now, finding something of keen interest on the nail of his ring finger. He didn't want to look at anyone, even Rafa, and with a sinking heart, Rafael realized there was a good chance he would still decline. Again.

He opened his mouth to say something, when somebody banged at his door hard enough to make it tremble.

"What the…"

He looked around the table, but every man and woman he had invited sat at the table, looking to either Al or him.

Al frowned, his glance darting back and forth between Rafael and the door, Irv leaned back as if he couldn't wait for the next installment of this drama, and whoever was at the door used both fists to bang now.

"Rafael. Fuck it. Open up. Now."

He would have known that voice anywhere. Drunk or sober, awake or asleep—only one man sounded like this, even when he was in a panic. Rafael jumped to his feet and opened, just as the other man raised a fist again.

"Connor?"

"Barry."

"What the—what are you doing at my door at this time of day, no matter what you want to be called?"

"Never mind that." Barry pushed past Rafael and into the dining room, where he was met by a dozen curious eyes. "Never mind that now. I think somebody just killed Tadeo Ivers."

He didn't act like Connor. Hell, he didn't even act like Barry—whoever that was. He looked as if he had spent the night in the gutter somewhere. For starters, he wasn't wearing a coat, his trousers looked filthy, and his hair stood on end in 15 different directions.

"You look like shit."

"Did you hear me, Rafael?" Barry grabbed him by the arm and shook. "Did you hear me? Somebody fucking killed Ivers."

"What are you talking about, Barry? What's going on with my father?"

Al pushed forward and took Barry's hand off Rafael's arm—carefully, but insistently nonetheless. "And what's this nonsense about him being killed?"

"You talk to your father today, Al?"

"I have—well, yesterday."

"No point in trying again. Because the cops knocked on my door this morning, wanting to know where I was while Tadeo Ivers was being shot. Oh, and sorry for your loss... you too, Dante."

"You're not joking, are you?" Al finally said and pushed back on Barry's shoulder. "You're not joking. But..." He ran his fingers through his hair, eyes darting wildly around the room. "Why the—why wouldn't they have called me? Or Dante, or... Why do I have to find out like this? This is ridiculous."

"They couldn't get a hold of you, or Dante," Barry said dryly.

Kayla stepped forward and enveloped Al in an enormous hug.

"I'm so sorry, Al. No matter how any of us felt about him, he was still your dad."

"This can't be real. He had those bodyguards... And why would anybody..."

"Roberto dismissed those guards." Barry recovered his usual arrogance and spitfire rather quickly. "And why wouldn't anybody? He was an ass most of the time—and the rest of the time. Let's just say he was an ass most of the time."

"Watch your mouth, Wentworth."

"Why? Because your family are all such choirboys? I think your father didn't have to look far for enemies."

"And this is why the police felt they needed to knock on your door first?"

Al and Barry stood squared off like prizefighters, while the rest of them tried to digest Wentworth's first sentence. Tadeo Ivers had been killed.

Nick stood and put his hand on Dante's shoulder. "Dante—I am so sorry."

"Somebody tell me what you have to do with this," Irv asked of Barry, who merely shook his head.

"Nothing. They're fishing. We had an argument in the board-room yesterday."

"Must have been a pretty big one."

"Fine—yeah, Moody. You ever argue with business partners? Everybody does. Doesn't mean you're going to go and kill them, right?"

"Still, they don't come looking…"

"Leave it be, Moody. Come to think of it, what are you—what are any of you doing here in the first place?"

"Not sure if you looked at the address, Connor, but this happens to be my house."

"Will you stop calling me Connor, Rafael? I came here to get some advice from you, and what I'm getting is grief—and all these people who are just itching to give me more."

"What kind of advice?"

"I said the police wanted to speak to me. I didn't say I actually went and spoke to them."

"Ah, so you took off again? Like the last time? Great. Just great."

"Give me a break, Rafael. Just where were you last night when Ivers was shot?"

"Here."

"Alone? Fantastic! That'll go over well as an alibi. He just fired you. I'd work on that if I were you. Ivers was an asshole—we all know that. And unless either of you has a nice set of witnesses for last night," his eyes rested on Kayla for a minute, "I'd start preparing for being questioned."

Dante looked down at his feet, Kayla folded her hands as if she were praying, and Nick dropped heavily into a chair.

"That's right, people. All of us had pretty good reasons to want Ivers gone, including the absent brother here, Roberto. All of us."

"You're not wrong," Rafael said softly. "This is going to get real messy real quick."

"Why do you think I am here, Rafael? I need to save the company—my company."

"If the police are investigating you for murdering Tadeo Ivers, this might not be the best time to try to take over as CEO."

"Well, I didn't do it."

"Oh, well, why didn't you just say so right away?" Rafael rolled his eyes, leaving the second part of his sentence unsaid: *You also said the same thing last time.*

"Fine, you want to look at your own motive? He fired you—after everything you've done for the bastard."

"Stop. All of you stop, right now," Al said, his voice raised enough that it made everyone in the room obey. "Stop. You're perfectly right. When this hits the newswires, the shareholders are going to go crazy. We have to prepare for the worst."

"No shit, Sherlock. Do you have some answers?"

"I might at that," Al said slowly. "And I might be the only one in this room who actually can save your company at this point."

"You're going to leave your filthy hands off PerCan, Ivers. Who says you didn't kill him? I hear he wanted to throw you to the wolves—the Vietnamese gangs—while he and his other sons played CEO for a bit. You've got just as much motive as any of us."

"Possibly," Al said, polishing the nail of his index finger yet again. "Quite possibly. The old man and I have not been getting on for the past few months, correct."

"There you have it. Now leave the house, if you will. Rafa and I need to make plans."

"Wrong, Wentworth. Thanks to an inebriated driver, I had to spend the entirety of last night in the most alibi-worthy place in the entire city—the downtown police station."

He waited for a moment for that little tidbit to sink in, then squared his back and straightened his shoulders.

"And unless my father did something completely stupid and unadvisable, I, as the eldest son, will inherit all of his business interests. So says the family trust."

He waited again and looked around the room, his eyes lingering a little longer on Dante. Was he trying to apologize, Rafael wondered, and, if so, for what?

"So, with that, and the fact that I'm the only one here with a guaranteed alibi, I am taking over as CEO of Perfect Cannabis Corporation, effective immediately."

FIFTY-FIVE

"Connor Beauregard," the young detective said and snapped a picture of Barry J. Wentworth to the magnet board in the conference room. "Always knew I'd see his ugly mug again. Everybody's favorite suspect. Current location—on the run."

"Temporary." His partner grinned. "Just take a bit more time. Long as he doesn't run off to the South Pacific again."

"He's not getting away from me twice, that much I will promise you, Chuck."

"Listen up, people. Sammy here is putting money on catching the Cannabis Preacher. You really think he did it?"

"Don't you?" Sam rolled his eyes as if he had a hard time confronting that much stupidity. "One, he had a big-ass motive. Ivers stole his company. Two, he had the opportunity. No explanation where he spent last night or who with. And three, he probably had the means. He changed his name and identity—wouldn't be too hard for a guy like him to get his hands on a handgun. There was an incident a couple of years ago involving a loan shark, Beauregard, and a handgun. I say we track him down, bring him in, indict him, bada boom."

"Bada bing?" An older detective entered the conference room and headed for the ancient coffee maker. "You're making it a bit easy on yourself, aren't you there, pal?"

The young detective, who hated being called pal, made a fist and forced a grin. Not much point in riling Robertson. And anyway—the guy had retirement written all over him.

"Why go looking further than we have to? If it walks like a duck and it talks like a duck… I think we might be looking at a duck here."

"One of many, perhaps. All in the same pond. And it's our job to get them in a row."

"You've got somebody else in mind?"

Detective Robertson pulled a sheaf of photographs out of a file and snapped them onto the board as he spoke.

"His youngest son Dante…"

"Dante? As in…"

"Dante, usually called Dan. Had an argument with his father in the boardroom yesterday—got fired? Reportedly, the words 'you are dead' were mentioned."

"No shit."

Out came another picture. "The next son, Roberto Ivers. Real winner, that one—spent a few years in one of our institutions to become a better person. I guess the lessons didn't take because he teamed up with Mr. Wentworth here, making young Roberto suspect number three."

Out came another picture, one in which a younger Rafael Covin posed before a high-rise under construction downtown. "Rafael Covin, erstwhile partner to our Mr. Wentworth slash Beauregard. Had a bit of a falling out, I gather. But he saved the company from certain ruin—and what does our friend Ivers do? One, he never pays him. Two, he fires him when things are finally running again. Suspect number four."

"Yeah, but Robertson, a lot of guys get fired. It makes 'em mad—not killers."

"Indeed," Detective Robertson said, waggling another picture in his hand. "Meet Miss Kayla Montecito…"

"The gossip queen."

"The very same. For those of you who are paying attention, she and Mr. Barry Wentworth were engaged at one point or another."

"Woman scorned," Sammy said, nodding. "But what does that have to do with Ivers and his killer?"

"Pay attention, young man, and don't say I didn't warn you. Because according to my sources, our gossip queen here," he snapped her picture beside the one of Rafael, "shacked up with the scorned business partner. Two for one. Ain't revenge beautiful?"

The young detective whistled and sat down hard.

"I beg your pardon, Robertson. This might not actually be as clear-cut as I thought."

"Not hardly."

Detective Sean Robertson took a broad black marker and wrote in careful lettering on a piece of plain paper.

"Numerous business partners who had dealings with Tadeo Ivers and lost out," Sam read. "People he screwed over?"

"If you would like to put it that way, yes. People he screwed over. Now…"

Robertson put down his marker and looked from Sammy to Chuck and back.

"Guys, we have our work cut out for ourselves. And I don't need to mention to you that with someone as high profile as Kayla Montecito involved, mistakes are not an option we can afford."

"Yeah, but…"

"No buts, Chuck. We need to bring these people in—one at a time—and have a nice and friendly chat with them. Feel them out. See how they felt about Ivers. As you can see…" Robertson pointed at the magnet board behind him. "He pissed off each and every one of them at one point or another. And if he didn't piss them off, surely Wentworth did. If I don't miss my guess, a few people will do a little happy dance if Wentworth goes to jail."

"A total nightmare," Chuck groaned. "Could have been any of them, for any motive at all… Jesus."

"He's not going to help you out here, Chuck Caslon. And you are quite correct. I would think the only person in the entire group who is not a person of interest right now is the oldest son, Al Ivers."

"Right. I just bet he was sitting in church, confessing his sins?"

"He was in fact sitting in the only place better than that, Sam—he was right here with us reporting a motor vehicle accident and drunk driver."

"Lucky bastard."

"Correct. And probably the only time a man would consider himself lucky for being rear-ended. In any case, I hear he has at this point taken over control of Perfect Cannabis Corporation. When this news starts hitting, he'll have his hands full, what with half his staff being questioned about their former shareholder's murder. He'll have loads of fun."

"You're sure then he had nothing to do with it," Chuck asked, and Robertson spread his hands and laughed.

"Sure? No, I'm not sure about anything after 45 years on the job, but you gotta start somewhere. I will give Mr. Al a quick phone call and get his take on all of it, but unless he does something stupid…"

"Like getting caught paying a guy he hired to off his own father?"

"I would classify that as stupid, yes. And unless he does something like this, he is in the clean."

"Fucking mess," Sam said and planted himself before the situation board. "Where the hell do you even start here?"

"You start at the most logical point, pal. And that is still Barry J. Wentworth. Hit the ground running. I want to know everything he did and said from the moment he got away from us two years ago. I want to know how he ended up a reverend in the South Pacific, I want to know how he got the money and where he hid it, I want to know how he managed to take over this company, Mariposa, and I want to know if and how he blew up the first merger with Green Technologies."

"I think they're just about to go bankrupt. That wouldn't have anything to do with this case, though, would it?"

"I don't know—yet. That's why I want to look at it, turn it over, smell it, and decide if it's related somehow. Get me the information. That's your task, Sammy. You…"

He turned around and pointed a finger at Chuck. "You, on the other hand, talk to the whole lot up there on the board and make an appointment to come in and speak to me. Nobody is being suspected of anything. Yet. We just want to talk."

"And you?" Chuck asked. An impertinent question perhaps, but one that fit with the rough and sometimes challenging tone the men from the downtown precinct had with one another.

"I—oh, I have picked out the juiciest one for me. I am going to find our man Wentworth, make sure he has no plans to go anywhere anytime soon, and get the real juice on what happened between him and Ivers. He slipped away from our team wanting to ask a few questions, but he left his hotel room wide open. And guess what we found there sitting on the desk, broad as daylight."

He reached back into the folder one last time and brought out a photocopy, carefully flattening it on the desk before him. It was an image of a piece of paper they had found on Barry's desk.

"Notes," Robertson read. "Could the Vietnamese gangs be used against Ivers, question mark? To scare him out of my company, question mark. Or worse, three question marks."

"Fuck," Sammy said.

"My sentiments exactly, but it continues. Tell him I put a hit out on him, three question marks."

Robertson took his reading glasses off, folded them carefully, and put them down beside the copy on his desk.

"You see, Sammy, you're not all that far off when you consider Mr. Wentworth the main suspect in our book. He's got a lot of things going for him right now. All the same, the DA is not going to indict on just this. And with the media already involved…" He nodded at the picture of Kayla Montecito. "I'm going to make damn sure we've exhausted every other possibility and ruled out every other suspect before we make a move. I don't actually care how long it takes, boys."

***

From the moment he heard and understood that Tadeo Ivers had indeed been shot and killed, Rafael couldn't form a clear thought. Everything seemed to move through a thick haze, as if his brain were packed in marshmallows.

After Al declared he was taking over the company, everyone felt the sudden urge to head home. No point in pursuing the new company idea quite yet, not while everything—their own fates included—hung in the balance.

Finally, only he and Barry remained. He, because it was his house, and Barry because he had nowhere else to go.

How many evenings had they spent hanging out at various bars together? Talking about everything and nothing, business and the world, women, politics, and sports? Most of their lives? Right now, Rafael couldn't think of a single thing to say to the man he had once called a friend.

"So," Barry said finally. "You're gonna come out and ask me if I did it?"

"Nah."

"You know I didn't. Rafael, you damned well know I didn't do it. I'm not a killer. Jesus."

"Don't bother, Barry. I know whatever you say in the moment—any moment—you actually believe it. It's your truth, and frankly, I don't want to hear it. I don't need to hear it."

"But I didn't do it, Rafa. And I want my company back."

"Still the same guy." Rafael shook his head. "Barry, take my advice— go home. Talk to the police. Tell them, not me. I have to figure out how to get my own head out of this fabulous new sling we have here.

And I just got fired if you remember. I don't actually care about the company any longer."

"Bullshit. Of course you do. You and I started this company—it's ours. How can you not…"

"You walked away, and I got fired. And then you fired me again, for fuck's sake."

"You cannot tell me you want to leave that moron Al in charge. He will…"

"You want to know something, Barry? Like, really know it? Al is actually a talented businessman, loyal, dependable, and quiet. No flash, no ego, just…"

"Like I said—he's a moron. That's why I need you. You need to take this company back until I convince everyone I'm innocent and…"

"Innocent," Rafael laughed and clapped slowly. "If there's one thing you're not now, and never have been, Barry, it's innocent. Now go home. Talk to the police, straighten this out. And if somebody somewhere, by some foolish reason, actually lets you run a marijuana company again, call me."

"Rafael…"

"Go, Barry—now, before I throw you out."

"What do you want from me?" Barry grabbed Rafael's shoulders, perhaps a bit too hard for Rafa's taste, and held him an arm's length away. "What do you want me to say?"

Rafael pushed away—gently but firmly. "Did you do it?"

"No, I already told you. I did not do it."

"Good, then that takes care of that. Now, if you please." Rafael pointed toward the door.

"I didn't do it, and I want my company back. I need your help to do this, Rafael."

"Do you now?"

"The cops are going to stop looking when they get to me—I'm their favorite suspect. You know that."

"Can't say I disagree with you. Still don't see how that involves me."

"They're not going to bother working the case. It's up to you to find out."

"What am I finding out then?"

"If we ever want to run Perfect Cannabis Corporation together, we have to find out who did it. You and I have to figure out who killed Tadeo Ivers."

Rafael shook his head, quietly opened the front door, and pushed Barry outside just as firmly as he had pushed him away a minute ago. He closed the door behind him and rested his hand on the locking handle for a moment. Well, if that wasn't the question everybody in town would be asking themselves. Who killed Tadeo Ivers?

***

Across town, the PerCan building literally hummed with the news of Barry J. Wentworth's return, Tadeo's death, and the implications of both of these on the company. Work was being done, but it was being done quickly and by sheer routine while the people paused to look at one another and ask, 'What do you think?'

Al Ivers opened the front door, and all conversation in the entry hall stopped, as if someone had thrown a power switch. No one was sure of anything at the moment. *Now what?* they all thought, and Al could read it on their faces.

"Good morning, Sheila." He nodded at the receptionist and walked right on through the little group of employees, on to the office that had been Rafael's. Still was, if he had anything to do with it.

For the moment, the company needed one leader, one CEO to look to, and, for the sake of the company and its employees, he would fill that need. For a while. Only until Rafael had been cleared in Tadeo's murder. Which he would be, of that Al was certain. Perhaps he need not have resigned either, but for the sake of their license to produce marijuana and its byproducts, they needed to avoid the nightmare and disaster of having their CEO under suspicion of murdering a shareholder and potential CEO.

It wouldn't take long, Al reassured himself, unlocking Rafael's office.

He was only keeping the seat warm. It wouldn't take long at all, and the rightful CEO would move back in here. He'd gladly vacate; that much he knew right away.

Slowly, he put down his old battered portfolio and looked around his office—Rafael's office. He wasn't going to change a thing. Perhaps the name at the door, but that was it.

He slipped into Rafael's chair and tried to get comfortable in it.

"Just so one thing is clear, Rafa," he muttered under his breath, carefully placing the framed picture of Kayla into a drawer. "I'm only agreeing to do this until you come back. You—not that fake reverend what's-his-worth either."

He rolled his shoulders and straightened up just as his intercom buzzed.

"Mr. Ivers? You have the Minister of Health's office on Rafa's—on the private line, asking for the current CEO of Perfect Cannabis Corp. Should I...?"

Al sighed and touched a button. The one that glowed would surely do the job, no?

"Put him through, Sheila," he said, forcing more courage than he actually felt. "Put him through, please."

ACKNOWLEDGEMENTS

I would like to express my deepest gratitude and appreciation to all those who have contributed to the creation and completion of this book. Your support, guidance, and encouragement have been invaluable throughout this journey.

First and foremost, I would like to thank my family (human and canine alike 🐾) for their unwavering love and belief in me. Your constant encouragement and understanding have been the pillars of strength that kept me going, even during the most challenging times.

I am immensely grateful to my editor and the entire publishing team at PRB for their expertise, dedication, and commitment to shaping this book into its final form. Your insightful feedback and meticulous attention to detail have greatly enhanced its quality.

To my mentors and advisors, thank you for your wisdom, guidance, and invaluable insights. Your expertise and willingness to share your knowledge have been instrumental in shaping my perspective and enriching the content of this book (Shawn, you've saved me from so many mistakes 😊).

I would also like to acknowledge the readers and reviewers whose feedback and engagement have provided valuable insights and perspectives. Your enthusiasm and constructive criticism have played an integral role in shaping this work.

Lastly, I want to express my heartfelt gratitude to all the individuals who have touched my life in ways both big and small. Your support, kindness, and belief in me have fueled my passion and determination to bring this book to fruition.

Writing the "Cannabis Preacher" series has been a labor of love, and it would not have been possible without the contributions and support of each and every one of you. I am humbled and honored to have had the opportunity to work with such an incredible group of people.

Thank you.

Sabine

www.ingramcontent.com/pod-product-compliance
Lightning Source LLC
Chambersburg PA
CBHW070152120726
47909CB00001B/74